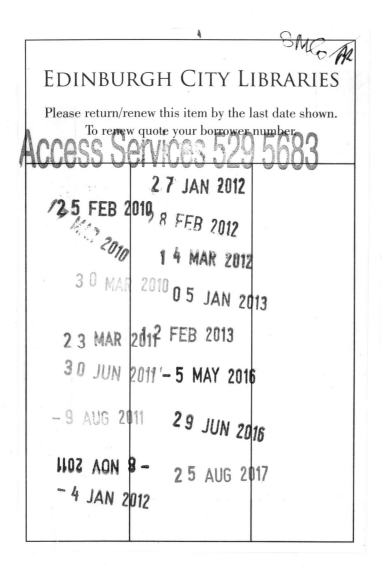

THE
SPIRE

THE
SPIRE

A NOVEL

RICHARD NORTH
PATTERSON

MACMILLAN

First published 2009 by Henry Holt and Company, New York

First published in Great Britain 2009 by Macmillan
an imprint of Pan Macmillan, a division of Macmillan Publishers Limited
Pan Macmillan, 20 New Wharf Road, London N1 9RR
Basingstoke and Oxford
Associated companies throughout the world
www.panmacmillan.com

ISBN 978-0-230-70565-4 HB
ISBN 978-0-230-71130-3 TPB

1 3 5 7 9 8 6 4 2

A CIP catalogue record for this book is available
from the British Library.

Printed and bound in Great Britain by
CPI Mackays, Chatham ME5 8TD

Visit **www.panmacmillan.com** to read more about all our books
and to buy them. You will also find features, author interviews and
news of any author events, and you can sign up for e-newsletters
so that you're always first to hear about our new releases.

For Justin Feldman

and

Linda Fairstein

The Offer

SIXTEEN YEARS AFTER THE MURDER OF ANGELA HALL HAD precipitated the decline of Caldwell College, Mark Darrow returned to campus, standing in the shadow of the Spire.

Darrow had come at the urgent request of Dr. Lionel Farr, his professor and mentor, one of the seminal figures in Caldwell's history and in Darrow's life. It was the end of the spring semester and blossoming dogwood trees, set between generous oaks, brightened the landscape with pink. Even here, Darrow could detect Farr's influence; since becoming provost, Lionel Farr had overseen the planting of pine trees and neatly tended gardens, giving the foliage both variety and order. But the buildings spaced throughout had no particular theme: the oldest—elaborate brownstones with Gothic steeples and towers—were mixed with square, staid structures from the late nineteenth century and newer buildings in a variety of architectural styles, some more nondescript than others. As a student, Darrow had found this hodgepodge engaging, a stone-and-brick record of the growth of Caldwell College over time. Though the campus would never resemble that of a picture-book college, these structures had housed generations of students and nurtured much learning—including, as Darrow gratefully remembered, his own.

The current students looked much like Darrow's classmates had all those years ago. With the subdued, somewhat dazed look of college kids facing finals, they wandered past him, taking little notice, Darrow reflected wryly, of the former campus legend, now a late-thirtyish lawyer in a business suit, headed for his meeting with the presidential search committee of a small Ohio school in crisis. Then Darrow looked up at the Spire, recalling the most vivid hours of his youth, and all trace of humor vanished.

Erected two decades before the Civil War by the school's founder, the Reverend Charles Caldwell, the tower remained as Caldwell had intended: the epicenter of campus, with four brick pathways radiating outward like spokes, the other buildings set at an appropriate, almost reverent distance. At its base was chiseled, CHRIST, THE CHIEF CORNERSTONE. From there, at Caldwell's insistence, over two hundred feet of sandstone rose above everything but sky.

The founder's aspirations had been realized—the Spire dominated both the landscape and the psyche of Caldwell College. Its image graced the yearbook, the alumni magazine, the school's letterhead, and, for over 160 years, had decorated every diploma issued to a graduate of Caldwell. Part of Darrow's fraternity initiation had been to memorize *Webster's* definition of a spire: "a structure that tapers to a point at the top, as in a steeple." Just below the steeple, in a space with four long openings, the great bell of the college hung, its deep resonant clang reserved for moments of celebration or sadness. The lawn beneath the Spire was the scene of graduations, weddings, pep rallies, and memorial services. In the week before Caldwell's annual football grudge match with its hated rival, Ohio Lutheran, students guarded it at night from vandals: by long tradition, the Spire was where, if Caldwell emerged triumphant, the celebration would begin. It was on such a Saturday in November that a twenty-one-year-old Mark Darrow had ascended the Spire for the first and only time, never imagining that, within hours, this memory, and this place, would turn dark for all the years that followed.

A scant hour before, Mark had thrown the last of four touchdown passes, sealing Ohio Lutheran's defeat; Coach Fiske, whose privilege this was, had designated Mark to ring the bell atop the Spire. Very rarely was a student admitted to the bell tower—the Spire's oaken door had been padlocked since 1938, when a drunken celebrant had fallen from the Spire to his death. The new president, Clark Durbin, had opened the door for Mark and passed him the ceremonial bronze axe with the chip in its blade, the spoils of Caldwell's victory. Then Mark stepped inside.

Alone, he paused inside the shadowy tower, filled with awe and reluctance. Since early childhood, Mark had loathed confined spaces; the absence of light frightened and depressed him. The winding staircase, dark and dank and steep, led, in Mark's imagination, to a chamber suitable to druids or high priests. Battling claustrophobia, conscious of his responsibility to commence the celebration, Mark started climbing. He felt his chest tighten, a nameless terror choking his breathing. As a distraction, he counted each stone step to confirm that—as his fraternity had also required him to remember—the Spire had 207 steps, each one foot high.

Reaching the top at last, Mark opened its door. The square chamber was bare, its mortared stone walls adding to its severity. Hanging over him was a massive brass bell. Mark's other aversion was heights: though the four long openings of the tower began at his waist, he approached the one he had chosen gingerly, as though some invisible hand might send him hurtling into space. But as he surveyed the throng below, a surge of triumph overcame his fear.

The lawn was covered with students, many of whom had already embarked on an alcohol-fueled bacchanalia that, for some, might last until dawn. Among them stood Lionel Farr, his wife, Anne, and their twelve-year-old daughter, Taylor, who had waited with the others for Mark to appear. Mark spotted them and then, for Farr more than anyone, he brandished the axe, his grin of triumph spreading as Taylor waved back with an adolescent's adoration. Seeing him, the crowd let loose with a deep-throated roar. Then, heart pounding, Mark reached for the heavy iron chain . . .

Staring up at the tower, Darrow could still hear the deep tolling whose echo had nearly deafened him. But now there were spotlights placed around the Spire, so that darkness never came here. This, too, was the work of Lionel Farr.

THE MOMENTS BEFORE he had first met Farr—an encounter that changed his life forever—were also imprinted in Darrow's memory.

He had been a seventeen-year-old in a small Ohio town, a star football player but a middling student. With no real family or any future he could see, he hoped only to wrest one timeless moment from a high school athlete's transient glory. His chance came down to the last play of his final game as quarterback of the Wayne Generals. The air was crisp, carrying the smell of popcorn and burnt leaves; the field, a bowl of light in the darkness, reverberated with the enthusiasm of a football town of seventeen thousand, perhaps half of them here huddled against the cold, screaming and stomping the wooden bleachers with booted feet, the small minority of blacks quieter and seated in their own clusters. There were six yards to go, four seconds left, three points between Wayne and its first defeat in an otherwise perfect season. The Generals broke the huddle, seven linemen in blue jerseys loping toward the line of scrimmage, their shadows moving alongside, as Mark, two running backs, and a flanker spread out behind them. Opposite them was the Cloverdale defense, eleven boys in green uniforms, their four defensive backs—poised to thwart a pass or run—portraits of taut alertness.

For an instant Mark took it all in—the light and darkness, the primal roar of the crowd, the illuminated clock frozen at 0:04. Pulsing with adrenaline, he positioned himself, setting his hands between the center's legs, conscious of his halfback, George Garrison, slightly behind and to the right. Time slowed for Mark; the cadence of his voice seemed to come from somewhere else.

The ball snapped into his hands.

Spinning, Mark slid the ball into George's stomach, then withdrew it as George, the decoy, hit the line as though determined to break through. Alone, Mark sprinted toward the sideline with the ball. Two linebackers ran parallel, barring his path to the end zone while his own blockers fanned in front of him. Without seeming to look, Mark saw the flanker, Steve Tillman, suddenly break toward the center of the field, two feet ahead of the back assigned to cover him.

At once Mark decided. Stopping abruptly, he threw the ball, praying that Steve would reach it before it fell to earth. Desperately, Steve leaped, feet leaving the grass as he stretched, arms extended, grasping at the ball. Then he clasped it, clutching it to his stomach as he landed near the goal line amid the crowd's thin cry of uncertainty, awaiting the referee's signal that Steve had either reached it or fallen short, the difference between victory and defeat.

Mark's heart raced. Then, gazing down at Steve, the referee thrust both hands into the air.

Tears came to Mark's eyes, a swift surge of joy and loss. This was it, he was certain: the last clear triumph of his life.

The first teammate to reach him, George Garrison, hugged him, his round black face alight. But when Steve Tillman wedged between them, George turned away. "You're the best," Steve said. When Mark reached out for George, he was gone.

The next half hour was a blur—the screaming crowd; the shouted questions from sports reporters; the celebration in the locker room, joyous yet shadowed by the seniors' awareness, so vivid in Mark's mind, that this was the end, deepened by his own deflating knowledge that he had no plan or even hope for where his life might take him now. When he emerged into the chill night with Steve, his sole vision of the future was to take Steve's station wagon and, armed with beer and whiskey, meet two girls at the reservoir.

A man stood in their path, hands thrust into his pockets. "Mark?"

Mark paused, impatient to be on his way, regarding the stranger with mild annoyance. "I'm Lionel Farr," the man said in a voice of calm authority. "I teach at Caldwell College."

Though Mark had met other professors at Caldwell—all of them parents of his classmates—Farr looked like none of them. An inch or two taller than Mark, Farr had strong features and the erect posture of an athlete or a soldier. Unlike most of the townspeople, he was bareheaded; instead of a jacket, he wore an olive wool coat, belted at the waist, adding to his martial air. Nodding to Steve, Farr asked Mark, "Can we talk for a moment?"

Shooting a glance at his friend, who was obviously mystified, Mark saw George Garrison leaving with a pretty classmate, Angela Hall. He thought to call out to them; then, not knowing the black girl, and aware of Steve and George's aversion to each other, he stifled the thought. "I'll meet you at the car," he told Steve.

Steve walked away, casting a last look of bemusement toward his friend. Turning to Farr, Mark said, "What is it?"

The brusque inquiry evoked the trace of a smile. "I've been watching you all season," Farr responded. "You have great presence of mind and understand the game. You could play football in college."

Mark shook his head. "Too small, too slow."

Farr continued to look amused. "I didn't mean at Ohio State. The right college—Division III-A, where small but slow has a chance to survive."

Mark shook his head, feeling the obscure resentment of someone being baited. "Those schools don't give scholarships. For grades, maybe, but not football."

"What *are* your college plans?"

Mark looked down. "I don't know. Money's a problem." He hesitated. "So's my transcript."

Farr waited until Mark met his eyes. "I understand. I know something about your life, Mark. The money and grades seem to be related."

Instinctively, Mark bridled at this intimation of sympathy.

"I have friends at the high school," Farr added mildly. "I hope you don't mind that I did a little checking."

In the semidarkness, Mark studied the professor's face. "It sort of depends on the reason."

Despite Mark's curtness, Farr looked unfazed. "A good one, I think. But this isn't the time and place to discuss it. My wife and I would like you to come for dinner."

Mark was unsettled. He did not know this man at all, let alone what this was about. Seeing Mark's reluctance, Farr continued, "Why don't we say Monday. You can come to my four o'clock class, then home with me. A small taste of college life."

Bereft of words, Mark responded to the stranger's understated but palpable force of personality. "I guess so. Sure."

"Good. I'll call the Tillmans with directions."

With this last suggestion that Farr was uncomfortably conversant with Mark's life, Farr extended his hand.

As though responding to an order, Mark took it.

YEARS LATER, MARK Darrow wondered if his interest in justice and morality, the seeds of his law career, had wakened that next Monday in Farr's four o'clock seminar.

Mark did not know the campus; for him it existed as a rarefied world, in which young people smarter and more privileged than him engaged in a mysterious rite of passage, learning punctuated by drunken parties. "Brundage Hall is behind the Spire," Dr. Farr had told him, and so he made his way toward the tower, which before he had only glimpsed above the trees that shrouded the campus. He took one path, then another, until the campus opened to the large grassy circle at its heart. Positioned at the center of the circle, the Spire was austere but strangely powerful: weathered and stained by time, it was topped by a graceful steeple so high that Mark had to lean back to see it. Hurrying past, he managed to find Farr's class.

Dressed in boots, khakis, and a wool fisherman's sweater, Farr paused momentarily in his lecture, nodding briefly to Mark as he found a desk in one corner of the musty classroom. Turning back to the dozen or so students clustered near the front, Farr said, "Friedrich Nietzsche was hardly the first philosopher to challenge the concept of objective morality. Who were his most convincing predecessors?"

Several hands shot up; Farr pointed to a bearded, red-haired kid in an army jacket. "Callicles and Thrasymachus," he answered, "in Plato's dialogues. Both argued that the idea of 'justice' is a sham, a subjective means of social control, and that therefore a wise man subverts 'justice' to his own ends."

"Then what makes Nietzsche distinctive?"

The redhead answered swiftly, eagerly: "He attacked two thousand years of Western thought, where philosophers promoted 'morality' as a kind of social glue."

Farr nodded. After barely a minute, Mark had grasped how completely he commanded the classroom, how intensely the students wanted his approval or, at least, to interest him. "So if moralists are charlatans or fools, Mr. Clyde, what did Nietzsche think was at the root of our foolishness?"

"Religion," a pudgy student in wire-rimmed glasses responded. "The Christians and Jews were weak; the Romans who ruled them were strong. Therefore these religions used the idea of morality as a defense against the Romans, who, by accepting 'morality,' would be more likely to allow them to survive."

"If," Farr asked, "our most sacred moral precepts—even the Ten Commandments—are merely a tactical invention of the weak, what does that imply?"

Mark felt the desire to object—he had learned the Ten Commandments in Sunday school, and the subordination of self from a string of coaches. "Racism," a dark-haired female student said sharply. "If Jews are weak, and morality a fantasy they invented to survive, there's no reason not to exterminate them."

Farr gave her an arid smile. "To be fair, Nietzsche also says some rather nasty things about Christians, Germans, and his fellow philosophers."

"But he *can* be read to justify evil." Glancing at her notes, the young woman read, " 'As the wicked enjoy a hundred kinds of happiness of which the virtuous have no inkling, so do they possess a hundred kinds of beauty.' Hitler would have agreed."

Farr eyed her narrowly, his leonine head still, as though deciding whether to play this out. "What is Nietzsche positing about man's inherent nature?"

"It suggests that we have within us the desire to be cruel and the need to dominate."

Farr cocked his head. "Let's put that to the test, Ms. Rosenberg. Suppose you ordered one of your classmates whipped or beaten. How would you feel?"

I couldn't do that, Mark thought automatically. The young woman answered promptly, "I'd feel guilty."

Farr's cool blue eyes glinted. "To Nietzsche, justice is merely a mechanism through which the state exerts its will, dressing it up in moral sentiments to disguise its exercise of power. What does this do to the concept of guilt?"

The woman hesitated. "That it only exists in our own minds," a clean-cut blond man interjected. "Nietzsche suggests that guilt is a mechanism of social control, keeping us from exercising our own free will."

Once again, Farr nodded briskly. Mark felt the relationship between teacher and class as an organic entity, in which, directed by Farr, minds fed upon one another.

As the debate continued, Mark was surprised to discover that he grasped its core: Does whoever is in authority make the rules to suit themselves, or are some rules a simple matter of right and wrong? "For our next discussion," Farr concluded, "I ask you to consider your own nature. Do you refrain from theft or rape or murder because you're afraid of getting caught or because you'd feel guilty? And, if so, is your guilt based on anything more than what you've been trained to feel?" A smile played on Farr's lips. "I expect an answer from each of you by Thursday."

With that, the students began slowly filing out, as though still pondering the question. Picking up a trim leather briefcase, Farr asked in a tone of mild inquiry, "Do *you* have an answer, Mark?"

Looking up at the keen face of this professor, Mark felt the same need to please him he had seen in the others, even as he tried to find the bones of a response. Instinctively, he said, "I don't think the rules were just made up. If there weren't any, we'd all end up killing each other. You can't always count on being the strongest."

Farr laughed softly. "I should introduce you to Thomas Hobbes. We can talk about *him* on the way home."

A FEW MINUTES later, Mark entered yet another world.

The Farrs' home, a rambling red-brick structure located on a tree-lined street, was strikingly different from the shotgun ranch house Mark had lived in for most of his seventeen years. It dated back to the 1850s, Farr explained. Lovingly restored, the living room featured a hardwood floor covered by rich-looking Oriental rugs; shelves filled with hardcover books; and paintings that, because they resembled nothing in life, Mark assumed to be modern art. But perhaps most striking was Anne Farr, extending her hand with a smile at once gracious and reserved, her jet-black hair showing the first few strands of gray, her handsome, chiseled face so pale Mark thought of porcelain, her eastern accent suggesting what people called good breeding. "Excuse me while I see to dinner," she told him pleasantly. "You two just enjoy yourselves."

Looking around, Mark noticed a sunroom containing white wicker furniture and a slender young girl seated at an easel. He could see only her back; dark-haired like her mother, she painted with total concentration, applying a new brushstroke so carefully her hand barely seemed to move. Noticing Mark's curiosity, Lionel Farr led him to the sunroom, speaking gently as though not to break the girl's spell.

"Taylor," Farr ventured, then added with pleasant irony, "this is Mr. Darrow."

The girl turned. Mark guessed that she was seven or eight; blue-eyed and grave, she regarded him in preternatural silence, as though assessing how she should feel about this stranger. If Anne Farr was still a beauty, someday this child would become one. "My name's Mark," he amended with a smile.

Silent, she continued her deep appraisal of him. Awkwardly, Mark asked, "Do you paint a lot?"

"Yes," she answered with surprising directness. "But I'm not very good."

Her painting was a child's landscape. Though the sky was pale blue, its sun was partially obscured by clouds. Beneath it, the figure of a girl stood in shadow, gazing down at a patch of sunlit grass. "Looks to me like you're good," Mark said.

This induced her first smile, skeptical but pleased, even as her serious eyes still focused on Mark's face. "It *is* good," her father offered. "We'll let you finish it, Taylor."

Farr led Mark to a book-lined study with two leather chairs, a rolltop desk, and an antique world globe featuring countries that no longer existed. For Mark, the life of privilege this suggested was as alien—though more refined—as what he saw on *Beverly Hills 90210*. "Taylor's like her mother," Farr was remarking. "Somewhat reserved, and very artistic. Anne paints as well, though her real forte is poetry."

Mark could not think of a response. Then his eye caught an oil painting of an officer he guessed might be from the Revolutionary

War and, near that, a map of Vietnam. "That's General Wayne," Farr said of the painting, " 'Mad Anthony'—the man who gave your football team its name. He cleared the Indian confederacy out of Ohio, gaining a reputation for military genius and a mercurial temper. I don't know that he was mad, though sometimes genius and madness feed upon each other."

Mark turned to the map. "Were you there?"

"Vietnam? Yes. I was an officer in the Special Forces."

Mark thrust his hands in his pockets. "What was it like?"

He felt Farr weigh his answer. "Suffice it to say I learned things there that West Point hadn't prepared me for, including what men are capable of doing when there's no constraint on their impulses or desire. Which, I suppose, was the point of today's lecture."

Mark turned to him. "I wish I knew more about that philosopher."

"Not all my students find Nietzsche uplifting." He waved Mark to a leather chair, settling into his own. "Nevertheless, it's important to examine the choices you make, and the freedom you feel to choose. Do you know anything about Jean-Paul Sartre?"

"Not really, no."

Translated, Mark's answer meant "Never heard of him." Nodding benignly, Farr continued: "Sartre contends that the human condition is one of absolute freedom. His argument is that we're free to make choices that reflect our authentic self. So let me ask you this, Mark: If you could define yourself, who and what would you choose to be?"

The abrupt shift to the personal made Mark fidget. "I haven't really thought about it," he confessed. "I mean, what's the point?"

Farr's face seemed to harden. "What do *you* think it is? From your test scores, you're far brighter than your grades suggest."

Mark felt defensive and exposed. "Why not just call me an underachiever."

Farr looked unfazed. "Because I think that's oversimplified. Tell me how you came to live with Steve Tillman's family."

Mark had sensed that Farr already knew. "It's simple," he said in a flat tone. "My mother's been put away—she's a drunk, and she's crazy. My dad's just a drunk. Being with them was like living alone, only worse."

Farr nodded, seemingly less in sympathy than in acknowledgment of a truth. "It must be difficult not to feel cheated."

"Mostly I don't give a damn." Feeling Farr's probing gaze, Mark felt himself speak against his will. "Sometimes I got pissed off at them. I still can."

"Understandably. But your problem is that the world doesn't care. The only person you're hurting is yourself."

Mark heard a knock. Anne Farr leaned in, looking from her husband to Mark. "I hope I'm not interrupting. But I thought you two might like your dinner warm."

The dining room was as elegant and subdued as the living room was bright. Taylor was lighting candles, the only source of illumination. "We do this every night," Anne explained. "In Boston, where I grew up, my parents made a ritual of it. Candlelight slowed us down, my father said, gave us time to talk."

Over dinner, fish in a surprisingly tasty sauce, Mark sensed that he was expected to converse. Groping for a subject, he asked about Anne's poetry. She was published in literary magazines, he discovered, too obscure for him to know. "I'm sorry," he apologized. "The only ones I read are *Sports Illustrated* and *Field and Stream.*"

Farr laughed. "Anne and Taylor are the aesthetes in the family. There's more beauty in one of Taylor's paintings, or a line of Anne's poetry, than in the entire book I'm writing now."

Mark had never known anyone who had written a book. "About Nietzsche?"

Farr smiled. "Yet again. But it's more a psychological study, relating his life to his beliefs—the why of them, I suppose. Including the idea that a man's supposedly objective beliefs are so often a product of his needs."

Anne Farr appraised her husband with a neutral expression. "You do believe that, don't you."

Her husband's smile faded. "Yes. Unfortunately, perhaps."

Quiet, Taylor watched them. Noting this, Mark turned to Taylor and asked about her painting. Somewhat wistfully, the girl said, "I know what's beautiful. But I can't paint it in real life."

"You will someday," Mark assured her. "When I was seven, I couldn't throw a football."

"Can you now?"

Mark smiled. "A little."

After dessert, a caramel flan, Mark offered to help clear the table. "The women can tackle it," Farr said dryly. "Let's finish our discussion."

Settling back in the den, Farr said, "From our talk on Friday, I assume you'd continue playing football if you could."

Despite their courtesy, Mark realized how much at sea he felt in the Farrs' household. Hesitant, he answered, "Sports is the only place I feel at home."

"You can find others, Mark. But first you have to change your destiny. For so many kids in Wayne, life after high school means a job making auto parts, or copper fittings, or maybe helping to fabricate Sky Climbers to wash the windows of buildings in big cities most of them will never see. I assume you must want more than that."

Once again, Mark felt on edge, grasping for the threads of a response. "Maybe go to community college. I thought someday I might want to coach."

Farr shook his head. "I was watching you in class today. A full scholarship to Caldwell College would open worlds you've never imagined."

Mark struggled to absorb this. It took a moment for him to realize how long he had been silent. "Sorry. I mean, how could that happen?"

"I'm the chairman of Caldwell's scholarship committee. You certainly qualify financially. If you can get your grades up this semester, I'm sure the committee would take notice. We want to reach more kids who lack opportunities."

Mark still could find no words. "Amazing," he finally murmured.

"You don't know *how* amazing," Farr said firmly. "A solid education. A chance to play sports, and then to do far more than that—become a lawyer, a teacher, a business leader, or anything your gifts entitle you to do. You'd graduate debt-free. All it will take to begin your change of destiny is two months of working harder at high school than you've ever worked before. From what I can see, you have it in you." Farr paused for emphasis. "If *you* think you do."

Mark imagined explaining this to Steve.

"What is it?" Farr asked.

Mark struggled to crystallize his thoughts. "I was thinking about the Tillmans—I mean, they took me in. Steve's almost as poor as I am, and he's got better grades."

Farr smiled fractionally—it did not seem in his nature, Mark realized, to exhibit unambiguous good cheer. "If you're asking whether we can extend similar largesse to your friend, I think Mr. Tillman may lack your potential. But I'll see about him."

Abruptly, Farr stood. "You should go home, and I've got work to do. It's become my job to read books to Taylor. She chooses rather precocious ones, I'm afraid."

Mark trailed Farr to the living room. Anne Farr sat on the couch, sipping wine. It struck Mark that she had an ethereal quality, and that, although lovely, she did not appear strong or healthy—unlike his mother, who, drunk or sober, sane or crazy, would burn fiercely until the end. Smiling, Anne said, "Please come again, Mark. Lionel suffers from a surplus of females."

"Thanks," Mark said, then added, "I only counted two of you."

Anne's smile became ambiguous. "Even so."

As they walked to the door, Mark saw Taylor in the living room, studying her painting as if she had not captured what she imagined—or could not. Suddenly conscious of his gaze, she turned, studying Mark with the same quiet gravity. Farr waited until Mark faced him again. "I thought you might ask about Steve Tillman. If I try to help him, Mark, do we have a deal?"

For an instant, Mark felt himself standing on the edge of the unknown. Then, drawn by the sudden promise of hope and the force of Farr's personality, he answered, "If you can help me go to school here, I'll do whatever it takes."

EVER SINCE THAT day, Mark Darrow had done exactly that. But he had not risen by his efforts alone. Lionel Farr had touched the scales of his life, and every privilege he had stemmed from that. Farr had not ordained his tragedies, only his successes.

Two weeks before his return to Caldwell, Farr had telephoned Darrow and asked if he could come by Darrow's law office in Boston. Farr had not explained himself, and Darrow had not requested him to. Awaiting Farr with curiosity, Darrow had gazed out the window of his corner office in the Prudential Center, rewarded by a panoramic view of the Public Garden and the Boston Common. Five months prior, Darrow had won a $120 million verdict in a financial fraud case stemming from the subprime mortgage meltdown, adding to a fortune already swollen beyond his wildest imaginings. On his desk the bones and sinews of a complex shareholder suit—financial statements; an expert deposition in which Darrow had eviscerated an arrogant investment banker—were neatly arranged before him. But as Darrow recalled his last visit with Farr, his eye turned, as it so often did, to the photograph of his wife.

Dark and pretty, Lee stood at the bottom of a ski slope, flushed from a breakneck run, her grin of triumph cracking clean and white and sharp. In the photo she was twenty-eight; in Darrow's mind, she was forever twenty-nine, in the fifth month of her pregnancy, waving to him through the window of the taxi that began her final trip to Iowa. In the two years since, Mark Darrow had turned thirty-eight. He had not seen Farr since Lee's memorial service.

Even among the throng of friends and relatives and Lee's colleagues from MSNBC and the *Boston Globe* who'd crowded the darkened church, Farr had stood out: at sixty-five, he was tall and astonishingly fit, with thick gray-blond hair and the erect posture of the Special Forces officer he had been before he had resigned his commission to pursue a doctorate in philosophy at Yale. That day he had been a quiet presence, offering a few words of sustenance to help Darrow endure this bleakest of winter afternoons. But Farr had lingered for two days after the service, until Darrow had fulfilled his obligations to Lee's parents, then taken him to dinner at the Federalist.

For Darrow, their reunion was shadowed by the day thirteen years before when, in a strange reversal of roles, the young Mark Darrow had called on the newly widowed Farr. Then Mark had managed only to recite a few words of concern for his mentor and his daughter, Taylor; years later, Farr offered him a stiff martini and companionable semisilence until—amid the elegantly appointed room, the quiet talk and laughter of couples taking their normal life for granted—Darrow had asked simply, "What do I do now?"

Sipping his scotch, Farr studied Mark across the table. They were similar enough in appearance that, at times, people mistook them for father and son: Farr's blue eyes retained the clarity of youth, and his still aquiline nose and seamed face, though betraying his years, showed no trace of dissolution. Answering Darrow, his features seemed graven with his own hard memories. "What I did, I suppose. Each day I picked out a task or two, and tried to perform it like the doing mattered. Teaching helped; I had an audience whose faces revealed how I'd done. So did being a parent, though there I functioned far less well." He grimaced. "Perhaps I was better at performing for students than consoling a young daughter shattered by her mother's death. But each morning I tried to look no further than the day ahead.

"There was no bright line, no turning point. More a slow acceptance of what could not be helped, and the realization over time that a greater portion of any given day held a measure of happiness—or, more realistically given who I am, satisfaction. I had my work, however cerebral and self-contained; you have yours, more engrossing in that it's filled with challenges and surprises and because, when you're ready, it will present you with new people to know." Farr gave a brief, reflective smile. "Eventually the life that goes on all around you, indifferent to your sadness, will sweep you up again. For better or worse there's a certain Viking hardiness in our natures, an appetite for more."

Darrow caught Farr's tacit suggestion: however unthinkable now, there would be women—then *a* woman—beyond Lee Hatton. "I've lost a wife," Darrow answered, "and an unborn child. How does one come back from that?" He paused, then added softly, "Anne died thirteen years ago, Lionel. You're still alone."

Farr seemed to look inward. "Perhaps Anne, not solitude, was my anomaly." He shrugged the remark away. "In any case, I was at a different stage of life than you, more than a decade older, with a daughter who needed whatever solace I could muster. As you'll recall, Caldwell College is a bit out of the way, and Wayne, Ohio, hardly a magnet for the bright, attractive young people who flock to Boston." He held up a hand. "Not that it matters in the face of such a profound loss. I'm simply offering my excuses. It would be tasteless to say more beyond the obvious—that you're young, successful, and live in a vibrant city among close friends. For which I, to whom you mean a great deal, am profoundly grateful."

Darrow stared at his half-empty martini glass. Then Farr reached across the table, grasping Darrow's forearm in a gesture of solidarity and consolation. Darrow was touched—Lionel Farr was not given to overt gestures of affection. Which had made his response to Lee's death all the more telling: though it was seldom expressed, since their first meeting, a great portion of Farr's empathy and respect, so sparely given, had resided with Mark Darrow.

Between that dinner and Farr's unexplained reappearance in Boston, Darrow had forced himself to live each day as if it mattered. But even after two years, his life seemed to matter less. Making money—if it had ever been—was no longer Darrow's purpose.

His intercom buzzed, announcing Lionel Farr, and then Rebecca, his assistant, opened the door to wave Farr inside.

Standing, Darrow embraced him. Then he leaned back, giving his mentor a look of mock appraisal. "You look pretty good, Lionel. I could still pick you out of a lineup."

Farr grimaced, a pantomime of doubt. In truth, Darrow saw a change; though still fit and handsome as he entered his late sixties, Farr looked more tired than Darrow could remember, the flesh beneath his eyes appearing slack and a little bruised. They sat in Darrow's wing chairs, Farr appraising the younger man with affectionate curiosity.

"So," Farr inquired after a time, "how are you?"

Darrow shrugged. "All right. I'm still living out the clichés of grief: anger, pain, acceptance. Some days are okay. Then, on a random morning, I'll wake up and, for a moment, Lee's still alive. I reach across the bed, touching where she used to sleep, and feel her loss all over again. I suppose someday that will stop."

Farr nodded in sympathy. "Eventually. Does your work help at all?"

"Sometimes." Keen to change the subject, and curious about the unstated reason for Farr's visit, Darrow asked, "How's your life as provost?"

Farr gathered his thoughts. "Troubled, as is the school. You remember the impact of Angela Hall's murder: we experienced it as no one else could have—except, perhaps, Steve Tillman. When I recall the loss of a young woman with so much promise, murdered in such a terrible way, I still feel disbelief.

"But what remains is the impact on Caldwell College. Sixteen years later, it still lingers: however unfair to the school, the perception of a murder tinged with race caused a falloff in applications, donations, minority students, and—as a result—the quality of the student body. For a short but crucial period, our endowment dipped, limiting our ability to give the kind of scholarships you and Angela received. We've never really recovered."

Darrow was surprised. "I thought the place had stabilized."

"In a fashion," Farr answered sardonically. "We've achieved a slower but steady decline. You'll recall that you turned down an appointment to the board of trustees, enabling you to preserve your sense of optimism. But the precise rate of decline hardly matters now, for reasons you must keep in strictest confidence."

A bit stung, Darrow answered, "Who would I tell?"

" 'Who would give a damn' do you mean? Both of us, I hope." Farr stood, reminding Darrow of how restless he could be. "Mind if we take a walk, Mark? It's been years since I strolled through Boston."

It was a fine spring day, breezy but sunny. Passing the pond in the Public Garden, filled with tourists in swan boats, they stopped at a food stand to buy Polish dogs smothered in grilled onions. Sitting on a park bench, Farr observed, "I always liked this city. You chose well, Mark."

Finishing his hot dog, Darrow saw a nun glance at them, smiling to herself—even now Darrow could be taken for Farr's son. Still, the resemblance was not precise. Even before Farr's hair grayed, Darrow's had been blonder; his face, however well proportioned, lacked Farr's striking angularity, the look of warriors; though obviously fit, little about Darrow, now prone to cuff links and Savile Row suits, suggested the Spartan bearing of a soldier. But the most striking difference was in their smiles. Orthodontics, Darrow's mother's last sacrifice before descending into schizophrenia, had purchased what

Lee once called his killer smile, which before her death had marked the chief difference between Darrow and Farr. Farr's smile, when it came, was less a show of teeth than a manifestation of his pervasive sense of irony.

"So," Darrow said. "Caldwell."

They began walking again. "Put simply," Farr responded, "nine hundred thousand dollars of endowment money has vanished."

Darrow turned to him. "How is that possible?"

Farr looked off into the distance, as though pondering the question. "Deciphering financial chicanery isn't my specialty. But as provost, I'm obliged to try. From what I know, the signs point to our president. You'll recall Clark Durbin."

"Durbin?" In his astonishment, Darrow almost laughed. "The man's a classic academic—remember how you had to prop him up after I found her body? I can imagine him writing a paper about embezzlement, complete with footnotes. But not stealing."

"Clark's weak." Farr's voice was etched with disdain. "Faced with hardship, the weak step out of character—or, perhaps, discover it. Clark's wife is an invalid, and his son's a drug addict who needed extensive treatment; heroin, as I observed in Vietnam, grips a man by the throat. Add that Clark has the investment skills common to many of my colleagues: none."

"So how did a man who can't pick stocks develop a talent for theft?"

Farr stopped to contemplate a dog chasing a Frisbee thrown by his youthful master, the animal's stubby legs leaving him endlessly short of the red plastic disk. "That dog," he observed, "will have a coronary. It's the downside of trying too hard to please. As for Clark, our board has an investments committee, with your old friend Joe Betts as chairman."

"Joe?" Darrow felt his amazement growing. "In college, his idea of high finance was sending his bloated credit card bills home to Dad."

"People change," Farr responded. "As you'd be the first to acknowledge. Joe Betts is now a partner in a respected investment
advisory firm that oversees our endowment. Durbin was on Joe's
committee, each of whose members was entitled to direct transfer
of endowment funds beneath one million dollars.

"The funds in question were certificates of deposit. What seems
to have happened is that Durbin e-mailed Joe's firm, directing that
the CDs be transferred to a bank account in the name of Caldwell
College, set up by Clark himself. From which, at his direction, the
money was transferred to a bank account in Geneva—"

"Then you can forget it," Darrow said flatly. "The Swiss are a
black hole."

Farr nodded. "In theory, everyone on the investment committee is suspect. But Durbin sent the e-mail, and his signature is on
the papers used to open the bank account in Wayne that received the
money."

"Are there other possibilities?"

Farr shrugged. "The other person seemingly involved is Joe himself, who transferred the money based on Durbin's e-mail. But it's
hard to see how Joe could send that e-mail to himself, or gain access
to Durbin's computer. It all comes back to Clark."

Pausing, Darrow watched a young couple walking hand in hand,
careless of anything but each other. "Still, nine hundred thousand
isn't that much. How large is our endowment?"

"Less than seventy million. The timing of Angela's death killed a
capital campaign we desperately needed. And historically the school
has never done well with its money—until the last few years, our investment committee might as well have put it under a mattress. We got
heavily into equities just in time for the dot-com meltdown, then the
near collapse of our financial system—too heavily, it turns out. By the
time Joe's firm took over, we'd lost over a third of our endowment.
And now this." Farr shook his head in disgust. "Stupidity and crimi-
nality are a lethal combination. Piety is even worse: church-related

schools, I'm finding, don't have the financial safeguards they should—
they were founded on notions of man's goodness. What pure-hearted
Christian would suspect Clark Durbin of being a crook?"

"Or just clever enough to be a fool," Darrow answered. "Embezzlement's a dead-end crime: sooner or later, the thief always gets
caught." He faced Farr again. "If it's money you need, I can make up
the nine hundred thousand. More, if you like."

Farr smiled faintly. "Who would have ever thought, Mark? I
guess lawyering *does* pay better than coaching, your original ambition.
But, with deepest thanks, the missing money is not Caldwell's problem. It's reputation.

"As the events surrounding Angela's death suggested, reputation,
once lost, is hard to regain—especially among the donors we need to
survive. We were planning a hundred-million-dollar capital campaign
when the board got wind of this. All that's needed for disaster to
strike, I've realized, is for Caldwell to dream up a new fund-raising
effort." Farr's voice softened. "Clark's embezzlement has become an
existential threat. How do you ask people for money when they don't
believe you can safeguard what you have?"

Darrow stopped, hands in his pockets, facing Farr. "You've just
redefined your problem, Lionel. It's public relations. How much does
the media know?"

"Nothing, yet. *That* problem is still hanging over us."

"Then if you've come to me for advice, I've got some. I assume the
board is hiring a forensic accountant to sort out how Durbin's supposed to have done this."

"As we speak."

"Have them draw up a new system of financial controls, to assure
the alumni—and the media—that nothing like this can ever happen
again." Squinting into the afternoon sun, Darrow put on his sunglasses. "The next thing is to engage an outside public relations firm.
You'll need to write this story before somebody else does."

Farr folded his arms. "The board's current hope," he responded in a dubious tone, "is to keep this quiet until we find out all the details. There's some thought that Clark will help us retrieve the money in return for a low-key resignation because of 'health.' Durbin has reason to cooperate—if he refuses, and this leaks out, some on our board want to press criminal charges. I doubt a mild-mannered heterosexual like Clark will want to make the kind of 'special friends' he'll encounter in state prison."

Reflexively, Darrow thought of Steve Tillman. "At least Durbin won't have spent his life there."

From the glint in Farr's eyes, Darrow saw that he'd grasped the reference. "True enough. But let's hope, for Clark's sake, that one prisoner from our community is enough."

"Whatever the case," Darrow said, "get all the facts, then make a complete disclosure. Dribbling out partial information is almost as bad as stonewalling." He looked at his mentor keenly. "But you know all this, I'm sure. So tell me what else I can do."

Farr was silent for a moment. "That depends, I suppose, on how you feel about your current life. And what plans you have for the future."

Darrow slowly shook his head. "I can't help but think about the first time you asked me that question. My answer's much the same: I don't really know. Before she died, Lee and I talked about what we'd do if she got tired of chasing after campaigns. But all that was complicated by the idea of starting a family . . ."

His voice trailed off. "What about the law?" Farr asked.

Darrow shrugged. "I'm a very good trial lawyer, no doubt. I've proven that. But there are other talented lawyers who can bring these cases, and I can't tell myself that I'm doing God's work. My dilemma is that it's easier to feel restless in the present than to define a different future." Giving Farr a fleeting smile, he finished: "It's like you said when we first met. I'm lacking in direction. But if you still want me to join the board, I will."

Briefly, Farr paused. The look in his eyes struck Darrow as speculative. "Actually, I want you to consider becoming president of Caldwell College."

This time Darrow did laugh. Removing his sunglasses, he said, "You're joking."

"Hardly."

"Then you should be. I've got no academic credentials; no administrative experience; no background with an educational institution of any kind. I haven't even kept up with the school. I've already offered the only thing I'm good for—money."

Farr folded his arms. Fleetingly, Darrow imagined how they looked to others: two men in business suits in the middle of the Public Garden, talking quietly but forcefully about something very serious. "If your model of a college president is someone like Clark Durbin," Farr said bluntly, "God help us. That's the last thing we need. Even colleges that aren't in trouble are making nontraditional hires: Oberlin just hired Michigan's outside lawyer, and the Stanford Business School's run by a former CEO."

"That makes a kind of sense," Darrow said. "This doesn't."

"No?" Farr countered dryly. "You spent five years prosecuting criminal cases—including homicides—and eight more years untangling every financial scam known to man. Given Caldwell's recent history, some might say you're perfect."

"*That's* pretty sad."

"But true. More fundamentally, you embody the best of Caldwell College: a small-town boy who made good through attending a school that stresses teaching instead of research. To be plain, you're here because of Caldwell."

"And you," Darrow answered softly. "I'm well aware of that."

"As the alumni are of you. You're an athletic hero, enshrined in our Sports Hall of Fame. You're a graduate of Yale Law, a nationally renowned lawyer. You've been on the cover of *U.S. News,* the *ABA*

Journal, American Lawyer, and—three times already—our alumni magazine." Farr spoke with quiet urgency now, brooking no interruption. "You're young, attractive, and gifted with considerable charisma. You know the school. And what the school needs is a leader with élan and a sense of humor, the vitality to lift our morale, redefine our message, refocus Caldwell on its future, and, in a year or so, help restart the capital campaign required for us to *have* a future.

"For you, the job wouldn't be a stepping stone to somewhere better. You'd be saying you believe in Caldwell College—that if you invest, others should."

Darrow held up his hand. "You need more than a symbol. You need someone with qualifications."

"The first qualification is judgment, which you have. Critical for the fix we're in, you're not remote, authoritarian, or rigid—in fact, you've always been adaptable, the quickest study I know. You won't have to learn the culture of Caldwell or the town." Farr's tone became emphatic. "With you as president, we can address our problems squarely. You're more than just a symbol, Mark. You're a human Hail Mary, a concrete sign that Caldwell can rise again. Anyone else is second best."

Stunned, Darrow felt a surge of doubt, the stubborn urge to dissent. " 'Anyone,' Lionel? What about you?"

"The board will make me interim president, if that's necessary. But I'm too old to do what's needed. We need a fresh face, one that doesn't look like a relief map of Afghanistan." Seeing Darrow smile, Farr added swiftly, "If you wish it, I'll stay on as provost—for any president, a good relationship with the provost matters. I can walk you through the budget, issues regarding the faculty and board, where the figurative bodies are buried. Whatever you need to ensure that you do well."

"You talk like all you need is my consent. Don't you have a search committee?"

"To be sure, and you'd have to meet with them. But I'm not here on some frolic of my own. There's substantial support for this idea—starting with Joe Betts, who seems to recall you more admiringly than you remember him."

"We were friends," Darrow demurred. "With a reservation here or there, I liked Joe, whatever his role in Steve Tillman's trial. But Joe no more knows me in the present than I know him."

"He thinks otherwise. So do I. By your senior year, your essential character was apparent. You were, and are, a leader."

"Of what, precisely? The football team?"

Farr looked nettled. "Don't be obtuse. People were drawn to you; you had a gift for empathy rare in someone your age. You can't be in the dark about why you've done so well with juries." Farr softened his speech. "Even the timing is right. It's April—if you start in June, you'll have two months of paid rehearsals before the students arrive. During which you can focus on our alumni."

Darrow smiled at this. "As usual, you've thought of everything. Except whether the timing's right for *me*."

Farr's face clouded briefly. "Only you can say for sure." Glancing at his watch, he said, "It's past four-thirty. Suppose I buy you a drink at the Ritz Carlton."

"Won't help, and the Ritz is now the Taj, a cog in the global economy. But sure—the bar's the same, and it still makes a good martini."

Silent, they walked across the gardens in lengthening shadows, crossing Arlington Street to enter the hotel. The first-floor bar faced back toward the gardens; its paneled walls, leather chairs, and oil paintings of hunting scenes reminded Darrow faintly of Farr's study. With a look of satisfaction, Farr sat across from him at a marble table by the window and ordered dry martinis for them both. Farr permitted Darrow a first bracing sip before saying, "About your timing, I *do* have thoughts."

"So do I. My life in Wayne, Ohio, seems like a thousand years ago. And as you confessed after Lee's memorial service, the dating pool is not exactly infinite."

Farr raised his eyebrows. "At last, you refer to a personal life. Is there one?"

Darrow pondered this. "Call it a half life. On a good day, three-quarters."

"There's a woman, then?"

"Plural." For a moment, Darrow fell quiet. "Physically, I function well enough. But my emotional equipment feels a little stuck."

Farr contemplated the table, considering his next words. "Forgive me if this sounds tactless. But it seems you're free to leave Boston without uprooting anyone, including yourself. This may be your time for something new."

Darrow smiled a little. "Whose idea *was* this, Lionel?"

Farr gave him an ironic smile of his own. "Mine. But the last idea I had about your life turned out pretty well."

"Except when it didn't," Darrow answered mildly. But that was not Farr's doing. In all but one respect—that which had come to matter most—Darrow was the luckiest man he knew. His debt to Caldwell College, it seemed, was indistinguishable from his debt to Lionel Farr.

As if reading his thoughts, Farr spoke quietly: "There's no place where you could make such a difference. In a few years, you could give our college what it needs. Perhaps you need that as well."

Darrow sorted through the jumble of his thoughts, the minefield of memory. The apogee of his young life, and his greatest trauma until Lee's death, had occurred at Caldwell College in the space of sixteen hours. Perhaps that was why he had never returned. "Do you ever visit Steve Tillman?" Darrow asked.

This seemingly irrelevant question would have puzzled anyone but Farr. "On rare occasions. These days we struggle for subjects. As you'd expect, it's very sad."

Despite his own guilt, Darrow heard no rebuke. The two men lapsed into silence.

Darrow finished his martini, feeling its initial jolt filter slowly through his system. "Give me a day or two, Lionel. You took me by surprise, and there's a lot for me to sift through. And remember."

Farr's eyes held understanding and compassion. "Perhaps more than anyone, I know. That morning we stood at the Spire, looking down at her, is something no one could forget. Certainly not the two of us."

PART

I

The Shadow

1

SIXTEEN YEARS LATER, DARROW'S MEMORY OF THAT TERRIBLE night and morning remained as fresh as yesterday, as disorienting as the aftershock of a nightmare.

Moments after ringing the great brass bell, he had descended from the Spire, less triumphant than grateful for his release from its stifling gloom. For a while he was caught up in the jubilation of the crowd. Then he headed for a celebration at the Delta Beta Epsilon house, his pleasure fading into a slightly melancholy sense of life's transience.

What the campus called fraternity row was, in fact, a grassy oval, surrounded by red-brick houses. Sheltered by trees, each house varied in style: one had filigreed balconies reminiscent of a New Orleans mansion; another reflected the Georgian revival; two had pillars that evoked southern plantations; still another, the greatest departure, resembled a suburban ranch house. The DBE house was a mixture of styles. Three stories high, it had a small portico at one side as its entrance, and steps in the rear that rose from a parking lot to a generous porch. At the front were six tall windows through which brothers congregating in the living room could monitor the abode of their fiercest adversaries, the SAEs, whose stone lions, situated by the front steps like sentries, stared fiercely across the oval.

For Mark, the sight of the lions summoned a memory shared by

only one other person. After the Ohio Lutheran game two years before, he and Steve Tillman, armed with tear gas canisters, had gassed
the second floor of the Sigma Alpha Epsilon house at four A.M. This
act of daring, attributed in legend to suspects as varied as students
from Ohio Lutheran and a local motorcycle gang, had caused a
cluster of SAEs to flee the house, weeping and vomiting, as the two
adrenalized perpetrators watched from DBE's darkened living room.
Reaching the house, Mark wondered what memories *this* night would
bring.

On the lawn, Mark passed a band of would-be athletes—his fraternity brothers, fueled by beer—playing a desultory game of touch
football. Declining their shouted invitation to join them with a wave
and a smile, Mark entered the house. Though it was not yet six
o'clock, the sound system was pumping out Pearl Jam, and revelers
were gathering in the living room and library—so called because, although no one ever used it for studying, its shelves of athletic trophies
were interspersed with leather-bound books no one ever opened.
Avoiding notice, Mark climbed the scuffed linoleum stairs to the second floor, still in search of his best friend.

Like Mark and several other football players, Steve had a room in
the stadium itself. Mark had not found him there. As a junior, Steve
had ripped up his knee in this emblematic game, leaving him with a
permanent limp and no physical outlet for his competitive nature; the
pain of no longer playing, Mark knew, sometimes caused Steve to
separate himself. But Steve was one reason Mark had no date this year,
just as on the same night one year ago he had postponed his date to go
with Steve to the hospital. Out of friendship and solidarity, Mark had
resolved to spend this special Saturday with his friend.

On the second floor, Mark went from room to room, looking into
each cramped living space. Most were empty; none held Steve. Instead,
sticking his head into Jerry Feldman's room, Mark found Joe Betts, a
fellow denizen of the football stadium, sipping from a whiskey bottle
as he watched a video.

"Seen Steve?" Mark inquired.

"Nope," Joe answered with indifference, riveted by the video.

Mark hesitated, mentally taking Joe's emotional temperature. Tall and rangy, Joe had been a decent enough flanker before dropping football altogether. Whereas Mark and Steve had strained to make the most of whatever ability they had, Joe's self-indulgence and aversion to training was so marked that Coach Fiske had given him a choice: work harder or leave. Joe had left. Now Joe looked a little soft, the outlines of his handsome face more indistinct, though his round glasses and swept-back hair still lent him an air of eastern prep school panache. That he had started in on whiskey was not a good sign. Otherwise contained and somewhat aloof, when drunk Joe could be mercurial and foul-tempered, prone to outbursts that ripened into fights. Mark sometimes wondered what psychic trip wires lurked inside Joe Betts; in three years of college, Mark had grasped that his own wounds were not unique, and that he often understood very little about the inner recesses of people he considered his friends. Drawn by Joe's fixation on the screen, Mark stepped inside.

The tape was a sex video. The naked female, a sturdy blonde, looked somehow familiar. "Tonya Harding," Joe said in a tone of satisfaction and contempt. "Trailer trash turned Olympic skater. Seems like her career's gone downhill since her ex-husband hired that douche bag to kneecap Nancy Kerrigan."

Mark eyed the screen. "Downhill's one thing," he observed. "This is more like free fall."

Joe shrugged, still watching the screen. "Her husband videotaped it, then decided he was Steven Spielberg. You and I are the incidental beneficiaries."

"She's all yours, man. I need to find Steve."

Joe flushed, as though Mark had insulted him. "*I'd* fuck her," he said with unsettling vehemence. "I'd fuck anything right now."

Mark flashed on Joe's girlfriend, Laurie, an attractive but reticent blonde whose attachment to Joe, given his volatility, had always puzzled Mark. Mildly, he said, "I thought you had that covered."

Joe's eyes narrowed. "Think harder."

Mark sensed that he had touched a nerve. "See you downstairs," he said, and left.

On the door of the stairwell was posted a list of duties for freshmen—cleaning bathrooms and scrubbing floors—the aim of which, a hygienic DBE house, was largely aspirational. Opening the door, Mark found Steve Tillman seated on the steps, beer in hand. Above them, an anonymous whoop of laughter issued from the third floor.

Surprised, Mark asked, "What the hell are you doing *here*?"

"I love the view." A shadow crossed Steve's open midwestern face. "Nice game."

This sounded sincere. But Mark understood Steve's clouded expression. Their trajectories had crossed: after Lionel Farr's challenge, Mark had finished high school with straight A's and, as though the scales had fallen from his eyes, had worked hard to continue the pattern at Caldwell. Once a better student than Mark, Steve—as Farr had guessed—found college academics more difficult. When his knee had gone, it seemed, so had Steve's sense of self; ever since, he had been mired in the C range, hoping for the career to which Mark had once aspired, that of high school coach. Now, aided by Farr, Mark was set on getting into Yale Law School, and it was Steve who had no vision of the future. Sometimes Mark imagined that they had traded places the night Farr first set Mark on his path, leaving Steve Tillman an afterthought.

Awkwardly, Mark said, "Wish I'd thrown those touchdown passes to you. If I hadn't played with you in high school, I wouldn't have been out there today."

Steve drained his beer. "You ran with it, chief. Not your fault no one shredded your knee." He stared at the cinder-block stairwell. "Shouldn't you be at the party?"

Mark shrugged. "I'll get there. It hit me today that *my* career's ending, too, like I thought it would in high school. No more football, just life. I wanted to hang with you awhile."

For a moment, Steve bit his lip, struggling with some unspoken feeling. Then he summoned a grin. "Tell you what," he said. "You have a beer, and I'll have another beer, and together we can work up a few minutes of real sentiment."

Mark looked into Steve's face. Beneath the short haircut, the same as in high school, was a face less bright, eyes less innocent. Sitting beside him, Mark answered, "Maybe we can fill up a whole hour."

So they sat as Steve killed most of the six-pack, reminiscing. At length, Steve placed a hand on Mark's shoulder. "You're my best friend," he confessed in a somewhat slurry voice. "Maybe the best I'll ever have."

"Keep drinking, pal. I get better."

"Nope," Steve said with sudden resolve. "We could drink all night, and you'd never be a woman. Let's go downstairs and see what our future holds."

2

In the living room, Mark paused with Steve, taking in the scene.

The night was building. Some couples had gathered in front of the stone fireplace engraved with the DBE insignia, drinking and watching the fire; others crowded together on the couches, their gestures animated by alcohol and adrenaline. On the front lawn Tim Fedak and Skip Ellis had rigged up a catapult with steel rods and surgical hose, and had begun launching water balloons at the SAE house, the rubbery spheroids traveling in an arc of impressive distance and velocity. "Those fucking balloons will kill someone," Steve opined. "Unless the SAEs kill those guys first."

Mark shrugged. "Either way it's no great loss. Let's go find the party."

Heading for the stairs to the basement, Mark spotted Carl Hall sliding through the front door. A slender young black man, Carl had wary eyes that constantly assessed his surroundings, making him seem older than he was. But even in high school, Carl had always struck Mark as a guy who would not live to see old age; his vocation—drug dealer—and a certain slippery quality suggested to Mark that someday one of his commercial calculations, skewed by self-interest, would prove fatal. Nodding toward Carl, Mark inquired of Steve, "You ask him here?"

"Nope. Only his sister." Steve frowned. "He shouldn't be at this party. If Scotty invited him, it's a bad move."

The disapproving reference to Jackie Scott, a basketball star who was the only black fraternity brother, evoked Mark's sympathy: Scotty lived in a twilight zone, perched uncomfortably between his white peer group and his connections to Wayne's black community, the nearest thing to the neighborhood from which he had come. "No matter," Mark answered. "No one's getting busted tonight. 'Zero tolerance' means 'Don't snort coke in Clark Durbin's driveway.'"

Steve gave a delayed but knowing laugh. In all the time they'd been there, the college had never enforced its drug and alcohol policy—draconian in theory—preferring ignorance to raids and spot inspections. Whatever surprises happened at the party, they would not involve the campus cops. As Carl Hall slipped into the basement, the two friends followed.

The room was dark, the lights dimmed so low that Mark could see only shadowy forms. Tom Petty's "Don't Back Down" blasted from the sound system—sooner or later, Mark could expect to hear the Smashing Pumpkins, the Gin Blossoms, Green Day, the Beastie Boys, and, inevitably, Kurt Cobain fronting Nirvana. A few of the shadows were dancing; others were drinking from paper cups full of beer or liquor; a guy and girl were sharing a joint next to an anonymous couple making out in a corner of the room. "Right on schedule," Steve murmured.

Glancing around, Mark spotted a form he thought was Carl Hall facing the chubby outline of a guy who must be one of his customers. Instinctively, Mark felt less sanguine than he had sounded to Steve. By coming, Carl had crossed a line, undefined but real, introducing an element of unpredictability into an already combustible environment.

"Mark," Shawn Hale's voice called out. "Hey, man."

Someone started clapping. Before Mark knew it, Shawn, Charlie Ware, and Jim Neeley had picked him up, one leg on Charlie's shoulder, the other on Shawn's, and were carrying him through the crush of bodies, yelling "Ice Man . . . Ice Man . . . Ice Man" in a tribute to his coolheadedness against Ohio Lutheran. Some at the party cheered; others took no notice. Pleased but embarrassed, Mark jerked Shawn by the hair. "Put me down," he shouted above the din, "before you three clowns drop me."

Shawn said something to the others. Abruptly, they tossed Mark to the floor. Stumbling forward, he found himself facing Angela Hall.

Carl's twin sister was alone, her eyes half slits, dancing with no one. It was strange, Mark thought—though they had gone to high school together, then college, until three weeks ago his only impression of Angela had been that she was shy. But until three weeks ago, when Steve had asked Mark to come along, he had never been to the Alibi Club.

THE CLUB WAS in the black section of Wayne, on the corner of a randomly zoned street that included a small grocery, a beauty shop, a shabby apartment building, and wooden houses and duplexes in various states of repair. Though near the border of Colored Town—as Wayne's older whites often called it—the street was a few blocks from fraternity row, marking an uneasy intersection of cultures where underage college kids sought out the Alibi Club for drinks and the drugs they could buy from Carl Hall, the son of the club's owner.

A neatly maintained red-brick structure, the club had a blinking neon sign that beckoned customers at night, its reflection flashing in the windows on the second floor, where the proprietress lived with her family. Though its primary clientele was black, the shadowy convergence of race and class served the community as well as the college: since high school, Steve Tillman, like other whites, had come here for what he could not get elsewhere. Though this was unspoken, the police treated the Alibi Club as they did the campus: short of murder, they left it alone.

What rules the club had—its own—were strictly enforced by a three-hundred-pound black man named Hugo. On the evening Steve first took Mark there, Hugo was at the door, his broad, impassive face revealing nothing as he nodded them inside.

The room was dark and smoky. An old jukebox blared soul music; black working-class men hunched at the bar; black couples sat at tables; a pair of white college kids huddled in one corner, drinking what looked like screwdrivers and keeping to themselves. When Steve went to the end of the bar, Mark took the stool beside him, noting the incongruity of two young white faces in the mirror fronted by rows of liquor bottles. Then he saw Angela Hall serving drinks at the other end.

She held herself tall, suggesting pride and a certain distance. As far as he could remember, they had never spoken. He knew only that her father was dead—much like Mark, she had fended for herself. They had both been in one of Farr's philosophy classes; she had impressed Mark as smart and conscientious, though on occasion, exposed by Farr's sharp questions, she seemed to have fallen behind.

Now Mark took in how pretty she was. Spotting Steve, she gave him a smile that, while fleeting, seemed friendly enough. Casually, Steve waved.

The brief interaction made Mark curious. "Thought you didn't like black folks."

"Times change." Gazing at Angela, Steve added softly, "Who wouldn't like that?"

Angela came up to them. "Hey," she said to Steve.

"Hey, yourself. How's life?"

Angela laughed ruefully. "What life? I go to class, I tend Mom's bar, I go upstairs to the flat I got born in and crack the books until my eyes close. Not exactly *Melrose Place*—which, by the way, I don't have time to watch."

"Life's tough," Steve allowed. "Maybe I should take you away from all this."

Her smile was at once flirtatious and amused. "Like to a movie, you mean? I'll be waiting by the phone." She glanced at Mark. "So what do you guys want?"

"Two beers," Steve answered. "Is Carl around?"

Displeasure seemed to surface in her eyes, and then they fixed on the door. With quiet distaste, she said, "Speak of the devil."

Mark turned. Gliding through the door, Carl stopped to look around. He summoned an expression of mild surprise at the sight of Steve Tillman, then came over to the bar. Ignoring his sister, he asked Steve, "Passing the time with Princess Angela?"

There was an edge in his voice, though Mark could not tell whether it was for Angela or Steve. "Yup," Steve said evenly. "Waiting for you to show up. You guessed right again last Sunday—your goddamn Pittsburgh Steelers beat the spread."

Her face closing, Angela turned away. She surely recognized, as Mark did, the charade through which Carl sold pot and powder cocaine to his Caldwell clientele. They gave him money in advance, paying off a fictitious "bet"; a day or so later they found a bag behind some musty tome in a corner of the public library, or beneath the rear seat of an unlocked car. But at the Alibi Club Carl was, at worst, a bookie.

Steve passed him a wad of bills. "Got a second?" he asked.

Carl glanced mistrustfully at Mark. "Let's grab a table."

Steve put a hand on Mark's shoulder, excusing himself. Mark nodded his understanding: in Carl's mind, Mark was a potential witness, a needless risk to a business built on subterfuge and discretion. When Angela brought back two beers, Mark was sitting alone. The dislike she clearly felt for her twin brother had left her silent.

Awkwardly, Mark said, "I'm Mark Darrow, by the way."

Angela laughed at this. "The whole damn campus knows who you are. Even the people you never talk to—in college *or* in high school."

Embarrassed, Mark said, "So let's talk now."

Angela put her hands on her hips, a mocking gesture. "Concerning what?"

"How about what you're studying so hard for. Seems like you've got a plan besides running Mom's bar."

She paused to look at him, and then her expression became serious. "My plan—if you really want to know—is to put this whole period of my life in the rearview mirror. Right along with Wayne, Ohio."

"And go where?"

"Same place you are, I guess. The best law school that'll pay me to show up. Which narrows the field a little." Picking up a cloth, she began wiping the bar. "So what kind of law are you thinking about?"

Mark shrugged. "Not sure yet. Maybe criminal, I guess. And you?"

Still wiping, Angela said, "Not that—I've seen enough criminals to last a lifetime. Corporate law, I'm thinking. Or maybe teach if I do well enough."

Though quiet, her voice held a determination close to longing, the sense—or hope—that she was bigger than the life she had been given. At once Mark intuited how alone she must feel. "I'll be rooting for you," he said. "Maybe Yale has scholarships for both of us."

Glancing up, Angela gave him a wry smile. "Aren't you worried that being white is a competitive disadvantage?"

"Is it? I hadn't noticed."

"You'll get by." Her smile softened a little. "Good luck to us both."

Steve came back, glancing from Mark to Angela. "Thanks for keeping my buddy company," he told her.

Mark wondered if he imagined something proprietary in Steve's tone, or at least familiar, suggesting more than a barroom friendship.

Angela shrugged, briefly meeting Mark's eyes. "He's really not so bad," she told Steve, and went back to tending bar.

Now SHE SMILED at Mark again. "Congratulations," she said above the din of the party. "Big day for you, seems like."

She was holding a drink and her voice seemed thick, her balance compromised. Though Mark did not really know her, this surprised him. Gesturing at the crowd, he said, "In fifteen minutes, they'll forget me."

She took a deep swallow of liquor. "In fifteen minutes," she countered, "they'll probably forget everything. Like I mean to."

Troubled, Mark sensed that she had come here to lose herself. "You with anyone?" he asked.

Blinking, she looked at him more closely. "Steve invited me, whatever that means. Other than that, I'm with no one in particular."

Mark hesitated. "Neither am I. If you need someone to get you home, I'm here."

"Tonight? You're supposed to be celebrating."

"True. You'd be saving me a hangover."

The look she gave him combined a question and a challenge. Defensively, she said, "Are you saying I should leave now?"

Mark shoved his hands in his pockets. "I'm wondering, that's all."

She shook her head, moving close to him. Softly, she said, "Gonna be a long night for me, I think." She gave him a quick, darting kiss on the lips. "You're kind of sweet, Mark Darrow."

Surprised, Mark thought he saw tears in her eyes. Then she turned, wandering aimlessly into the crowd, alone.

MARK WENT TO the makeshift bar in the corner, pouring himself a Jack Daniel's on ice. He felt a hand on his shoulder.

Turning, he expected to see a friend, perhaps to hear a few drunken words of praise. Instead Carl Hall demanded in a hostile tone, "You get off on fucking around with black girls like Tillman does?"

Mark felt a flash of temper. Removing Carl's hand from his shoulder, he said, "If you mean your sister, that's not what's going on."

"Looked like that. In fact, looks like you want to fuck her."

Mark stared at him. "This can't be some sort of principle for you. You've never had any."

Hall's eyes flashed. "Look," Mark said more evenly, "Angela's already over the line. If you care about her at all, take her home. Might be a good idea for both of you."

Hall stood taller. "Don't like me at *your* house, white boy?"

"That's not it," Mark answered. "I don't like you anywhere. So you'd better back off right now."

Carl gave him a measured look, as though assessing the difference in their strength and will. Then he turned abruptly, vanishing as his sister had.

3

For an hour or so, Mark drank and danced with whoever came along.

In the dark he felt an odd detachment, the numb whiskey glow spreading through his limbs as the forms and faces in front of him kept changing. Then the newest face became Joe Betts's girlfriend. "Hey, Laurie," he said with foolish surprise. "It's you."

He waited for the smile he could expect from Laurie Shilts. Instead, she shook her head, speaking quietly beneath the cacophony of the party. "This isn't any good."

"The party?"

"Everything."

With fraternal affection, Mark pulled her closer. Her small, pretty face looked pained; the cheek beneath her right eye looked bruised and puffy. Silent, she leaned her head against his shoulder.

"Maybe we should talk," Mark suggested.

Laurie's laugh was mirthless. "Here?"

Without speaking, Mark took her hand, leading her to the back of the room. He pushed open the stainless steel doors to the kitchen, where, six nights a week, their cook prepared meals for sixty brothers. As the doors closed behind them, partially sealing off the sound, Mark switched on the lights.

Laurie winced at the new brightness. She looked small, diminished, her blond shag straggly. The bruise beneath her eye was a faint blue-purple.

Disturbed, Mark motioned her to one of the stools in front of the oversized sink where, for most of his sophomore year, he had earned money by peeling potatoes or washing iron pots. They sat next to each other, quiet for a time.

"I came looking for him," she said in a monotone. "So stupid—he was already drunk. I was stupid for staying with him so long."

Her blue-green eyes looked at once miserable and angry. Uncertain of how to respond, Mark said, "Joe's okay when he's not drinking."

Laurie crossed her arms. "So which Joe's the real one?" she asked bitterly. "Both of them, actually—they're the same fucking guy. Drinking just rips the surface off his anger." Her voice faltered. "You don't really know him, Mark. Deep down, Joe hates women."

Despite his own haziness, a memory came to Mark. It had been late Saturday night exactly a year ago, the end of a long evening during which he had gone with Steve to the hospital, spent time at the party with his date, and then, devastated by Steve's injury, wound up drinking with Joe on the front lawn of the DBE house, their backs against an oak tree. Sipping from his silver flask, Joe had said, "Keeps the cold away, doesn't it."

"Yup."

"Only problem is, it makes me think about dear old Dad."

His tone wavered between sardonic and sentimental. Two months before, Joe's father had dropped dead from a massive heart attack. Mark assumed that the sentiment was for his father, its acrid undertone a drunken attempt at emotional distance. "Yeah," Mark commiserated. "That must be hard."

"You've got no idea, Mark." Joe's voice softened. "I loved him, and I hated him."

Mark turned his head, face against the rough bark of the oak. "How's that?"

Joe took a deeper swallow. "Jekyll-Hyde, man—Jekyll and fuck-ing Hyde. Used to get drunk and beat the shit out of my mother. Next day he'd sit around all quiet and ashamed. You never heard a house so filled with silence."

Surprised, Mark thought of his own parents—that one got drunk had inspired the other to follow. "Maybe she should've gotten him to stop."

Joe's bark of laughter held disdain. "Too weak. Her father was just like mine, a red-faced drunk who no doubt beat up Grandma. Deep down I think Mom wanted that—my old man was what she thought a man should be. At least that's what all the textbooks say." He took a deep swallow of bourbon. "Who gives a shit now, right? The bastard's dead, and Mom can blubber over his memory in peace. It's done . . ."

Now, facing Laurie, Mark believed that it was not. "Did you ever ask Joe not to drink?"

Briefly, Laurie's crescent eyes shut. "Try 'beg.' "

"What happened?"

"I picked the wrong time. More and more with him, there's *no* right time. I found that out again tonight." Her voice, though soft, had new intensity and clarity. "Joe's got bigger problems than drinking. Way bigger. This is about my own survival."

Mark hesitated. Glancing at her cheek, he asked, "Want to tell me about it?"

Laurie looked slowly around the bright industrial kitchen, as though rediscovering her surroundings and herself. "No," she said firmly. "I need to go back to the dorm, start respecting myself. My new plan is to forget Joe Betts and everything that's happened."

Mark pondered his obligations. "Can I do anything?"

Looking at the whiskey in his cup, Laurie's laugh was free of rancor. "Tonight? Maybe we can find some better time." Her voice softened. "But you're a good listener, Mark. Drunk or sober."

"Seems like this is my night for it." Looking at her, he saw a small, cute girl with a bruise beneath her cheek, carrying a memory not easily erased. "I'm sorry, Laurie."

Laurie grimaced. "I'll be fine. It's Joe's next girl you should worry about."

Touching his arm, she left. Alone on the stool, Mark watched the metal doors swing in her wake.

He supposed the only cure for how depressed he felt was whiskey.

ANOTHER HOUR LATER, taking his own advice, Mark sat in the living room drinking whiskey with Rusty Clark.

A slight redhead with the countenance of a shrewd but amiable badger, Rusty was feeling valedictory. Gazing at his gin and tonic, Rusty gestured at the couples by the fireplace. "Tonight it hit me that we're leaving in six months. We may never see these people again."

Mark laughed thickly. "I'm not sure we're seeing them now."

Rusty gave him a faux-sententious look. "Aren't you feeling a little nostalgic?"

Mark shrugged. "A few hours ago I was. Now I feel like it's getting to be time to go."

Rusty nodded solemnly. "To law school, right?"

"For sure. I can make a living defending drunks. They're a recipe for trouble."

Rusty raised his cup. "Maybe *I* should go. Got a truckload of clients right here."

"They're leaving, remember? You'll never see them again."

"True." Rusty thought for a moment. "There's always the good citizens of Wayne."

Mark turned to him. "Don't get stuck, Rusty. It's time for us to bail."

On a nearby couch, Bobby Gardner took his date's hand, pulling her upstairs. Watching, Rusty said, "I always thought I'd meet someone here. Maybe settle down."

Mark took a swallow of whiskey. "You sound like you're about to die. We're twenty-fucking-one."

Rusty looked offended. "Easy for you to say—you run through girls like potato chips."

"Mixed metaphor, Rusty. I can feel the crumbs between my toes."

"Come on, man. You know what I mean."

Mark reflected. What he could not say to Rusty was that, in great measure because of Lionel Farr, his idea of himself had changed. Whoever he would become, he knew he was not yet there; he should wait for the woman the future Mark Darrow would know was right. Nor was he inclined to reveal that his parents, who had married right out of high school, had poisoned the ideal of young love. Even drunk, Mark knew that he was better at listening than self-revelation. "Yeah," he temporized for Rusty's sake. "I know what you mean. I just haven't found her yet."

Mollified, Rusty settled back on the couch. Mark realized that he had drunk too much already—the room was starting to expand and contract; voices beyond Rusty's seemed to come from a great distance. "Well," Rusty announced, "look at *this*."

Turning, Mark saw what this comment was about: Steve Tillman had emerged from the basement with Angela Hall, his arm around her waist. At the top of the stairs they paused, kissing. "True love strikes," Rusty said. "Aren't you sorry you're such a cynic?"

Mark found the sight jarring—not because of Steve or Angela but because of what he knew to be, at least until now, Steve's small-town disdain for blacks. His face close to Angela's, Steve whispered something. Then he turned, heading for the first-floor bathroom, his limp briefly becoming a stagger. In the tone of a TV color commentator, Rusty opined, "Looks pretty fucked up to *me*, sports fans."

Gazing at Angela, Mark did not answer. Alone, she faced the living room; spotting Mark, she gave him a small wave and a smile, fey and wistful and embarrassed. This is what the night had brought, her expression said; the idea that whatever might follow was a premeditated act of carelessness, somehow sad, penetrated Mark's fog. It crossed his mind that this night might be—perhaps should be—the last epic drunk of his life. Then Joe Betts came reeling up the stairs.

When Mark glanced over, Rusty was smiling to himself, gone to another place. But Mark was at once alert: Joe's expression was purposeful and closed to reason, and his eyes were fixed on Angela.

She stood with her back to him, gazing at the tile floor. When Joe put his arm around her, she started. Joe pulled her closer, his face flushed with alcohol and desire.

Steadying himself, Mark rose.

Joe turned Angela's face to him. As Mark started forward, Steve emerged from the bathroom, stopping at the sight of Joe. "What the fuck you doing?" he demanded.

Joe spun, eyes widening with surprise. Three feet separated them when Joe raised his fist at Steve. "*No*," Angela cried out.

Startled, Steve teetered back as Joe's roundhouse swing struck him on the arm. Swiftly Mark stepped between them, grabbing Joe by the shirt collar and staring into his eyes. Joe's breath was rank with whiskey, his gaze wild and opaque. "Stop," Mark told him in a low, savage voice. "You've seen this movie before, remember?"

Joe stiffened, his body taut with fury. Heart racing, Mark snapped to Steve, "Get out of here. Angela, too."

Steve hesitated, then stepped forward, grasping Angela's hand. Struggling, Joe grabbed Mark's wrists. "*Look at me*," Mark ordered.

Joe did. Mark heard the door open, felt the cool night air before Steve slammed the door behind them. Feeling Joe's fingers tighten, Mark jerked him upright. "Stay right here, Joe," he said more softly. "I've got the next dance."

For a few precious seconds more, Joe froze, forehead shining with sweat. Then he wrenched himself away and hurried toward the door.

Mark went after him. As Joe ran toward the parking lot, Mark saw the red taillights of Steve's Camaro careen into the night. He felt himself expel a breath. When he looked for Joe again, he saw no one.

Coming from behind him, Carl Hall's voice was etched with anger. "Guess your buddy wins the prize. Maybe you two can share her."

Mark turned and stared at Carl. "Too bad she's not an only child, Carl. Just the only one smart enough to leave."

Without awaiting an answer, Mark brushed past him. Rusty was standing in the doorway. "Night like this," he said, "no one should be driving." His face clouded. "Never seen Joe *that* bad before."

Mark thought of Laurie Shilts. "Maybe we haven't been looking."

They went back to the living room. Already the couples remaining, dulled by drink, seemed to have forgotten the incident. His face brightening, Rusty saw Tim Fedak and Skip Ellis, coinventors of the DBE catapult.

Turning to Mark, Rusty announced, "I've got a plan. Hang here."

Rusty hurried over to Tim and Skip. As their heads came together, Tim's eyes widened with delight, and Skip began laughing and nodding. "You got to hear this," Rusty called to Mark.

When Mark came over, Rusty convened them in a mock huddle, their faces nearly touching. "Here's the play," Rusty said. "Joe's car is still here. He shouldn't touch the wheel tonight, okay? So we go to the parking lot, lift his Miata, and carry it back up here. He's way too drunk to drive back down the steps."

"You're putting it where?" Mark asked.

Rusty pointed toward the library. "There."

Mark felt the beginning of awe, the germination of another piece of DBE lore. "You're serious."

"We *all* are," Tim replied. "You the quarterback, or not?"

Mark laughed. "For one last play."

With purposeful strides, the four friends went outside, threw open the double doors leading to the living room, and took the steps down to the parking lot. Joe's Miata awaited them, conveniently parked at the foot of the steps.

The cool night air brushed Mark's face. "Think we can carry it?" Skip asked.

Rusty smiled. "C'mon, man. It's fucking tinfoil."

The strongest of the quartet, Mark and Tim took the front bumper, preparing to back up the steps. Knees bent, Skip and Rusty put their hands beneath the rear. As if calling signals, Mark barked, "Hut one . . . hut two . . . hut three."

Muscles straining, the brothers slowly lifted the car. Elated, they started up the steps, their effort punctuated by grunts and muttered encouragement. As they reached the porch, onlookers gathered in the doorway. "Make way," Rusty called out in martial tones. "We bring you the spoils of victory."

Laughing, the revelers stood aside; some, catching the spirit, moved the couches to clear a space in the living room. What Rusty proclaimed as "Team Betts" deposited Joe's Miata with great ceremony, as though unfurling the flag at Iwo Jima or toppling the statue of a dictator. "Aren't we going to the library?" Mark asked.

"Got to clear the road." Rusty reached into the Miata, producing Joe's car keys. "It's your day, Mark. You get to drive."

Rusty was not usually a leader—it struck Mark that, for him, inspiring this teamwork meant more than the perpetration of a prank. "Whatever you say, Captain. From this night on your name will forever live in legend."

With pleased solemnity, Rusty issued directions. As Tim and Skip pulled the library table to one corner, Rusty handed Mark the keys.

Sitting inside, Mark turned the ignition far enough to put Joe's top down, then started the motor. To cheers and applause, Mark slowly drove the Miata through the open double doors, into the library.

He killed the engine, then sat there, mildly astounded. Rusty handed him a cup of whiskey on ice. "Why don't you try out the sound system," he suggested.

Mark took a deep, harsh swallow of whiskey, then reached into the glove compartment for a tape. It was Bon Jovi, a favorite. Surrounded by friends, Mark leaned his head back, listening to the music as he slowly closed his eyes.

WHEN MARK AWAKENED, the library was dark.

He felt sick. His head pounded, and his mind filled with rueful self-recrimination. The illuminated clock in Joe's Miata read 3:04.

He needed to get back to his room. But he lived in the bowels of the stadium, a good three-quarters of a mile away. Too far to walk at night—too far, period.

Still drunk, he reached for Joe's car phone.

Steve owed him, he reasoned—Mark had saved him from certain death at the hands of Joe Betts. Early-morning taxi service was not too much to ask.

With a trembling hand, he punched in the number to Steve's room.

The phone rang once, then twice. At fourteen rings Mark hung up. "Wake up, you sonofobitch," he murmured.

Nothing.

Mark dialed again, counting to fifteen rings.

Slowly, he replaced the phone. Never again, he promised himself. Then he shut his eyes once more.

4

WHEN MARK AWOKE AGAIN, HIS SKULL THROBBED AND HIS mouth tasted sour. The stale air smelled of beer and whiskey and cigarette smoke, the faint pungent whiff of marijuana. Adjusting to the dark, his eyes were slits. He could not remember feeling so stupid.

The clock in Joe's car read 5:43. Soon dawn would break, providing enough light for him to stagger home. He craved fresh air and his own bed.

Slowly, Mark extracted himself from the Miata.

The living room was empty except for a body sprawled on the couch. Rusty Clark. Passing through, Mark cautiously opened the side door, as though expecting to find himself in a foreign country. He took one deep breath of chill morning air and started on his way.

The first thick ribbon of orange-gray dawn appeared above the trees outlined in the semidark. In the distance, Mark discerned the steeple atop the Spire.

He headed there. Between the fraternities and campus, a gently sloping walkway flanked by trees and gardens passed modern buildings constructed of red brick—the library, the student theater, the alumni center, and, newest and most impressive, the architecturally striking student union, a steel-and-glass marvel that was the pride of Caldwell. But as with most other paths at the college, this one led to the Spire, towering above all else. As the sky lightened, the steeple emerged more clearly, creating the illusion that it was moving toward him from above the trees. There was a dusting of frost on the ground.

At the foot of the pathway, a black metal clock, eight feet high, told Mark that it was now 6:07. Passing it, Mark entered the main campus, demarked by a sandstone gateway. For the next few minutes he wended his way through the buildings, varied in size and style, that housed his classes in English, history, philosophy, and science. At midday, he promised himself, he would go for a very long run and afterward, head cleared, resume his pursuit of a place at Yale Law School. Then he reached the lawn surrounding the Spire.

He paused there, recalling the tumult he had inspired hours before, the primal roar of the crowd as he'd brandished the bronze axe. Now the site of the Spire was so quiet and empty that it evoked a vanished civilization. Gazing up at the steeple, he remembered the harsh severity of the bell tower, his brief attack of vertigo. With a sense of awe, he again approached the tower.

He stopped abruptly.

A dark form lay on the grass. Completely still, it was too long and angular to be anything but a person. He stepped forward, wondering if someone had passed out here, deeply afraid that this was something worse.

It was a woman. Arms outflung, her body faced the sky. A terrible sense of familiarity hit him as he moved closer.

He stopped abruptly, sickened.

Angela Hall lay at the foot of the Spire like a sacrifice on an altar. She stared up at him, her eyes too fixed to be alive. Her lips were parted in an expression of pain or anger, exposing her white teeth.

A cry of animal anguish issued from Mark's throat. He forced himself to kneel, touching her wrist. It was not as cold as he had imagined or as warm as he had hoped. Feeling this contact like an electric shock, he fought back the reflex to vomit.

Mark stood. There was no telephone, he realized, no way of calling for help. Instinctively he began running across the lawn, heading for the one house he knew near campus, Lionel Farr's.

AGAIN AND AGAIN he rang the doorbell, jabbing the button as though willing Farr to answer. At last, minutes later, someone jerked open the door.

It was Farr, his strong face lined with sleep, his eyes keen with a displeasure that changed to surprise. He was still adjusting his sweater, and his gray-blond hair was mussed. "For God's sake, Mark. What is it?"

Mark's throat was parched. "Angela Hall. I found her near the Spire." Voice catching, he finished: "I think she's dead."

For an instant, Farr's eyes froze. Then he snapped, "Wait here."

Mark stood on the porch, shaken yet relieved. Farr hurried through the door. "I've called the police," he said. "We'll meet them there."

Together they rushed down the street toward the Spire. Between breaths, Mark said, "I saw her last night."

Loping beside him, Farr asked sharply, "Where?"

"The DBE house."

"Tell me."

As they entered the campus, Mark began a hasty outline of the party.

"She left with Steve?" Farr interrupted.

"Yes."

They reached the grass, Mark hoping against hope that this was a dream. The landscape was empty but for Angela.

Slowing, Farr approached her. His military posture vanished. Kneeling beside the body, he looked into her face, his eyes narrowing in scrutiny until, briefly, they shut. "She's been strangled."

"Strangled?" Mark repeated.

"Look at her eyes," Farr responded softly.

Mark forced himself to do that. There were red pinpoints in the whites of her sightless eyes. In a monotone, he said, "I should have taken her home."

Farr turned. Following his gaze, Mark saw two uniformed policemen running toward the Spire. "Whatever happened," Farr said with quiet urgency, "tell them everything . . ."

"What about Steve?"

"Everything, dammit. You can't know who it helps or hurts. But concealment helps no one—especially you."

One of the policemen was George Garrison—his high school teammate and Angela's friend. Staring at Angela, George slumped. "Sweet Lord," he said to the body. "What happened to you, baby?" It was not the voice of a cop.

When Mark looked up at him, George was staring back. The other cop, white and older, put his hand on George's shoulder. Then he spoke to Mark and Farr. "The detectives are coming," he told them. "I want you over on that bench."

The next several minutes were a blur. Seated at the edge of the grass, Mark and Lionel Farr watched the police tape off the grass around the Spire. A photographer and videocam operator focused on Angela; a youngish blond woman carefully examined her body; two plainclothes detectives took notes. Mark tried to remember whether he had seen, or only now imagined, a bruise on Angela's face.

At length the two detectives walked toward the bench. "Tell them everything," Farr repeated. "Leave nothing out."

The older, red-headed detective identified himself as Fred Bender; the bulky man with a worn, sad face was Jack Muhlberg. Standing over them, Muhlberg said evenly, "So what happened here?"

With quiet efficiency, Farr traced their movements from Mark's arrival at his door. The detective pointed to a nearby garden. "Let's talk over here," he told Farr.

They left Mark alone. Disbelieving, he watched men in white jackets examine the ground near Angela's body. The morning sun, he noticed, was turning the frost to dew.

If only.

If only Steve had not invited her. If only she had left before. If only Steve had not left with her. Mark could not decipher cause and effect, only its rudiments. He kept seeing Joe's glazed eyes, Steve's taillights swerving into the night, Angela's wistful smile. Somewhere between that moment and dawn, tragedy had waited for her.

The two detectives returned with Farr. "Okay, Mark," Muhlberg said. "We'll need to go over just what happened." Turning to Farr, he added, "You can leave now, Professor."

"I'd like to stay."

Bender shook his head. "That's not how we do things."

"Is Mark in custody?"

Glancing at Muhlberg, Bender said, "Of course not."

Farr crossed his arms. "Then you should understand that he's much more than a student to me. It comes down to this: either I stay, or I'm hiring him a lawyer. Your choice."

Muhlberg looked nettled. "How do you feel, Mark?"

Mark sorted out his thoughts. "Professor Farr said to tell you everything. I'd like him here with me."

When Bender turned to him, Muhlberg shrugged in resignation. Silent, Mark saw George Garrison watching over his murdered friend. He stood so still he could have been in a trance.

"Okay, Mark," Bender said briskly, and the questioning began.

THE TWO DETECTIVES were dogged and thorough. Reluctantly, Mark described the night: drinking with Steve, encountering Angela, confronting Carl, breaking up the fight between Steve and Joe. Under persistent questioning, Mark explained his relationship to each. "Before you found her," Muhlberg asked again, "when did you last see Angela alive?"

It dawned on Mark that he was a suspect. "When she left with Steve," he answered tiredly. "Just like I told you before."

"Where does Steve live?"

"Where I do. We both have rooms in the football stadium."

The two detectives glanced at each other. "Can you tell us anything else?" Muhlberg asked.

For an instant, Mark hesitated. "Yeah. You should talk to Laurie Shilts, Joe's girlfriend. She was at the party, too."

Muhlberg sat beside him. "I thought Joe went after Angela."

"They'd broken up, Laurie told me."

"Did she say why?"

"You'd have to ask her." Mark stared straight ahead. "All I know for sure is they'd had a fight."

Bender wrote this down. Moving forward, Farr asked, "Can Mark go now?"

Nodding, Muhlberg gazed at Mark. "Do us a favor," he said, "and also yourself. Don't talk about this to anyone. I know these kids are your friends. But we need to get their independent memories."

Silent, Mark nodded. To his surprise, Muhlberg put a hand on his shoulder. "You were a great quarterback, Mark. I always liked watching you play."

"I always liked playing," Mark answered.

THE TWO DETECTIVES left.

"I don't care what they say," Mark told Farr. "I've got to find Steve."

"That would be a mistake," Farr said firmly. "It's also too late. I'm sure they've already gone to his room. All you'd do is walk in on them and make yourself look bad."

Mark felt the enormity of events crashing down on him, the world as he knew it spinning out of control. "Then what do I do now?"

"Stay out of trouble." Farr's taut voice brooked no dissent. "I have to tell Clark Durbin, and you're coming with me."

5

THEY RUSHED TO DURBIN'S HOUSE ON FOOT. STILL disoriented, unsure of his role here, Mark sensed that Farr meant to keep him close, away from Steve or Joe or the police. His face careworn, Farr said little. Only when they approached the door of the president's house did he pause, saying softly and sadly, "That beautiful girl." Then he stood taller, fully himself, and rapped the brass door knocker.

Opening the door, Durbin looked from Farr to Darrow, his reflexive half smile at odds with his expression of puzzlement. "There's been a terrible tragedy," Farr said in a low voice. "Angela Hall, a black scholarship student. Mark found her at the Spire, strangled. The police are already there."

Durbin stared at Mark, lips parting slightly. He had been president for three months. Yesterday at the Spire, when Mark had met him for the first time, his fleeting impression had been of a slight dark-haired man in his forties with a ready smile and warm blue eyes who gave off a jittery energy. Now his body seemed to sag; in his slack expression and softening chin, Mark saw only shock. For an instant, Mark compared his reaction to Farr's—Durbin seemed momentarily paralyzed.

"Come in," he said haltingly. "Please."

Mark followed Farr inside. The one-story house was modern and light, with an open floor plan and tall windows that looked out on a patio and garden. Durbin waved them to a couch, sitting across from them with his hands clasped, his expression more focused. "A student's lost her life," he said. "That's the worst thing that can hit any school. I need to hear everything you know."

Farr took a moment to gather himself. "That's why I'm here. Not many—if any—people know. By this afternoon everyone will. No matter the shock, you'll have to move quickly. But it's worth taking an hour now to design the best response." Farr nodded toward Mark. "From what I understand, this tragedy may have started with a party at the DBE house. Mark was there. He has a story to tell you that may bear on what you should do."

Surprised, Mark stared at Farr. "Go ahead," Durbin urged Mark. "Please."

Facing him, Mark outlined the events, culminating in Angela's departure with Steve. He could not shake the sense of betraying his friend. But Durbin listened closely, his expression open and even kind. "Thank you, Mark," he said, then turned to Farr. "Obviously, I need to address the school right away. The students will need a sense of calmness."

"That's only part of it," Farr ventured. "The police know all this from Mark—no doubt they're questioning Steve Tillman right now. Inevitably, this story will be tinged with drugs, alcohol, and overtones of racism. It heightens the risk of frightening our students and our applicants, including minorities. How you react in the next twenty-four hours, and then the next few days, will help determine how bad that gets." Farr leaned forward, saying gently, "I've had a few more minutes to think about this. May I offer some suggestions?"

To Mark, Durbin appeared freshly appalled by what he faced. "Please."

"First, call an all-school meeting for seven o'clock tonight—use the school's voice-mail system. Between then and now, phone Angela's mother to express our grief and ask what we can do. Call any leader of the black community you can find. Also our board chair and general counsel—you'll need their advice, and there'll be hell to pay if you don't take it. Especially about preventing a racial or town-gown conflict."

Durbin held up his hand. Walking to a desk, he took out a legal pad and pen. Sitting again, he asked, "How do you see this all-school meeting?"

"The purpose—as you say—is to calm the campus. Offer the students grief counseling. Announce a memorial service for Angela, and a day of reflection in our classrooms on what this tragedy means to Caldwell. Invite student leaders in for meetings—including leaders of minority groups."

"What about campus safety?" Durbin cut in. "I should hire more security guards."

"Agreed," Farr responded with quiet force. "But by itself that suggests that this place is dangerous. Have your VP for student affairs gather the statistics on previous campus crime rates—I've been here almost twenty years now, and I can assure you that it's pretty low. At tonight's meeting, tell the students that."

Durbin shook his head. "That would sound like I'm saying there's nothing to worry about. Plainly, there is."

"Then why not announce a new campus safety program— tonight. A buddy system where students are encouraged to walk together. A ride system for women walking back to their dorms or sorority houses at night. Telephones every fifty yards or so, connecting students to the campus police. A new lighting system to illuminate the campus after dark." Farr paused for emphasis. "Let them know that you won't rest until you're certain—and *they're* certain— that this will never happen again."

As Mark listened, it struck him that Farr's professorial persona was falling away, exposing the military officer he once had been, quick-thinking and decisive under stress. Durbin scribbled a few more notes, then looked up at Mark. "I can't imagine how you must feel, Mark. Still, I'd appreciate any thoughts you have."

For a moment, Mark studied a patch of sunlight on Durbin's tan carpet. "Okay," he said finally. "Don't just have this meeting. You should also go where we live—you, or the deans, or maybe some professors. Give every student you can find someone they can talk to. A lot of the guys I know won't relate to some psychologist they've never met."

Slowly, Durbin nodded. "Good advice."

"Also," Farr added, "you should announce another student forum in one week's time, to tell them what you've learned and whatever else you're doing. It's no good that you're in charge unless the students, board, faculty, alumni, and community know that. For the sake of us all, it's imperative that you emerge from this tragedy as the leader Caldwell needs."

To Mark, Farr's implicit warning was unmistakable. Whatever else Durbin did in the future no longer mattered—his presidency would be judged, favorably or not, based on how he handled Angela's murder. "I need to get our board chair on campus," Durbin said to Farr. "Also Ernie Sims—it might be good to remind everyone that our thirty-person board actually includes an African-American. As soon as possible, the three of us should visit Angela's family."

"If you like," Farr offered, "I'll go with you. I'm the head of the committee that gave Angela her scholarship. More than that, I'm the only one of us who actually knew her." A look of sadness crossed Farr's face. "Consoling her family is the hardest job we'll have, and one of the most critical. For the sake of Angela's mother, we can't seem distant from her dead daughter. And to be brutally practical, we don't want her suing the school."

Once again, Mark absorbed Farr's ability to anticipate potential consequences. "We'll need more outreach to the black community as a whole," Durbin said. "The town seems pretty segregated, and we can't let the blacks in Wayne fester in their own resentment and isolation."

Durbin was right, Mark knew. Blacks seldom went downtown; even at the high school, black and white kids rarely socialized. Racial attitudes, even if unspoken, were often adversarial. Uncomfortably, Mark thought of Steve Tillman and his casual, if infrequent disparagement of black classmates. "True enough," Farr was saying. "Then there's our alumni. As you well know, their donations help fund this place. You've got to reassure them quickly." Farr's tone became grim. "A big problem with *that* is the media. A white-on-black murder, if that's what we have, will be catnip for them."

Durbin frowned at this. "I'll get our public relations people on this right away."

"It's over their heads, Clark. Hire an outside PR firm with experience in crisis management. We need to bombard the media and our funders with Caldwell's story—the low crime rate, the new campus safety program, how we've gotten our own kids through this, how much we welcome minorities." Farr's tone was pointed. "They should also provide talking points for our admissions people. You can take it to the bank that our applications will drop. What we have is not just murder, but a combustible mix of race and drugs and alcohol."

"There we can point to our substance abuse policy," Durbin said. "It's one of the first things I asked about in the interview process."

"Did they mention that our policy is bullshit?" Farr inclined his head toward Mark. "Any student can tell you that this place is awash in alcohol and drugs, including the DBE house. I should know: I'm on the student-faculty disciplinary committee, and every so often some drunk or drugged-out kid destroys a dorm room or precipitates a charge of date rape. That's the only time we stop pretending there's no problem." He turned to Mark. "You said Angela's brother was at the party. He deals drugs out of the Alibi Club, right?"

Mark hesitated. "Yeah, he does."

"Not much we can do about *that*," Farr told Durbin. "Angela's mother owns the place. That leaves the fraternities."

"That's tougher, Lionel. A lot of the alumni I'm meeting feel like their fraternity was the heart of their experience at Caldwell."

"And a lot of them are morons," Farr responded. "Here's what I'd recommend. Conduct a full investigation of that party. Warn the presidents of every fraternity that their parties are no longer off-limits to school authorities. If fraternities tolerate drugs or underage drinking, it's not the particular student who'll go—it's the fraternity. Any kid caught once with drugs will get compulsory drug and alcohol counseling; twice, they'll be suspended; three times, they'll be expelled. Make sure they know what date rape is, and that any assault on a woman, of any kind, will be dealt with harshly.

"It's clear and it's fair, Clark. More alumni will praise you than resent you. Ask the ones who complain if they care more about the idiots in their old fraternity than about the reputation of the school and the safety of its students." Farr's tone was quiet but firm. "Tell them your job is to make Caldwell College the safest place on earth. Then do it."

Durbin frowned. "I came here to raise money from them, not to beat them over the head. This is my first presidency; fund-raising's my skill set. The board hired me to launch a new capital campaign and beef up our endowment."

"You can't right now," Farr said with muted impatience. "Not for at least a year. It's not just that there's been a murder after a fraternity party. In all likelihood, Angela Hall was strangled by a student at this college."

Durbin raised his eyebrows. "Specifically, Steve Tillman?"

At once, Mark began to fear that Steve might be railroaded to save the school. "Perhaps," Farr answered. "If so, it's possible that sex—consensual or nonconsensual—may become part of the mix. I know one thing for sure: if any student is charged, we have to expel them. Neither the school nor its students can live with anything less."

Abruptly, Durbin stood. "I need to get started. For the next few hours, Lionel, I want you at my side."

Farr nodded. "Of course. Just let me talk with Mark for a minute."

"Please." Facing Mark, Durbin said, "You've been through a lot since yesterday, when we first met. I know you have Professor Farr to lean on. But if there's anything I can do for you, at any hour, just call."

Even through his fog, Mark felt this man's essential goodness. "Thank you, sir. I will."

Farr touched his arm. "I'll walk out with you."

The two of them stopped on the front porch. In the driveway, a pale, uncoordinated-looking boy of about twelve was shooting baskets without much skill, oblivious to all that had happened. Mark turned to Farr and saw that his eyes suddenly looked tired and deeply sad. "It's hard to believe," he murmured, shaking his head. "She was full of promise, full of plans. I had so much hope for her." Looking intently at Mark, he asked, "Are *you* all right?"

Mark tried to imagine the next hours and days. "I guess so. But there's no way Steve could have done this. I'm starting to get scared for him."

"I know," Farr responded gently. "But there's no help for that now—or for any of it. There hasn't been, ever since you found her."

Slowly, Mark nodded. Farr placed a hand on his shoulder. "There's one more thing," he admonished quietly. "No one should know about this meeting. Whatever Clark Durbin does should be seen as his initiative. He's the president, and now it's his time to be a leader."

6

FILLED WITH DREAD, MARK WALKED SLOWLY ACROSS THE campus to the football stadium.

A quiet gathering of students ringed the Spire, cordoned off by yellow tape. Mark kept his head down, avoiding eye contact with anyone he passed. Within hours, he had gone from hungover to adrenalized to how he felt now—stunned and disoriented and filled with disbelief, yet constantly seeing Angela's stricken face. He felt a deep sadness for Angela, and a deep worry about the meaning of what he had witnessed the night before. His only hope now was that this tragedy, whatever its cause, would not touch Steve Tillman.

Like Mark's own, Steve's room was on the first floor of the worn gray football stadium, a relic of the twenties. But the entrance to Steve's dimly lit corridor was marked with yellow tape saying CRIME SCENE. From inside echoed male voices, too authoritative to come from students. Mark felt a nightmare closing around him.

He needed air. Caught between the need to find Steve and the desire to be alone, he chose a place where he and Steve sometimes went—a section of bleachers on the fifty-yard line where, concealed by night, he would sit with Steve while his friend smoked pot. These sessions were more common, Mark reflected, since Steve had torn up his knee and, it seemed, plunged into despondency. Now Mark hoped that this had not awakened something worse.

The afternoon was darker than the morning. The sun had been extinguished by the lowering lead-gray sky common to Ohio as fall deepened into winter, and though it was not raining, the air felt cold and damp. As Mark stared at the empty field, the noise and sweat and exhilaration of yesterday's game felt like a barely remembered dream. A white hot dog wrapper skittered across the field.

Mark sat there, grateful for solitude. Then he heard heavy thudding footsteps on the wooden stands, suggesting a limp, and turned to see Steve Tillman.

Steve's face was pale, his brown hair matted and askew. His gaze held a hint of pain and puzzlement commingled with dissociation. Then he said, "I guess you've heard."

Mark's own voice sounded foreign to him. "I found her."

Steve stared at him. "You told them about me."

"I had to," Mark said in weary protest. "At least about the party."

Steve shoved his hands in his pockets. After a moment, he nodded.

"What happened?" Mark asked.

He meant between Steve and Angela. But instead Steve answered, "The cops came to my room. I was so fucked up, I couldn't really say what happened, I'm not sure I *know* what happened."

"What did the cops ask?"

As Steve began talking, Mark envisioned the scene, a narrative of innocence and surprise he did not know whether to believe.

SOMETIME DURING THE early-morning hours, Steve had passed out. He awoke to a knocking on his door, then a male voice calling his name.

Eyes opening, he looked around his room in a fog. His bedside lamp was knocked over, its base shattered into pieces. There were drink glasses on the tile floor, a bottle of rum, empty Coke cans. His sheets, a tangled mess, were strewn across and beside the bed.

"Steve Tillman?" the rough voice queried.

Judging from the light behind the curtains, it was day. "Wait a minute," Steve shouted back.

He was naked. Grabbing boxer shorts and a T-shirt, he struggled to put them on. When he opened the door, Steve saw two grim-faced men he knew were not from the school.

"You're Steve?" the red-haired guy said.

"Yeah."

Swiftly, the man's eyes took in the mess that was Steve's room. "I'm Detective Bender, Steve, and this is Detective Muhlberg. Can we talk with you for a minute?"

There was cocaine hidden in his drawer, Steve realized, bought from Carl Hall. "Let me get dressed," Steve said hastily. "I'll meet you outside."

The cop's voice was softer now. "It might be better if we talked in private."

Steve looked at the other guy, Muhlberg. "We need your help," Muhlberg told him. "A female student's been murdered."

Steve felt pinpricks on his skin, then a numbness that made his limbs feel heavy. "Who?"

"Her name was Angela Hall."

Steve sat down on the bed.

Muhlberg pulled up the desk chair, stationing himself in front of Steve. His sad eyes filled with sympathy. "I know this must be a shock, Steve."

Steve was aware of Bender looking around his room. "She's dead?" Steve heard himself say.

"Strangled, seems like."

"Where?"

"We don't know where, Steve. That's what we're trying to find out." Muhlberg's voice was reasonable, unthreatening. "We're talking to people who knew her. You were with her at the DBE house, right?"

Steve hesitated. Cautiously, he answered, "Right."

Haltingly, Steve let them extract his story—drinking beer; meeting Angela; switching to whiskey; the near fight with Joe Betts; heading with Angela for his dorm room.

Muhlberg wrote it all down. "What happened then?" he asked.

"I couldn't remember," Steve told Mark now.

Sitting in the bleachers, Mark felt his disbelief become fear. "What do you mean?"

"I was too fucked up. I think maybe I did a line of coke, drank some rum." Steve began rubbing his temples, elbows resting on his knees. "It's like I have these images, but I can't be sure they're real. You know those lights that flash at parties?"

"Strobe lights?"

"It's like that. There's light for a second, and you can see—then it's dark. Remembering her is like that." He covered his face, fingers splayed. "I can't believe she's dead, Mark."

Mark inhaled, the nausea of the previous night returning. "What *do* you remember?"

Softly, Steve answered, "I think we must have had sex."

As HIS FRIEND spoke, Mark tried to link the scattered images Steve evoked.

A flash of light, Angela undressing. Slim hips. Full breasts. Nipples with dark brown areolas.

Another flash. She slid down her panties, exposing the tangle of her fur as she looked into his eyes.

The light came back on. She had turned to show him her firm round buttocks.

Do you want me?

Steve pulled her to the bed, something crashing in the darkness. The scent of her skin suffused his senses . . .

I have to go.

Steve struggled to comprehend this. *Leave?*

I have to.

MARK STRUGGLED TO imagine this. But it made no sense.

Filled with doubts, he asked, "Did you leave with her?"

Steve shook his head. "No way."

I tried to call you, Mark wanted to say. *From the house, at three in the morning.* Instead, he asked, "Did you go anywhere at all?"

Steve looked over at him. His pale face had turned blotchy, his expression suddenly guarded. "When?"

"Anytime that night."

"I must have been passed out." Steve shook his head, as though in wonder at the wreckage of his memory. "I can't bring anything back. I don't know, man. I don't get what's happening at all."

Mark tried to sort out his thoughts. "After you left the party, did you see Joe?"

"Nope." Steve's tone was faintly hostile. "They asked me *that,* too."

Mark looked out at the football field. The sky was lower yet; in an hour or so, he guessed, the gray would darken with impending night. Facing Steve, he asked, "Got a place to sleep tonight?"

"I'm going to my folks'." Steve shook his head again. "They don't even know about this. When those cops took me to the station, they kept me too busy to call."

Mark's foreboding deepened. "What did they do?"

"They swabbed my mouth, scraped under my fingernails, drew some blood." His voice became resentful. "Then they ordered me to strip, and took pictures of me buck naked. Hope *those* don't get out."

"What else?"

Steve gazed out at the empty field. "They asked me if I'd hit her. I said I didn't do that kind of shit to women."

But Joe Betts might, Mark thought. His mind a kaleidoscope of confusion, he tried to remember whether Angela's face was bruised. Then he imagined Steve's parents—his plain, perpetually mystified mother; his bluff, kind father—struggling to absorb what might be happening. "Want me to go home with you?" Mark asked.

Steve grimaced. "Don't think so, man. This one I'd better do alone."

He stood, his bad knee buckling slightly. Turning, Steve asked, "You look at something for me?"

"Sure."

He pulled up his sweatshirt, exposing his pale back. "See anything?"

The red scratches on Steve's back resembled welts. Quietly, Mark said, "You've got some scratches, pal. Bad ones."

Slowly, heavily, Steve sat down again. "Yeah," he mumbled. "It feels like that."

Mark lapsed into silence. "Maybe I fucked her," Steve said. "But that doesn't mean I killed her."

To this remark, disturbing in so many ways, Mark had nothing to say.

7

IN THE DAYS THAT FOLLOWED, STEVE WAS BARELY SEEN ON campus.

For Mark, time was a blur—the all-campus meeting, President Durbin announcing the measures Farr had crafted for him; nights of sleeplessness; bleak dinners at the DBE house; the refuge of an evening at the Farrs'; a memorial service for Angela held in the chapel of College Hall. Mark managed to avoid Joe Betts. Then on Thursday afternoon, when they emerged from a history class devoted to discussing what—if anything—the murder revealed about Caldwell College, Joe caught up with him.

"Hear you were the driver," Joe said in a sardonic tone.

Mark shrugged. "It was a selfless act, Joe. You didn't need to be driving."

To Mark's surprise, Joe did not protest. They headed across campus, pausing at the green around the Spire.

A crowd had gathered, alien to Caldwell—some white but mostly black, carrying signs demanding JUSTICE FOR ANGELA, with reporters and video cameras interspersed among them. Though Mark had lived here all his life, many of the demonstrators were strangers to him. An imposing black man in a clerical collar addressed them. "We come here today," he said, "to demand that Caldwell College search its soul.

It is not enough for a school to say that it welcomes students of color. Caldwell College must create an environment where our young women leave the school in a cap and gown, not a coffin."

Applause burst from the crowd. Accompanied by Farr, Clark Durbin made his way toward the speaker. Farr placed a hand on the clergyman's shoulder, speaking to him quietly. Nodding, the minister passed the microphone to Durbin.

Though Durbin tried to stand taller, the reverend towered over him, and the president's voice was high and reedy. "You have come," he said, "to challenge our consciences. I welcome that, and make two promises. First, we will ensure that this is a safe place for students of all origins, offering those opportunities that our society all too often forecloses. As of next fall, the Angela Hall Memorial Scholarship program will offer four years at Caldwell College—free tuition and room and board—to worthy minority students."

At the tepid applause, Durbin raised a hand. "I recognize that we gave such an opportunity to Angela. I recognize that we failed her." His voice grew firmer. "It will never happen again. And we will do everything we can to help the authorities find the perpetrator of this loathsome crime—whoever and wherever they may be."

The applause, deeper now, mingled with an outcry of a crowd in search of justice. As a black-and-white placard of Angela's high school graduation picture thrust from their midst, a pleasant-looking man took the microphone from Durbin.

Dressed in a suit and tie, he had a ruddy complexion and russet hair and projected an air of calm. "I'm Dave Farragher," he said, "the prosecutor for Wayne County. I've come to assure you that we are working night and day to solve this terrible murder." He paused, his gaze sweeping the crowd, focused on the video cameras. "We expect to have an announcement soon—"

For four days, the authorities had said nothing. Now Mark felt an invisible web enveloping Steve Tillman. Unable to repress the thought, he murmured to Joe, "I think Steve's in trouble."

"I know he is." When Joe turned toward him, his eyes held a pleading look Mark had never seen before. "Let's get out of here, okay?"

JOE SUGGESTED THE Carriage House, a wood-paneled restaurant-bar long favored by students and locals that provided booths where patrons could talk in relative privacy. He sat across from Mark with slumped shoulders and a look of troubled abstraction, as though burdened by the weight of his own thoughts. When Mark ordered a beer, Joe asked the waitress for a Diet Coke on ice.

"No beer?" Mark asked.

He meant it as a casual remark. But Joe stared at the table. "I don't feel like it. I may never feel like it again." He looked up at Mark. "I'm an asshole when I drink."

Joe's expression, more often cynical or superior, was so vulnerable that his practiced veneer of prep school toughness vanished. He seemed to expect a response. "Sometimes," Mark agreed.

Joe nodded slowly. Cautiously, he asked. "How was I at that party?"

Mark eyed him with puzzled skepticism. "You don't remember?"

Joe winced. Removing his glasses, he wiped the lenses with a paper napkin, as though to improve his vision. "Kind of." He met Mark's eyes again. "I shouldn't drink at all, should I?"

Weighing his response, Mark reflected on the mercurial relationship among Joe's personae: the supercilious but amusing child of privilege; the wounded son of an angry father; the abrasive, abusive drunk. Why, Mark wondered, were he and Joe so different when both their childhoods had been train wrecks? Maybe it was innate; maybe it was that Mark had Lionel Farr. Or maybe it was that his own parents, unlike Joe's, were equals in their irrationality and rage. "When you don't drink," Mark responded evenly, "you're a good guy. When you do, you're more than an asshole—you're dangerous. I don't know you anymore." Mark paused, then decided to take a chance. "Maybe I'm meeting your father, Joe. The guy who kicked the shit out of Mom."

Eyes closing, Joe became very still. Mark felt his friend withdrawing to another place—some bad memory or deep within his most hidden thoughts. Then he opened his eyes again. Softly, he said, "I don't want to know that person anymore."

The statement sounded literal, the expression of a strong desire—even a need—to exorcise something within himself that Joe despised and feared. Mark felt a troubling shadow pass between them, his own unease about what lay beneath his friend's confession. Then Joe said with quiet fervor, "I need to make someone a promise, Mark. I've chosen you."

Mark cocked his head. "Not Laurie?"

A flicker of emotion—perhaps fear, perhaps shame—crossed Joe's face. "Too late." He put his hand on Mark's wrist, as though establishing a bond. "My old man's dead now. From now until I die, I'm never taking another drink."

"I believe you."

In truth, Mark was not sure. But Joe gave him a look of deep relief, as though Mark had absolved him. "Thanks, man. I mean it. I know the last few days have been hard for you."

Now it was Mark who stared at the table. At length he said, "I keep remembering her face." He paused, then finished in a monotone: "I'd never seen anyone dead before. All I can think is that no one should die that way."

Joe grimaced. "She looked bad, I guess."

"Yeah."

Through his own discomfort, Mark wondered what lay behind the question—compassion, morbid curiosity, or something deeper. Then Joe asked, "The night she died, when was the last time you saw Tillman?"

Mark met his eyes again. "When he left with her."

"What did *I* do?"

"You ran after them. After they got in Steve's car, you just disappeared."

Joe contemplated the remnants of his Coke. "I guess I went back to the dorm. I was asleep when the cops started pounding on the door."

"That's what Steve says, too."

Joe touched his eyes. "There's something else about that night," he said at last.

Once more, Mark felt pinpricks on his skin. "About Steve?"

"Yeah. I saw him."

"With Angela?"

Joe shook his head. "In the middle of the night, I woke up feeling like I was about to puke. So I went to the window and cracked it open, trying to suck in air."

Mark tried to envision this. Joe's room was on the second floor, a level above Mark's and Steve's. Save for lights at the entry to the dorm section, the stadium at night was dark. "And?" Mark prodded.

"Steve was outside." Joe's eyes narrowed, as though refocusing his memory. "It was only a second or two. But I could see it was him, passing through the light as he came toward the stadium. No one else limps like that." His face became grim. "I heard his key, the downstairs door opening, then closing."

Mark tried to gauge the importance of this. "Could you tell where he was coming from?"

"He was outside, that's all. Like I said, it was only a few seconds."

"Do you know what time it was?"

"Yeah, 'cause I remember looking at the clock. It was a little after three."

From the reluctance in his voice, Mark knew that Joe understood the danger inherent in his story—were Steve outside the stadium, he could have left with Angela, potentially placing him near the Spire.

Then what neither Joe nor the police knew hit Mark with a jolt. At 3:04, Mark had called Steve's room, then called again; for whatever reason, his friend had not answered.

A flush was spreading across Joe's face. "Thing is, I told the cops about it."

Mark stared at him. In a pleading tone, Joe said, "Don't tell anyone at the house, okay? They'll feel like I ratted Steve out. But you just don't lie to those guys."

Unless you had good reason to lie, Mark thought. But now he had an uneasy conscience of his own: uncertain of its meaning, certain only of the damage it might do, he could not bring himself to tell anyone about his phone call.

"I won't tell anyone," Mark promised.

Joe seemed both somber and relieved. "Let's go up to the house," he said abruptly. "We're almost late for dinner."

WITH THE HELP of their fraternity brothers, Joe had liberated his Miata from the library. Silent, they drove from downtown Wayne to the DBE house, parking close to the rear steps, where, in what Mark thought of as a more innocent time, he and three inebriated friends had lifted Joe's convertible.

Sliding out of the passenger seat, Mark saw the back doors of their fraternity house open.

Framed in the doorway, Steve Tillman was flanked by two policemen, one at each elbow. Steve's hands were cuffed behind him. Stunned, Mark saw that one of the cops was their former teammate George Garrison, Angela's high school friend.

At the head of the steps, Steve stumbled, his damaged knee buckling. When he saw Mark, his mouth twisted in an odd, chagrined smile, as though he had been busted with a nickel bag of pot. On the other side of the car, Joe softly murmured, "Jesus . . ."

Mark wanted to say something. Instead, he froze, paralyzed by confusion and what he had learned from Joe. With the force of a blow, Mark understood that their lives had changed in a profound and frightening way.

The police trundled Steve into a squad car. Without speaking to Joe, Mark hurried off to the only place he could go for help.

HE ARRIVED AT Lionel Farr's out of breath, pursued by his memory of running there only days before. To his surprise, Taylor answered the door.

Unlike most adolescents, she seemed to be skipping the gawky stage: at eleven, Taylor was part child, part the dark-haired beauty prefigured by her mother. But already she had the preternatural seriousness, sometimes disconcerting to Mark, of an adult guarding her private thoughts. Anne had dryly remarked that Taylor reserved her brightest smiles for Mark, practicing for when boys her age became halfway human, and sometimes it seemed so. But tonight the girl simply stared at him, her eyes so filled with sorrow that he guessed she must know why he had come.

"Is your dad home?" he asked.

Reluctantly, Taylor opened the door, inching aside.

Farr sat beside his wife in the living room. Though Anne greeted him pleasantly, her voice was soft, her face ashen. Farr looked tired; all the energy and resolve Mark had seen since Angela's death seemed to have drained from him. In a voice more weary than welcoming, he asked, "What is it, Mark?"

"They've arrested Steve."

Anne looked down. Standing, Farr touched her shoulder, an overt gesture of tenderness Mark had seldom seen from him. "Let's talk in the den," Farr said.

WHEN FARR SAT across from him, Mark thought briefly of his first dinner here, the night that had changed his life. But now Farr's manner was far less expansive. Bluntly, he said, "You must have felt as if you were walking into a séance. The trouble is that Anne's not well."

Despite his own anxiety, Mark was startled. "Is she okay?"

"In a manner of speaking. At least for now." Farr's voice softened. "Anne has a heart condition. It's something all three of us live with, though Taylor is simply afraid of her mother dying. Sometimes Anne's blood pressure drops so precipitously that she passes out. In truth, that's one of her lesser problems. But today Taylor found Anne on the kitchen floor and thought that she was dead."

This explained Taylor's greeting, Mark thought—in fact, it might explain much more about her. "So," Farr said in a flat voice, "they've decided Steve's the one. I know how that must upset you."

Mark felt deflated. "I think he needs a lawyer."

"I'm quite sure he does." Watching Mark's face, Farr inquired, "Are you so sure he didn't kill her? I learned long ago how little we know about others, even those we're certain we know well. You also know nothing about what may have happened between those two. People can do strange things when liquor unleashes their darker natures."

Mark felt himself resist this. "That's not Steve."

"Then who did this?" Farr parried. "Murder by strangulation is not an impulsive act. It took someone a long time to suffocate her like that."

Farr's voice betrayed an undertone of anger. Chastened, Mark realized that Farr had felt closer to Angela than to Steve, and had admired her far more. It was even possible, Mark thought, that his own presence reminded Farr of why Steve had been given a scholarship, and that, with Angela dead, Farr bitterly regretted his role. "Steve's my friend," Mark said. "His parents took me in. I've got to help him somehow."

Farr regarded him closely. "Discussing this is difficult," he said at length, "given my relationship to the school and my feelings about Angela. But if Steve's a murderer, it's quite certain he was impaired. That's the basis for *some* sort of defense. I suppose it's even possible that he's innocent."

Mark felt the whipsaw of his own doubt, the secret lodged within him. He waited for Farr to speak again. "I know a decent lawyer in town," Farr continued. "Griffin Nordlinger. I expect he might do better than some overworked state public defender from who knows where. At least Griff might be good for some advice. I'll see if he'll agree to visit your friend."

The new reality hit Mark: Steve was in jail now, his expulsion from Caldwell certain. It felt like another death.

CROSSING THE DARKENED campus, Mark reached the stadium filled with apprehension and despair.

He found Joe in the recreation room, watching a local TV station. Dave Farragher spoke from behind a podium. "With this arrest," the prosecutor said firmly, "our community and the college can start to feel safe again."

Standing to one side, Mark regarded Joe's face in profile. Neither acknowledged the other's presence.

8

"KEEP MOVING FORWARD," FARR URGED MARK MORE THAN once. "All you control is whether you do your damnedest to get into Yale Law School. Don't let Angela's murder kill your dreams as well."

Days became weeks, then months. Mark studied relentlessly. He rarely dated, and avoided parties altogether. He told no one about Joe's story, or the phone calls Steve had failed to answer. He learned nothing more about the case against his friend.

The trial was set for September, four months after the graduation ceremonies that would no longer include Steve Tillman or Angela Hall. Mark never discussed the impending trial with Joe Betts; they seldom spoke at all. For Mark, except for his studies, college was done. His main activity beyond class was visiting Steve at the county jail.

Separated by Plexiglas, they met every Sunday, speaking through miniature microphones. Mark offered encouragement; sometimes they reminisced. But Steve's lawyer, Griffin Nordlinger, had forbidden him to discuss the charges in any detail. Perhaps he could not have, Mark thought; unless Steve was lying, he seemed to live in a fugue state, unable to recall or reconstruct the events that now controlled his fate. He seemed crushed by the fear of never being free.

"Just think," Steve murmured. "That may be the last time I ever touch a woman, and I can barely remember it."

Mark did not know how to respond. Once again, he thought of his three o'clock phone calls.

Winter passed; spring came. And then, in April, Mark's senior year became cemented in his mind as the year of death.

IT WAS A week before Mark expected to hear from Yale. He walked into Lionel Farr's nine o'clock Philosophy of Mind class, a choice driven less by its subject matter than by a desire to experience, for one final time, the stimulation that had first drawn him to Caldwell. But another professor, Michael Dunn, appeared—Farr had been called home abruptly, interrupting his eight o'clock class. Anne was dead; Farr's classes were canceled until further notice.

Mark waited until late afternoon, thinking of Farr and Taylor, struggling to accept that Anne had died. Then he went to their home unannounced, hoping that Farr would not take it amiss.

Farr himself answered. His gaze was spectral, although he managed to summon a wispy smile. His voice was unusually gentle. "Hello, Mark. It's good of you to come."

Awkwardly standing on the porch, Mark shifted his weight from one foot to the other. "I'm just worried about you, that's all. And Taylor."

"Her mother would thank you for that." Pain surfaced in his eyes. "Taylor found her, Mark. Her deepest fear became real."

The image of Taylor discovering Anne sent a frisson through Mark. He tried to imagine how she must feel, a twelve-year-old girl facing life without her mother. "Is there anything I can do?" he finally asked. "Maybe in a couple of days, I can take Taylor somewhere."

Farr placed a hand on his shoulder. "Thank you, Mark. Right now she's sedated, or I'd let you see her—she's very fond of you. But her grandparents are coming to help care for her."

Slowly, Mark nodded. "I only wish there was some way I could help. All three of you mean a lot to me."

"And you to us." Farr's grip on Mark's shoulder tightened, then relaxed. "There'll be a memorial service, I'm sure. We'll hope to see you then."

THEY HELD THE service in the shadow of the Spire.

Perhaps this was Farr's true memorial to Anne, Mark reflected, allowing her death to rededicate this site through a commemoration that, however premature, had occurred in the natural order of things. The day was breezy and pleasant; the lawn chairs were filled with family and faculty and students, a scattering of friends from Wayne and elsewhere. Sitting with Joe Betts and Rusty Clark, Mark was glad of this. But the Episcopal service performed by the school chaplain, while consistent with Anne's eastern heritage, came to Mark as a meaningless drone, divorced from life on earth or the woman who no longer lived here.

"I am the resurrection and the life; he that believeth in me, though he were dead, yet shall he live . . ."

Farr sat with Anne's parents, two dignified and stoic New Englanders. Anne's mother held her granddaughter's hand. Taylor looked blank, as though she, like her mother, had gone elsewhere. The chaplain's litany continued.

"I know that my redeemer liveth, and that he shall stand at the latter day upon the earth; and though this body be destroyed, yet shall I see God . . ."

Mark closed his eyes.

At last Farr spoke for himself and Taylor. The woman he described was articulate and graceful, her voice the music of their household, her love the touchstone of their lives. He spoke of Anne's countless acts of kindness, performed with a tact and lightness that called no attention to itself and asked for nothing in return. It struck Mark as true to his sense of her: though her sensitivity was plain to see, there were few light anecdotes to share. He, with so few good memories of family, wondered what Taylor would remember.

Still she stared ahead, as though she were alone.

AFTER THE SERVICE Mark spoke to Farr, who embraced him, then to Anne's father and mother, to whom, clearly, he was just another stranger in a pageant that filled them with unspoken horror, two parents who had outlived their only child. But when Mark paused in front of Taylor, her stoic mask dissolved. Silent tears ran down her face.

Instinctively, Mark held her. When at last he drew back, Taylor's eyes locked his with something akin to desperation. "I missed you," she whispered.

"I'm sorry." He clasped both of her hands in his. "You still have your dad, Taylor. You can lean on him now. That's what he wants you to do."

For a moment, she looked as though she had not heard him. Then she squeezed his hands, keeping him there an extra moment before her grandmother introduced her to a woman she did not know. As Mark moved on, Taylor turned back to look at him.

That afternoon, as on every Sunday, Mark went to see Steve Tillman.

9

WHEN YALE LAW ACCEPTED HIM, MARK WAS LESS ELATED than relieved. He was moving on—life beyond Caldwell was tangible now. His graduation a month later was not so much a culmination as a way station. Though Farr congratulated him warmly, the ceremony reminded Mark that, unlike his classmates, he had no family to inflate the moment; nor, given their own pain, could he have asked Steve's parents to come. Tactfully alluding to Angela Hall, Clark Durbin said nothing about the person Mark missed most keenly, his closest friend.

He spent his final summer in Wayne working construction, losing himself in the doing of tasks, the oddly pleasant ache of joints and muscles. On the Sunday before he left for Yale, Mark paid Steve a final visit.

Steve gazed at him through the Plexiglas. "So you're off to law school," he said.

Mark felt a stab of guilt. "Yeah."

"You're on your way, pal." Steve's lips compressed. "My lawyer thinks *I'm* going to the pen."

"Did he say that?"

Doubt and anger surfaced in Steve's eyes. "Not exactly. But he asked me to think about involuntary manslaughter—letting the jury consider that along with a murder charge. If I was too drunk to know what I was doing, Griff says, maybe I can get off with ten years."

Mark wondered if Steve was asking for advice. He had none to give. Something about Griffin Nordlinger bothered Mark—an air of distraction, a sense of always running behind, combined with Mark's knowledge that the lawyer's bills were likely to cost Steve's parents the only home they had ever owned. But in the last few weeks Mark had heard vague rumors of another witness who bolstered the prosecution's case. Mark was bedeviled by the thought that this person might help corroborate Joe Betts's story, making Steve's failure to answer Mark's phone calls seem more damning. Cautiously, Mark asked, "What did you tell him?"

Steve's mouth set in a stubborn line. "Going for involuntary manslaughter would be like saying I killed her but can't remember. Who'd believe that? They'd just convict me of murder." His tone was at once pleading and insistent. "I may not remember things, but alcohol and a little coke didn't turn me into some other person. Besides, I liked her."

Once more, Mark had a terrible sense of randomness, a death at once tragic and banal. "Can you remember *anything* else about what happened?"

"No." Reading the doubt in Mark's eyes, Steve snapped, "If you don't believe me, don't come back for the trial."

Mark did not have a choice. Farragher might want him to testify about the party; Nordlinger would call him as a character witness. Quietly, Mark answered, "I'll be there for you."

Tears surfaced in Steve's eyes. Mark had known him since they were twelve; now he could not console him, or even hug him. Briefly, Steve leaned his forehead against the Plexiglas. Then he straightened again, summoning a strained smile for his friend.

"Do good at Yale," he told Mark.

*   *   *

ON THE NIGHT before Mark left, Lionel Farr took him to dinner at
the Carriage House.

Mark had little to say. After a while, Farr observed, "You don't
seem very excited, Mark. I gather Tillman still weighs on your mind."

Mark nodded. "I'm feeling like I should stay here," he admitted.
"Hardly anyone visits him now."

Farr put down his scotch. "And postpone Yale? Or, worse yet, *lose*
Yale?" His face hardened. "I refuse to let you throw your life away because Steve ruined his. Not to mention taking someone else's life."

Mark bridled at his mentor's certainty. "I'm not sure he did."

"That's what trials are for, Mark." Farr modulated his tone. "Your
boyhood friend did a foolish thing, perhaps a terrible thing. He's got
an able lawyer. It's not your fault you saw him leave that party with
Angela."

"Maybe not. But I started this by telling the police that. They
came down on Steve before he knew what hit him."

Narrow-eyed, Farr looked off into the middle distance. "I don't
know if this helps," he said at length, "but I've spoken to Dave Farragher. He won't need your testimony at the trial. So that part, at least,
won't be on your conscience. You needn't come back at all."

Mark shook his head. "I will, though. Griff Nordlinger wants me
to be a character witness."

"To say what?"

"That Steve's truthful. That I've never seen him act violent, or
even be angry enough to hit someone."

"Is that so?"

"I've known him half my life." Mark felt the burden of his secret
overtake him. "There's something else, though. Something I haven't
told anyone."

He felt Farr appraising him closely. "Then maybe you should tell
me, Mark. Better now than when Farragher cross-examines you."

Mark paused a final moment. Then, haltingly, he told Farr about the two phone calls.

Listening, Farr steepled his fingers, placing them to his lips. Then he looked around, as though concerned that the other diners—couples and college students and families with kids—might overhear. "Let me make sure I get this," he responded quietly. "Joe Betts will testify that he saw Steve returning to his room at three A.M. or so. Farragher could use this secret you've been keeping—that Steve didn't answer when you called him—to help confirm Betts's story. The implication for you is this: you think Steve may be guilty but don't want to help convict him. You also don't want to lie on the witness stand—for the sake of your own integrity, and because you don't want to commit perjury to protect someone who may have murdered an admirable girl. Does that cover it?"

"Yes," Mark answered miserably.

"Then there's only one solution, however imperfect. Don't go anywhere near that trial."

Mark gazed past Farr, torn between the desire to stand by Steve and the need not to seal his friend's fate or lie on the witness stand. "Do I have a choice?" he asked.

"I'll talk to Griff Nordlinger." Farr's tone became both kind and weary. "However *I* feel about this information, I doubt Griff will want you back here."

Awash with both relief and a sense of betrayal, Mark felt himself separating from Steve Tillman, even as he felt guilty about making Farr complicit in his secret. When their steaks arrived, Mark did not pick up his fork. "Eat something," Farr said mildly. "You've got a long drive to New Haven tomorrow."

Mark began cutting a piece of meat. It struck him that he had asked nothing about Farr's life. "I still don't know how *you* are," Mark said simply.

Farr smiled faintly. "Keeping busy, at least. It seems that Clark

Durbin and the board want me to consider becoming provost of Caldwell College."

The idea of Farr not teaching seemed unfathomable. "You wouldn't be a professor?"

"Maybe I'd teach a class. But there seems to be a feeling, shared by Clark, that I helped keep the school going in the wake of Angela's murder."

"Not a feeling. You did."

Farr shrugged. "Whether that's true or not, it's difficult to say no. Especially given that taking on a new challenge would be helpful to me personally. To understate things, Anne's death lingers."

Mark sipped his beer, watching a family in an adjacent booth, two parents and three kids cheerful in one another's company. "What about for Taylor?" he asked.

Farr frowned. "That's my one reservation. Taylor can't seem to reconcile herself to Anne's absence. She's become withdrawn, almost angry." Pausing, Farr issued an uncharacteristic sigh. "These things take time, I know. But I'm worried about our future as father and daughter, so I don't want to lose myself in work."

Mark felt sadness for them both. "Is there anything I can do?"

"No, thank you. The question is what *I* do."

The statement had a dismissive sound. Farr lapsed into silence, seemingly lost in his own thoughts. Then he said softly, "About this other thing, Mark: I'll take care of it. But let's not talk of it again, between us or to anyone else. For both our sakes."

Once more, Mark felt that he had led this man, who had done so much for him, into a moral gray zone. Nodding his assent, he tried to focus on his steak.

After dinner, they stood outside the restaurant as twilight descended, deepening the valedictory mood Mark felt enveloping them both. Farr was too much a man of his generation to hug Mark. Instead, he shook his hand, bracing Mark's arm as he did. Realizing how much he had depended on Lionel Farr, Mark suddenly felt alone. "I'll miss you," he said simply.

Farr shook his head. "There's so much ahead for you now. Standing here, I think of the night I first approached you." He paused, his voice rough with banked emotion. "I can't express how proud I am of you, and how proud you should be of yourself. Take what you've achieved and make your place in the world. Leave the past behind."

Mark tried, and occasionally, over the next few months, he succeeded. In mid-October, as he prepared for midterms, Steve Tillman was convicted of first-degree murder and sentenced to life without parole.

The Return

1

ON THE FIRST SATURDAY IN JUNE, HOURS AFTER HIS RETURN as the seventeenth president of Caldwell College, Mark Darrow called on Lionel Farr at home.

He had shipped his possessions ahead and driven from Boston to Wayne in his Porsche convertible. Reaching central Ohio, he found the countryside just as he recalled it, green and flat for miles on end, with a gentle roll now and then. But, he noted wryly, he had long since become a creature of urban culture, somehow surprised to pass more cemeteries than hybrid cars. The people of Wayne believed in tradition—they buried, rather than cremated, their dead. Darrow's mother was one; he supposed he should visit her.

The president's house—where he and Farr had met with Clark Durbin, now his predecessor—felt strange to him. Driving to Farr's, Darrow put the top down, a favorite indulgence when he and Lee had taken weekend trips to Cape Cod. The feel of the air—warm, a touch muggy—brought back his youth; the sight of Farr's house infused old memories, both pleasant and painful, with a startling immediacy. As he stepped from the car, Darrow felt a curious dislocation, as though he were the unsettled youth he once had been rather than the presumptive savior of Caldwell College. Resolving to act his current age, Darrow knocked on the door.

To his surprise, it was opened by a young woman in her twenties. Framed by raven hair, her chiseled face was at once aristocratic and startlingly beautiful, with deep blue eyes that gave an impression of wariness, intelligence, and, as she studied him, amusement. Darrow had the odd sense that he knew her, though surely they had never met: hers was a face he would not forget.

"Hello, Mark," she said. "I'd still recognize you anywhere."

Darrow stared at her, then emitted a startled laugh. "You're supposed to be eleven."

"Twelve," Taylor Farr corrected him. "Except that I'm actually twenty-eight."

"And living here again?"

She led him inside. "Visiting," she answered. "I'm taking the summer off from teaching classes at NYU to work on my PhD dissertation."

He followed her through the living room. "In what discipline?"

"Art history." She smiled at him over her shoulder. "As an artist, I was always long on theory."

Darrow realized how little he knew about what had become of her. Farr's comments about Taylor, sparing and detached, had suggested an unspoken estrangement. "So what's it like being back?"

Turning, she paused in the living room, her expression openly curious. "I was going to ask you that."

After a moment's hesitation, he decided to acknowledge their shared history. "Weird, at times. When I first came back to campus, I found myself standing in the shadow of the Spire."

Her blue eyes seemed to darken. "That was the last place I saw you, remember? You were very kind to a twelve-year-old girl in pain."

"I liked you, Taylor. And I'd had my own experiences with pain."

Taylor seemed to study him. "And more since then, I know. I'm so sorry about your wife."

"Thank you." He put his hands in his pockets. "It seems that Lee's death changed things for me. After everything that happened my senior year, I planned never to come back here. But now Caldwell has a need, and maybe I do, too."

Taylor simply nodded. In her silence, Darrow felt disconcerted by their moment of near intimacy. But he supposed it was not surprising that he and Lionel Farr's daughter should retain a kinship. "I know my father needs you," she said. "He's in his study, more eager to see you than he'll admit."

She led him there. She was taller than her mother, Darrow noticed, though she had the same grace of movement, the indefinable air of separateness. Softly knocking, she opened the door to Farr's study.

Caldwell's provost rose from his familiar chair to shake Darrow's hand. "I see you've remet Taylor."

"Uh-huh." Glancing at Taylor, he said, "I recognized her right away. Hasn't changed a bit."

"But she has, of course. Taylor's become her mother." Giving Taylor a brief smile, Farr added, "That's a considerable compliment. But Taylor has talents all her own."

Taylor's smile was somewhat arid. "If you're going to talk like I'm not here," she told both men, "I'll make it easier by leaving." To Darrow, she said, "Do you need anything?"

"No. Thank you."

Briefly, she met his eyes. "Then just say good-bye before you go."

She left, closing the door behind her. Farr gazed after her. "She does resemble Anne, don't you think?"

Sitting, Darrow shook his head. "Actually, Lionel, she looks more like you than Anne, though the results are better than I'd have expected. She also *seems* more like you."

Farr raised his eyebrows. "How so?"

"More edge." Darrow hesitated. "Taylor also strikes me as more present. Anne as I remember her was kind but subdued."

"She wasn't well." A look of reflection crossed Farr's face. "As for Taylor, Anne's death seems to have created a wall between us that still exists. The tacit silence builds, and what we do say to each other leaves many things unsaid. I've often felt that our idea of family is a myth, the reality of which is bound to disappoint. As a father, I suppose I disappoint myself."

"Have you disappointed Taylor?"

"I'm afraid to ask. But a decade-plus of absence—physical and emotional—made that plain enough. This may be our last chance. That's why, despite any awkwardness, I'm glad to have her back." Farr leaned forward, speaking with more cheer. "I'm also glad to have *you* back, Mark."

Darrow smiled at this. "The least I could do."

"Oh, it's something." Farr gave a rueful wince, wrinkling the corners of his eyes. "The fig leaf of 'health' we used to cover Clark's resignation is in shreds. During your trip out, someone leaked word of the embezzlement. As of this morning, the media carried the story of our missing near million all over Ohio. I'm already hearing from alumni, and our board chair, Ray Carrick, is apoplectic."

Darrow's shrug was philosophical. "It was bound to get out sometime. The real problem is that we've lost control of the story. Do you know who leaked it?"

"No. But a good guess is any board member who wants Clark Durbin pilloried." Farr sat back. "This leak puts Durbin on the hot seat, and you along with him. Welcome back to Caldwell, Mark."

"This is why you hired me, isn't it? Tell me what else I'm facing the next few days, and then we'll think through this embezzlement."

Briefly standing, Farr reached into his rolltop desk and handed Darrow two stapled pages. "As we discussed, I've prepared a schedule for the next three weeks. Why don't we look at it now?"

Darrow scanned the pages. "You'll see," Farr told him, "that you've got meetings with key donors in New York, Cleveland, and Chicago, as well as alumni events in each city. When you're on campus, you'll meet with our CFO, the finance committee, and the investment committee, headed by Joe Betts."

"That reunion should be jolly," Darrow said. "In light of the em-bezzlement."

"Yes. You'll find Joe's feeling a little raw. Ditto with the faculty. Some have great ambitions for expanding our curriculum and won't be happy that Durbin's now-public defalcation may derail yet another capital campaign. Which is why," Farr added pointedly, "throwing Durbin to the wolves—or, more specifically, to Dave Farragher—would provide the discontented a welcome distraction from whatever cuts you're forced to make. There are times when your new job re-quires a certain ruthlessness."

"Much like my old one," Darrow answered crisply. "But before I castrate someone, I prefer the reasons to be my own. I'll decide about prosecuting Durbin when I know more."

Farr gave him a cool look of amusement and surprise. "Fair enough. Just remember that a part of this job is political awareness. Clark's no longer popular."

"I'll keep that in mind," Darrow responded amiably.

Farr paused a moment. "Turning back to the schedule, you'll also see meetings with community leaders."

Darrow read the names, stopping at the police chief. "Is that *the* George Garrison?"

"I'm only aware of one."

Darrow laughed in surprise. "That *is* progress."

Farr nodded. "Since Angela's death, black-white relations have changed a bit. Whites became more aware; blacks felt that justice was done, by the police and by Dave Farragher. That's the only good that came from that tragedy—an absence of more harm."

"Except to Steve."

"Is punishment for committing murder 'harm'?" Farr hesitated, then asked in a neutral tone, "When was the last time you saw him?"

"You know when it was," Darrow said more sharply than he wished. "Ten years ago, just after both his parents died. After that I stopped coming back at all."

"For which no one can blame you," Farr said calmly. "Especially if they knew about your phone calls to Steve that night. It's well to remember that the jury convicted Steve without that, and that you might feel even worse if they'd acquitted him. I know *I* would."

At this, the first mention of their shared secret since he'd departed for Yale, Darrow fell silent. At length he said, "Let's discuss our division of labor. I've done considerable reading about why college presidents succeed or fail—especially people who, like me, have no actual qualifications for the job. One major ingredient is a successful partnership with the provost."

As though relieved at the change of subject, Farr nodded his affirmation. "I suggest that you focus on the externals: alumni, the board, public relations, fund-raising, and the general infusion of inspiration and vision. I'll deal with the plumbing: curriculum, personnel, appointments, tenure, the physical plant, and student life." He held up a hand. "Which is not to say that you should allow me carte blanche. But I know the culture and politics of this place, the pitfalls and personalities—to borrow an unpleasant metaphor, where the bodies are buried."

"I appreciate that. And I could certainly use the help."

"A word then about our students and faculty. Kids come here with more psychological, familial, and personal problems than they once did—"

"More than me?" Darrow interjected with a smile.

"More and different. These days, we don't turn away students with learning problems—we try to work with them. And though we're tougher about enforcement, all these issues are still exacerbated by drug and alcohol abuse. So just be warned about that."

"And the faculty? Are all of *them* screwed up, too?"

Farr gave a short laugh. "Just more steroidal. During Clark Durbin's tenure, there was an enhancement of faculty power over academic matters, to some degree at the president's expense—"

"But not the provost's expense, I assume."

"No," Farr acknowledged. "As a former faculty member, I'll concede this was largely my doing, and it enhanced my own authority as well. But my reason was a sound one—the faculty are the experts in these areas, and honoring that attracts better faculty. That's one area in which Caldwell's grown stronger."

Darrow absorbed this, unsurprised. Farr was a natural leader, born to fill vacuums or—if need be—create them; Durbin was not. And Darrow was not Clark Durbin. But this, Darrow decided, was an issue for another day. "Is there anything else I should know?"

"Perhaps something you should consider. I'm sure you're accustomed to acting quickly and decisively. But if you're not facing a crisis, strike a balance between decisiveness and diplomacy.

"As provost, I learned patience. It takes time to win the trust of a community. The quality of one's decisions isn't enough—in any given case, the board, faculty, or alumni need to feel they're included. That means listening a lot, and discerning friends from enemies—aware that on any given issue, friends can become enemies overnight." Farr smiled. "Fortunately for you, academia's not your life; nor is money of any concern. Everyone knows that we need you way more than you need us. It's just better if you don't rub people's faces in it. Make your moves in a deliberative way."

"Good advice," Darrow answered. "Which brings me back to the embezzlement and Durbin. Where does that stand?"

Farr sat back in his chair. "As I told you, the board's hired an excellent forensic accountant—his investigation is well under way. As you suggested, new safeguards are already being crafted. "Embezzlement isn't pretty, but at least it's not the murder of a student. The accounting details are in good hands, and we've hired an outside PR firm. Your major worry *is* public relations: assuring alumni that this will never happen again and deciding what to do with Durbin."

Darrow nodded. "Still, I'd like to meet with this accountant. When alumni ask questions, I'll need command of detail."

"That makes sense. Conveniently, he'll be here on Monday, along with Joe Betts. I'll make sure they see you."

"Good." Durbin stood. "I'd better get settled in. Durbin's old house is filled with my boxes. Where *is* Clark, by the way?"

Farr grimaced. "Living in a furnished apartment, consulting with lawyers while awaiting his fate. A melancholy outcome to a career."

"And a surprising one, I still think." Darrow paused. "The schedule is fine, by the way. Go ahead and set it up."

Farr nodded. "I'll see you Monday, then. Your first official day as president."

They shook hands warmly. "Don't bother to walk me out," Darrow said. "I promised Taylor I'd come find her."

She was in the sunroom, a stack of papers on her lap. When she looked up, Darrow said, "As I remember, this is where you used to paint."

Smiling, she put the papers aside. "I'm working on another thing of beauty—my dissertation." She stood, walking him to the door. "Did you two have a satisfying summit conference?"

"Of course. The renaissance of Caldwell College has begun."

"Just in time," she said in a tone that contained good-humored mockery with truth. "Thank God you're here."

"I suppose." Darrow paused at the door. "But except for Lionel, I barely know anyone now. Do you?"

She shook her head. "I've spent the last fourteen years avoiding that. The center of our life in Wayne is the same man—your friend, my father."

Darrow considered this. "Then maybe we should expand our social circle. Can I buy you dinner Monday night?"

Despite her poise, Taylor looked pleased. "Think I'm old enough now?"

"Yup. Unless you think I'm *too* old."

"Not yet," Taylor answered philanthropically. "I'll make reservations at the Carriage House. Some things don't change; it's still the only place in town."

THAT NIGHT, UNABLE to sleep, Darrow listened to the distant sound of a train whistle.

This, too, had not changed. In high school, bereft of family, he had lain awake in the bedroom he shared with Steve, listening to the same whistle. It had become the symbol of the larger world, life bypassing Wayne, Ohio. But now he was back.

Tomorrow he would visit his friend.

2

ONCE AGAIN, DARROW FACED A PLEXIGLAS SHIELD. THE shield had a small oval with metal grids through which they might speak. A door on the prisoner's side opened, and then Steve walked toward him.

The first thing Darrow noticed was that his limp remained. As Steve sat on his side of the Plexiglas, his eyes seemed to drill into Darrow's core. His skull was shaved, his face hard. In his jumpsuit he looked fit and well muscled, as though he had channeled his energy and anger into making himself invulnerable. He looked so alien that Darrow cringed inside.

Some of this must have shown in his eyes. With their faces two feet apart, the smile he gave Darrow was sardonic and unwelcoming. "Think you'd have recognized me, Mark?"

The question mingled accusation with curiosity, making Darrow feel more defensive. "Only by the surroundings," he answered. "How are you, Steve?"

"Better off than my parents. That jury sentenced them to die of shame and misery. I'm merely in prison for life, still wondering what happened to me."

His speech and phrasing seemed more studied than that of the small-town boy Darrow had grown up with, his emotional range flatter, yet suffused with subterranean anger. Awkwardly, Darrow asked, "How do you cope?"

"Exercise. And reading. You name it: history, politics, philosophy, anything but prison novels. My professors would be amazed—right now I'm into the new translation of *War and Peace*. But my favorites are books on repressed or recovered memory." His eyes bored into Darrow's. "So why did you show up now? Curiosity?"

Darrow chose not to answer. "I'm back in Wayne. They've made me president of Caldwell."

Steve flashed a wolfish smile. "So I hear. You buy them a building or something?"

"They didn't have the bargaining power."

"Guess not. Lionel and the rest must be pretty desperate these days. First Angela; now Durbin's fingers in the cash box. That day you won the Lutheran game was the end of our Age of Innocence." The mirthless smile returned. "Yeah, I even read Edith Wharton."

Darrow had a profound sense of a life wasted. He took in the tile floors and cinder-block walls, yellow under the light from fluorescent tubes.

"Books keep me from going insane," Steve continued. "And memories. Sometimes I relive college a week at a time, from freshman year until that night, remembering what it felt like to be free. Except now that kid I was seems like a blind man, headed for some terrible moment hidden in the ambush of time." His voice softened. "Sixteen years now, and I still don't know what happened between Angela and me. I've filled notebook after notebook with scribbles about that night—scraps of memory that might have happened, but I'm not sure of; images I might have imagined because I'm so fucking desperate to know. It's like strip-mining a played-out vein of coal. Nothing left but dust."

To Darrow it sounded hauntingly like the truth. Either Steve was a gifted liar and always had been, or he was tormented by the fear that he had killed someone, or he was innocent. Of these, the hardest to imagine was a murderer so drunk that he had strangled Angela to death, then awakened wondering what had happened. Buffeted by doubts, Mark could not resist asking, "Do you remember leaving the dorm in the middle of the night?"

"No," Steve answered tersely. "You'd have to ask Joe about that. He fucked me over at the trial."

Darrow had a piercing memory of hearing Joe's story, coupled with his own foreboding about phone calls Steve did not answer. "How, exactly?"

Anger and confusion clashed in Steve's eyes. "According to Joe, he had to lean out the window to keep from puking. I happened— just happened—to be strolling back from the general direction of the Spire. I didn't see him; he didn't say a word to me. Only to the cops." Steve's voice became quietly caustic. "You should have seen him on the witness stand, so hangdog, so sorry to testify that he couldn't even look at me. I barely recognized the arrogant prick you and I used to live with. Hope Mr. Prep School's not still suffering too much."

Darrow felt more disquiet: he, too, held a potential piece of evidence, perhaps corroborating Joe's story. "Joe couldn't have convicted you by himself," Darrow said. "What else was there?"

Steve tilted his head, staring at Darrow through the Plexiglas. "Why all the questions?"

Darrow did not care to answer. "Maybe habit," he finally said. "I spent the first five years after Yale as a prosecutor. Asking questions becomes a reflex; if you're any good, so does doubt. Sometimes lawyers or cops who want an outcome arrange the facts to fit what's convenient to believe."

"I certainly was convenient," Steve said with corrosive sarcasm. "Not just for the prosecutor, but for Caldwell College. Once they put me away, the campus was safe. You could send your daughter there knowing I couldn't choke her to death."

Darrow could find no adequate response. Finally, he said, "Is anyone still working on your case?"

"On what, exactly? That I sort of remember Angela saying she had to leave? What kind of sense does *that* make?" Steve's tone was suffused with pain. "I'll tell you what makes no sense to me. That I'm a murderer but don't remember being one. That I'd want to hurt a woman, let alone kill a woman I liked enough to sleep with."

Mark thought of Angela at the party, seemingly bent on losing herself. "You both were drunk. The next day, you said you could barely remember whether you'd had sex with her or not."

Tillman stared at him. "I liked her sober, Mark."

"So did I." Saying this, Darrow felt twisted up inside. "I should have stayed in touch, Steve. I haven't known how to deal with everything that happened. Including my own role."

Steve's gaze was unyielding. "That's a lot of guilt to carry. Wondering if you failed me, then wondering if I strangled her. I can't imagine how hard it must be for you to wonder if I might be innocent."

Again, Darrow chose not to respond. "Maybe you don't want to see me," he said at length. "But if you don't mind, I'll come back next Sunday. Maybe there's something I can bring."

Steve gave him a crooked smile. "They don't usually let you 'bring' stuff. Just your own psychic baggage."

Darrow's own smile was strained. "Sixteen years, and you've become portentous."

"And you've got a truckload of new baggage. The price of freedom, I guess." Steve's voice became less biting. "Sorry about your wife—I saw the reports on television. Locked up here, you forget that life outside this place has moments of darkness."

"More than a moment." Darrow hesitated, then said, "Our time ran out. Sometimes people forget that all of us live a few feet, or a few seconds, from tragedy—some random accident that just misses us without our even knowing. I should have a wife and a two-year-old son. Instead Lee hit a patch of ice she could have missed."

After a moment, Steve nodded. "I think that's what happened to me, Mark. I only wish I knew."

THAT NIGHT DARROW stood in the semidarkness of what had been Clark Durbin's home. It needed more lighting; the furniture was sterile; the representational art on the walls was at odds with the decor and Darrow's tastes. But then, it wasn't his home. It was still the place where Lionel Farr had prepared Durbin to cope with Angela Hall's murder. Coupled with the arrest of Steve Tillman, that crucial hour had enabled Durbin to survive so that, sixteen years later, he could bring Caldwell to the brink of permanent decline again.

Darrow thought of Steve's fate, then Durbin's; in each case, their guilt in some way served to insulate Caldwell from further damage. It had been hard to imagine his friend a murderer; now, if one believed the available evidence, Durbin was a thief. It was another humbling example, Darrow supposed, of the mysteries of character—how little you understood the people you thought you knew unless, by chance, you happened on some unguarded window on their lives. For a moment he wished Lee were here. Then he remembered that, in ways that shamed him now, he had not truly known her either.

Darrow went to the bedroom and unpacked another box.

3

Darrow's first day as president of Caldwell College began quietly.

He walked from his residence to College Hall, the site of his office, a 160-year-old Gothic brownstone with a steeple far more modest than the Spire. The morning was already warm, and summer students were heading to early classes in T-shirts and jeans or shorts, among them a few kids from India or the Far East, a much rarer sight when Darrow himself had attended Caldwell. With a sense of mild wonder at his return, Darrow climbed the steps to the front entrance.

Inside, the floors were marble, the hallways hushed and shadowy, the wood-paneled walls darkly stained. Along the spacious corridor leading to Darrow's new office were oil paintings of the past presidents of Caldwell College—save Clark Durbin—beginning with the Reverend Caldwell himself, whose deep-set brown eyes stared at Darrow with a fierce and unbending rectitude. Darrow remembered these portraits well; it struck him that, if he helped save the school, his own would hang here long after he was dead. He found the thought amusing and more than a little jarring.

Feeling like an impostor, he proceeded to the president's suite. He greeted his assistant, Lisa Forbes, then stepped into his office and shut the door. Instantly the spacious room felt sealed off, its decor—a Louis

XIV desk, leather chairs and couch, an oil painting of the Spire—like a movie set waiting to be occupied. In fifteen minutes, when Joe Betts appeared, Darrow's history at Caldwell would resume. He used the time to carefully consider his approach to this most delicate of subjects, the embezzlement that had triggered his return.

WHEN THE DOOR opened, Lisa ushered in the forensic accountant hired to investigate Durbin's theft, followed by Joseph C. Betts III—as the day's schedule had listed him—chair of the investment committee of Caldwell's board of trustees.

Joe stopped in the doorway, eyeing Darrow with mock astonishment. "Oh my God," he said. "He's b-a-a-ack."

Darrow emitted the appropriate laugh. "Just like Freddy Krueger."

Crossing the room, Joe gave him a quick embrace. "It's terrific to find you in this office, man. Truly." Turning to his companion, he said, "Mark, I'd like you to meet Greg Fox, financial bloodhound par excellence."

Darrow took in Fox, a small, neatly dressed man in his forties with salt-and-pepper hair, black eyes, and a shrewd expression that suggested quiet confidence. Shaking his hand, Darrow said, "Thanks for coming. I hear you do terrific work."

Smiling, Fox took a chair beside Joe, enabling Darrow to take a closer look at his old friend. Joe looked youthful and healthy, his face virtually unlined, with modish swept-back hair, horn-rimmed glasses, and a jovial demeanor somewhat at odds with his watchful eyes. He seemed the epitome of an East Coast financial adviser, sound as a pre–9/11 dollar, save that Darrow caught—or imagined—a glimmer of the uneasy college student beneath. "Is it true," Darrow asked him in a parody of amazement, "that some misguided woman actually agreed to marry you?"

It was not, Darrow realized at once, the most artful thing to say: for an instant Joe's face darkened, as though Darrow were reopening old wounds. But he answered lightly enough. "Not only to marry, but to procreate. We have a boy and a girl—both blond-haired paradigms of brilliance. Clearly Katie's kids. All I did was light the match.'"

Greg Fox, Mark noticed, took in this badinage with smiling but careful attention, as though listening for distant signals on a crystal set. "Congratulations," Mark told Joe. "As Somerset Maugham once said, 'Luck is a talent.'" He smiled again. "It's really great to see you, Joe."

"Likewise," Joe rejoined dryly. "As the spider said to the fly."

At once Darrow became serious. To both Joe and the accountant, Mark said, "Dealing with this embezzlement is critical. I'm grateful for all you're doing."

Joe's eyes narrowed slightly, as though Darrow had rebuked him. "I'm just trying to help fix what I helped screw up. If I hadn't been so trusting, Clark couldn't have stolen close to a million bucks."

Glancing at Fox, Darrow shook his head. "*I'd* have trusted Durbin, Joe—certainly about money. But I'd still like your take on how it all happened."

"Stupidity," Joe said with a grimace. "Greg can give you an outline. More, if you like."

Darrow shook his head. "For now the Cliffs Notes version's fine."

Fox glanced from Joe to Darrow. "Okay," he said briskly. "Caldwell's board has a five-man investment committee. Including Joe, all the outside members—Ed Rardin, Paul Johns, and John Stewart—are well-off and financially sophisticated." Fox's midwestern twang sharpened. "The fifth member was Clark Durbin.

"Each member of the committee had the authority to direct transactions under one million dollars—"

"Obviously a mistake," Darrow interjected.

"Which we're correcting," Joe said swiftly. "Going forward, we'll require the written authorization of three committee members, a majority."

"In any event," Fox told Darrow, "we had nine hundred thousand dollars sitting at Joe's firm, Buckeye Capital in Columbus. Durbin e-mailed Joe, directing that he transfer the proceeds to the Wayne County Bank, where Clark had opened an account in the name of Caldwell College. His signature is on all the papers."

"I sent an e-mail back to Clark," Joe put in, "confirming his instructions and copying the bank. It all checked out."

Darrow nodded. "And from there, it appears, Durbin transferred the nine hundred thousand to an account in Switzerland. Cutting off our ability to get the cash back, or even find out where it went."

"Exactly," Fox responded. "As I expect you also know, the only entity that can persuade the Swiss to lift their veil of secrecy is the U.S. government. In our case, Uncle Sam won't even try. The money's not enough to care about, and our government reserves its leverage for tracking transfers by known terrorists."

Joe shook his head in disgust. "Durbin turned out to be smarter than I'd ever have imagined."

"To a point," Darrow said. "I gather our auditors tumbled to this soon enough."

"Routinely," Fox confirmed, "and inevitably. They tried to verify the amount of the CDs at Joe's firm and wound up tracing the money all the way to Switzerland. At which point they contacted the audit committee of the board."

Darrow considered this. "What's so jarring is that Durbin was clever in the service of a stupid crime. Embezzlers always get caught; the only difference here is that most crooks steal money in small amounts, hoping to escape detection—at least for as long as possible. Stealing a larger amount of money, as Durbin did, exponentially accelerates the timetable for getting caught. Unless the embezzler disappears."

"He was desperate," Joe said simply. "His kid was a junkie; his wife has Lou Gehrig's disease; his own investments went south. Serial disasters caused Durbin to look into his character and find a thief." Joe's voice softened. "Then he looked at me and must have seen a fool."

"You'd be surprised," Fox told both men in a mollifying tone. "At small schools like Caldwell, people know each other over long periods of time. So trust builds up. That explains the lax policy on transfers of money—which, I might add, was known to every member of the committee. The only reason Joe became the fall guy is that his investment firm served as advisers to the school. So Joe was sitting on the money Durbin wanted."

"At my suggestion," Joe told Darrow hastily, "we've decided that no member of the committee should profit in any way from Caldwell's investments."

"All good," Darrow concurred. "By the time your work is through, I'm confident that what Durbin did would be impossible. What still troubles me is accepting that he did this in the first place."

Joe shook his head. "Why, Mark? It's Occam's razor—sometimes the simplest explanation is the right one."

Still unsatisfied, Darrow turned to Fox. "Up until a few weeks ago, my job was trying financial fraud cases. Mind if I have one of my old experts take a look at what happened here?"

For an instant Fox looked mildly annoyed; then his expression eased. "Sure," he answered. "As I always say, two heads are better than one. As long as they're not on the same body."

Darrow smiled at this. "Then I won't take more of your time."

Both men stood, Darrow shaking Fox's hand. With a final thanks, Darrow walked Fox to the door, closing it behind him.

Joe stood with his hands in his pockets. "Not that you weren't gracious, Mark. But Greg's top-flight, and you may have stepped on his pride a little. Sure you need to bring in your own expert?"

Darrow nodded. "Maybe you're right, Joe. I'll ponder it." He waved Joe to the couch, sitting companionably at the other end. "So tell me how you've been."

"Good." Nodding in self-affirmation, Joe said, "Really good, actually. In college, I never thought marriage could be this great. As you'll recall, my parents' marriage sure as hell wasn't."

"How *is* your mom?"

"Good enough. In her mind, my dad's become a saint. I guess it helps that he's still dead." A moment's unease crossed Joe's face. "About Lee, I don't know what to say. I can't even say that I know how you feel. Only that I feel for you."

Darrow mustered a smile. "That's all anyone can say, Joe. In a very real sense, we all go through life alone. Although some days alone is lonely any way you slice it."

Joe nodded in commiseration. "So what's it like for you, being back?"

"A lot of different things—I guess you could say it's complicated." He looked at Joe more closely. "Yesterday I went to visit Steve."

Joe blinked. "In the pen? How was he?"

"Different. Extremely buff, not to mention an eclectic reader. Also highly articulate."

"You're joking, right?"

Darrow shook his head. "Not at all. Steve's a stellar example of what can happen if you take an inherently good mind and eliminate all distractions."

Joe looked away. After a moment, he said, "I guess you know about the trial."

"Of course."

Joe nodded to himself, eyes still averted. "Did my name come up?"

Mark weighed his response. "It did. Steve has a point of view, and he's had sixteen years to perfect it." More quietly, he added, "Whatever you saw that night couldn't be helped, Joe. No reasonable person could expect you to lie on the witness stand."

Joe looked up. "Did Steve talk about that?"

"Only that he doesn't remember being outside the dorm. But then he claims not to remember much about Angela, either. Including whether he strangled her."

"That's bullshit," Joe said with sudden harshness. "Either he killed her or he didn't. But he sure as hell didn't forget about it."

"Yeah. That's what I think, too."

Joe seemed to ponder this. Then he stood, mustering a reasonable facsimile of the smile he had entered with. "It really is wonderful to see you, Mark. And even better that you're doing this for the school."

Darrow shrugged. "I owe this place," he answered. "I only hope I can give Caldwell what it deserves."

ALONE, DARROW CONSIDERED the last hour, then called Mike Riley, the forensic accountant he had used in Boston.

"Mark," Riley said in a jocular tone, "I thought you'd returned to the Poison Ivy League."

"Fucking Harvard snob," Darrow said. "Though it pains me, I'd like a moment of your time. The halls of ivy are crawling with crooks."

"Explain, please."

Darrow summarized the meeting. "So what bothers you?" Riley asked. "That a gentleman and scholar can open up a Swiss account? Or steal that much money without any sensible exit strategy?"

"Maybe both—I'm not quite sure yet. It's more a feeling I have."

"You've had them before," Riley answered. "Now and then you were even right. Problem is, I'm a little busy. Can't this wait two, three weeks?"

"Sure. The money's gone."

Riley laughed. "Okay, then. I've always wanted to visit Wayne, Ohio."

Hanging up, Darrow glanced at his schedule. Thanks to Lionel Farr, for the rest of the day there was barely time to breathe, let alone think. Ruefully, he recalled that the Reverend Caldwell had believed in total immersion baptism.

WHEN DARROW EMERGED from his office, his watch read seven o'clock, and he was running late for dinner with Taylor Farr. The evening was still light, the air muggy. Darrow put his top down, smiling at this gesture to his Porsche-less youth.

The main drag of Wayne, Scioto Street, bisected the town's commercial area. Downtown seemed much as it had been when Darrow left: two-story buildings that housed a hardware store, a haberdashery, a barbershop, and offices for real estate agents, accountants, lawyers, and insurance salesmen. Except for an outdoor café, a novelty, haute-bourgeois chic still seemed alien to Wayne. But the parking meters, Darrow noticed when he stopped, remained a bargain—four quarters bought two hours, ample time for dinner at the Carriage House.

The restaurant was at the end of the block. Two cars away, a slender black man with thinning hair stood by a silver Mercedes, sticking quarters into the meter. Turning, he examined Darrow with cool but ostentatious interest. "Well," he said in a silken voice, "Mark Darrow himself. And still the hero, seems like."

It took Darrow a moment to be certain. He glanced at the quarter between the man's fingers. "And you're still dealing in cash, seems like."

Carl Hall emitted a short laugh. Nodding toward Darrow's Porsche, he said, "Nice ride."

"Yours, too. So what are you up to, Carl?"

Hall gave him a complacent smile. "This and that. You know how it is."

"I certainly remember." Darrow waited for a moment. "I remember a lot of things, in fact. Yesterday I went to see Steve Tillman."

Hall's smile turned canine, more a show of teeth. "As they say, that's mighty white of you."

Casually, Darrow propped his arm on a parking meter. "He still insists he didn't kill her, Carl. That Angela told him she had to leave."

"Sure, at two in the morning. Must have had an appointment to get those white teeth cleaned."

Darrow repressed his visceral dislike. He waited for an elderly couple to pass them on the sidewalk, then asked in a tone of mild curiosity, "Did your sister have a relationship?"

Hall scrutinized Darrow more closely. "A secret boyfriend, you mean?"

"If you do."

"How would I know? The princess and I weren't that close."

Scumbag, Darrow thought. "Funny," he told Hall. "You had enough brotherly feeling to warn me off her at the party."

"That was about *you,*" Hall shot back. "I never minded taking money from white college boys. But I didn't like you people fucking my black sisters, related or not."

Darrow stared at him. "Fucking's not killing."

"Your buddy," Hall said flatly, "was a racist. Ask any black kid who went to high school with him. Surprised *you* missed it, actually. Assuming you did." He shook his head in weary scorn. "Stupid white men have been abusing black women since time began—that's how Angela's skin became that tawny shade you boys prefer. Tillman just took things one step further. So live with it, Mr. President."

Abruptly, Hall turned and walked away.

4

Walking into the Carriage House, Darrow entered a time warp, a place unchanged since he was in college. The commodious bar had three shelves filled with wine, liquor bottles, and painted signs touting extinct beers; the two rows of wooden booths still featured Tiffany lampshades overhead and sports memorabilia decorating the walls—jerseys, pennants, pictures, and framed articles capturing athletic triumphs. The place was packed with couples, old and young, and families across the generations; one long table included a pregnant woman, her husband, three restless kids, and a weary but patient grandmother. A man Darrow did not know waved in recognition, as though he had watched Darrow play football a week before. Friendly and unpretentious, the atmosphere suggested ordinary people going about their lives, uninterested in the concerns of Darrow's friends in Boston, who were so often focused on politics, travel, the arts, or vacation homes. Searching for Taylor, Darrow spotted Dave Farragher sitting with his wife and decided not to approach him.

Taylor occupied a booth near the back of the room. She wore blue jeans and a red silk blouse, which, Darrow thought, suited her color well. Approaching, he saw that she sat beneath a picture of the young Mark Darrow, thrusting the ceremonial bronze axe from the steeple of the Spire. He sat across from Taylor, glancing at his own image. "I can't seem to escape myself."

Taylor considered the photograph. "I remember that moment exactly—my parents and I were so excited for you. Looking at this picture now, I wish that were all I remembered."

"So do I."

She faced him, her expression pensive. "The owner meant well, seating us here. But you and I have a unique relationship to the Spire. For you, it's Angela; for me, my mother. I wouldn't mind crossing the campus someday and seeing that thing gone."

"No chance of that. There'd be an alumni revolt." He resolved to lighten her mood. "Nice blouse, by the way."

Taylor smiled. "If you see me again, you'll see *it* again. Part-time college instructors lack extensive wardrobes—the rewards of academic life are purer than that." She raised her eyebrows. "How was *your* first day in academia?"

"Terrific," he answered dryly. "The faculty's nervous; the alumni restive; and my predecessor—so it appears—was a criminal. A less optimistic man would say Caldwell's in trouble."

"So my father says. What will you do about it?"

"What I'd like is to start an endowment drive. But I can't just say to alumni, 'The last guy stole your money, so give me some more.' So I'm hitting the road, hoping to change the conversation from 'How the hell did this happen?' to 'How can I invest in Caldwell and its dynamic new leader?'" Darrow glanced at a waitress, drawing her attention. "In the meanwhile," he concluded, "I've hired a consultant to help me assess the priorities of the school. Before I try to raise a hundred million dollars, I need a fresh vision of what Caldwell can be."

The waitress, a wiry middle-aged blonde with a nice smile but tired eyes, took their drink orders. It gave Darrow time to absorb once more how attractive Taylor was. When the waitress left, Taylor said,

"It sounds like a lot of work. Does Caldwell really mean that much to you?"

Darrow considered his answer. Abruptly he decided to give this woman the truth as best he knew it. "When I left here," he acknowledged, "I meant to leave this place behind. Not just Caldwell, but the town. My family life was miserable; I'd grown up wanting to escape but never believing that I would." He paused, parsing his complex thoughts. "It's strange. I walked in here tonight and remembered all that's good about this town: that most people are friendly and straightforward; that they're bonded by clubs or civic groups or church; that they connect with one another in a way lost to e-commuters and the residents of gated communities; that despite their blind spots—race being one—they tend to be generous to anyone they actually know. And yet I also had this spasm of fear: that somehow I'd reverted, and was coming back for good.

"But the reason I left is the reason I returned. Caldwell—and your father—changed my life. If I'd turned him down, it would be like denying the central fact of my existence: the act of generosity that made me whoever I am now."

Abruptly, Darrow felt as though he had said too much. But Taylor regarded him with a look of sympathy and reflection. "Was it hard to leave Boston?" she asked.

Their drinks arrived. Darrow sipped his whiskey, pondering how much more to say to a woman he barely knew but for whom, given their shared history, he felt an affinity. At length he said, "Like Caldwell, Boston has its ghosts. Suddenly what remained felt empty."

Taylor regarded the table, as though considering what to say. Then she looked up at him again. "When I read that your wife had died, I thought about writing you. But it seemed gratuitous, a condolence note from someone who remembered you more clearly than I'm certain you remembered me. I imagined my note being more puzzling than consoling. So I didn't."

"I wouldn't have minded, actually. Now and then I've wondered about what became of you. How is it for *you,* being back?"

Taylor tasted her gimlet. "Funny," she answered. "Dad's still a stranger, although I feel him trying. And for some odd reason I don't sleep well in that house. But then I haven't had much practice since I was fourteen."

"Fourteen?"

Taylor nodded. "I went away to the Trumble School, in Connecticut. My grandfather Taylor went there—my uncle, too. So my grandparents offered to pay my way." Taylor paused, her eyes pensive. "They seemed to sense that my dad and I were both adrift. He didn't know what to do with me; worse, I think I resented him—terrible as this is to say—for being the parent who survived. Looking back, my grandparents were giving us both some breathing space. But when I left, I left for good."

When the waitress returned, they paused to order dinner. Picking up the conversation, Darrow thought of Joe Betts. "What was Trumble like?" he asked. "I always imagined prep school as a gilded prison."

Taylor laughed. "Oh, there's a little of that. Sometimes I think parents pay schools like Trumble a ridiculous amount of money to warehouse the puberty-maddened, imposing rules that Mom and Dad would never dream of trying. Imagine your mom conducting room inspections."

"I can't."

Registering his sardonic tone, Taylor smiled faintly. "No, I guess not. But add to that hall monitors who called you out for wearing headphones, sign-in sheets for breakfast, and a schedule where every hour from seven A.M. to nine at night was planned." She laughed softly at herself. "I make it sound like Alcatraz. The fact is, Trumble was good for me, and mostly I adored it. Suddenly I had friends from everywhere—my three closest girlfriends were from Ghana,

Hong Kong, and Spanish Harlem. Our classmates called us the 'four corners of the world,' which we wore as a badge of pride." Taylor's expression grew reflective. "I missed my mom, of course. There were so many times I wanted to talk with her about friends or boys or social pressures or dreams about the future, and I couldn't. But no one had a mom on-site. Instead, my friends became like a second family."

Thinking of Steve Tillman, Darrow nodded. "As a teenager I remember feeling like we were a secret society, conspiring against clueless adults."

Taylor smiled in recognition. "The four of us certainly had our secrets. When Lupe, from Harlem, was the first to sleep with a guy, the rest of us knew within hours. But no one else did, ever—except for all the people *his* friends told, of course."

Darrow cocked his head. "I'm curious about the logistics. Where did Lupe go to pull this off?"

Taylor grinned. "Sedgwick Chapel—the holiest of holies on the Trumble campus, laden with history: graduations, memorial services, addresses by storied alumni. No student was supposed to have a key, but someone always did. I've often thought the richest part of chapel lore was its unofficial history. Which no one ever acknowledged."

Darrow glanced at the photograph. "Sounds something like the Spire."

"I suppose so. But nothing died in Sedgwick except virtue, and most of us were dying to be rid of it." Taylor's expression grew serious. "Trumble was where I learned to cope with whatever happened to me. I left there as an adult, more or less."

It struck Darrow that Taylor, weaned from family, in some ways had become even more of a loner than the girl he remembered. "After prep school," he asked, "how were things with Lionel?"

"Much the same. Even at Trumble, I spent summers as a camp counselor, or with my grandparents on Martha's Vineyard. Same thing when I went on to Williams. During my junior year, my grandfather Taylor died, then Grandmother six months later. So I decided to leave the country altogether."

Their steaks arrived, pronged with small plastic signs that said, CERTIFIED ANGUS BEEF and promised that both were cooked medium rare. Darrow smiled at this. "The Carriage House," he told her, "has the virtue of being utterly resistant to fashion. It's been open for half a century now. In London or San Francisco, restaurants open and close in a year."

Taylor cut a decorous sliver of steak. "Have you spent much time in London?"

"A little." He hesitated. "That and Paris were Lee's favorite cities. We split our honeymoon between them."

Taylor took this in. "I lived in London for almost three years, taking a crash course in art dealing at Sotheby's, then getting my master's at the Courtauld Institute. It's probably the city I know best."

"Did you like it?"

"Quite a bit," she answered. "In fact, I thought about staying. But the best doctorate program anywhere is at NYU. So I went there, and learned to love the West Village. Now I need time off to finish my dissertation. So here I am, in Wayne."

"So here we both are—you living with your dad, me in what I still think of as Clark Durbin's house."

"The President's House," Taylor amended. "What's that like?"

"Not exactly to my taste. It feels a little like one of those furnished apartments that serve as a halfway house for husbands whose wives have thrown them out." He sipped his drink. "Perhaps it's my state of mind. In my former life we had a town house near the Common, filled with things we'd chosen over time. To me home is something organic. This is a place to sleep."

Taylor gave him a curious look. "Do you still own the town house?"

"Uh-huh. But it's begun to feel like a remnant of some other life.

There's too much of Lee there, and it seems empty without her." Embarrassed, he stopped himself. "God, I'm sounding sorry for myself. Lord knows why I'm subjecting you to this—I'm generally pretty okay."

Taylor shook her head. "You don't sound sorry for yourself, Mark. Just honest."

Darrow shrugged. "Then you can take it as an inverted compliment. I don't much like talking about myself."

Taylor smiled a little. "As I remember you at my parents' dinner table, you never did. Sort of like me. I guess we've been saving it up."

They finished dinner, chatting easily. Leaving the restaurant, Darrow was conscious of heads turning—perhaps for both of them; no doubt for Taylor Farr.

He walked Taylor to her car. They faced each other in the twilight. "I've been thinking," she told him. "Maybe you should do something to the President's House."

"Such as."

"Change it a little, or a lot." Her tone became wry. "At your own expense, of course—I gather you can afford it. But it's no good being in new surroundings if they depress you."

Darrow considered this. "That's not a bad idea, actually. Except for the time it would take." He tilted his head in inquiry. "Think you could advise me?"

Taylor laughed. "About what? Just like I'm not an artist, I'm not an interior designer. Besides, my specialty is postmodern art—any suggestion I made would terrify you. By the time I finished, you'd be sleepless, too, just knowing what horrors were lurking in your living room."

Darrow shrugged. "At least I'd be entertained."

She looked at him, her smile lingering. "You're serious."

"Completely. I'm curious about whatever you'd come up with.

Besides—as you pointed out when we met again—you're not twelve anymore." Though still light, his tone softened. "Truth to tell, I enjoyed myself tonight."

Slowly, Taylor nodded. "So did I, Mark. If you want my advice, just call me."

5

By Thursday evening, Darrow had spoken to alumni groups in Cleveland, Chicago, and New York. What daunted him was being introduced as the savior of Caldwell College; what pleased him was that, when he finished, the applause was louder than before he had begun. Besides the embezzlement and, in one case, the lingering effect of Angela Hall's murder, alumni concerns varied: in New York, the penultimate question was how Caldwell could let Huntley Stadium become so shabby; the last question, more to Darrow's liking, was, "Describe how you envision Caldwell College in five years' time."

"With a new football stadium," Darrow deadpanned. When the laughter died, he said, "New facilities will help us attract the best faculty and students. But what concerns me even more is where our students come from."

Pausing, his gaze swept the crowd, three hundred alumni assembled for dinner in a hotel ballroom. "Look around you," he suggested. "We're mostly white and uniformly prosperous." Darrow flashed a smile. "Mind you, I've got nothing against rich white people, and neither did the search committee. But the years since I graduated— thanks, I might add, to our school's generosity—have marked a decline of opportunity, not only for minorities but for middle-class kids squeezed out by rising tuition. Too many other Americans, fortunate themselves, have begun to live in gated communities of the mind, where no one asks them to care about people outside their own direct experience."

The audience was quiet now. Sensing their discomfort, Darrow continued firmly: "The Hall tragedy diminished what I want Caldwell to offer—excellence in education for students whose only barrier to college is money. *That* will make our school a place that enriches our country by expanding its promise. *That's* the heart of *my* vision for Caldwell College, and *that's* the effort I will ask you to support . . ."

To Darrow's surprise, the alumni gave him a standing ovation.

IN THE TAXI to the airport, Darrow's cell phone rang. "I'm calling about Pamela Hartman," Lionel Farr said without preface, "an associate professor of history. Her husband killed himself tonight."

"Good God," Darrow said reflexively. "Does anyone know why?"

"He lost his job." Farr sounded weary. "But who knows why anyone takes their own life. This man left Pam with two young kids."

Darrow realized that a woman he did not know, suddenly a widow, would need his consolation and support. "How's she doing?"

"Not well. Apparently her husband kept things buttoned up tight. Right up until he shot himself."

Darrow thought swiftly. "Let me know whatever she needs from us," he instructed. "If she wants to take a leave from teaching, we'll make the necessary arrangements. As soon as she's ready, I'll go see her."

Darrow stared out the window at the darkness. Remembering the call from Iowa telling him that Lee was dead, he felt this woman's grief and pain and, he imagined, guilt. Then he recalled Clark Durbin's kindness to him on the day of Angela's death. For the first time, he fully accepted that he was president of Caldwell College.

ON FRIDAY MORNING Darrow called on Professor Hartman. Then he drove to Huntley Stadium, the scene of his athletic triumphs, the place where he had once lived with Steve Tillman and Joe Betts. Farr was already there, gazing through the iron gateway from the parking lot to the football stadium. When Darrow approached, Farr asked, "How was Pam?"

"She still doesn't believe it. Part of her won't for a very long time."

"I know," Farr answered softly. "We both do."

The two men fell quiet. The weather was gentle enough, Darrow reflected, unlike the raw gray day after Angela's death, when he and Steve had sat in the bleachers. But even in sunlight, the stadium looked dingy, its walls darkened and eroded by time and wind and dampness. The stands were worn, the field patchy. "At the time I thought it was a dumb question," Darrow said, "But that alumnus who asked me that was right. This place is a dump."

Farr smiled a little. "It always was. You were just too young to notice. For you, Huntley was the Garden of Eden. And why not?"

They began to walk toward the center of campus. Turning back to look at the stadium, Darrow asked, "What about the wing where I used to live?"

"Padlocked. It's a storage area now. No one's lived there since you graduated."

Silent, Darrow gazed up at the window that had once admitted light into his room and, next door, the window through which Joe Betts—at least by his account—had seen Steve Tillman returning from the direction of the Spire. Glancing at Farr, Darrow asked, "Have time to walk with me awhile?"

The main campus was empty save for a man and woman heading for the science lab. The walkway they followed was flanked by the safety measures Farr had suggested to Clark Durbin: lights every fifty yards or so and, along the way, telephones connected to the campus police. Darrow was silent until they reached the grass surrounding the Spire. Then he turned, gazing back at the stadium. "How far would you say it is from Huntley to the Spire?"

Farr glanced back at the tower, then toward the stadium, blue eyes crinkling at the corners. It was the look of eagles; at that moment Darrow pictured the combat officer Farr once had been. "Two hundred yards," Farr estimated. "Give or take."

"Do you know if Steve's lawyer asked for the jury to come out here?"

"No. I don't."

Darrow gazed at the grass where he had found Angela, watching the play of light and shadow cast by swiftly moving clouds. "There are two possibilities," he said at last. "Either Steve killed her near the Spire or he carried her body two hundred yards, dumping it in the heart of campus. Neither makes much sense to me. Especially the latter."

Farr considered this. "It doesn't seem logical, does it? Of course, drunks aren't always rational. And assuming he killed Angela in his room, even a drunk would know her body couldn't stay there."

"True," Darrow conceded. "But Steve had a car that year. Why not throw her body in the river? Why walk all that way, with a bum knee, and risk letting someone see him?"

Farr looked at Darrow keenly. "You're asking the wrong man. But for the sake of argument, consider the hour. As you know all too well, the party action had moved to the fraternity houses." Farr paused a moment. "The time for kids from Ohio Lutheran to vandalize the Spire had passed, so no one would be guarding it. By two A.M. on a deserted campus, Steve would know that the pedestrian traffic was nil. Better to leave her here than get snagged for drunk driving with a corpse in his trunk."

Darrow faced the provost. "Fair enough," he said. "But did Steve Tillman ever strike you as capable of strangling Angela to death?"

Farr grimaced at the question. "Put that way, no. But who does? Certainly not anyone you've ever imagined you knew."

Briefly, Darrow thought of Joe Betts at the party, the puffy discoloration on his girlfriend's face. "There's a deeper reason," Farr went on, "why your question has no meaning to me."

"Vietnam?"

Farr studied the same swath of grass. "When we found her, I knew at once that she'd been strangled. That wasn't a guess. In my last year of service, our unit had what one might call unusual assignments. Perhaps made easier by latent—or not so latent—prejudice against an Asian populace where we couldn't tell enemy from friend.

"After that, I was never quite the same. Vietnam became a great silence; perhaps that's what Taylor senses in me. As did her mother." Farr straightened his shoulders, as though sloughing off the past. "That's done. But it left me with one advantage, if you care to call it that. You've never been forced to confront the full range of what you—or anyone you know—is capable of doing. I have."

Darrow had no response. More quietly, Farr said, "Follow your curiosity, Mark—I'm not trying to dissuade you. Exorcise Angela, if you can. But don't be disappointed by whatever you may find."

6

AT NOON, DARROW LEFT THE CAMPUS. LATER THAT DAY, HIS tasks involved Caldwell's budget: discussing potential cuts with Farr and the vice president of finance, followed by a meeting with faculty department heads, accustomed to their prerogatives, to broach the same subject as tactfully as he could. But his immediate mission was external—speaking to the Wayne Chamber of Commerce about his plans for the school.

He found himself facing almost a hundred citizens, mostly men, after a generous introduction by the mayor. Scanning the faces, he saw Dave Farragher, George Garrison, and, to his pleasure and surprise, a prosperous-looking man who could only be Rusty Clark. The welcoming ovation gratified Darrow as well—remembering him as an athlete, the town took satisfaction in his success and pride in his return. His speech was an appreciation of what Caldwell and Wayne had given him, sincere in what it expressed and artful in what it chose to omit. Its focal point, a promise to give deserving local students the same chance Darrow himself had received, drew warm applause.

Afterward, he sought out Rusty, who, he discovered, was practicing law in town. "Who knew?" Darrow said of them both, and made plans to meet Rusty for breakfast. Shaking more hands, he suddenly faced George Garrison.

In the uniform of Wayne's chief of police, Garrison looked bulkier. His perfunctory smile accompanied a look of shrewd appraisal that lent maturity to his still-youthful face. "Good speech," Garrison told him. "You've come a long way since we pulled out that last game."

"Seems like we both have." Darrow glanced around. "I'd like a moment, if you have one. Can you walk with me to the parking lot?"

Garrison checked his watch. "I can spare a moment," he answered. "After all, I'm the chief."

THEY STOPPED BY Garrison's squad car. "So," the chief said, "life's been good for you. At least mostly."

"Mostly. And for you. You're pretty young to be chief."

Garrison gave him the same measured smile. "And you're pretty young to be president of anything. As for me, the mayor seems to think I've got more to offer than just police work. I'm a big believer in community relations, and our black and white communities still need some relating."

It was strange, Darrow thought: in the social pattern of Wayne, he and Garrison had lived parallel lives, been classmates and teammates without knowing each other well. The last time Darrow had seen him—as a young cop, standing over the body of a murdered girl he had known far better than Darrow had—underscored their separateness. Now both had new and demanding jobs, entrusted to them, at least in part, because of what they symbolized. Curious, Darrow asked, "What's it like to be a cop in the town where you grew up?"

Garrison shrugged. "You know this place. The black folks live on the southeast side, the middle-class whites in the northwest, blue-collar whites in between. Only the Hispanics are new, and they keep to themselves, too. A lot of them are illegals and don't want anything to do with the police." Garrison's tone was dispassionate.

"In certain ways the separation helps—you don't get a lot of overt conflict. The problem is that blacks and whites and Hispanics don't talk to one another much, even when they need to. That makes my life as chief a little harder."

"Was it hard for you to get the job?"

Garrison considered his answer. "What was hard, at first, was being the only black guy on the force. Bust a drunken white guy and he'd call me 'nigger,' trying to get a rise. Older white folks forgot my name and left messages for 'the colored officer.' As for blacks, a fair number treated my questions like accusations; kids didn't wave when I drove through the old 'hood; when I arrested some badass, no matter for what, it was like he couldn't believe a brother was doing this to him. But my colleagues were always pretty good—we're mostly college graduates, even if some of us went at night, and all of us went through psychological testing before they hired us. We've even got a woman now. All in all, the people on the force seem to accept me fine. But among my own, I still tread a little lighter."

In sixteen years, Darrow reflected, George Garrison seemed to have become a solid man—philosophical, pragmatic, measured, and observant. Perhaps those qualities had always been there and the young Mark Darrow had seen them less clearly. Casually, Darrow asked, "Ever go by the Alibi Club?"

Garrison looked at him harder; to Darrow, the quiet stare suggested that they were edging toward more difficult subjects. In the same even tone, the chief said, "Now and then. Mrs. Hall's attitude is still that the club takes care of its own problems until there's something they can't handle. Not much of that. You remember Hugo."

Darrow smiled. "The doorman. He was big enough to block the sun."

"Yeah. Second year on the job they sent me out there to bust him for a stack of parking tickets he'd never paid." Garrison shook his head. "No way I wanted to do that at the club. So I just told Hugo he ought to come on down in the next week or so, pay those suckers off. For a while he just looks at me, sitting in that chair like a potentate receiving an ambassador from China. Then he nods and tells me he appreciates my attitude.

"A couple of days later, he paid off the tickets. Ever since, if I have to go to the club, Hugo says, 'I got your back, boy.' No more 'I smell bacon' from the guys drinking at the bar—on account of Hugo, everyone's real polite." His tone became pointed. "It helps that anyone who knows Mrs. Hall also knows that after Angela died, I was there for her. Carl wasn't much use."

Darrow nodded. "So," Garrison said, "you just wondering about life in Wayne, or is there something more particular?"

Darrow considered his answer. "I ran into Carl the other day, which piqued my curiosity. What's with Carl's Mercedes?"

Garrison's smile was no smile at all. "Carl," he answered, "is chief executive officer of a small but successful business."

"The same business?"

"More or less. Also the same clientele, including kids from Caldwell with just enough brains to know that the college still protects its own." Once more Garrison spoke with a slight edge. "Kind of like the kids at the last party Angela ever went to. Only change is her brother's product line. Back then it was weed and powder cocaine; now Carl's branched off into heroin. The irony here, in terms of Caldwell, is that we think Carl was the one selling smack to Clark Durbin's boy."

"A sad case," Darrow remarked. "Not to mention expensive—Clark's rehab bills for his son ran over a hundred thousand."

Garrison nodded. "I heard. Guess that was part of why his fingers got so light."

"So people think. You ever try to shut Carl down?"

"If we could, we would. But Carl's still smart. He communicates by prepaid cell phones, uses different stash houses to conceal his drugs. Living in a small town, he's got a nose for narcs or anyone wearing a wire. Plus he gets his heroin through illegals, who can't drop the dime on him without getting deported." Garrison eyed the asphalt at their feet. "Truth is, Carl's not exactly a law enforcement priority."

"Why's that?"

"We don't have unlimited manpower. So we care less about the drugs than the trouble they cause for law-abiding citizens." Garrison looked up again. "That's why we focus on crystal meth and crack cocaine, drugs that make users crazy and violent—we don't want them raping, mugging, and killing innocent folks at random. So we keep after the scum that sells that shit. That's another way Carl's smart: the product he peddles doesn't cause his clients to kill anyone. Except maybe themselves."

Darrow considered this. "I'd think running a cash business would create a problem for him. That's how the feds got Al Capone—not murder but tax evasion. I guess Carl must launder his profits through the Alibi Club."

"That's what we assume. You can also bet he's put that Mercedes in someone else's name." Garrison scowled. "In recent years, it seems like Carl's expanded his operation a whole lot: buying more, selling more—heroin, especially. The guy who runs the county's drug task force thinks Carl got financing from somewhere. But no one has the time or resources to try and nail that down."

"A shame."

"I suppose. But so many things are." Garrison's expression seemed to harden. "I'm standing here, looking at you. Do you know what I see? Not the quarterback for the Wayne Generals or even the president of Caldwell College. I see you standing over her body. Then I look at you again, and all I see is Tillman."

Darrow met his gaze. "That was a bad morning, after a bad night. Lives changed."

"Especially hers." Garrison's tone was quiet. "Except for my wife, she was the sweetest and smartest girl I ever knew. Leaving out lethal injection, your friend got what he deserved."

Darrow shoved his hands into his pockets. "I went to see him last Sunday. I'm not so sure he's glad to be alive."

"Then I guess I'm glad he is."

"Are you *that* sure he killed her?"

Garrison's eyes widened in a pantomime of astonishment. "Guess no one told you about the trial."

"Not in detail, no."

"That's where they present evidence," Garrison said caustically. "Sort of like they taught you about in law school. According to the *evidence,* Steve Tillman was a murderer with a mile-wide streak of racism."

"Steve was thoughtless," Darrow retorted. "He said cruel or stupid things by rote, like a lot of people in Wayne. None of whom are murderers."

"Most of whom," Garrison shot back, "probably don't have weird pathologies about sex between blacks and whites." He paused, then spoke more calmly. "After you found Angela, the force kept me out of it—didn't want me involved in a case where I'd gone out with the victim, even if it was only high school. But there was plenty of evidence on how Tillman felt toward *us* without me telling the jury about the date I *didn't* have. The one with your buddy's kid sister."

"Mary?"

"You never heard about that? That surprises me some, seeing how you lived with him. But then maybe Tillman's racist talk was all white noise to you." Garrison paused, then spoke with the same weary patience. "Senior year, I asked Mary out. She said yes—we liked each other, so why not? Then Steve pulled me aside after practice and said, 'Keep your black hands off my sister.' He looked and sounded like whatever he imagined us doing made him sick.

"Mary never went out with me—after that, she couldn't. But that didn't keep Tillman from wanting Angela." Garrison's voice was softer yet. "Maybe after sex, he felt so sick that he had to kill her. All I know is that he did. Funny he can't remember."

"What Steve says he can't remember," Darrow answered, "is whatever happened in that room. Do *you* know for sure? I don't. But I *did* know Steve, and I *did* see him with Angela. And I'm pretty damned sure that sexual revulsion was *not* Steve's motive."

"No one knows," Garrison said flatly. "And who cares now? You don't need a motive to prove murder."

"It's just more satisfying that way," Darrow answered. "I wasn't looking to pick a quarrel, George. But my feelings about this are more complicated than yours. If I knew for sure Steve killed her, then I could accept where he is."

Garrison put his hands on his hips. "Then let me tell you a story. A couple of years ago, at the high school, a white teacher started sleeping with a seventeen-year-old black girl. When the school found out, the girl claimed that he'd coerced her into sex in exchange for grades.

"Maybe it happened that way, maybe it didn't. But both blacks and whites got mighty riled. The man ended up losing his job, his wife, and his kid." Garrison's gaze was steady. "Suppose Tillman raped Angela. What would have happened to him if she'd lived to tell someone? Like with that teacher, nothing good."

"*Did* he rape her?"

Garrison scowled. "There's rape, and there's rape. No one but Angela could say exactly what this was. But she couldn't, could she?"

Darrow had no answer. "Look," Garrison said. "I wish you luck with being president. I'm sure you wish me luck being chief. I never thought you were a bad guy, and now we've both got our jobs to do, problems in the here and now. Why don't we leave the past where it was."

Darrow nodded. Wayne's chief of police extended his hand, shaking Darrow's, and then they went their separate ways.

7

O N SUNDAY MORNING, DARROW DECIDED TO WALK through the residential part of campus, toward fraternity row.

It was ten o'clock, and the slanting sunlight, warm and moist on his skin, presaged a hot, cloudless day. Taking a brick pathway past a colonial-style dormitory dating from the 1870s, Darrow had a sharp, sudden memory: a bright spring day, its warmth lingering into early evening, the light sound of women's voices through a window as he passed this very dorm. Even then he had marked the moment, combining the irretrievable preciousness of a time soon to be lost with the promise of a future still ahead—in which a woman yet unknown to him might be taking a path that would someday merge with his. So much had happened since, for good or ill. But it was no use, at thirty-eight, to mourn his youth: he was still young, and he could hope that the best moments of his life waited for him yet.

He tried to date the memory. Surely it had been late May, or perhaps even early June. Since that time, the school year had been shortened, cutting off the weeks to which the moment belonged. No doubt it made sense, from Caldwell's perspective, to charge more tuition for less schooling. But the young Mark Darrow had savored the arrival of spring on campus: the greening of trees and the bright flowering of dogwoods; the careless interplay of young men and women outdoors as their clothing became lighter; a sense of awakening on campus that felt almost sensual. A long time ago, Darrow thought.

FRATERNITY ROW WAS also much as Darrow recalled it; the trees around the grassy oval were somewhat fuller, the large brick houses sixteen years deeper into their aura of solidity and permanence. But while the SAE house across the street was, like most others, reasonably well maintained, the DBE house evoked the House of Usher: the white paint on the wooden trim was peeling; the scabrous lawn was pocked with crabgrass; and the screen of an upstairs window was askew, like an idiot's glasses. Even had Darrow not suspected the cause, the portrait of decline was plain enough.

In summer, the house would be manned by a skeleton crew of students. Chary of what he might find, Darrow walked inside.

The living room was empty, the furniture worn. Darrow could have sworn that he had sat on that same couch when Steve and Joe had fought over Angela. For a moment Angela's tipsy, poignant glance at him seemed as fresh as yesterday. As he gazed at the library, another flashback struck him: awakening in Joe's Miata, blinking at the dial of its clock, and then, on the car phone, vainly trying to call Steve. His thoughts from that time, a sort of stupefied irritation, struck him as innocent compared to the guilt and uncertainty their memory surfaced now.

Darrow went downstairs to the basement.

There should have been ten tables, accommodating sixty or so college boys for dinner on any given night. But now there were only four. The tiles, worn and scuffed with dirt, were certainly the same tiles he had stood on when he and Angela had exchanged their final words.

If you need someone to get you home, he'd said, *I'm here.*

She had shaken her head, moving close to him. *Gonna be a long night for me, I think.* Then she had given him a brief kiss on the lips. *You're kind of sweet, Mark Darrow.*

Standing there alone, Darrow shook his head.

Crossing the room, he peered into the kitchen. Laurie Shilts appeared in his mind, barely twenty-one. *You don't really know him, Mark. Deep down, Joe hates women.*

Briefly, Darrow closed his eyes. He tried to imagine Angela Hall, perhaps with the sheets pulled up around her, telling Steve that she had to leave. But he could not summon the image; it was not his memory. Nor, perhaps, was it Steve's.

Darrow went back upstairs.

He stopped in the stairwell where he and Steve had drunk beer on the night of the party. It had still hurt Steve to walk; the knee injury had banished him from football one year before. And yet if he had strangled Angela in his room, Steve must have carried the dead weight of her body at least two lengths of a football field.

Surely Steve's lawyer had focused on this incongruity. And yet a jury had found him guilty.

To George Garrison, and perhaps to the jury, Steve had been a racist. Maybe this was so. But his attitudes had always struck Darrow as rote village bigotry, more reflexive than embedded in Steve's psyche. Garrison saw him differently. No doubt George had the right; most people changed with the eyes of the beholder. But few changed so completely or so tragically.

Entering the second floor, Darrow glanced into the room where Joe had watched the video of Tonya Harding. To his surprise, it was occupied by a bulky kid watching ESPN. With a one-day growth of beard and what looked like barbecue sauce smeared on his T-shirt, he seemed in roughly the same state of disrepair as the house itself. He eyed the trim stranger in sport coat and blue jeans with a look of torpid wariness.

"Sorry to bother you," Darrow said. "But I used to live here. I guess that makes us fraternity brothers."

It took the kid a few seconds to compute this. "You're President Darrow."

Darrow smiled. "So they tell me."

The boy got to his feet and shook Darrow's hand. "I'm Skip Penton," he said, summoning a sheepish grin. "I'm president of the DBEs."

"How's it going?"

The grin became a skeptical smile. "You can't tell?"

"I can guess. The house looks kind of sad."

"No help for it. When you guys were here, how many brothers in the chapter?"

"Sixty-plus."

Skip grimaced. "We're down to twenty-one. After that black girl was killed, everything changed. And when that guy Tillman was found guilty of murder, it sunk our reputation."

"Not to mention Steve's," Darrow answered mildly. "What happened was bad all the way around. Angela Hall was a good person, and Steve was my closest friend."

Skip seemed to consider his response. His tone mingled apology with grievance. "Whoever's fault it was, we suffered for it. The school watches us like hawks. Except for hard-core loyalists like my dad, the alumni punted us too, like we were a pack of drunken, drug-crazed, racist murderers. Even on the weekend of the Lutheran game, they never come here anymore."

So this, too, had become part of house lore, repeated by its oral historians like the epic achievements of its athletes, or the famous "Nude Olympics" party of '67, after which, it was said, three female guests turned up pregnant. But Darrow knew other stories, far more common but less often told, of loyalty and kindness and friendships made for life, like those he had once imagined having with Steve Tillman or Joe Betts—the good qualities encouraged, the frailties tolerated unless they needed to be addressed. And one of Darrow's more recent memories involved the numerous and desperate appeals for help from chapter presidents, the latest being Skip's letter, which Darrow had chosen to ignore. "How's your maintenance budget?" Darrow asked.

"A lot like the school's. Only worse."

Ruefully, Darrow laughed. Then he took his checkbook from his coat pocket and, leaning on the desk, scrawled out a check for twenty thousand dollars before handing it to Skip. "This should cover painting, landscaping, and new furniture on the first floor. When I come back here this fall, I want to see them all."

Skip gaped at the check, then at Darrow. "I don't know what to say."

"Nothing," he answered. "It's an anonymous gift. But it might help with fraternity rush, or when you invite alumni back over Lutheran weekend to see the improvements you've made. If they think other alums are supporting you, *they* might."

Leaving, Darrow checked his watch. In an hour, Sunday visiting time would commence at the penitentiary in Lucasville.

FACING HIM THROUGH the Plexiglas, Steve looked mildly surprised. "You came back."

Darrow's smile felt synthetic. "I said I would. This may sound strange, but I've never shaken what happened. Especially to you."

Steve's laugh was a derisive bark. "Then this is a new record for delayed reactions."

"I keep getting reminded." Darrow looked into Steve's eyes. "I saw George Garrison the other day. He's chief of police now."

Steve's reaction was contradictory—a sardonic smile, a guilty flicker in his eyes. "So I heard. Seems like everyone's moving up but me. George isn't exactly a fan of mine, is he?"

"Not exactly. Before he thought you were a murderer, he just thought you were a racist prick."

"Guilty," Steve said with sudden softness. "At least on the 'racist prick' count. In high school, we had a little incident."

"Over your kid sister?"

"Yeah." Steve looked down. "As best I remember, I told George I didn't want him trying to stick his black dick into Mary."

Darrow winced inside. "George left that part out. But it helps explain why *he* remembers the moment so clearly. Also why he thinks you might be a psychopath when it comes to interracial sex."

Steve's head jerked up. "So how does Sigmund Freud Garrison square that with me and Angela doing it? That I'm a racist *and* a hypocrite?"

"*And* fucked up. In George's estimate, you turned on yourself. And her."

"Jesus fucking Christ." Steve's voice became a whisper. "It's like a curse, man. It never expires."

Darrow watched his face. "I don't follow."

Steve's eyes misted. "What I'd said to George about my sister. I told Angela about it. She was tending bar and I was drinking—"

"You must have been, to bring it up. Especially there."

Through the grid, Darrow could hear Steve exhale. "It was something I'd begun feeling shitty about. So I told her what I'd said to George, kind of like an apology."

"What did she say?"

"That George had told her about it, years before. And that maybe I should be apologizing to him." Steve shook his head. "For a minute, I thought she was pissed off—like she was my all-purpose black confessor, stuck listening to a stupid white boy purge his conscience of bigotry. Then she admitted she'd ripped into George for asking out a white girl. 'I wonder if it's something we learn,' she told me, 'or it's just hardwired in the species. Either way it's pretty sad.'

"She went to serve drinks at the other end of the bar. I just sat there for a while, thinking. That's when we started to be friends."

Gazing at Steve, Darrow pondered the story. It might not be true; Steve had had sixteen years to invent, or even imagine, a redemptive tale. But the story accounted for the casual friendliness between Steve and Angela—perhaps hinting at more—at the Alibi Club when Angela and Darrow had first spoken. It also explained why Steve had invited her to the party, and why she had felt inclined to leave with him. And it turned George Garrison's theory of Steve's psychology inside out.

Thought you didn't like black folks, Darrow had said to Steve.

Times change. Gazing at Angela, Steve had added softly, *Who wouldn't like that?*

"I was over that crap," Steve said now. "But they wouldn't *let* me be over it."

"When?"

"At the trial." Steve's voice filled with anger. "What was Caldwell College supposed to be *for*? Making you think, right? Being challenged by people like Lionel Farr to question your assumptions and prejudices." Steve's voice thickened. "Part of my deal with Angela was about that—wanting to learn more about her, find out what her life was like. I think that's why she went with me that night, when we'd never been alone before. I wanted to *know* her, not strangle her." His voice steadied. "I even think that's why Farr comes to see me once in a blue moon. Caldwell—Durbin and Farr—may have thought it was convenient for me to be a sacrificial lamb. But I think deep down Farr sees that giving me a scholarship to Caldwell made me a better person, and that now I've been thrown away."

Darrow wondered. Farr was too deeply skeptical of human nature and, it seemed clear, of Steve's innocence. In Darrow's estimation, Farr had helped Steve find a lawyer only because Darrow had asked; if, after the trial, Farr had shown Steve kindness, it was because—despite his deeper fondness for Angela—Farr knew that men were too complex to be defined by the worst moment in their lives. But all Darrow said was "Farr's a good man, Steve. I'm sorry I'm not a better one."

Steve simply nodded.

8

DARROW BEGAN HIS SECOND WEEK AS PRESIDENT BY meeting Rusty Clark for breakfast at the Bluebird Grill.

The first to arrive, Darrow took one of three booths at the rear, surveying the once-familiar setting. To accommodate more customers, the wooden counters were configured around two T-shaped spaces in which waitresses served breakfasts or lunches to diners on both sides. All were white. Most of the men wore jackets and baseball caps with the logos of local employers; the women tended toward pantsuits and short hair, often stiffly lacquered. In the eyes of some women, Darrow detected a vaguely fretful, worried look, reminding him that surrounding Caldwell College sat a small midwestern town where jobs were limited and paychecks finite. Most of the diners seemed to know one another; they chatted sporadically, laconically, their speech uninflected. Eyeing that morning's specials, scrawled in Magic Marker on a board over the open grill, Darrow saw Rusty hurrying through the door.

His college friend waved, giving Darrow a wide smile that seemed to melt away years. "Had to drop my oldest boy at school," Rusty explained as he slid into the booth. "Takes after his old man—slow to wake up. By ten or so he'll resemble human life."

Darrow laughed. "How many do you have?"

Rusty whipped out his wallet, displaying a picture of a pert, pretty woman with a red-haired boy and two strawberry-blond girls flashing smiles just like Rusty's.

"These aren't children," Darrow adjudged. "They're clones."

Rusty chuckled with pleasure. "At least I know they're mine. Meg says that all she did was perform a storage function."

"Other than that and tolerating you, what else does Meg do?"

"Teaches English at the high school—she loves the kids and likes her colleagues. And I've cobbled together a decent practice out of what happens in a place like Wayne: death, divorce, real estate trans-actions, and petty crime. Together we'll get our kids through college without going into hock. Some days it's a mini–rat race, but life's turned out okay." He smiled again. "Remember Tim Fedak?"

"How could I not? He helped us stick Betts's Miata in the library."

Rusty seemed momentarily sobered by the underside of memory. "So he did. Anyhow, Tim's into real estate development around here. His family, mine, and two other couples with kids take a group vaca-tion every year at a small lake in northern Michigan—the kids fish, swim, and water-ski while we cook steaks and keep them all from drowning. With any luck, someday us and our kids will be trekking up with *their* kids. We grandparents will be happy, and our children can do the cooking."

Smiling, Darrow absorbed his friend's contentment. If Rusty was spared life's random tragedies, Darrow had little doubt, the future would unfold much as he intended: marital fidelity, attentive parent-ing, deepening roots in a chosen place and time. Though he envied Rusty what fate had taken from him—a wife and child—Darrow knew that he had become incapable of choosing a course so circum-scribed; for him, and for Lee before she died, hell was knowing with utter certainty what one's path would be. But it pleased him that Rusty was realizing his fondest hopes. "I'd say you were lucky," Dar-row told him. "But as Lionel Farr once told me, luck is a talent."

Nodding, Rusty acknowledged the compliment. "I figured out what I wanted and went for it. So did you." He paused, adding quietly, "What happened to you surely wasn't fair."

Perhaps not, Mark thought—too often, the consequence of not fully comprehending someone close to you far exceeds the sin. But he had never expressed to anyone his fear that Lee's accident was not, in one sense, accidental. "My life has its fair share of compensations," he answered. "Certainly compared to Steve's."

Rusty studied the table. "I keep thinking I should visit him," he said at length. "But I've been thinking that for almost fifteen years. I can't get past what Steve's inside for."

The plump young waitress arrived. Rusty ordered scrambled eggs; Darrow, English muffins. "Sorry," the waitress told Darrow. "We don't have those. Only toast."

When Rusty smiled at Darrow's look of perplexity, Darrow realized, yet again, how far he had journeyed from Boston. After Darrow ordered wheat toast, Rusty asked, "Have *you* seen Steve yet?"

Darrow took a sip of coffee. "Twice."

"Does he still 'think' he's innocent?"

"So he says. You know the story. He's never had a better one."

"He never had a *good* one. The racial thing didn't help him, either."

Once again, Darrow felt a lingering guilt about avoiding his friend's trial. "I gathered that. Did you know his lawyer?"

"Griff Nordlinger? I met him maybe once—he quit practicing about the time I got out of law school."

Surprised, Darrow said, "He wasn't that old. Mid-forties, I'd have said."

Rusty furrowed his brow. "I think something happened to him, maybe medical. Of course, a case like Steve's would give any lawyer around here a heart attack."

"How so?"

"We get a couple of murders a year, max. That's no way to build up expertise." Rusty added more sugar to his coffee. "Plus, homicide cases are ballbusters—no lawyer wants to get a client executed or locked up for life, like Steve. But there's no money to pay for the time you need to put in, no private investigators in town to help. So you end up relying on the cops who helped indict your client in the first place."

"That's no good," Darrow said flatly.

Rusty spread his hands. "What else can you do? A solo practitioner like Nordlinger has got no one to cover his other cases, and a client like Steve's got no money to cover his lawyer's time. They're both screwed." Rusty's voice lowered. "I tried one homicide, Mark. I swear to God I'll never do another. By the time I pled the guy out on the eve of trial, I was a nervous wreck who could hardly pay my overhead, reduced to praying that my guy was as guilty as he looked. He'd have been better off with a public defender—that's not what most people think, but it's the God's-honest truth. At least the PD's office has investigators and a budget."

The waitress served their breakfasts. Darrow's wheat toast was soaked in butter. When the woman left, Darrow said, "Heart attack on a plate. How do people in this town ever become old?"

Rusty patted his stomach. "Prepaid quadruple bypass. My insurance guy is working on a plan."

Darrow smiled at this. "As near as you could tell," he asked, "what was Nordlinger's reputation?"

"For high-end criminal work? I don't think he had one." Rusty took a bite of his eggs. "To be fair, Steve didn't give a lawyer much to work with."

"Ever think about how *you* might have defended him?"

"You mean if they'd held a gun to my head?" Distractedly, Rusty moved his eggs around the plate. "I'd go into every aspect of his relationship to Angela. Then I'd scour his memory of the day she died, hour by hour, and whatever the cops did with him after that—interrogation, tests, any clue to what he was up against." He looked up at Darrow. "You can't assume the police are rubes—they're smart and highly trained. Like the lawyers, all they lack is murder cases to practice on."

"So the next step is replicating what the cops did?"

"Exactly. Interview everyone at the party—you, me, Carl Hall, anyone else who saw anything at all. Including Joe Betts. *Especially* Joe, even if he hadn't turned out to be Farragher's star witness." For a split second, Rusty hesitated. "You knew him better than I did. Was he doing coke that night?"

"I don't think he needed to be. That night seems to be why Joe quit drinking."

"Whatever it was, I didn't want to be anywhere near him." Rusty took a quick gulp of coffee. "Speaking as a lawyer, you'd want to find out what *Joe's* thing about Angela was, and what he did after he left the party. Not to mention whether he saw what he *says* he saw on a pitch-black night—including inconsistencies, or any reason he'd want to nail Steve." Abruptly Rusty's voice softened. "I'm just thinking like a defense lawyer. Joe is make-or-break—his story is either true, or a mistake, or a setup."

"Then one more thing," Darrow added quietly. "He's also your alternative suspect."

Rusty focused on his eggs. "I'd sure like to have a motive, Mark. Jealousy seems like a stretch to me."

"So what was Steve's motive? Even drunks and bigots have a sense of self-preservation. Why kill her when you'd be such an obvious suspect?"

Rusty looked up. Quietly, he said, "She's stayed with you, hasn't she?"

"Her face has. It wasn't a drive-by shooting, Rusty. This was personal."

Rusty took his last bite of sausage. After a time, he said, "Steve didn't seem like that, did he?"

"Not to me." Darrow hesitated. "Even now, that bothers me. Especially after seeing him again."

"So, as a lawyer, a big question is whether you'd have put him on the stand. That's what Nordlinger did. It's also what a good lawyer *should* do, if he can. I've never believed that relying on the presumption of innocence and a defendant's right to silence cuts it with a jury."

"I agree. But the downside would have been leaving Steve wide open to whatever Farragher's got. If you make the wrong decision, he's done." Signaling the waitress for more coffee, Darrow turned back to Rusty. "What are the chances of looking at the transcript of Steve's trial?"

"You personally?" Rusty asked in a tone of surprise. "If you wanted to, you could—Ohio has an open-records law for old files. The practical problem is what kind of shape they're in. The last old files I dug up had been stored in an attic infested with hungry rats and sparrows—they'd converted the most critical papers into pellets and bird poop. Hopefully Steve's files aren't as appetizing."

"What about files from the autopsy and forensics?"

"Those should be fine. Our coroner's just a functionary. When an autopsy is called for, he farms it out to the ME in Columbus. Same with the crime lab. The Bureau of Criminal Investigation stores the records."

When the waitress brought the check, Darrow grabbed it before Rusty could. "This is on me," Darrow said. "I could use a favor, though. If I become a paying client, think you could copy Steve's files?"

"Sure, at cost. But not without Dave Farragher knowing who wanted them."

Darrow shrugged. "That's okay."

Rusty gave him a dubious look. "Is it? You've just come back here, and you've got big problems at the school. For years Farragher served on Caldwell's board of trustees, and he's still got lots of friends there. I can imagine someone asking why you're wasting time reading the transcript of a fifteen-year-old murder case."

"Who would care that much?"

"Farragher. Our local congressman's about to pack it in, and Dave wants to take his place." Rusty frowned. "That was the biggest case Dave ever had. The only thing between him and Congress might be for someone to suggest that he convicted an innocent man."

"I'm not suggesting anything, Rusty. I'm just curious about how and why Steve got convicted. Maybe the only way to ease my mind is to read the trial transcript."

Rusty glanced at his watch. "Up to you, pal." He paused again, then added, "If you're poking around, the police chief's where you can do some business."

"Garrison? You didn't go to high school here. He despises Steve."

"Maybe so. But George has graduated, all the way to chief of police." Rusty leaned forward. "Farragher pushed a white guy for the chief's job, a Republican friend of his—pushed him hard, in fact. But the mayor chose George. So there's no love lost between our chief and our county prosecutor; Farragher's still a threat to George's job, and George still has something to prove. Undoing Farragher's finest hour would not break George's heart."

"Small towns," Darrow said with a smile. "All I want is a look at those files. I'm a long way from threatening anyone's ambitions."

Rusty stood. "Including your own, I hope. For a lot of us, Caldwell College is a very special place. We've got a stake in your success."

"I'll remember that," Darrow promised.

9

THE MAJOR EVENT ON DARROW'S SCHEDULE THAT DAY WAS A midmorning meeting with Ray Carrick, the chairman of Caldwell's board of trustees. Darrow intended to spend the preceding two hours reviewing budget projections, calling prominent alumni, and scanning plans for a new science building—which, although badly needed, would require $20 million Caldwell did not have. Then a sharp knock punctuated his thoughts, and Lionel Farr leaned through his office door. In a tone drenched with irony, Farr said, "As Sartre once remarked, 'Hell is other people.'"

"Which people?" Darrow inquired.

"In this case, your faculty. A potential charge of sexual harassment."

Grimacing, Darrow waved him to a chair. "What's the genesis?"

"Stupidity. You took a history course from Tom Craig, right?"

"Uh-huh. A good professor, I thought."

"He still is. Also easily bored. So he decided that sleeping with a student might, as it were, help him fill the void." Farr's tone held weary exasperation. "The *wrong* student—a young woman from India of considerable volatility, spiked by cultural misunderstanding. Whatever the reason, Ms. Kashfi imagined that Tom planned to leave his wife."

"Which he didn't."

"Of course not. So our student showed up at Tom's house two days ago, threatening Anita with bodily harm. Dr. Craig has become a bystander—for Anita, the price of marital peace is having Ms. Kashfi deported."

"Is she crazy?"

Farr emitted a mirthless laugh. "For my money, they both are. But now we own the problem."

Darrow sighed in irritation. "Ms. Kashfi requires counseling, not expulsion—let alone deportation. As for Craig, any time a professor's screwing a student you're risking angry parents, potential lawsuits, and the possibility of trading grades for sex. Not to mention an erosion of student respect for the faculty and damage to Caldwell's reputation. So what *is* our policy on faculty-student involvements?"

"There is none," Farr conceded. "We have 'guidelines.' In all of these cases, you're dealing with two people who are over the age of consent—"

"Granted," Darrow cut in. "But also with a power differential ripe for abuse. Describe these so-called guidelines."

"We strongly discourage romantic relationships between faculty and students, listing all the reasons you suggest." Pausing, Farr added dryly, "In reality, we're asking for a modicum of judgment and discretion among consenting adults. For faculty, the unwritten message seems to be 'It's okay to marry a student, but please don't date them first.' At least not where anyone can see you."

Darrow shook his head. "That's like sitting on nitroglycerin. As we both know all too well, people kill each other over sex. What if Ms. Kashfi had shown up at midnight and Anita Craig had put a bullet through her brain? Or vice versa? And even short of murder, the whole thing reeks.

"Bring our general counsel in. We need to craft a stronger policy, clearly understood. Our faculty should know that I'll go after anyone guilty of abusing their power over students—if I could, I'd bar these relationships outright. But if any professor still insists on dating a student, we should require them to disclose that to their department head *and* to you, and to refrain from teaching anyone they're involved with. If they don't, I'll do my damnedest to get rid of them."

"The faculty may bridle, Mark. Some will call it an invasion of privacy."

"No doubt. But it would cut down on the threat of lawsuits and put the fear of God in married faculty that their spouses will find out." Darrow's own voice held a trace of sarcasm. "I'll solicit faculty responses, of course—I'm sensitive to their prerogatives, and I'll hate cutting down their dating pool. But reasonable professors will understand, and the rest will be wary of making themselves conspicuous. Especially if we cite Tom Craig's embarrassment as a teachable moment."

Farr smiled a little. "I'll call our general counsel, Mr. President. Are you ready to face the chairman of our board?"

THE SPIRE WAS Ray Carrick's favorite place on campus, and so his tour of Caldwell's facilities ended in its shadow. He walked between Farr and Darrow, his paunch preceding him, his movements ponderous and heavy-shouldered. He had the self-satisfied countenance of a provincial worthy with, in Darrow's estimation, the sensibility to match: tough, shrewd, reliable, loyal, and wholly unoriginal. In better times, Darrow judged, he would have been a proper steward of Caldwell's affairs. But becoming a leading business magnate in a central Ohio town had dulled Carrick's self-perception and inflated his self-regard. Though no friction had developed between Caldwell's new president and its board chair, Farr had counseled Darrow to treat Ray Carrick with care.

Now Carrick turned from the Spire, facing Darrow. "We need money," he summarized peremptorily. "The science building's outmoded, and so's our field house. As for Huntley Stadium, it looks more like a soccer stadium in downtown Baghdad."

Darrow smiled. "Never seen one, Ray. But I'll take your word."

Carrick's mouth clamped down. "It's no joke, Mark—we've got to get cracking on a big endowment drive. Why do you want to cancel our feasibility study? Walter Berg's all ready to go."

"No doubt. But I don't want to pay Walter's consulting firm a hundred grand to tell me what I already know—that we can't raise a hundred million until the alumni believe that I've straightened this place out." Glancing at Farr, Darrow finished: "Lionel and I have talked about this. In the short term, the best way to engage our alumni is to ask them not for money but ideas. If I can enlist them in defining our needs and goals, they'll pony up when I ask them to."

Carrick turned to Farr. "Mark's right," Farr said simply. "For the next year or two we just have to keep the school afloat."

Carrick crossed his arms, eyeing the grass at their feet and then Mark Darrow. "You say the alumni need to know you're cleaning things up. Isn't the best way to ask Dave Farragher to indict Clark Durbin? Let's place the blame where it belongs and put the Durbin era behind us."

"Perhaps. But I don't want to do that yet, Ray."

"Why not?" Carrick asked with palpable annoyance. "Most folks on the board see this as a moral issue. If Durbin won't cooperate by helping us trace the money, then he deserves a stretch in jail. Give the bastard a choice, I say. Where's the virtue in shilly-shallying when a man we trusted turns out to be a crook?"

"Because Durbin's not the problem anymore. Assuring alumni that another embezzlement won't happen *is,* and I've begun to do that. As for Durbin," Darrow continued in the same calm tone, "he's not running off to Paraguay. Within a month the accountant I'm bringing in can help us decide what to do with him."

Carrick's eyebrows shot up. "What about Joe Betts's man? Doesn't he already have this buttoned up?"

"Fox is good," Darrow answered. "So's my guy. I want him to look at this without preconceptions."

"Durbin stole the money," Carrick snapped. "Isn't it obvious?"

"It seems so. But there are a couple of things about the embezzlement I'd like to nail down. After that we can consider the benefits of prosecuting Durbin or letting him go quietly." To placate Carrick, Darrow added, "You're right about the money—assuming there's any left. If Durbin's guilty, we can give him some hard choices."

With a dubious expression, Carrick turned to Farr. "What do *you* think, Lionel?"

Farr inclined his head toward Darrow. "That we hired Mark to make these calls. Besides, he knows more about financial chicanery than both of us combined. If there's something here that bothers him, I think we'd do well to listen."

Carrick wheeled on Darrow. "*Is* there, Mark?"

Darrow found himself cornered. "I can't tell you, exactly. Maybe *that's* what troubles me. It's too neat."

Carrick gave a snort—half laugh, half resignation. Then he turned again, gazing at the base of the Spire. "Such a tragedy," he said with surprising quiet. "All our troubles started *here,* when Tillman killed that black girl. To associate a murder with such a special place makes it that much sadder."

Darrow thought of Taylor Farr. "The other day," he told Carrick, "someone asked if we'd consider tearing the Spire down."

Carrick gave him a hard sideways look. "Over my dead body, Mark. Over my dead body."

"That," Farr ventured mildly, "is an unfortunate turn of phrase."

Carrick shook his head. "Damn Steve Tillman," he said to Farr with muted vehemence. "I wish you'd never given him that scholarship."

"So do I, Ray. But that's how we got Mark."

This exchange, Darrow discovered, touched the nerve ends of his guilt and obligation. Facing Darrow, Carrick said softly, "So it was, and I'm glad for that. Once you finish those alumni calls, Mark, let me know how they went."

The two men shook hands. Extending his hand to Farr, Carrick said with genuine warmth, "Thank you, Lionel. Without you, I don't know where we'd be."

Shaking Carrick's hand, Farr smiled. "You have no idea, Ray. But neither do I."

Carrick chuckled, and headed off for the parking lot.

Darrow and Farr watched him go. "Thanks," Darrow said. "It's clear you've got more credibility than I do."

"More years, anyhow." Farr turned to him. "You know how Ray is. He's smart enough to know you're smarter, and spoiled enough not to enjoy it. Mind if I reiterate a word of advice?"

"Of course not."

"Don't alienate him over Durbin. Do whatever you need to feel more comfortable, then move as quickly as you can. As a practical matter, feeding him Clark Durbin will buy you Ray's goodwill on bigger issues. It's the kind of callous act that makes a leader great."

Darrow laughed softly. "I'll remember that, Chairman Mao."

DARROW PLACED ALUMNI calls through lunch, then used the afternoon to catch up with his schedule. A little after five o'clock he stuffed the budget figures in his briefcase, pledging to revisit them before he went to sleep, and left his office for the day.

The police station was new since Darrow had graduated, a two-story building constructed of red brick, its modernity suggesting that Wayne was now on the cutting edge of law enforcement. Darrow went to a reception area protected by bulletproof glass and, reminded of his visits to Steve Tillman, spoke through a grid to the receptionist. A moment later George Garrison leaned through a metal door. "Come on back," he said.

Darrow followed him to his corner office. One bookshelf was filed with tomes on criminology; on another, next to George's college diploma and certificates of completion from advanced policing courses, was a picture of a smiling, round-faced woman and two bright-eyed kids. Families everywhere, Darrow thought.

"Have a seat," Garrison said brusquely. "To what do I owe the pleasure?"

"A couple of things. For openers, I went to see Steve again."

Garrison's face turned opaque. "And?"

"He told me about the incident involving you and his sister. He also claims that he told Angela about it shortly before the murder, apparently by way of apology."

"*That's* what you came to tell me?" Garrison paused, then muted his tone of incredulity. "You don't just 'get over' a prejudice so deeply ingrained. Even by your account, Angela was Tillman's one black 'friend,' and his idea of racial amity was fucking. God knows what happened between them in that room."

Darrow shifted in his chair. "Maybe so. But murder's an extreme form of prejudice. Did your investigation come up with any other instance where Steve became violent—whether with women, blacks, or otherwise?"

"Not that I know of," Garrison said. "But suppose you believe, like Tillman says, that Angela left his room alive. Then who killed her? Someone lurking by the Spire at two A.M.? A random murderer walking across a deserted campus, looking for some equally random victim to strangle but not rape or rob? Some drunk who had the sudden inspiration to kill the first woman he saw?" Once more, Garrison modulated his tone. "Why don't you ask Fred Bender. Should be easy enough—in case you've missed it, Fred became Caldwell's chief of security. He'll know who the suspects were, if any."

"What about Griff Nordlinger?" Darrow asked. "I'd ask *him,* but he seems to have disappeared."

"All the way to heaven. Nordlinger died in Phoenix, several years ago."

"Of what?"

"Heart attack, I think. The man had worked his ticker overtime." Garrison seemed to sit more heavily. "A couple of years after the trial, I busted him for possession of cocaine. By then—or so his ex-wife said—he had a wicked cross-addiction to powder cocaine and whiskey. Nordlinger was finished as a lawyer—I had him ready to flip, name Carl Hall as his supplier. But instead of pressing charges, the chief let Griff's daughter hustle him off to rehab in Arizona. Not my call—I wanted Carl pretty bad. Needless to say, Nordlinger never came back to Wayne."

Darrow parsed the implications of this. "During Steve's trial, was Nordlinger screwed up?"

"Thought you'd ask that," Garrison answered with a trace of asperity. "As far as I recall, no one ever said so during the trial. In Tillman's case, I doubt it would have mattered. Anything else you want to know?"

"One thing. Who performed the autopsy on Angela? All I remember is that she was blond."

Garrison nodded. "That would be Carly Simmons."

"Know where I can find her?"

"Yeah. She lives here in the county, out by Cahaba Road." Garrison leaned forward, gazing at Darrow across the desk. "I don't know what you're up to, Mark. But I don't have the time or the manpower to excavate the past. Or, in Tillman's case, a reason. So the next time we discuss him, it'll be because you've got something real to say."

Darrow thanked him. Leaving, he walked swiftly to the parking lot, hoping to beat Taylor to his door.

10

TAYLOR FARR, DARROW NOTED, WAS A PUNCTUAL WOMAN—AT six-thirty she arrived at his door, wearing jeans and a sweater and carrying a thick black binder. Pointing at the binder, Darrow asked, "Is that my homework?"

"More or less," she said briskly. "A survey of postmodern art, culled from the Internet and screened through my quirky sensibilities. But after you called me, I tried to be gentle. There may be something in here that you actually like."

"It's fat enough." Motioning her inside, Darrow said, "Ready to inspect the chamber of horrors?"

She walked past him into the living room, her swift, graceful strides reminding him of both an athlete and a runway model. From the back he watched her look from piece to piece: the pastel watercolor portraying spring; a winsome girl with saucer eyes; the nondescript Swedish modern furniture; the dining room table of blond wood; the glass coffee-table top set on the lacquered stump of a redwood tree; and, over the fireplace, an oil painting of the Reverend Charles Caldwell, his forbidding mien meant to signal rectitude but, to Darrow, more evocative of a hanging judge. She studied the Reverend Caldwell for a good while, her long raven hair tilting with the angle of her head.

"Well?" Darrow asked.

Taylor did not turn. "I'm speechless."

"Try."

Facing him, she knit her brow in mock concentration. "'Dreadful'? No. What word means both 'depressing' and 'horrifying'? The art's insipid, the furniture sterile, and nothing goes together. You're living in the Museum of Modern Dreck." Waving a hand at the Reverend Caldwell, she said, "Then there's him. If you look at him too long, you'll never have sex again. And if you *stay* here too long, you'll kill yourself."

"The thought's occurred to me," Darrow answered solemnly. "Tell me, are art historians always this scathing? Or is this lacerating commentary inspired by my decor?"

Taylor laughed. "Both. There's no art historian typology, really. But all of us tend to be passionate about art, and more than usually opinionated." Placing her binder on the coffee table, she added, "We're also trained to see things, though I think some of that's inherent. Even as a kid, I saw that what I drew wasn't as good as what I could perceive in someone else's work."

"I liked what you painted."

Taylor smiled up at him. "That's because you're inherently nice. You'd have said something kind if I'd painted a lopsided dollhouse with smoke coming out the chimney. But I wasn't an artist, like my mother; I was an interpreter and describer, like my father. Sometimes I think we're too much alike."

For an instant, Darrow thought of Taylor at eight or nine. The image he retained was of a lovely child, serious and very observant, who seemed to harbor more thoughts than she cared to express. "You're certainly less quiet than you were," Darrow remarked lightly. "And very clear about what you think. That's Lionel as I know him."

Taylor's smile was fainter. "So's the quiet. Beneath what my father chooses to express is a bottomless well of silence. I try to guess his thoughts and feelings, and all too often draw a blank. Perhaps he's lonely, an introvert by nature."

Though Darrow shared this sense of Lionel Farr, he had come to accept it as a given. "I've sometimes thought that," he responded. "Though I'm sure it's more perplexing in a parent than a provost. Would you care for some wine, by the way?"

"Yes, thanks. A white, if you have one open."

Darrow went to the kitchen. When he returned, Taylor was flipping pages in her binder, her concentration total. It gave him a moment to consider, once again, the evolution of child to adult. The child Taylor's beauty had a porcelain quality, contained within itself; the woman radiated a more vibrant beauty, a presence that filled a room even when, as now, she was silent.

He sat beside her, placing two glasses on the table. "So," he asked, "you think you're more like Lionel than your mother?"

Taylor took a sip of wine. "I guess I'd *like* to be my mother's daughter, if only because I remember feeling so loved by her. But my dad's a strong personality, and the genetic lottery has whims of its own." She smiled again. "One thing for sure—we both have way too many books. In my case, big ones, filled with paintings. Half my income is spent hauling tomes from place to place."

"Where do you want to end up?"

"I'm not sure yet. It seems like I've got two choices: teaching or a curatorship—the collection side of the museum world."

"Not running an art gallery?"

"God, no," Taylor answered with a laugh. "My senior year at Williams, they took us around to visit people who owned galleries. I met a bunch of glamorous women wearing expensive jewelry and Hermès scarves, more absorbed in bling than scholarship. It was like visiting a club where I could never belong." Her tone became self-mocking. "I'm way too *serious* a person, Mark. I need to work for a museum with a sense of adventure, or teach in a good school in a good city with smart students and colleagues, where I can further refine my extraordinary gifts. With all respect to your new position, I'd go mad in Wayne, Ohio."

"So what constitutes a good city?"

"New York, definitely. There's more *there* there—art, music, theater, varied ethnic influences, and every species of humanity you can think of. Assuming I can afford it."

"What about Boston?"

"It's not a *terrible* city," Taylor allowed. A mischievous smile played on her lips. "On the downside, it's painfully provincial—too many overeducated people with too little to do, except obsessing over the Red Sox and worshipping their ancestors. Plus it's jam-packed with racists, too muggy in the summer, and five degrees too cold in January."

Though intended to tease him, Darrow realized, the description had a certain jaundiced accuracy. "Picky," he said.

"Oh, I'd *look* at Boston, if the job were right. There are some very good schools there. And if the Museum of Fine Arts ever got serious about contemporary works . . ." She stopped, laughing at herself. "As if it's *my* choice. Right now, the only job I have is helping you attack this aesthetic nightmare. Care to look at what I've brought?"

"Sure." Darrow hesitated, then asked, "Are you hungry? I used to know a place that delivers Chinese food."

"In Wayne?" Her voice softened. "I'll stop being a critic, Mark. I'm always up for experiments."

LEAFING THROUGH THE pages, they nibbled passable chow mein and snow peas and started a new bottle of sauvignon blanc. To Mark's relief, he liked much of what Taylor had selected as examples of what he might look for: a chromagraphic print by Andreas Gursky of a bank tower at night; an installation by James Turrell, a field of colored light so cleverly designed that its elements looked like phantom shapes; a piece composed of Ektacolor prints by Richard Prince, four beautiful but strikingly different women, their heads tilted in the same direction to appraise some unseen object; a gelatin-silver print by James Casebere; and, though perhaps too challenging to live with, eight black-

and-white photographs by the German Anselm Kiefer, together forming a stark portrait of stone and gnarled trees disturbingly evocative of
Nazi art. Taken together, Taylor's compilation bespoke a keen eye,
considerable aesthetic judgment, and, flattering to Darrow, a great deal
of time and thought. Finishing, he imagined himself embarking on a
new project with a curiosity and enthusiasm he had not felt since Lee's
death.

"Can you leave this here?" he asked. "I'd like to look it over some
more."

"Of course. That's why I put it together."

Darrow closed the book. "Thank you, Taylor—really. It's enjoy-
able to think about redesigning a space again."

Taylor sipped her wine. "What was your town house in Boston
like?"

"As light as we could make it, and filled with modern art." He
touched the notebook. "Though *not* this modern. Among other
things, we had a Vasarely, an Agam, and a Dalí print. But our criteria
was less the artist than how we felt about the piece."

"Did you have an art consultant?"

"No. Lee and I made it our project. Fortunately, we had similar
tastes—bright colors, bold images, abstract forms. No paintings of
horses, hunting parties, dilapidated barns, or pastoral New England.
Half the fun was looking at a space and imagining the right piece for
it; the other half was finding it. By the end, every object in the house
came with its own story."

The smile Taylor gave him seemed reflective, even wistful. "Is
that why you didn't bring anything with you? Even photographs?"

"I left in a hurry. I figured there would be time to settle in later."
He took another sip of wine, then decided to give Taylor a deeper version of the truth. "To a degree I didn't fully appreciate, at least until
now, the town house became the museum of our marriage. But I
couldn't seem to change anything, because I couldn't ask Lee about
it." He gazed into his wine glass, speaking quietly. "Even her closet

stayed the same. Shortly after the first anniversary of her death, I made myself give her clothes to charity. It felt weird, like I was losing another piece of her. I remember staring at the empty closet and not knowing what to do."

Pausing, Darrow felt the ache of memory. Softly, Taylor said, "I'm sorry."

"For asking? Don't be. I never say these things, and maybe I should. Perhaps it would help to talk about her to another human being."

He felt Taylor watching his face. "I remember her, actually."

Darrow looked up at her. "How?"

"Since college, I've been an election junkie. Lee was on MSNBC a lot—I remember thinking how smart she was, with a wicked, almost subversive sense of humor. Not to mention that she was *really* pretty. Anyone would have been drawn to her."

"Oh, they were. The night we met—at a cocktail party, of all things—I had loads of competition."

Taylor smiled at this. "But you won out, of course."

"I had certain natural advantages. Lee and I were both self-invented: kids from small towns whose parents never got past high school, and whose families were utterly dysfunctional." Darrow poured more wine. "Lee was from Virginia, the smartest kid around. Her dad sold insurance; her mother kept the books; Lee worked in the office after school. When she left for the University of Virginia, she never looked back. Ever."

"And you were like that, too."

"Uh-huh, especially after what happened at Caldwell. Both of us hell-bent on the future. We never took success for granted, because we'd never had a lot. That made us different from almost everyone around us—on an almost instinctive level, we got each other." Darrow looked down again. "For Lee, her career was more than an identity. It was the thing that kept her from being like her alcoholic father or, worse, a mother so scarred and narrow that what she felt for Lee was jealousy."

Taylor considered that. "She hardly looked like a woman in danger of regressing."

"No way. Still, on one level I could understand her—as I said, I still have the superstitious sense that I'll become who I was before Lionel changed everything. But Lee had a depth of fear beyond anything she could express, or I could fathom. The idea of becoming her mother tied her in a psychic knot." Almost against his will, Darrow felt himself edging closer to the source of his unspoken pain. "The decision to become pregnant was extremely hard for Lee. But she knew how much I wanted to give a child the love and security I'd never had." His voice softened. "Up to the day she died, I worried that she'd just given in. But I never asked. I was too afraid of the answer, and what it might cause her to do."

All at once, Darrow knew that finishing the story would be too hard. He felt Taylor appraising him and then, without words, deciding not to press him. "Lately," she said, "I've thought about having kids. In a wholly abstract sort of way."

Relieved, Darrow turned to her. "What did you conclude?"

"That I want them. It came to me when I realized that the guy I was involved with imagined being the only child of our marriage. I'd like to be a mother, as good as I believe my mother was. But for the right reasons."

"Which are?"

In Taylor's silence, Darrow watched her framing the answer with care. "For me, parenting can't be a means of making up to myself for what I missed, using my child as a surrogate. There's too much narcissism in the way some people parent, and I don't want to become an obsessive mother. Moms or dads like that too often warp their children, or force them to fill parental needs in some fairly unhealthy ways." After taking a sip of wine, she finished quietly: "The gap between the myth of what family should be and the sad reality of what it often is can be pretty hard on everyone."

Perhaps Taylor was talking about her own family, or the better family she hoped to have. But, however tactfully, she had also held Darrow's own image of fatherhood to the light. He felt torn between the desire to say something and uncertainty about what he wished to say. Then Taylor checked her watch. "I forgot this was a school night, Mark. It's getting late for both of us."

Darrow felt a stab of disappointment. Awkwardly, he said, "I hope we're not finished."

She gave him a swift, sidelong glance. "With your surroundings? We've barely started."

Darrow walked her to the door. "This weekend," he ventured, "why don't we do something?"

Taylor looked amused. "Something? Whatever it is, I'm willing to discuss it."

Later, falling into bed, Darrow felt restless. Then he remembered finding the package Rusty Clark's assistant had left on his doorstep, a partial transcript of Steve Tillman's trial. Turning on the light, he began reading.

11

THE NEXT MORNING, DARROW MET WITH THE PUBLIC relations expert hired to deal with the embezzlement. It was brief and efficient: all statements by the school would come from Darrow himself, whose focus on imposing strict accounting controls seemed to placate restive alumni. But the next meeting, with Provost Farr and faculty department heads, was longer.

It was the last such gathering before the faculty went off for their various summer studies, trips abroad, or retreats to produce works of scholarship. As a group, Darrow had discovered, the heads represented the usual mix of personalities—wry, enthusiastic, detached, rancorous, intemperate, and ingratiating. Though most accepted his proposal to restrict faculty-student dating, their other complaints were many. Some lobbied to improve the lives of students; others, to assert the primacy of their departments in the battle over Caldwell's slim resources. There was not enough money to satisfy them all—or any of them. Instead Darrow solicited a written summary of their departments' needs and ambitions, promising that, in due course, he would consider these in framing an endowment plan—which, however, must also finance his aim to recruit disadvantaged students. They departed in various states of hope and discontent. It was, Farr told him afterward, the best Darrow could hope for.

His workday ended with a conference call from Joe Betts and Greg Fox, scheduled at Joe's urgent request. With evident satisfaction, Fox reported the discovery of a second account in the name of Caldwell College, opened at the local branch of the First Columbus Bank, for which the signature card bore Clark Durbin's name. "What's different here," Fox explained, "is that the money didn't *leave* for Switzerland—it came back."

"How much?" Darrow asked.

"Fifty thousand dollars, transferred three months ago."

"This clinches it," Joe Betts's voice broke in. "Durbin laundered the money through Switzerland and sent it back to himself in Wayne."

"It seems circular to me," Darrow said. "Why would Durbin do that?"

"Concealment," Joe answered promptly. "He was trying to make it harder to trace the flow of cash. This is the last piece of evidence we need to prosecute."

Darrow scribbled two words on his notepad: "Why Columbus?" Then he asked, "What do you think, Greg?"

"I'm with Joe," Fox answered crisply. "Durbin outsmarted himself. Most embezzlers do."

"True enough," Darrow answered. "I'll let Mike Riley know about this. He'll be in touch with you soon."

"Your guy?" Joe's voice rose slightly. "Do we really need him after this? Seems like a waste of time and money."

"Time, maybe. Not money. I'll pay him myself."

After a moment's silence, Fox allowed a note of strained patience to seep into his voice. "I'll be waiting for his call."

Hanging up, Darrow scribbled, "Missing: $850,000." Then he left a voice message with Mike Riley in Boston, and hurried out the door.

IT WAS A soft summer evening, lightly humid, and the rolling landscape outside Wayne evoked a slice of Darrow's teenage years: aimless drives with friends, radio blaring, cold six-packs of beer hidden in the trunk while they searched for a place to drink it. But the once-verdant farmland was now dotted with pseudobaronial homes, their acreage demarked by rustic fences—the retreats of Columbus-based businessmen like Joe Betts, designed to suggest the horse country of Kentucky. Only Carly Simmons's place had been there twenty years ago: a rambling white nineteenth-century farmhouse, with a barn that still displayed a worn advertisement for Red Man chewing tobacco, its yellow letters peeling, its fierce-looking Indian head fading into commercial history. The sight made Darrow smile.

Simmons waited in a fenced-off area in front of the barn, throwing a wooden stick to a black terrier who returned it eagerly and repeatedly. As the wheels of Darrow's Porsche crunched the gravel driveway, Simmons turned and waved by way of greeting. Even after sixteen years she looked familiar, though the blond woman who'd once knelt by Angela's body was stockier now, her curls tipped with gray. Her ruddy face flushed from exercise, she gave him a firm handshake.

"So you're president of Caldwell," she said without preface.

"Yup."

"A lot to do, I imagine." Her tone flattened out. "You also found her body, I remember."

Darrow nodded. "It's something you don't forget. Now that I'm back, I've started thinking about all the things I still don't know."

"Don't blame you," Simmons said matter-of-factly. "It was one of my first cases, and it sticks in the mind. Partly because of the victim, partly because I pretzeled myself to get things right."

The statement was factual, and undefensive. But her large brown eyes seemed to examine him closely. "So," she finished, "you're back, and now you're nagged by unanswered questions. What do you want to know?"

"Several things," Darrow said, "in no particular order. For example, how drunk was Angela before she died?"

The terrier nudged Simmons's leg, stick between its teeth. Reaching down, Simmons retrieved the piece of wood and threw it toward the fence. "Drunk enough," she answered. "It's hard to be precise. But tests on the two glasses we found in Steve's room showed they'd both kept on drinking. Though from the toxicology report, Angela had begun to metabolize the alcohol before she died."

Darrow watched the dog scamper for the stick, tail bobbing. "What does that tell you?"

The lines at the corners of Simmons's eyes deepened slightly. "That she'd stopped consuming alcohol. Also, possibly, that she'd had some form of physical activity."

"Like walking?"

"Maybe. Or sex."

"How drunk was Steve?"

Simmons smiled faintly. "That was kind of critical, given his story. You don't black out on a couple of Miller Lites. Let alone suffer gaps in memory." She paused, ordering her thoughts. "By his own account, Tillman was a seasoned drinker, much more so than she was. That means he metabolized alcohol more quickly.

"By the time we took his blood sample, maybe nine hours later, he was a hair below the legal limit of .08 blood alcohol concentration. Once you stop drinking, you drop about .0125 every hour. So put Tillman up around 2.0 at the height of his intoxication."

"That's pretty drunk."

Simmons nodded. "I can't tell you at what point the kid's lights would start going out. But yeah, that's pretty drunk. Not to mention he'd done some coke."

"So we've got a drunk with a bum knee lugging a dead body around campus."

Simmons threw the stick again. "So they say. Maybe the coke jacked him up. I don't try the cases; I just do the corpses."

"Any chance she was strangled near the Spire?"

The question made her turn, eyes focused on the question. "Are you familiar with the concept of lividity?"

"Uh-huh. Once the heart stops pumping, gravity governs the flow of blood. Depending on the position of the body, blood flows to its lowest point." Darrow shoved his hands into his pockets. "I found Angela lying face-up. So the blood should have gravitated to her back."

"Which it did."

"Nowhere else?"

Simmons slowly shook her head. "I checked her fingers and toes. No lividity."

"What did *that* suggest?"

Crossing her arms, Simmons ignored the dog at her feet. "There are two possibilities. The first is that the killer carried Angela to where you found her quickly enough that the blood didn't flow to her extremities. The second is that she was strangled much closer to the Spire."

Darrow felt his instincts quicken. "So there's no medical evidence affirmatively suggesting that she was carried there?"

Simmons shook her head again. "I can't rule that out. Nor can I rule it in."

Watching the terrier paw Simmons's pant leg for attention, Darrow tried to organize his thoughts. "What about time of death?" he asked.

Simmons threw the stick again. "That's more art than science. We go on body temperature. But there's all sorts of variables: ambient air temperature, moving air currents, type of clothing, how long the body had been outside. Angela was slender, causing her body to cool more quickly. But she was wearing a heavy coat. So it was hard to be exact."

Listening to the vicissitudes of science, Darrow remembered Angela herself—her face at the party so human and vulnerable, in death a mask of agony.

"The range we settled on," Simmons continued, "was that she'd been dead from six to twelve hours. But my best estimate was she'd died between two and three A.M. Which, as it turned out, was more or less consistent with the trial testimony."

"From Joe Betts, you mean?"

"Yeah, and that waitress."

"What waitress?" Darrow asked in surprise.

Simmons threw the stick still farther, grunting with exertion. "I forget her name—she worked the night shift at Donut King. As best I recall, she was taking a shortcut across campus. She claimed to have seen the outline of a man beneath the Spire laying down what looked like a body."

"What time was it?"

"Shortly after three A.M., I think she said."

Darrow struggled to reorganize the puzzle pieces to accommodate a new one. Joe Betts claimed to have seen Steve outside the dorm around three o'clock; apparently the waitress believed that an unidentified man had deposited Angela's body a few minutes later. But, despite this contradiction, both accounts suggested that Angela had been carried to the Spire. At length, Darrow asked bluntly, "Was Angela raped?"

Simmons pursed her lips. "There was evidence consistent with rape. That the sperm was Tillman's only proved they'd had sex. Ditto that both their pubic areas contained each other's hair. But there were scratches on his back, and skin under her fingernails—Tillman's, according to the DNA. Add the contusion on her cheek and you can come up with a sexual assault."

"What about forcible penetration?"

"There weren't any vaginal tears. That doesn't mean the sex was consensual. Angela wasn't a virgin, it's clear. And she could have given in to avoid a beating, or just passed out. That's still rape. But you just can't know."

"Yeah. I keep hearing that."

Kneeling, Simmons took the stick from the terrier's mouth, ruffling the fur on its neck. "Enough, Diablo. You're wearing me out." She stood again, gazing at the landscape in the gently slanting light. Evenly, she said, "We didn't have all the medical evidence we might want. But there was an absence of any evidence helpful to Tillman. There was no one else's DNA on Angela's body. I tried to get something off her neck—the murderer's fingerprint, or even DNA from the moisture on his fingers. Either one could have further inculpated Tillman or, conceivably, exculpated him. But those were long shots, and neither panned out." She gave a fatalistic shrug. "So we lived with what we had. With the witnesses, it turned out to be enough."

Darrow absorbed this in silence. After a moment, Simmons faced him again. "There's something else you should think about," she said. "Ever try to strangle someone?"

"I've considered it once or twice."

Simmons's expression became grim. "It's an extremely unpleasant act—for both the victim and the murderer. To asphyxiate another human being by strangulation takes about three minutes. The killer doesn't just need to be strong—he needs to be determined. Whoever decided that Angela Hall needed killing remained firm in his intentions despite ample opportunity to reconsider. Even a drunk had time for second thoughts." Finishing, Simmons spoke coolly and incisively: "What that means, Mr. Darrow, is that first-degree murder was the appropriate verdict. This was an intentional homicide, carried out by someone who wanted to make sure this young woman never saw another day, or spoke another word.

The murderer was either very cold-blooded or very angry. Maybe both."

Darrow thanked her.

Driving to his empty residence, he watched the blue-gray of twilight envelop the horizon. He already knew what part of the trial transcript he would read.

12

IN THE MORNING, DARROW TRIED TO SET ASIDE WHAT HE HAD discovered in the trial transcript. He began his workday by reviewing Joe Betts's plan to tighten Caldwell's financial safeguards; with one addition, which Darrow scrawled in the margins, it seemed prudent and comprehensive. Then he prepared to meet with Fred Bender, now Caldwell's head of security, by scanning the campus safety program—which, he knew, tracked what Farr had suggested to Clark Durbin on the morning of Angela's murder. Finishing, Darrow reflected that both plans, sound in themselves, existed to prevent disasters that had already occurred.

The next problem on his desk, though new, had been exacerbated by the old ones. The campus employees no one thought much about—the maintenance crew, cafeteria workers, and distributors of campus mail—were seeking a raise they clearly deserved; Caldwell had little money to give them. Picking up the phone, Darrow asked Farr what the employees might accept.

"Whatever we give them," Farr answered bluntly. "The job market's brutal; their skills minimal; the economic trends Darwinian, winnowing out the less gifted or educated. Your faculty—which also deserves more money—knows that. So does our board of trustees.

Give them a choice between a happy maintenance staff or renovating a building, bricks and mortar will win every time."

"Maybe so," Darrow said. "But why should I choose *for* them? If they want to screw these people, let them say so."

"Why expend your political capital on mere charity?" Farr replied sardonically. "Especially when you're telling the board to put off a new capital campaign. Besides which, as of an hour ago, you can't afford an act of human kindness."

"Because?"

"A leaky pipe in the IT center has caused the supports to rot. Which means, I'm afraid, moving our entire computer system, at considerable expense, infuriating whatever department whose office space you jam it into. And, of course, the board will blame our maintenance crew, however underpaid and understaffed they happen to be. George Armstrong Custer himself wouldn't ask Ray Carrick to approve a raise."

The sense of choicelessness, Darrow found, deepened the depression seeping into his brain. "First things first, then. We'd better solve the IT problem."

As though registering Darrow's mood, Farr said equably, "It's four-thirty now. Why not come for a drink at six. We can figure this out then."

Why not? Darrow thought. A martini could not hurt, and he would not mind seeing Taylor. "By six," he responded dryly, "I'll expect you to have answers for all our problems."

WHEN DARROW ARRIVED, Taylor was nowhere in sight.

The evening was warm and breezy. Ties loosened, Darrow and Farr sat in the intricately landscaped backyard, Anne Farr's legacy—Farr drinking Scotch, Darrow a martini. By the second drink, the two men had moved the IT center to the basement of the old art building and resolved to defer any pay increases with a promise of better raises in better times. Sipping his martini, Darrow paused a moment, then spoke to the roots of his disquiet. "The last couple of nights," he told Farr, "I've been reading Steve Tillman's trial transcript."

Farr's eyebrows shot up. "Oh?"

"Call it a professional compulsion. Now that I'm back, I can't help thinking about how Steve got where he is."

Farr studied him. "Reach any conclusions?"

"No. But I have some distinct impressions."

"Such as?"

As Darrow ordered his thoughts, the door from the sunroom opened and Taylor Farr stepped onto the brick patio, miming shock at the sight of sunlight. "I've been locked up with my dissertation all day," she announced. "Hibernation isn't meant for summer." Turning to Darrow, she said, "Hello, Mark. Hope you've taken the Reverend Caldwell off your wall."

"I'm giving him to you," Darrow answered her. "As thanks for all the advice you gave me the other night."

Taylor laughed. Farr looked from Darrow to his daughter, eyes keen and head slightly tilted, as if listening to notes no one else could hear. After a moment, he asked, "Care for a drink, Taylor?"

"White wine, thanks. I'll get it myself."

As she left, Farr resumed his appraisal of Darrow. "You said you had 'impressions.'"

"Several. What they add up to is whether Steve should have been convicted at all."

Farr cradled his drink, unsipped for the last few moments. "The jury thought so. Frankly, so did I. The evidence seemed good enough."

Taylor emerged with a glass of wine. Gauging the two men's expressions, she sat at the edge of the wooden table, watching them in silence. "Maybe in the abstract," Darrow was saying to Farr. "The key witnesses against Steve were the two homicide cops, principally Fred Bender; Carly Simmons, the pathologist; a waitress returning home from the doughnut shop; and, critically, Joe Betts."

"There were also Steve's own statements to the police," Farr amended.

"True, and they weren't helpful to him. But the essence of the case was this: Angela left the party with Steve. They went to his room. They drank some more and had sex, leaving scratches on Steve's back and, perhaps, a bruise on Angela's face. To the police, that suggested rape, as did the fact that the room was disordered and Steve's bedside lamp knocked over.

"Two witnesses strung these pieces together. The waitress claimed to have seen a man about Steve's size and build setting down a body near the Spire around three A.M. But Joe Betts was the clincher: by swearing he saw Steve returning to his room from the direction of the Spire, he made Steve out to be a liar—and therefore a murderer. Without Joe, Steve might well have walked."

Still quiet, Taylor looked from Darrow to her father. "But there *was* Joe," Farr proferred mildly. "The only alternatives are that *he* was lying or that Steve didn't remember leaving his room. The latter's not plausible."

"Assuming he'd returned from carrying a body. Suppose he was just a drunk in search of fresh air—which was Joe's stated reason for sticking his head out the window."

Left unanswered were the implications of Farr's first alternative. Carefully, Farr asked, "Who else do you suppose wanted to kill Angela?"

"That *is* the question," Darrow concurred, "as Dave Farragher emphasized in his closing argument. 'Don't leave your common sense at home,' he told the jury. 'Do you really believe Angela just wandered away and was strangled at random?' "

Narrow-eyed, Farr put down his tumbler, contemplating its contents. "Perhaps I'm out of my depth. But I was there, and I watched the jury's faces. For me, the key was when Dave said something like 'Sometime during your deliberations, I want you to remain silent for one hundred and eighty seconds, the time it took the murderer to choke the life from Angela Hall. Then ask yourself these questions: Was her death the product of a momentary impulse or was the murderer implacably determined to kill her? And would a murder so deliberate, so remorseless, so angry, and so intimate be committed by a stranger?' What's *your* answer, Mark?"

Darrow felt Taylor watching him closely, her own mind at work. "If *that's* the question, Lionel, my answer is clearly no."

Farr nodded briskly. "Meaning that whoever strangled Angela knew her and was driven by what seemed to him—and it's fair to assume it was a him, given the strength it took—an extremely powerful motive. Who else but Steve Tillman?"

Darrow chose not to answer. During his silence, Taylor looked at the two men's empty glasses. "Can I offer either of you a refill?" she asked. "Perhaps some wine?"

Intent now, Darrow shook his head, glancing at Farr.

"No," Farr said curtly. "Thank you."

After giving her father a swift glance, Taylor turned to Mark. "What *did* the defense lawyer do?" she asked.

"Nothing good," Darrow replied. "If Nordlinger did any pretrial investigation, it isn't evident from the transcript. When he called on Steve in his own defense, Steve wasn't prepared for what happened to him."

"Which was?"

"Accusations of racism," Darrow said crisply. "Farragher went after all the times in high school someone heard him say 'nigger.' He also forced Steve to admit that he had confronted George Garrison about asking out his sister."

Taylor finished her wine. "Not pretty. But that doesn't make Tillman a murderer."

"Exactly. If it did, back in the nineties a chunk of our population would have been on death row. At the least, Nordlinger should have objected like crazy."

"On what grounds?" Farr inquired. "That there's a difference between racial animus and murder? Or that wanting to sleep with a black woman is the opposite of wanting to kill her?"

"The legal frame," Darrow answered, "is that racist statements are more 'prejudicial than probative'—they create bias against Steve without providing any evidence of murder. I knew *that* much before I passed the bar."

Farr sat back, emitting a barely audible sigh. "You drive me to a painful admission. During the trial, Griff Nordlinger didn't look right to me—I thought he might be sick, literally. Months later I heard that his marriage was falling apart, and that the cause might be some serious substance abuse. If I'd suspected that Griff might have been impaired, I never would have suggested he take Steve's case. But by then the trial was over.

"On appeal, the public defender's office replaced Griff. I told myself his problems didn't matter—or, if they did, that the appellate courts would consider them. And I believed then, as I do now, that Steve Tillman strangled Angela." He glanced at Taylor, and his voice went softer still. "Racism makes savagery more thinkable. So do cocaine and alcohol—beyond question, Steve had overindulged in both. If he was guilty, I concluded, Griff's overindulgence was beside the point."

Uncharacteristically, Farr sounded pained. Choosing silence, Darrow felt Taylor watching his face. "If *you* had been Steve's lawyer," she asked him, "how would you have defended him?"

It was the same question Darrow had asked himself. Mindful of Farr's sensitivities, he organized his thoughts. "It's not an easy case," he acknowledged. "There are only so many defenses: 'somebody else did it'; 'I did it, but I'm insane'; 'I did it for a good reason'; or, as Nordlinger tried, 'reasonable doubt.' I would have combined 'reasonable doubt' with 'somebody else did it.'

"You'd start by attacking the physical evidence. There's no doubt Steve and Angela had sex. But she had no vaginal tears, and the scratches she left on his back might simply have reflected Angela's involvement in the moment."

A corner of Taylor's mouth twitched. "Is that often your experience?"

Darrow smiled faintly. "As to Steve's messy room, my experience—and I'm sure yours—is that college boys have messy rooms and drunks knock over lamps. The physical evidence, by itself, does nothing to establish murder."

"What about the bruise on Angela's face?"

"That's more problematic, I'll admit. But how did she get it? She could have bumped into a wall."

"Or Tillman could have hit her," Taylor interrupted coolly. "As a prelude to rape. And what about the witnesses?"

In the enveloping dusk, Darrow noted, Farr had dropped out of the conversation, watching the exchange between Darrow and his daughter. "Contrary to popular belief," Darrow answered, "eyewitness testimony is pretty unreliable. And what did the witnesses actually say? The waitress merely claimed she saw a shadowy figure of about Steve's size and stature—which, as it happens, could also describe the two men on either side of you.

"Only Joe Betts claims to have actually seen Steve. But Joe was neither reliable nor unbiased—he was as drunk as Steve, and they'd fought over Angela just hours before. Even if you believe Joe's story, placing Steve outside the dorm doesn't put his fingers around Angela's throat." After glancing at Farr to underscore his point, Darrow again faced Taylor. "Let me ask you this: If Steve Tillman raped Angela in his dorm room—given the freezing night, the only location that makes sense—what does it tell you that she was found by the Spire, fully dressed?"

"That Steve carried her there—"

"Despite his leg and his condition?"

Taylor gave him a mock-patient look. "What I was going to say, before being interrupted, is that what's strange to me is the 'dressed' part."

Darrow smiled again. "Why's that?"

"Because it suggests that she dressed herself following sex, perhaps a rape. Which means that Steve didn't kill her during, or immediately after, whatever happened in his bed."

Beside her gifts in her chosen field, Darrow was perceiving, Taylor had Farr's talent for linear thought—though not a lawyer, she had swiftly integrated the known facts with the probabilities of human nature. "Or," Darrow added, "that she was dressed when they had sex."

"Then why the scratches on his back? If it was consensual, they'd both be naked. And if it was rape, why would he undress?"

Darrow had considered this. "There's a grim alternative—that Steve forced her to undress, raped her, then strangled her. After which he dressed her body and carried it to the Spire."

Taylor shook her head. "Unlikely. Dressing a corpse can't be easy. It also suggests a cold-blooded guy with real presence of mind. That doesn't sound like a drunk to me." Taylor's face closed. "I can't tell you about the scratches. But like most women, I've been in a couple of scary situations with a guy who couldn't hear no. I've sometimes wondered what I'd have done if things had spun out of control."

Darrow brushed away this unwelcome image. "What did you conclude?"

"That I might have given in, however much I hated it, rather than have someone beat me up or tear my vagina to shreds. She also might have passed out before penetration." She turned to Farr. "Sorry, Dad. But the lack of vaginal injury tells me nothing."

Both Farr and Darrow fell quiet again. "After all this it may seem odd," Taylor told them, "but I'm getting hungry. You must be, too. Mind if I order a pizza?"

Farr looked distracted, as though lost in the exchange between Darrow and Taylor. "Pizza's fine," he said. "Mark?"

"Anything you want," Darrow told Taylor. "Vegetarian's okay with me."

Taylor flashed a smile. "That's very thoughtful. But I'm a carnivore, remember? On our first 'date' we both ate steak."

Standing, Taylor went back into the house. Darrow followed her with his eyes, then became aware that Farr was watching him watch his daughter, his own expression thoughtful and enigmatic.

AFTER LIGHTING A candle, Taylor poured three glasses of chardonnay, then distributed slices of pepperoni pizza. "So," she asked Darrow, "what did the prosecutor say Steve's motive was?"

"He didn't," Darrow said. "Your dad makes a good argument that people in extremity are capable of the worst. But the Steve Tillman I knew was never abusive to women or aggressive toward anyone off the football field. And Farragher found no one to say otherwise. That makes strangling Angela a pretty startling anomaly.

"You asked how I would have defended Steve. After raising reasonable doubt, I'd have hammered on motive, then tried to find an alternative suspect. If Nordlinger had done that with any plausibility, my guess is that they'd have acquitted Steve."

Farr did not touch his pizza. "What I keep returning to," he said slowly, "is that two courts of appeals upheld the guilty verdict."

"True," Darrow answered. "But Nordlinger lost the appeal by screwing up the trial. Appellate courts don't reopen the evidence. They just review the record before them—in this case, one made by a skilled prosecutor and a lousy defense lawyer, perhaps an impaired one. And judges don't like finding lawyers inadequate. Even—and this is an actual death-penalty appeal in Texas—a drunk who slept through his client's trial. If there *was* enough evidence to keep Steve in jail, they don't care what the trial was like. And there was enough evidence—barely."

Farr stared at the flickering candle. "Then perhaps there's nothing for it," he said at length. "I'm sorry, Mark. But I can't help thinking about all you're facing in the here and now, and all the board and alumni expect you to do for Caldwell. If they sense you've been distracted from that, they'll never understand the reason."

Darrow felt nettled, perhaps because he saw the truth of this. "I don't expect them to," he answered. "And they won't have to. I'll do the job I came to do. But two years ago, Lionel, life conspired to give me some spare time. So instead of reading bedtime stories to a two-year-old boy, I'm reading trial transcripts.

"I was once a criminal lawyer, and Steve Tillman was once my friend. Knowing he'll die in prison after a trial like this one gives me a restless conscience."

Taylor, Darrow noticed, had become pensive. She remained so throughout dinner.

13

I N THE EARLY-MORNING LIGHT, DARROW STOOD BY HIS
mother's untended grave.

Oak Hill Cemetery was quiet. A few robins chirped; the damp
overgrown grass had a fresh day's sheen of newness. NEILA DARROW,
the headstone read, WIFE OF GEORGE, MOTHER OF MARK. No one
knew George Darrow's whereabouts. Steve Tillman's parents had
paid for the marker; they knew better than to make more elaborate
claims.

"Well," Darrow said softly. "I'm back."

But she would not have known him. Even in his teens she barely
did; the insanity that enveloped her made her perceptions a distorted
mirror. And the Mark Darrow gazing at her worn headstone was, as he
had acknowledged to Taylor, his own invention—even Darrow's eru-
dition of speech, a departure from his plainspoken youth, was derived
from listening to Lionel Farr, and summer nights spent reading the
books Farr suggested. Neila had given him life and, Darrow profoundly hoped, little else: her last years had frightened him almost as
much as how she had chosen to end them. Surely he had transcended
her madness, her terrible dissociation from others.

But only Neila had a son.

Enough, he told himself. The past was done. He would spend this day, then whatever days fate gave him, as best he could.

He went to meet Fred Bender.

SITTING BESIDE BENDER on the bench where they had first met, Darrow had the ironic perception that—despite his credo, and by his own acts—his past had resumed tugging at his present.

Bender smoked a Camel. His once-red hair was steel gray; the mottled skin of his face was so close to the bone that it evoked a mummy. But the seen-it-all cop's eyes staring from this weathered carapace remained a clear and lucid blue.

"President Darrow," he commented wryly. "Who knew."

"Who indeed. It's 'Mark,' by the way. Like on the day you questioned me."

Bender took a drag, then exhaled. "A long time now."

"A long, safe time. Thanks to you, in part."

As two female students passed by, laughing, Bender watched with the air of a silent guardian. "More thanks to Lionel Farr. The campus security plan he designed has stood the test of years. Phones every hundred yards, a buddy system, and monitors at campus entry points."

"The technology's different," Darrow pointed out.

"True. Now we use computers to warn students of any problems and remind them of what they shouldn't do—drinking too much or tearing up their dorms. But we still deal with our issues in-house. Parents don't send their kids here so we can turn them over to the Wayne police." He gave a faintly sarcastic laugh. "No matter how many FBI training courses Garrison sends them to.

"What's different is that Caldwell's stopped being a sanctuary for bad behavior. Angela Hall's murder started with drugs and alcohol. Now we bust kids for public intoxication, conduct periodic sweeps for drugs, monitor fraternity parties, discipline underage kids for going to places like the Alibi Club, and let outsiders like Carl Hall know that they're not welcome here. All that's Lionel's doing—the Hall murder hit him hard. I just oversee things."

Darrow gazed up at the Spire. "How'd you come to take the job?" he inquired. "With all that Lionel's done, seems like Caldwell might be too quiet."

Bender took a ravenous puff, flicking ashes off his sport coat. "After the Tillman trial was done, he approached me about coming here. Farr's pitch was pretty much the same, I guess, as the one he just gave you—you can have all the systems you want in place, but it's people who inspire confidence. Even with the school's fiscal crunch, he dangled more money than I was making, then sold the idea to Durbin." He paused, adding softly, "Who knew about *him,* either.

"Anyhow, I came here. Since then we've had a couple of assaults, a few brawls, and our share of petty theft. But no rapes in sixteen years. And, thank God, no murders."

"Seems like Lionel and you made my job a little easier."

Bender shrugged. "Lionel Farr is a leader. Guess he's been one since he left West Point. Hope you can do as well."

Darrow found that Bender's awe of Farr both nettled and amused him. "That's what I'm praying for," he answered mildly. "I still can't walk on water, but I'm learning how to skate."

Eyeing Darrow anew, Bender gave a hollow chuckle. "Somehow I think you'll do just fine. So what else can I do for you?"

Fred Bender was no fool, Darrow reminded himself. "I know it's ancient history. But Steve Tillman was my closest friend, and being here brings all that back. Especially because I helped put him where he is—"

"Tillman," Bender interrupted harshly, "put himself there—not you, and not us. We just followed his bread crumbs."

"Mind if we talk about that?"

"You're the boss. Anything in particular?"

"Several things. I'm curious about what you did after you questioned me."

Bender ground out the cigarette butt on the sidewalk, then tossed it into a metal trash bin, a smoker retrained. "We started wondering about you—it wouldn't be the first time the real killer dropped the dime on somebody else. So we sent George Garrison to the DBE house to ask about what you did the night before." He paused, then added with satiric wonder, "George Garrison as chief is another 'who knew.' But George more or less cleared you. By then we'd been to Tillman's room."

As though reverting in time, Darrow felt events closing around his friend. "How was he?"

Bender lit another cigarette. "Seemed pretty fucked up. His room sure was—broken lamp, sheets half off his bed, drink glasses on the floor, a trace of white powder on his desk. With the naked eye I could see come stains on the mattress, a couple of dark hairs on the pillow that didn't look like his. Even before we brought in the forensics people, you could feel that something might have happened in that room."

Darrow tried to envision this. "Think we can take a look?"

Bender appraised him, then shrugged. "Why not—I've got the keys. The walk will give me time to finish off my smoke."

DARROW AND BENDER stood at the base of the football field. Inserting a key, Bender gave the door a savage jerk, and then Darrow stepped into his own past.

The entryway was barren, the lights dim, the tile as scuffed and worn as he remembered. Turning to his right, he walked through the bleak corridor toward Steve Tillman's room, as the young Mark Darrow had countless times before.

The door was unlocked. Pushing it open, Darrow found—in place of the bed and desk and posters summoned by his mind's eye—

a storeroom jammed with ancient audiovisual equipment. Memory plays tricks, Darrow reflected—the room was smaller than he remembered. Stale air filled his nostrils. Darrow's stomach felt sour.

"Different," Bender observed. "No one's lived here since she died here."

The thought haunted him, Darrow found. Drawing a breath, he sat on a giant loudspeaker that lay sideways, gazing through the open door. Arms folded, Bender leaned against the cinder-block wall. "Bring back memories?"

"I'm more interested in yours. Remind me of what the crime lab found."

"A lot of what I already knew. The sperm was Tillman's; the hairs, Angela's. Two glasses contained traces of rum and Coke; the powder turned out to be cocaine."

"What about fingerprints?"

"Yup. His and hers, each on one of the glasses."

Pensive, Darrow tried to imagine Steve and Angela's drunken arrival and, crediting Steve's story, her mystifying departure. Once more his eyes lit on the doorway. "What about on the doors?" he asked. "Both to the dorm and to Steve's room. On the outside *and* the inside."

Bender's eyes glinted. "Let me see if I follow you. The lab might well find Tillman's prints on both sides of those doors or doorknobs—after all, he came and went all the time. But not Angela. Her prints on the inside of either door might suggest she'd left here still alive. You're wondering if we thought of that, and what we might have found."

"All these years, Fred, and you're still ahead of me."

Bender smiled without humor. "Yes, we thought of that. And no, she left no prints on the inside of either door. Finding prints is hit or miss. But we found no evidence that she'd left this room alive. Unless you count Tillman's illogical story."

"You said he was 'fucked up.' Does that mean disoriented?"

"Maybe that. He still seemed drunk to me, like he couldn't

compute what was happening. His account was Swiss cheese—he claimed to remember almost nothing. But he had a small-town boy's manner: open, respectful of authority, hoping you'd like him. You didn't want to believe how things were beginning to look for him."

"But you *did* believe it."

Bender's eyes narrowed slightly. "In other words, did we consider other suspects or just take the easy way out."

"Not my question," Darrow answered. "All I know is that Angela was killed on Saturday and Farragher charged Steve with murder the following Thursday."

"That's Farragher. For our part we worked around the clock, interviewing anyone who might know anything at all—Angela's friends, the other kids at the party, her mother, her scumbag of a brother. Joe Betts, you already know about.

"Our big focus was Angela Hall herself. You had to figure she'd been strangled for a reason. So we went all over her life and anything she'd left behind—her room, her calendar, her medical records, her checkbook. We even tracked down an old boyfriend whose name we found on a postcard, and delved into their sex life." He took out the pack of cigarettes. "Before you ask, she left no scratches on his back. Or so he claimed."

Bender, Darrow saw, could track his thoughts with ease. "What about her academics?" Darrow asked. "Any changes?"

"We looked for that, too. We checked out her files and talked to her professors for the last couple of semesters—including Farr, who also ran the committee that reauthorized her scholarship every year. We found no sign of trouble, and nobody thought different. In fact, I seem to recall her grades were on the rise."

Stymied, Darrow sifted his impressions of Angela. "At the party, she seemed troubled to me—like drinking was an act of self-obliteration. Was there a hint of any new problems in her life?"

For an instant, Bender hesitated. "We couldn't be sure. Her

mother said she'd started going out in the middle of the night—one A.M., two A.M. College kids do that. But this was new for her, Mom said, and Angela wouldn't tell her where or why."

Darrow felt his nerve ends tingle. "Did you ever figure it out?"

Bender frowned. "No. We looked for suggestions of a drug problem, or even that she'd turned to hooking. No evidence of either— she seemed like a different proposition than her brother."

"And yet she'd started leaving at nights, and never saying why. Did you ever find anyone who'd admitted seeing her?"

"Nobody. That seemed to haunt her mother." Reaching into the pack of Camels, Bender began fidgeting with an unlit cigarette. "According to Mom, when Angela was younger she'd kept a diary hidden beneath her mattress. Her mother thought that she still did, though she swore she'd never read it. That was hard to believe—my wife sure as hell would have. But the woman was absolutely torn up—if she'd read the diary, she kept saying, maybe she could have saved her daughter."

"Based on what?"

"Grief and helplessness. Anyhow, we never found a diary. Wish we had. But we couldn't chase after something that might never have existed—or if it did, might not have told us anything of value. Whichever one, sure as hell the murderer didn't make it disappear."

"Did you ask her brother about it?"

"Yup. He gave us nothing: no diary, no boyfriends, except maybe Tillman. We had to lean on him about his drug dealing to even get him to talk about his murdered sister. All we got was what we already knew: that Carl was a greedy little shit. Which he still is, only now he's a prosperous little shit." Bender's lips compressed. "Too bad. What with his dislike of whites and his connections with bad people, I thought *he* might have something to do with her murder. That would have suited me fine."

Darrow considered this. "Where'd Carl go after the party?"

"Home, he said. To bed. We never found out different."

"Just like Joe Betts," Darrow observed. "That's how he got to be a witness. While we're here, mind if we look at his room?"

For a moment, Bender watched Darrow's eyes. Then he shrugged. "Why not," he answered. "If we open that window, I can smoke this cigarette."

14

DARROW AND BENDER LEANED OUT THE WINDOW OF JOE Betts's old room on the second floor, Bender smoking, Darrow watching a few summer students, clad in shorts and T-shirts, taking the pathways that radiated from the Spire. Shadowed by trees, its base was barely visible—the distance, Farr had calculated, was roughly two hundred yards. Darrow tried to imagine the scene on the night of Angela's murder.

"Exactly where," he asked Bender, "did Joe say he saw Steve?"

Bender pointed to a spot a few feet from the entrance. Gazing down, Darrow observed, "Seems like you'd mostly see the top of someone's head. There weren't any outdoor lights then, right?"

"Just by the door itself."

"And the moon?"

"Full." Bender took a drag, exhaling the smoke away from Darrow. "Muhlberg and I tried it two nights later, and I could make out who he was. It helped that I knew him. But Betts knew Tillman, too."

Darrow turned to him. "But if Steve was close enough to identify, Joe couldn't know which direction he was coming from—let alone that he was returning from the Spire. For all Joe knew, Steve could have been outside throwing up."

"No upchuck in the grass," Bender said tersely. "Or footprints we could trace to anyone—the ground was semi-frozen. As I said, we were thorough."

"But thanks to Joe you had your murderer?"

Bender did not react to this. Instead, he asked, "Back then, how well did you know Joe Betts?"

"Pretty well."

"Did you like him?"

Darrow parsed his feelings, then and now, conscious of their implications. "It depended on the moment. And whether he'd been drinking."

Bender flicked an ash. "Really? Betts was more or less sober when we found him. And I still thought he was a dick."

Surprised, Darrow asked, "How so?"

"He had attitude—not like Tillman at all. Betts was an East Coast kid, a preppy out of some rich suburb in Connecticut. We still get them at Caldwell—too lazy as students to make the Ivy League, thinking they're above whatever team they're playing on." Bender's tone was flat. "That was Joe Betts—he thought just getting born had made him better than anyone. That was his attitude toward us."

"Still, he gave you Tillman."

With a thin smile, Bender rejoined, "At first he gave us nothing. Based on what you'd told us, we started by asking him about the party. He refused to talk. Next thing we knew, his uncle had the kid lawyered up—a criminal defense specialist out of Columbus, expensive and smart. The lawyer kept him on ice for twenty-four hours, refusing to let us take a polygraph or meet with Betts at all.

"Finally, we let it drop to your old coach that Betts was looking good for the crime—a little psychology, to loosen Betts up. Like we knew he would, Coach Fiske passed the word. That was when Betts and his lawyer decided to give up Tillman."

Darrow recalled Joe's confession the day of Steve's arrest; Joe had told him none of this. "Didn't that make you skeptical?"

Bender laughed softly. "Back then everything about Joe Betts made me skeptical. Especially when he claimed to have stonewalled us just to keep from getting his friend Tillman in trouble. But his story cemented a decent circumstantial case. The question for us—and Farragher—was whether to believe it."

"Which you did," Darrow said.

"Not at first. We'd checked out *his* life, too—he was a bad drunk, it was pretty clear, and he'd just broken up with his girlfriend. Fighting with Tillman over Angela Hall made him the leading alternative; his story might have been intended to frame Steve for a murder Betts had committed." Bender took another puff. "Thing is, we never found anything tying Joe to the murder. No witness, no physical evidence. Nothing to say that he didn't walk back to his dorm room, like he told us, to try and sleep it off."

"Did anyone see him come in?"

"No. But as far as we could tell, no one saw him anywhere at all. We know he wasn't with Angela. Tillman was."

Darrow cocked his head. "What did Laurie Shilts tell you?"

"Joe's girlfriend? Nothing much. According to her, their breakup was nothing dramatic—she couldn't see a future, I guess you'd say."

"That's a way of putting it. Happen to notice a bruise on her cheek?"

"No." Bender turned to him, openly curious. "I remember she was wearing a lot of makeup."

"Maybe that day."

"So you're telling me Betts hit her?" Bender asked bluntly. "Just like we figure the murderer hit Angela."

Darrow fell quiet, reflecting on his moments with Laurie. *Deep down,* she had told him, *Joe hates women.* "Laurie never said," he answered. "But that was my impression."

For a time, Bender appraised him keenly. "You had more on your mind than we knew, didn't you?"

Remembering his calls to Steve, Darrow felt his unease deepen.

"Maybe so. But I didn't know what it meant, or anything about Joe's story. Since then I've gotten better at stringing things together."

"So it seems."

Beneath Bender's tone, though mild, Darrow heard a note of accusation. Quietly, he asked, "What do you know about Joe's father?"

"Only that he was dead." Bender's voice became weary. "I guess you're also going to tell me the old man beat Joe's mother."

"According to Joe. No reason to lie about that."

"*That* would have been of interest. You and I both know that men who abuse women often learned from Dad." After stubbing his cigarette out on the windowsill, Bender put it in the pocket of his sport coat. "But if it makes you feel better, in the end none of this would have mattered. We had nothing on Betts except the fight over Angela Hall. The only DNA we could get from her body belonged to Tillman. When the crime lab scoured Betts's room and found nothing, the one surprise was how neat it was.

"As a suspect, Betts looked better than he turned out to be—at least based on what we could find. And what would his motive have been? He'd have to have been so pissed off about what happened at the party that, four hours later, he followed Angela when she left the dorm and strangled her near the Spire. Even if you can imagine that, there's no evidence that it happened. That leaves Tillman."

Darrow found himself gazing at the Spire, burnished in the sunlight above the trees. "Maybe it does. But the scenario I still have trouble with is that Steve Tillman strangled her, dressed her, and then decided to deposit her body at the foot of the most iconic structure on Caldwell's campus."

Turning, Bender had a small, grim smile. "Who's to say he dressed her? You and I will never know what happened in that room. But, if you're interested, I can tell you what I think went on between the two of them."

Darrow felt a new tautness, interest combined with dread. "Sure."

"It's simple enough. Tillman and the girl were drinking and making out, both hotted up. Tillman had a little coke, and began wanting something more. Angela wasn't so up for that. But Tillman just had to fuck her, no matter how. When she resisted, he lost it. That was when he hit her."

Bender, Darrow realized, had thought about this long and hard; like Darrow himself, he needed a story that made sense and that, at least, conformed to the physical evidence. "So she gave in," Darrow said.

"A fateful choice," Bender answered softly. "Tillman made her undress, then used his finger to make her wet enough to enter, leaving no injuries. When he was done, she dressed herself. But Angela never left the room alive."

"You think she threatened to report him."

"Uh-huh. Everything we know says she was a strong-willed girl with real pride, nobody's victim. And she was too drunk or angry to realize that a guy capable of rape and battery might take the final step. But Tillman knew enough to understand that he could spend a stretch in prison, and was coked up enough for rage to overtake his reason." Bender took another puff, eyes narrow, as though reenvisioning the murder. "All your friend knew was not to let her talk. Three minutes later, she couldn't."

Silent, Darrow reviewed Bender's thesis. "If Angela let him penetrate her, why the scratches on Steve's back?"

"Maybe she changed her mind, or wanted to leave her mark." Pausing, Bender fished out another cigarette. "Nothing's perfect. Including the logic of a homicide involving two drunken kids."

"There's also this," Darrow rejoined. "Joe didn't have a car that night; he left on foot, and then we clever fraternity boys parked his Miata in the library. But Steve *did* have a car. Does illogic also cover a drunk with a trick knee carrying a corpse two hundred yards to a very public space—instead of dumping her in his trunk and throwing her in the river? Or dumping her body in a place—the old lime pit, for example—where you might never find her?"

Bender seemed unruffled. "No clue—Tillman sure didn't tell us. Maybe he thought she'd leave traces in his car. All we know is what he did with her."

"How do you know *what* he did? How did he carry her, for one thing? Did the forensic people find any drag marks on her heels?"

"No. But if he carried her over his shoulder, there wouldn't be."

"In which case," Darrow rejoined, "you'd think there might be traces of her saliva on his clothes. Were there any?"

Momentarily quiet, Bender considered the implications of the question. "Corpses drool," he said. "Maybe just not this one. At least not that the crime lab found."

"In other words, there's no evidence at all that Steve carried her to the Spire. All we know is that I found her there."

"Not all. Pat Flynn—the waitress from the Donut King—saw the guy who carried her there. She swore he was about Tillman's height and build."

"That could have been me, Fred. Or anyone." Darrow hesitated. "Does Pat still live in Wayne?"

"Yup. Same life, same job. Donut King's still there."

For a long time, Bender said nothing more. "Since you came back," he finally asked Darrow, "have you run into Joe Betts?"

"Once."

"Last few years, I've met him a couple of different times. By appearance, I could have picked him out of a lineup. But he seems like a different guy, and not just because he's sober." He turned to Darrow. "A decent guy, wouldn't you say?"

Darrow hesitated. "Yeah," he answered. "I would."

WALKING WITH DARROW back to his office, Bender paused at the foot of the Spire for a final smoke. For Darrow, the site evoked many things. But what he recalled now was stopping with Joe Betts to watch the rally where Dave Farragher had pledged before a swarm of TV cameras to solve the murder of Angela Hall.

"Tell me about Farragher," Darrow said.

Bender weighed the question. "At the time of the murder, he was still pretty new in the job—had only been prosecutor for three years. But he'd been an assistant prosecutor, known for being sharp. Legally and politically."

"Which mattered most?"

"In this case, both. Dave was up for reelection, so he was on the hot seat. No point indicting someone if you may well lose at trial, or just turn out to be wrong. Dave needed to be right."

"Within three days?"

"A fair question," Bender conceded. "Dave was under a lot of pressure, including from the black community, as well as from the college. And the media. You didn't need to be as smart as Dave to know this one was make-or-break, the biggest case he might ever see." Briefly, Bender interrupted himself by coughing. "No one thought his vision of the future ended with county prosecutor. Some folks used to call him 'Governor' behind his back. Only two things could derail him for sure—some sort of scandal or fucking up this case. He needed a conviction."

"So when did he decide that he could win a case against Steve?"

"When Muhlberg and I brought him Joe Betts's story. 'That makes Tillman a liar,' I recall him saying. 'If I can prove to the jury he lied about something that important, that could seal a conviction.'" Bender finished his cigarette. "I wasn't there when he met with Betts. But whatever Joe said was enough to convince Farragher that Tillman was the one. A few hours later, Dave had him arrested."

This was another detail, Darrow remembered, that Joe had not revealed to him. He felt Bender watching his face. "Look," the detective said evenly. "I know this is complicated for you. You found her body. Steve Tillman was your best friend, and you also knew Joe Betts pretty well. Looking back at it, I imagine you're remembering a lot of things, and maybe feeling some sort of guilt you can't quite put a name to.

"But this is a classic cold case, with gaps no one can fill in. The passage of fifteen years has made it worse." Dropping the cigarette in the grass, Bender ground it with his shoe. "The real problem is Angela Hall. She's what I'd call a legitimate victim—not some gangbanger anyone might have shot, where there are a lot of potential witnesses. Or suspects.

"People like Angela aren't courting death. With victims like her, often there's no witnesses except the killer. So you work with what you've got. And you learn to accept that that's probably all you'll ever have."

"Not easy."

Stooping, Bender picked up the butt, then faced Darrow. "Believe me," he said quietly, "I wish I had all the answers. This was the last case of my career. No one wants to end with an unsolved homicide. But no cop wants to die still wondering about his biggest success."

Bender put the dead cigarette in his pocket. Alone, Darrow went back to his office.

15

Darrow capped a review of Caldwell's finances by taking Joe Betts to dinner.

The venue was the Carriage House. As before, the owner seated Darrow in the booth below his photograph—the much younger Mark Darrow brandished the ceremonial axe from atop the Spire. "This seems to have become my table," Darrow remarked.

Eyeing the picture, Joe shook his head. "That was a moment. Too bad the day didn't end there."

The waitress took their drink orders. "Just give me Château Perrier," Joe told her amiably. "I hear May 2009 was a good month."

When the waitress left, Darrow said, "You really *did* give it up, didn't you?"

"Cold turkey," Joe answered. "After that night, I didn't need a twelve-step program. I *knew*."

He looked unsettled by the memory. "That was years ago," Darrow said. "You've done well, Joe. Certainly for Caldwell—given the times, our portfolio could have taken a far bigger beating than it has."

Joe grimaced. "Not many good places to put our money, what with the housing bubble and the rest. My great achievement was not losing more. Compared to letting Durbin embezzle close to a million bucks, I guess that's a point of pride."

Joe might have changed, Darrow thought, but not entirely; beneath the smooth exterior, he sensed the touchiness and insecurity Joe had tried to conceal in college. "No one figured Clark Durbin for a crook," Darrow responded. "The flaw was in the system, and your proposals for fixing it are sound. Once we get them in place, it'll close the books on this whole sad episode."

"We'll close the books, Mark, when we throw the book at Durbin. You ready to do that yet?"

Darrow sipped his martini. "Not quite. I still want my guy Mike Riley to take a look at this. Call me thorough."

To Darrow's surprise, Joe flushed with anger. "That's not diligence, for Chrissakes—that's necrophilia. Especially after we found the account where Durbin transferred money back from Switzerland. I'm with Ray Carrick: nailing Durbin to the mast is what the alumni need to see. New financial controls are good and well, but they don't satisfy the viscera."

"Whose viscera?" Darrow asked mildly. "I've been called a lot of things, but 'corpse fucker' is pretty novel."

Joe managed a sour smile. "Okay," he acknowledged. "The Durbin thing is personal to me. I feel like a buffoon, and now it's like you're second-guessing Greg Fox and me. For no reason either of us can detect except that you can."

"I'm way too busy for petty shows of authority," Darrow answered firmly. "So bear with me. I owe a debt to Caldwell College, and have ever since Lionel got me in. That's why I came back despite all the reasons I had to stay away."

Taking off his horn-rimmed glasses, Betts wiped both lenses with a napkin, removing spots only he could see. "I know that, Mark. Believe me." He paused a moment. "Have you gone to see Steve again?"

"Yeah. It's becoming a regular stop."

"Anything new?"

"Not much happening at the pen—or many distractions, either.

Prison seems to breed a certain monomania. It's fair to say he still blames you for his misery."

Joe put his glasses back on, fiddling with one of the stems. "That's pretty misdirected, wouldn't *you* say?"

Darrow shrugged. "I guess that depends on whether he killed her. Steve still swears she walked out alive and that he never left the dorm." He hesitated, then asked mildly, "Any chance at all the guy you saw was someone else?"

Joe's jaw set, defensiveness flashing in his eyes. "No matter what had happened between Steve and me, I wouldn't put a friend in jail unless I *knew*. Even if I hadn't glimpsed his face, the guy *limped*. I'd have known Steve Tillman if he'd been walking with fifteen other guys."

After a moment, Darrow nodded. In a tone of idle curiosity, he asked, "Do you remember what he was wearing?"

"Not really, no."

"Did you happen to notice the time?"

Joe was quiet for a moment, brow slightly furrowed. "I thought it was around three o'clock, but can't remember why. Leaning out that window, I still felt pretty fucked up."

Darrow thought quickly of his own memory, still undisclosed, that he had tried to reach Steve Tillman after three o'clock. Joe's sense of time, were his story true, would put Steve back in his dorm room an hour before. But the significance of this—if any—was unclear. "Between the party and whenever you spotted him," Darrow inquired, "did you see Steve or Angela at all?"

"You mean after he drove off with her? No." Joe bit his lip. "The mood I was in, if I'd known they were screwing one floor below, I might have busted in on them. Would have been better if I had—Angela Hall might still be alive." Joe's voice softened. "As it was, all I did was go home and puke in the upstairs john. I remember being on my hands and knees, grabbing both sides of the commode, then staggering up to look in the mirror. I hated what I saw there—not just how I looked, but who I was."

"A bad night, Joe."

Summoning a look of candor, Joe met Darrow's eyes. "No," he answered. "A bad *guy*. I'd lost my girlfriend. I'd fought with Steve. I'd made a fool of myself in public. All I wanted was to get off the earth somehow—not just leave the night behind; leave *myself* behind. Other than my own face, the last thing I wanted to see was those two cops, wanting to go through what I'd done, over and over. I didn't tell them about Steve until I had to."

The latent ambiguity in this last statement left Darrow quiet. Joe's expression became pleading. "I'm different now, Mark. My whole life is different. My career's good. Katie and I are good, and we've got two great kids. Now I'm on Caldwell's board, and I like to think, despite this screwup, that I'm repaying my own debt to the school." He paused, then added in a lower voice, "I didn't become my old man, after all. The guy you saw that night isn't me anymore. He's as dead as Angela Hall."

Darrow had a deep sense of sadness. He remembered Steve Tillman saying much the same thing after his arrest—"That's not me." Except that Joe Betts was disowning the person he had been, not the act for which Tillman was imprisoned. Beneath Joe's plea, Darrow felt the man's fierce desire never to reprise memories that, whatever his reason, frightened him too deeply to conceal.

"I understand," Darrow said gently. "Do you happen to have a picture of Katie and the kids?"

With evident relief, Joe pulled a picture from his wallet, sliding it across the table. In her tennis dress, Katie Betts looked athletic and well-groomed, a classic blonde from some wealthy precinct of Connecticut. Standing beside her, a bright-eyed boy and his gap-toothed sister were laughing at something off-camera.

"Nice," Darrow affirmed. "I envy you, Joe."

*   *   *

DARROW LEFT THE Carriage House a little after nine o'clock. He stood on the sidewalk, breathing in the lightly humid air and recalling the summer evenings he had savored before his senior year at Caldwell transformed his memory. Reaching back in time, he located Donut King in his mental map of the past.

It was next to the Greyhound bus station, a one-story building with the same red neon sign. As he entered he saw, sitting at the counter, a man in a windbreaker and another in the jacket of a bowling team drinking fruit drinks, a new offering since Darrow had last come here after his high school prom. But the place still smelled like the glazed doughnuts he no longer allowed himself to eat.

A waitress in her fifties, peroxide-blond hair tightly curled, greeted him with a smile that lit her gaunt face. "You're Mark Darrow," she said.

Darrow smiled. "Guilty. And you are . . ."

"Pat Flynn. What can I get you?"

"Black coffee. Wish I had room for a doughnut—after twenty years, I can still taste them."

Flynn laughed. "I've been here so long I smell like one. But they're still good. Sure I can't tempt you?"

Darrow grinned. " 'You're a long time dead,' somebody once told me. So, sure."

She returned with coffee and a doughnut. "You've still got that same smile," she informed him. "Guess you're back to clean up this latest mess."

"That's the idea. Really, *this* mess isn't that bad."

At once Flynn became somber. "You mean no one died this time."

"Yeah." Darrow took a sip of coffee. "That can't have been easy for you, Pat."

She looked unsettled for a moment, and then the expression passed—Wayne was a small town, her role in Steve's trial common knowledge. "All I said is what I saw. It wasn't my place to say what it meant." More sadly, she added, "Still, I remember Steve Tillman coming in here a few times. Always polite. Always friendly, the last person you'd imagine doing what he did. But that's probably what all those dead girls thought about Ted Bundy, right up until his mask slipped."

Darrow eyed his doughnut. "You just don't know, I guess. Anyhow, you never told them it was Steve."

"God, no. At the time, I wasn't quite sure what I'd seen. It was all, like they say, circumstantial." Her mouth formed a wispy smile. "Guess I watch too much Court TV. But his frat buddy's the one who nailed him. I couldn't have picked the guy I saw out of a two-man lineup."

"How'd you even happen to be there?"

"It was late, past three o'clock, and I was so tired I could hardly see straight. My car was in the shop, so I decided to take a shortcut home." She poured Darrow a refill of coffee. "I'd done that a couple of times before—to me it was better than walking through deserted streets. Anyone you'd meet might be out for no good reason, whereas—or so I thought—the campus would be empty. Dumb, huh?"

"Not that anyone would have thought." Darrow sipped his coffee. "Where were you when you saw him?"

"Near College Hall, a fair distance from the Spire. There weren't any lights there. But the moon was full, as I recall, and there weren't any trees nearby to block the light. When I saw him, I just froze—half scared, half just surprised. At first I couldn't see her at all."

"How do you mean?"

"He had his back to me. So I couldn't tell *what* he was doing."

Darrow put the cup down. "I'm trying to envision this. If you were by Caldwell Chapel, and he had his back to you, then he must have been more or less facing in the direction of Steve Tillman's dorm."

Flynn squinted, searching her memory. "I guess so, yeah."

"Which was closer to you, the Spire or the man you saw?"

"The Spire."

"So he had his back to the Spire and was facing toward the dorm."

"Uh-huh." Her eyes became wary. "He wasn't coming *from* the dorm, if that's what you mean."

Darrow gave her an easy smile. "I'm not sure what I mean. *You* watch too much Court TV; *I've* spent too much time in courtrooms."

Flynn's face relaxed. "No, this is interesting. Thinking back, I don't believe Steve Tillman's lawyer asked me about all this."

Nordlinger had not, Darrow knew. "Could you make out what this guy was wearing?"

"Some sort of overcoat, I thought. Seemed like I could only see his legs below the knee."

"When did you first realize that he was carrying a body?"

Flynn glanced at her two other customers, assuring herself that they were content. "He turned sideways, sort of looking around. That was when I saw that he was cradling something—maybe a sack, is what I thought. Then he started to lay it down, and her arm sort of dangled." Her voice turned thin. "That was spooky. I thought maybe the person was drunk. But when he laid her down, she didn't move at all. The guy just hurried off, like he was afraid of being seen."

"Could you tell in which direction?"

"No. Like I said, except for the moon it was dark. He disappeared in seconds." She shook her head. "I still didn't know what I'd seen. But it really creeped me out."

Darrow nodded in sympathy. "Other than thinking he wore a coat, what do you remember about him?"

"That he was tall, and pretty slim, it seemed. Nothing else to remember. I couldn't have told you his age, or whether he was black or white or Asian or had landed in Roswell, New Mexico."

"Or if he was wearing glasses?"

"Nope. The police asked me that. If I couldn't see his face, I sure couldn't make out glasses."

"Guess not." Darrow feigned thought, as though something had just occurred to him. "Was there anything funny about how he walked?"

"How do you mean?"

"A limp, maybe."

Flynn considered this. "Not that I remember. Of course, his legs were mostly covered. Mainly, though, I just wanted to get out of there. So I did."

"Yeah. I would have, too."

Slowly, Flynn nodded, and then eyed his plate. "You going to eat your doughnut? Or you want a bag for that?"

Darrow smiled. "How about a bag?" he said. "I'll enjoy having it for breakfast."

16

IT WAS CLOSE TO ELEVEN WHEN DARROW LEFT THE DONUT King—time, he supposed, for the normal thirty-eight-year-old college president to go home to his empty bed. Instead, still arranging and rearranging facts—the compulsion of an ex-lawyer and Steve Tillman's onetime friend—he found himself heading for the Alibi Club.

The neighborhood had not changed much: as with the rest of Wayne, on the southeast side the global economy was, at most, a rumor. As he approached the club, a clump of young men on a corner eyed his Porsche with envy and suspicion. Parking on the half-empty street, Darrow approached the door of the Alibi Club, feeling that he was about to turn back time.

Hugo sat on his stool by the door, more massive than ever, his close-cropped hair turned white. His eyes widened at the sight of the newcomer, his mouth forming a grim smile of displeasure before he curtly nodded Darrow inside.

In the darkness, the first thing that hit Darrow was the pulse of rap music. He half-expected to spot some white kids at the bar, where he once had perched, chatting with Angela, while Steve scored pot from her brother. Instead, the patrons appeared older—men and a few women drinking whiskey or beer and listening to a rapper who, if

Darrow's ear was good, might be Kanye West. The smell of cigarettes and beer evoked the DBE party on the night of Angela's death; like prosperity, the anti-smoking movement had bypassed the neighborhood. But Farr's campus control measures had clearly worked—the club was no longer a haven for underage would-be alcoholics from Caldwell College. Darrow was the only white man in the place.

An older woman tended bar. Though Darrow had never seen Angela's mother, he could not have mistaken her—slender, she had a faded version of Angela's prettiness and grace. As with many black women in middle age, her eyes were older than her face, staring at Darrow with hostile weariness from a lineless mask. She held his gaze until he felt impelled to take a seat at the bar.

As he did, two men at the other end shot him a glance. The woman approached him, looking hard into Darrow's face. "So," she said curtly. "Do ghosts drink liquor?"

Darrow did not respond to this. "Hello, Mrs. Hall."

She laid her hands flat on the bar. "You're the last person I'd expect to see here."

Darrow nodded slightly. "If that dredges up hard feelings, I apologize."

"Hard memories," she said coldly. "You were one of the last to see my daughter alive, the first to see her dead. Except for your friend. I don't need you to remind me of how she looked when he got through."

Darrow weighed his response. "I can't claim to know how you feel, Mrs. Hall. But Angela and I were becoming friends. How she died still makes no sense to me."

She stared at him, repelling sympathy. "Do you want a drink, or not?"

"Cutty Sark, neat." Darrow was glad he had not eaten the doughnut.

After a time, she brought him his scotch, then watched him take a sip. "*What* made no sense?" she demanded.

"Something feels like it's missing." Darrow hesitated. "The night I saw her, she was drinking to get drunk. I didn't know her that well, but it bothered me enough to offer to drive her home."

Her voice softened slightly. "Lord knows I wish you had."

"She didn't want to go. It was like she was on a mission that night, but wouldn't talk about it."

"Maybe you're seeing a mystery where there was no mystery." Maggie Hall looked around herself, then back at Darrow, a sudden film appearing in her eyes. "Maybe, for once, my daughter wanted to escape. That's nothing to die over."

Darrow cocked his head. "Escape from what, Mrs. Hall?"

"From being so *good* all the time. If you knew her at all, you must know that much—working to meet expenses, studying late at night to keep from losing her scholarship, always scared to death of failure."

"Or just driven to succeed. I know she was set on going to a good law school."

Maggie Hall's eyes grew distant. "That was always her dream. Angela was the child with dreams."

The last was spoken with deep sadness, perhaps a hint of disdain for the child who had survived. Softly, Darrow said, "Still, working like that had been her life for all four years. Did something happen to make that harder?"

She gave him a probing look. "Maybe my girl just wore out. Why does any of this matter to you now?"

"Because I became part of it, and it's still with me." He took another swallow of scotch. "I guess you know they made me president of Caldwell."

"Who doesn't? It's like the pope showed up, except you're not wearing a dress."

Darrow knew better than to smile. "Fred Bender's our chief of security. The other day, I asked him about Angela. Fred gave me the sense that her life had changed in her last few months."

The woman's face closed. Relinquishing secrets about a child was hard, Darrow surmised—even a dead child. Maggie Hall had spoken to Bender in anguish and then, perhaps, with Angela buried and Steve convicted, reinterred her daughter in memory as the near-perfect striver. Now Darrow was digging her up.

"What good is this?" Maggie Hall said flatly. "She's dead."

"The reason still matters," Darrow answered. "After law school, I spent time prosecuting homicide cases. I can't help thinking about Angela. How she died and where I found her aren't quite adding up for me."

In a guarded tone, Hall said, "I don't follow."

"Steve Tillman still says Angela told him she needed to go somewhere—"

"What *would* he say?" Hall snapped. "It was two o'clock in the morning. Think my girl was going to the movies?"

"I understand your feelings about Steve. But suppose, just for a moment, that he was telling the truth. You told Fred Bender that Angela had started disappearing at night—that you didn't know where, and it wasn't like her."

Staring at the lacquered bar, Hall briefly closed her eyes. "I thought maybe it was to sleep with someone. A new guy called for her a couple of times—sounded like a white college boy, but he wouldn't leave his name or number."

Surprised, Darrow asked, "Do you think it was Steve?"

"I didn't know. But I asked her about it, the whole business of sneaking out," she said in a muted tone. "Angela got real angry. Her late father hadn't left us anything, she said, and I wasn't *paying* for anything. So I had no right to ask about her life, or how she made her way in the world."

"Did she often get that angry?"

"This was more like being defensive," Hall answered in a parched voice, "like I'd said out loud she was selling herself. So I asked her if she was.

"The girl just stared at me. 'You don't understand me at all,' she said. 'You don't understand my life at all.'" Hall's tone became harsher. "I wanted to bury the hurt of what she said, and the trial helped me do that. Or I think I'd have died from the hole in my heart."

Darrow wondered what right he had to strip-mine this woman's pain. But in the brutal logic of the law, someone should have done it long ago—certainly Steve Tillman's lawyer. "Fred Bender said you thought she was keeping a diary. I guess you don't know what happened to it, or what was in it."

Hall shook her head, either in affirmation or refusal to speak. After a moment, she said, "Finish your drink, Mr. Darrow. And please don't come back here again."

Darrow nodded. Maggie Hall's decision not to spy on her daughter, he supposed, had become her deepest wound: she was afraid that by shrinking from the truth she had caused Angela's death. Only Steve Tillman's guilt could salve her own.

Darrow paid for the drink and left.

17

Looking ahead to Friday night, Taylor proposed to provide their dinner. She enjoyed cooking, she explained, and they had largely exhausted Wayne's cuisine. All she needed was to borrow Darrow's kitchen. "With all respect," she told him, "I don't want your provost hovering around."

Laughing, Darrow said that was fine. He found himself looking forward to the evening.

The day was crystalline—electric-blue sky, a light pleasant breeze, little dampness in the air. Taylor called him in midafternoon, suggesting a change of plans. "Would you mind going to the riverbank?" she asked. "I haven't been there for a very long time."

Something in her tone suggested that this was more than a whim spurred by lovely weather. "Sure," Darrow said. "Do you want me to pick up something?"

"Maybe some wine," she answered. "I'll pull together a gourmet picnic from the heartland."

For whatever reason, she sounded preoccupied. "I'll bring a nice bottle," he said.

Darrow picked her up in his convertible. As they drove up Scioto Street with the top down, he was suddenly aware of the impression—

or misimpression—they might make: the president of Caldwell and his provost's daughter cruising through town, wind blowing her raven hair. "I think maybe I should garage the car," Darrow remarked. "It's beginning to feel a little ostentatious."

Smiling, Taylor did not answer. After a time she said, "I should give you directions."

"I know the way. I used to go out there all the time."

"Up to no good, I suppose."

Darrow grinned. "Depends on your point of view."

"I can imagine. But if you don't mind not reliving your off-the-field highlights, there's a place I'd like us to go."

As they sped through the sloping countryside, nearing the river, Taylor became quieter. "You okay?" he asked.

She turned to him. "This is going to sound kind of weird. We're going where my parents used to take me when I was young, to swim and picnic. But the last time I went there was with my father, to scatter my mother's ashes. I've never been able to go back."

Darrow thought of visiting his mother's grave. "Memories have their undertow," he said. "Sometimes it's best to face them."

Taylor gave him a pensive look. Perhaps, Darrow realized, she thought he was remembering his wife. But, this time, he had not been.

FLANKED BY TREES and grassy banks, the Miami River resembled a wide creek, perhaps a hundred feet across, its waters so serene and still that they barely created a ripple. At once Darrow thought of riverbank parties, fraternity raft races, dope and beer and sex at night in the grass. But Taylor's images, it seemed, began with the dawn of her memory.

They sat on a blanket in the light of summer's longest evening, drinking red Tuscan wine from plastic glasses. "At first," Taylor told him, "my dad would carry me in on his shoulders. When I was five, he gave me swimming lessons—sometimes a bit impatiently, like I was in boot camp for kindergartners. But I learned to swim, and not to be afraid. Fear, he always insisted, should be mastered."

Darrow tried to imagine Lionel Farr as the father of a little girl. "Did your mother swim as well?"

"She watched us, mainly. Often she'd write poetry or something in a journal she kept; other times she painted. Sometimes I'd see her smiling at me." Taylor's face clouded. "Most of these memories are from when I was six or seven. I don't remember her coming here much after that. Maybe it was her heart."

"Was that always a problem?"

Taylor spread pesto on two crackers and put them on Darrow's paper plate. "I don't really know. What I recall so vividly is finding her on the kitchen floor, unconscious, blood coming from her nose. My dad stayed calm—by the time the doctor arrived, she'd recovered." Taylor gazed out at the water. "Both my parents tried to reassure me. But every day until she died I worried that I'd lose her."

Darrow watched her face, filling with remembrance of a child's fears. "I came over that night, remember?"

"Did you?" Turning, Taylor smiled a little. "I don't recall that, so I *must* have been devastated. When I was young, you showing up was a real highlight."

Though she said this lightly, Darrow sensed she was not joking. "I didn't know I'd made such an impression."

"Part of it was your smile." Saying this, Taylor's own faint smile lingered. "That, and the way you talked with me, and listened."

Recalling her own vulnerability, Darrow reflected, seemed to soften her a little. "I remember everything about that day," he told her. "I came to tell your dad that Steve Tillman had been arrested."

Taylor shook her head. "Something so important to you, and for me it's like you were never there. The only other part I remember is sitting in the living room, the two of them trying to reassure me. My mother had a heart condition, she explained—sometimes her blood pressure would drop suddenly and she'd just pass out. There was medication for it; I needn't worry. I fought back tears: somehow it was important to show them—him, really—that I wasn't afraid. Then my mother promised that she'd always be there for me."

Her deep blue eyes, though directed at Darrow, seemed focused on the past. "But you didn't believe her."

"No. Her promise scared me more than anything else they'd said. That was when I knew she wasn't like other moms, that she might leave me in an instant. After that, whenever I'd come back from school, I'd go through the house, heart in my throat, until I found her. When I did, she'd smile—in a sad and knowing kind of way, I think now—and give me a hug."

To fear losing a mother, Darrow reflected, must have been haunting for a girl that young. He wondered whether Taylor's fear had been more long-standing and intuitive, preceding her discovery of Anne lying unconscious on the kitchen floor. That might explain the solemnity of the lovely child he remembered and, perhaps, her retreat into painting and drawing. "She hugged me every day," Taylor concluded simply. "Five months' worth of hugs, and she was gone."

Darrow nodded. "I went to class that morning, and Lionel wasn't there. You found her, didn't you?"

"Yes." Taylor paused, as though summoning the will to say more. When she did, her words were so vivid that Darrow, listening, could imagine how she felt.

IT WAS A bright spring morning, a little before eight o'clock. That semester her father taught an early class, so Anne drove Taylor to school. But on this day her mother did not seem to have awakened.

Tentative, Taylor walked down the hallway to Anne's bedroom. Her parents had begun sleeping apart—her father was a restless sleeper, Anne had told her recently, with dreams that seemed to surface from the murky void of Vietnam. Leaning her face against the bedroom door, Taylor heard no stirring. She knocked on the door, and still there was no sound.

Taylor steeled herself, then cracked open the bedroom door.

She half-expected—deeply hoped—to find her mother stirring. Instead, Anne lay on top of the covers, still and very pale. Something about the cast of her face did not resemble sleep; it was as though, Taylor thought, her soul had left behind a shell.

Taylor could not touch her. Turning, she rushed out the door and ran toward the campus, heart pounding wildly, tears streaming down her face. She arrived at her father's classroom out of breath.

He saw her standing in the doorway and knew at once what must have happened.

Calmly, Farr faced his students and explained that he had to leave. Then he took her by the hand, his grip firm, and hurried across the campus, urging Taylor to run with him as fast as she could.

Reaching the house, he paused briefly at the door, then pushed it open. "Where is she?" he asked.

Mute, Taylor pointed toward Anne's bedroom. Her father swiftly climbed the stairs, Taylor following.

The bedroom door was open. Her father knelt by the bed, feeling for Anne Farr's pulse. Briefly, Taylor saw his eyes shut, and then he turned to her.

"She's gone," he told her gently.

LISTENING, DARROW REMEMBERED Farr kneeling by a murdered girl, the beginning of a terrible, tragic year. Now he wondered if Farr had thought of Angela Hall as he pronounced his own wife dead.

"I remember him calling the doctor," Taylor finished. "After that it's all a blur. Except that I still recall, very distinctly, how kind you were to me at her memorial service. I didn't want to let you go."

"I wish I could have helped more."

Taylor gazed out at the water. "I don't know what else you could have done. I went into a kind of fugue state, as though I were sedated. My next clear memory is when we came here with my mother's ashes." She turned to Darrow again, as if returning to the present. "I hope you don't mind my bringing you here. But I needed to come, and not with my father. I guess this is what you get to do for me, after fifteen years."

"A long time," Darrow said softly.

"Right now," she answered, "it's yesterday."

THE AFTERNOON HER father chose was sunny and mild; the trees were budding with new growth, and slanting sun lightened the blue-brown waters. When Taylor could not bring herself to open the urn that held her mother's ashes, Farr took it from her hands.

"This was always her wish," he explained. "Ever since she learned that her time with us might be too short. Your mother loved beauty—lived for it, really, when she wasn't living for you. When her heart began to fail, she told me that she wanted to be part of nature in a place we three had shared. A place where we could remember her fondest memories."

Taylor had no reason to dispute this. Nor could she imagine her mother trapped in a box, with six feet of earth between her and the light she so loved. Complying with her father's instructions, Taylor helped him scatter her mother's ashes on the glistening surface of the river, watching the gray and silver remnants recede from sight. Suddenly, Taylor was bereft: her mother had vanished from this place, and from her life. There was nowhere she could whisper secrets to her, even if her mother could not answer.

She looked up at her father. His smile, meant to be of comfort, made her feel angry and alone.

"EVEN THEN," TAYLOR told Darrow, "I knew it was unfair. He must have been hurting too, and he tried to give me solace. But he couldn't.

"Certainly, I was no comfort to him. For me he was Lionel Farr, the Special Forces officer and great professor. *She* was my mother."

Darrow found the story painful. He imagined two people, isolated by their own sorrow, without the gift to reach for each other. "How was Lionel as a father?" he asked.

Distractedly, Taylor sipped her wine. "In many ways, a stranger. *You* knew him better, I think. You were almost an adult, and I imagine he saw you as a quasi son he could launch into the world, a living reflection of himself.

"I don't mean that as harshly as it sounds—in the best of parents, love can't be separated from ego. But I was her daughter, not his son. I could never crack his code."

"Because you were a girl?"

"That's part of it, I think—he didn't know what to do with me." She paused, recrossing her legs, moving a little closer to Darrow. "He'd come of age in the fifties, then entered the most masculine environment there was—West Point. In those days, men not only weren't taught to understand women, they didn't think it was possible. Even a wife or a daughter."

"Maybe so," Darrow said. "But don't think my relationship with Lionel was warm and fuzzy—he's more a combat leader than a therapist. Not that there haven't been moments. When Lee was killed, he shared his feelings about your mother, as one man who'd lost his wife to another. And in college he always made sure I had enough money, like the time he got me a job taking around prospective students. But our relationship was about mentoring and exhortation, making sure I realized whatever potential I had." Darrow's voice softened. "I owe who I am to Lionel. But there were a few important things I had to learn on my own."

Taylor surprised him by smiling. "Like listening to girls?"

Darrow laughed. "And old friends."

Taylor shook her head. "I think you care about people, period. I also think you'd rather listen to others than talk about yourself. It's partly a strategy of avoidance."

The comment was so accurate that it took Darrow by surprise. "Am I that obvious?"

"Maybe to me," Taylor said. "But my course in Mark Darrow studies began when you were seventeen. You've changed a lot, and very little."

"That *is* disheartening," Darrow replied. "And more than a little scary. You were seven, Taylor."

"And very perceptive," she said briskly. "Then, and now. Which is why I'd guess that working with my father is not exactly problem-free."

This time surprise made Darrow laugh. "Not *too* problematic. But for someone in my position, Lionel has the faults of his virtues."

Taylor gave him a keen look of interest. "Such as?"

Darrow had meant to reveal these thoughts to no one. But Taylor's directness, and perhaps the wine, made elaboration tempting—especially given her insight into Lionel Farr. "In confidence?" he asked.

"Of course," Taylor said with some impatience. "In case you haven't grasped this, I've said more to you in one night than to my father in either millennium."

"Okay." Pausing, Darrow organized his thoughts. "As you suggest, your dad is a classic 'guy'—give him a problem, and he'll fix it; give him a void, and he'll fill it. Because he's also a born leader, regardless of whatever role he's in.

"In a crisis, he thinks faster and better than anyone. When Angela Hall was murdered, Lionel had the instincts Clark Durbin lacked. In a very real way your father cemented Durbin's presidency, as surely as he made me who I am. So in return for Lionel propping him up, Durbin turned over the internal management of the school.

"All in all, your dad is a man of prodigious gifts—that Caldwell's still afloat is mainly due to him. But Lionel amasses power like a magnet draws iron filings. Add his considerable force of personality, and people are very disinclined to tell him no. *That,* I realize more and more, is how I became president."

"You didn't sense that all along?"

"Of course I did. But it seems more troubling now that I'm here.

One example is the faculty—their power's too entrenched, and their sway over hiring, tenure, and curriculum reflect Lionel's own prerogatives. In some very important ways, Clark Durbin became a figurehead. Which suited your dad just fine, I think, right up to the moment a chunk of Caldwell's money disappeared."

Listening closely, Taylor frowned. "But you're a wholly different proposition than Durbin. My father may be willful, Mark. But he also can be quite subtle, and he's certainly no fool."

"Never that," Darrow agreed. "But extremely confident in his own vision. So sometimes he doesn't see other people as clearly as he usually does. I've noticed a couple instances of that, one regarding a female foreign student who was sleeping with her professor. To me, it was a delicate situation, and Lionel's touch a little off."

Taylor poured them more wine. "That's the old adage," she remarked. "My father can read the notes, but can't always hear the music. And I believe he knows it. That was part of our problem, I think. It may also be why he never married again."

Darrow scrutinized her, curious. "How are the two of you doing?"

Taylor shrugged. "Now that I'm an adult, I don't think I was always fair to him. Part of growing up is perceiving that Dad and Mom aren't Adam and Eve—that your parents had parents too. One reason I came back is to see if I could make things better."

"Are they?"

For a moment, Taylor was quiet, gazing at the tranquil river as its color dulled in the fading light. "A little. Maybe I'm just more accepting. Which would certainly be suitable for a twenty-eight-year-old."

To Darrow, this sounded more aspirational than heartfelt. Watching her face in profile, he found himself hoping that, before Taylor left, he could help bridge the lingering divide between two people he cared about.

The thought brought him up short. He had cared about Lionel Farr for over half his life, perhaps even loved him. Now—he did not know quite when—he had begun to care for Lionel's daughter. No doubt this connection was rooted in their past. But perhaps, he suddenly realized, there were reasons still to be discovered.

For a long time, neither spoke at all. Then, without wholly understanding the impulse, Darrow took Taylor's hand.

She did not turn. Her only acknowledgment that anything had happened was the slightest tightening of her fingers around his. Quietly, she requested, "Tell me about your mother."

The inquiry surprised him. Instinctively, Darrow had expected her to ask about his wife. But in Taylor, he had begun to understand, sensitivity followed perception.

"Not much to tell," Darrow answered. "She was a woman of moods—all mutable, many frightening. When you're a kid, it's hard learning to be scared of the person every instinct says should be your protector.

"I wanted to love her, but I couldn't. When they locked her in the asylum, I was relieved; when she killed herself, I felt nothing at all. Later on I learned that she came from a dynasty of schizophrenics, and understood how damaged she must have been. But the damage made her impossible to love."

Taylor absorbed this. "That must be hard, Mark. Even now."

"Not really. I moved on—I started my own life, began looking forward to a family of my own, nothing like the one I came from. I still try not to think about her much. Her legacy, if there is one, is that I try to do my best to see people whole, for who they are and what they've been through. Especially those who matter to me."

Taylor asked nothing more. After a time, she moved closer. Darrow could smell her hair, fresh and lightly scented. Suddenly he felt the pulse in his own throat.

Tentative, he turned her face to his. Her eyes were open, their expression both expectant and surprised. "What . . ." she began to ask.

Darrow kissed her. Pressing against him, Taylor's lips were soft and warm.

After a moment she broke the kiss, resting her forehead against his. "As I was saying," she murmured.

Darrow's skin still tingled. "Yes?"

He sensed her reluctance to speak. "Before tonight, you acted like I was still a child. Then I revert to childhood, talking about my mother—and now this. Is being a child-woman what you want from me?"

Though the wariness of her question startled him, it spoke to her honesty, her desire for this in others. "No," he answered firmly. "That's the opposite of how I've come to see you. I may be ten years older, but I'm way too young to be your father."

She rested her arms on his shoulders. Softly, she asked, "Then where do you think we're going with this?"

Darrow hesitated. "Home, I thought."

"Home?"

He sensed a smile in her voice. "My place," he answered. "Our original destination, if you'll recall."

As she drew back, looking into his face, Darrow detected a disbelief and wonder that seemed to match his own. "That was before you kissed me."

Darrow kissed her again, slowly and deeply. "Okay," Taylor said with a modest sigh. "Really, it was about time."

IN THE LIGHT and shadow of his bedroom, Darrow undressed her. What he could see of her body was as beautiful as her face.

Holding hands, they walked to his bed.

They touched each other, filled with desire, yet both wishing not to hurry. In time his mouth found all of her.

"Now," she whispered.

Darrow slipped inside her, still aware of her responses, yet lost in the moment. Only at the edge of consciousness did he sense something within her that Taylor still held back. Then he felt her shudder, heard the cry she repressed.

Briefly, Darrow wondered at this. Then he gave himself up to wanting her.

Afterward, they lay close together in the dark, feeling the dampness of their skin, the depth of what they felt. Darrow touched her face. "Are you okay with this?" he asked.

"More than okay." Her voice lowered. "I hope you'll give me time."

Darrow felt surprised. "I didn't know I was holding tryouts."

"It's not you," she demurred. "Definitely not you. But I've always been slow to trust, and sometimes it follows me to bed. I wish I could tell you why. But I worry about losing myself, or giving any man too much power over me."

"I don't want that. Or need it."

Taylor took his hand. "I think I know that about you. But then, in a way, I've known you for a very long time."

"Maybe so," Darrow said lightly. "But I'm sure *this* didn't occur to either of us. At least I hope not."

"When I was seven? Hardly—I didn't even know that I had a crush on you. But I did think you were the most beautiful person I'd ever seen." Taylor laughed at herself. "The first time I saw you again, I *still* thought that. Think that makes me shallow?"

"Then so am I. Even when you were a child, I thought you were very pretty. But looking at you now, you damn near take my breath away. Except you've no doubt heard similar things too often to trust them, either."

He felt Taylor's mood turn serious again. "I've just never been sure it mattered much. Especially at times like this one."

Darrow hesitated. Then, by instinct, he spoke aloud another thought that took him by surprise. "Then try this instead, Taylor. You're the first woman since Lee died who can make me forget her. Not just tonight. For moments at a time, I'm simply *with* you. That's a bigger gift to me than you can ever know."

Taylor moved closer, breasts touching his chest. "Then I guess I'll stay."

"Was there a question?"

"Several." Taylor paused again. "Like my father, sometimes I have nightmares. I don't want to wake you up."

She was serious, Darrow realized. "Nightmares about what?"

"The usual panoply, I suppose. Fears, random scraps from the subconscious, the dregs of one's imagination. It really doesn't matter."

But it did to Taylor, Darrow sensed. "I want you to stay," he affirmed. "Including for breakfast. That way you won't pass your father as he's going out the door for our squash game."

Taylor summoned a theatrical moan of horror. "God," she said. "That's absolutely Greek."

"I agree. So let's deal with it later."

Taylor gave him the complicit kiss of a co-conspirator. Later, Darrow lay awake, absorbing what had happened to them. Taylor slept through the night.

18

IN AT 10:00 A.M., DARROW AND LIONEL FARR PLAYED SQUASH at Caldwell's gym.

They had never played before. The game was Farr's idea: no quarter was given or sought; neither man liked to lose, Farr even less than Darrow. Punctuated by the quick, hollow thud of their tennis shoes, the green ball ricocheted off the white walls, pursued by an echo, a rubberized whine that carried into the next hit. Though swifter and younger, Darrow was less experienced; Farr's grim determination was aided by the guile of a veteran who had mastered the tactics and geometry of the nearly claustrophobic rectangle. For an hour they fought for dominance, playing with a trapped intensity until Darrow felt propelled by reserves of adrenaline, half conscious. On the final point, Farr slashed a wickedly angled shot to Darrow's right. With an instinct driven by the harsh lessons of the last hour, Darrow, anticipating this, lunged, skidding on his chest as he stretched to hit the rubber ball with a desperate flick of his wrist. The ball looped off the front wall just beyond Farr's reach. Darrow's point, Darrow's game.

Breathing deeply, Farr watched the ball dying in small bounces at his feet with a last rubbery whimper. Grimacing in disgust, he told Darrow, "You'll never do that again."

Sprawled on the wooden floor, Darrow laughed. "I'm never playing you again. To quote the immortal Rocky, 'No rematches.'"

"Unacceptable," Farr said curtly. "For someone who barely edged a man in late middle age—on a lucky shot, at that—you're far too pleased with yourself."

"No triumph too small," Darrow responded dryly.

Farr managed a sour smile.

There was no one waiting for the court. The two men sat, backs against the wall, drinking from bottles of mineral water. In a serious tone, Farr said, "There's something we should talk about."

The subject, Darrow guessed, might well be Taylor. "What is it?"

"The latest student contretemps—allegations of date rape, to be precise."

Shaking his head, Darrow turned to his erstwhile competitor. "What are the specifics?"

"They're fairly unsympathetic. Three nights ago, it seems, an inebriated sorority girl invited two guys back to her dorm room for a three-way. Both admit being quite enthusiastic—"

"Jesus," Darrow interjected. "Don't our summer students ever go to class? Or even to sleep?"

"Apparently not. As far as I can sort this out, one boy penetrated her to climax. Before the other could follow suit, her friends burst in and broke things up.

"That was Wednesday. Yesterday, our venturesome young lady charged the one who *didn't* penetrate her with rape, claiming that he'd intimidated her. I don't see that as likely, but she's becoming quite belligerent." Farr's tone became astringent. "No doubt some of this indignation reflects her assertion that the guy in question ripped her forty-dollar underwear.

"Grounds for moral outrage these days, I'm sure. Whatever the case, I get to deal with this farce. As provost, I'm the final arbiter in charges involving student conduct."

"A neutral arbiter, I'm sure."

"Naturally," Farr responded with weary disgust. "However un-sympathetic the complainant, or incredible her charges."

"Maybe on the surface," Darrow cautioned. "Likely this woman's claims are meant to cover her own embarrassment. But, if not, she may have been too drunk to report this right away." He paused a moment. "As both of us are well aware, in cases like this it's hard to ever know."

"Not every case is Angela Hall, Mark."

Darrow turned to him. "Nonetheless, I don't want to hang these guys for something too ambiguous to resolve. But we need to hear this woman out."

"Of course," Farr answered crisply. "But there's no guarantee she won't go running to Dave Farragher. Absent his involvement, I'll give our newly vehement complainant a hearing so dispassionate and thor-ough that your law professors at Yale would be proud."

"I never doubted it." Pausing, Darrow wiped the sweat off his forehead. "Speaking of Farragher, he called me at home this morning. Now that I've settled in, he said, he'd like to buy me a drink. You wouldn't happen to know what might have spurred this."

Farr sipped some mineral water, gazing at the opposite wall. "I think I do, actually. I imagine you do, too."

Darrow turned to him again. More sharply than intended, he asked, " 'Think,' Lionel? Or know."

Farr kept his own voice casual. "Ray Carrick called me yesterday. To paraphrase his bluster, he wonders why you're more concerned with exhuming a sixteen-year-old corpse than with prosecuting Clark Durbin for stealing Caldwell's money."

Darrow was irritated. "Setting aside Ray's characterization, who told him that I was?"

"It seems Dave Farragher's tumbled to your bedside reading. As you well know, once you asked for the transcript, Dave was bound to hear about it. What you may not have known is that Ray is one of Farragher's closest friends."

"Terrific."

Farr placed a hand on Darrow's shoulder. "Caldwell's small, and so is Wayne. So's the core group of men who run our board of trustees." His tone became avuncular. "For all our sakes, it's not the time for your interest in the Hall case to become a focus of their attention. Please treat Farragher with the exquisite tact you'd have me lavish on our female complainant. Like her, Dave may feel a little aggrieved. Perhaps for better reasons."

Unsettled, Darrow wondered whether Farr's involvement in this matter ended with Carrick's phone call. "Is there anything else I should know?" he asked.

For a moment, Farr was quiet. "Nothing important, Mark. Once you consider your options, you'll know what to do."

IN THE EVENT, Darrow's hour with Farragher was mainly pleasant; Dave Farragher was an amiable man, with a ready smile and a forthright air, burnished by fifteen years spent shrewdly tending the political capital engendered by the conviction of Steve Tillman. The venue, Wayne's country club, was unpretentious and relaxed, a rambling white wooden structure from the twenties where everyone knew everyone else. Sitting near the bar, for a half hour the two men talked about predictable subjects—how much Farragher admired Darrow's athletic and professional successes; how the community and college had changed and not changed; the shock of Clark Durbin's misconduct, now so evident; the resulting challenges Darrow faced as president. Only during the second drink did Farragher mention the murder of Angela Hall.

"Look," he concluded with an air of puzzlement. "I know Steve Tillman was your closest friend. But what in particular has caught your eye? You're a smart guy, Mark, and I'm wondering if there's anything I missed."

With his ruddy, open face and clear blue eyes, Farragher was a portrait of candor. But the question was so disingenuous that Darrow repressed a smile. Amiably, he answered, "I don't think you missed a thing, Dave."

A flicker of relief showed in Farragher's eyes. "Really?"

"Really. In fact, there are two things I don't doubt at all. That you and the police were extremely thorough, and that you're a way better lawyer than Griff Nordlinger."

Farragher chuckled briefly. "You give me too much credit."

"Not at all," Darrow assured him. "In fact, if Nordlinger had been the prosecutor and you'd been Steve's defense lawyer, I think he might have walked."

Farragher picked up his scotch, then put it down unsipped. "The court of appeals," he responded, "upheld Steve's conviction. So did the Ohio Supreme Court. Both rejected inadequacy of counsel as grounds for a reversal.

"I know what you're thinking—that doesn't make Griff adequate. But the case against Tillman was there, and the appellate courts so found."

Darrow nodded. "I've read both opinions. But, as a practical matter, why do *you* think the jurors found Steve guilty?"

The thrust of the question, directed at third parties, seemed to make Farragher relax again. "You can tick them off," he said. "Tillman and Angela Hall had sex. There were scratches on his back, a bruise on her face. If you believed Joe Betts—and the jury did—Steve lied to them on the witness stand.

"Add to that the absence of any other plausible suspect. Disparage Griff as you will, but there was nothing anyone could pin on Betts—or, for that matter, Carl Hall. Nor, despite her nocturnal wanderings, could any of us locate a boyfriend in Angela's recent life; at best, her mother remembered an anonymous white guy calling once or twice. No one found *him*, either."

"And the diary?"

Farragher spread his hands. "Who's to say it ever existed? And if it did, who in the world could have taken it from under her mattress?"

"An excellent question," Darrow concurred mildly.

"*We* thought so." Farragher took a gulp of scotch. "Believe me, we didn't stop investigating just because we'd arrested Tillman. We even checked out whether there were any known stalkers in the area, although the idea that someone like that would be on campus at three A.M. was pretty far-fetched. Nothing.

"In the end, Griff had no alternative killer. There was none. The jury had no choice but to return a guilty verdict." Farragher looked squarely into Darrow's face. "As for me, I wouldn't have brought the case unless I was morally certain that Tillman strangled Angela Hall. Why, only *he* knows for sure."

Darrow held his gaze. "As I recall, you gave the jury a couple of possibilities to ponder. One was that, in high school, Steve had broadcast his racial bias. You pretty much clobbered him with that on cross."

"Tillman was a bigot," Farragher said crisply. "And Angela *was* black."

"And Griff Nordlinger opened all that up by putting Steve on the witness stand, then not objecting to your questions."

"I don't know that he *could* have objected. Once Tillman claimed to have cared so much about Angela, he opened up questions of credibility. I'd have been derelict not to bring out Tillman's racism." Farragher shrugged dismissively. "I'm sure the jury viewed all that as secondary. On closing argument, Griff argued quite vigorously that we'd never offered a motive."

Darrow sipped his martini. In an even tone, he observed, "Still, you had the last word on rebuttal, including with respect to motive. That was the first time you floated Fred Bender's theory—that Steve strangled Angela Hall to stop her from reporting a rape. Maybe I missed something. But I couldn't find any evidence in the transcript to support that. And the suggestion itself is lethal. Had you been Nordlinger, you'd have asked for a mistrial." Matter-of-factly, Darrow finished: "Which makes my original point, I think. From beginning to end, you were a whole lot sharper."

Though blandly delivered, the double-edged compliment induced in Farragher a somewhat cornered look. "My statement on rebuttal implied facts that *were* before the jury—that Angela was a proud and assertive woman committed to women's rights." Farragher paused a moment, then added in a straightforward manner, "You were once a prosecutor, Mark. In a situation like that, wouldn't *you* have been tempted to do the same?"

"That's hard for me to say, Dave. I never faced a defense counsel quite that bad." Darrow finished his drink. "A cynical colleague once said that a trial is where twelve people gather after a performance to vote for who they thought was the best lawyer. If so, you won."

Farragher regarded him with a quizzical smile. "Seems like we'll just have to agree to disagree. I wish you luck at Caldwell, Mark."

They parted with a civil handshake.

19

ON SUNDAY MORNING, DARROW AND TAYLOR PLAYED TENNIS. At Darrow's invitation, Taylor drove them in his Porsche. On the way to the municipal courts, Darrow asked, "What is it with the Farrs and smacking balls with rackets?"

Taylor kept her eyes on the road, a smile playing on her lips. "I heard you played squash with Dad. How was it?"

"Brutal. Even worse was that I won. He's not a happy loser."

Taylor's enigmatic smile lingered. "How well I know it. When *I* beat him, he sulked for half a day. I'm hoping you're a better sport."

Darrow stared at her. She did not seem to be joking.

They parked beside an empty court. Taylor hopped out and walked ahead of him, eager to get started, long legs moving in swift, confident strides. She did not appear to have an ounce of body fat.

Standing at the service line, she said, "Want to hit some practice serves?"

"Sure. You first."

Darrow went to the opposite side, crouching behind the service box. Eyes narrowing in concentration, Taylor tossed the ball in the air and then, stretching her five feet eight inches until she stood on the tips of her toes, extended the racket high above her head and uncoiled a swing so smooth and powerful that the ball became a blur, skidding past Darrow before he could even react.

"Guess I'm ready," she said laconically. "Your turn."

Darrow walked to the net. "Anything more you'd like to tell me, Taylor?"

Unable to contain herself, she grinned. "Okay, I was captain of the women's tennis team at Trumble. I also played at Williams—which is probably why they let me in. So please don't be too hard on yourself."

Darrow lasted two sets. Though fit, he was untutored; despite a little rustiness, Taylor covered the court like a greyhound, swift of foot and eye, settling into a rhythm, one smooth stroke after another speeding the ball to where Darrow was not. By the end of the second set—another 6–2 loss for Darrow—he was winded. Taylor met him at the net, the light of not-so-innocent triumph in her eyes. "You did great," she told him generously. "It's probably just the difference in our ages."

Darrow laughed. "You're certainly a gracious winner. I can guess who first taught you how to play."

"Of course he did. Those were among our better moments, at least after I could hit with him—silent communication, like a dad and son playing catch. And my dad was a good teacher. But I could never shake the feeling that he wished I were a boy."

"That would have been a waste," Darrow answered with a smile. "Think he knows what's going on?"

"With us? I'm not sure. But if we continue like we did the other night, he will."

Within this comment, Darrow sensed, lurked a question about their relationship and one unspoken aspect of it: in other circumstances, that Farr was Darrow's provost would be inherently problematic. Tilting his head, Darrow asked, "What would you like to do tonight?"

Taylor bit her lip in pretended thought. "Well," she said at length,

"I suppose I could always shower at the museum of bad taste you call home—there's a change of clothes in my duffel bag. What do *you* want to do?"

Leaning across the net, Darrow kissed her. "I was hoping for a re-match," he told her.

As SHE STEPPED into the shower after him, Darrow gazed at her in open appreciation. Everything about her, he thought, was beautiful: her face, her elegant neck, rounded breasts with brown areolas, flat stomach, womanly hips that tapered from the black fur in the midst to long, slender legs. An athlete, he thought again, or a runway model—both and neither. She was uniquely Taylor Farr.

She looked into his face, not shy. "Have you never showered with a girl before?"

Not since Lee, he thought. "It's as I said, Taylor. Sometimes you don't leave room for anyone else."

"For me," she answered simply, "there's no one else in the way."

After the shower, they slipped into bed.

The sheets felt crisp and cool, Taylor's skin warm. Darrow's lips found her stomach, her nipples, the hollow of her neck. He could feel her breath catch, hear the soft murmur of desire in her throat. When at last he entered her, she spoke his name.

After that, the only sounds were not speech but guides to the movements of their bodies, synchronized by instinct until both shud-dered as one. Eyes opening, Taylor looked up into his face. "Mark Darrow," she murmured. "So nice of you to find me after I grew up."

QUIET, TAYLOR LAY in his arms.

As he held her, Darrow found himself remembering doing this with Lee, lazy Sunday mornings at their town house in Boston. He felt a moment of confusion: the tug of past loyalties, eroding the sweet-ness of this moment with Taylor; and yet the sense that, by replicating an act of tenderness he had once shared with his wife—and, at last, by wishing to—he was slipping further away from the past. "What are you thinking?" Taylor asked.

"Many things. Including about you. I was also remembering Boston, and the place I used to live."

"And where all your things still are."

Not just his things, Darrow thought; as Taylor's remark implied, the house was filled with memories. He supposed that was why he never brought another woman there. "Speaking of Boston," Taylor told him, "I had some news yesterday. The Museum of Fine Arts has offered me an interview. Seems they're developing an interest in postmodernism, after all."

Darrow was surprised. He propped his elbow on the pillow, cradling his head in his hand. "I thought you didn't like Boston."

Taylor smiled. "Now that there's some interest there, I've decided I just don't *know* Boston. So I told them I'd come in."

"When are you going?"

"I'm not sure yet. We're still working that out."

Darrow thought for a moment. "Why don't we go together. My former partners want me to consult on a couple of cases I turned over, and I owe my town house an inspection. If you like, I can try to fit my dates with yours."

Taylor gave him an inquiring look. "Is that something you really want to do?"

"Sure," Darrow said, even as he realized that they might be crossing another bridge. "I can show you around a little. It might be fun for us to get away from Wayne."

Taylor kissed him. "As long as you can find us a place to stay."

THAT AFTERNOON, AS was now his custom, Darrow visited Steve Tillman at the penitentiary. Speaking through the slits in the Plexiglas, Steve asked sardonically, "So how was *your* week?"

Darrow did not blink. "Fine, Steve. And yours?"

Steve gave him a crooked smile. "They're great believers in

structure here. We're a 'special needs' community—surprises might unsettle the student body. As usual, I've been using my leisure time to read."

"Anything in particular?"

"My current area of concentration," Steve said with mock gravity, "is twentieth-century Europe. Specifically, the rise of the Nazis in Weimar Germany. The topics include the role of World War I, the Versailles Treaty, inflation, economic collapse, and, of course, anti-Semitism. Hanging over all this, naturally, is the specter of the Holocaust—the central question being 'Why Germany?' A lot for me to think about, wouldn't you say?"

However ironic, this disquisition was so unlike anything that might have issued from his college friend that, again, Darrow was overcome by a sense of waste. "Actually, I've been thinking a lot about the Hall case."

Steve stared at him. "I *always* do, Mark. For you, it's optional." He paused, then spoke more evenly. "Don't think I held a grudge about what you told the police. That part you couldn't help. What sticks in my craw is that you just disappeared—fewer visits, then letters, then fewer letters, then nothing. You did a very thorough job of moving on. Maybe that's what you're best at."

Stung, Darrow tried to distance himself from his own emotions. "Sometimes I wish I were better at it. But about drifting away from you, no excuses. Except maybe for the last couple of years, when it felt like I was seeing the world through a very thick pane of glass."

"Like Plexiglas?" Steve gibed. "From where I sit, you seem pretty okay to me. Better than you did when you first showed up."

Darrow waited a moment. "Let me ask you something, Steve. Do you know anything about Angela keeping a diary?"

"No. What was in it?"

"I don't know. But her mother says she kept one. If so, it's disappeared. Which is also what Angela herself began doing, late at night, in the weeks before she died. Was any of that time spent with you?"

Steve inhaled, eyes fixed on Darrow. "Mark," he said slowly, "I don't have a fucking clue about any of this. If Angela and I had been screwing in the dorm, you'd have known about it."

"Yeah, I guess so."

"Guess?" Steve's laugh, though brief, held a hint of humor. "How many times were both of us in and out of each other's rooms? Remember when I walked in on you and Connie Coolman?"

Darrow smiled. "That *was* a bad night—for Connie, and for me. She was so embarrassed she completely lost interest."

"Connie was always old-fashioned. Guess she didn't count on *two* guys seeing her naked." Steve's expression darkened. "Wish you'd barged in the night I was with Angela. By now all three of us might have been able to laugh about it."

The sad image silenced Darrow for a moment. "Before that night," he asked, "had you ever called Angela at home?"

"No. I don't think I even had her number."

"Then how did you ask her to the party?"

"I was at the club when she was tending bar. I had a couple of drinks, and it began to seem like a good idea." Steve looked down. "This may sound pathetic, but I still didn't know her all that well. I don't even know what I had in mind. We just seemed to like each other."

Darrow nodded. "That fall, I don't remember you going out with anyone. Were you?"

"No," Steve answered curtly. "Maybe you've forgotten, what with all you've had to think about in life. But I spent a whole damn year brooding over Laurie Shilts dumping me for that asshole Betts. If anyone held a grudge, it should have been me."

At once Darrow remembered this: the hurt of losing Laurie had compounded the wound inflicted by the sudden end of Steve's football career, accelerating his downward spiral. "Have any idea why Joe was so pissed off that night?"

"About me and Angela? Betts didn't need a reason. It only took a drink or two to release his inner jerk."

"Did they have some sort of relationship?"

"Not that I know about. Betts was still with Laurie, remember? I couldn't figure out why he wanted Angela. Except maybe that she was with me."

"Maybe so. But I ran into Laurie that night, Steve. She and Joe had just broken up."

"No shit? Did she say why?"

Darrow hesitated. "Not directly. But for her part, Laurie was very clear that she and Joe were through."

Intent, Steve pondered this. "Then maybe it *was* about Angela. Guess you'd have to ask Laurie. Any idea where she is?"

"No. But I could find out easily enough. To escape our development office, you have to enter the witness protection program."

Steve did not smile. "If you find her," he said softly, "tell Laurie I said hi."

To Darrow, the statement was at once wistful and bitter. "I know you've gone over this a thousand times," he said. "But do you have any idea at all why Joe said he'd seen you outside the dorm?"

"Besides that he's spiteful enough to lie?" Steve's voice became hard. "I've thought about that for fifteen years—my brilliant lawyer made quite a point of asking who would have killed her, then carried her body all the way to the Spire. But he never gave the jury an answer. Thanks to him, I've had the time to develop one on my own. Joe Betts."

Though Darrow had been expecting this, hearing it spoken aloud was jarring. "It's a theory," he allowed. "But Joe would have had to maintain an insane level of anger for several hours, wait for her outside the dorm, then strangle her. That's obsessive to the point of madness. It also raises the question of where you imagine Angela was going."

A new brightness made Steve's eyes glint. "Still, I can see I'm not alone. You've thought about it, too. So who strikes you as likeliest to kill a woman? Betts or me?"

Darrow did not answer. "Is there any way that you could be innocent and Joe still be telling the truth?"

"How? Because I blacked out, and sort of sleepwalked out of the dorm? Or maybe wanted a gulp of air at the same time Betts did? Or maybe I followed Angela in a drunken stupor to the Spire, changed my mind about killing her, then left before somebody else did. And then literally forgot about it." Steve shook his head in seeming bewilderment. "Of course, I forgot a lot of things that night. The last thing I remember, or *believe* I remember, is Angela saying she had to leave. And what sense does that make?"

"I don't know. There are a few things about this no one can make sense of."

"One person can," Steve said succinctly. "The guy who actually killed her. *He* knows everything. Including why he did it."

That night, alone again, Darrow pondered this. He could not seem to sleep.

20

THE FIRST TELEPHONE CALL OF DARROW'S WORKDAY SURPRISED him.

"Mark," the thin voice said, "this is Clark Durbin."

"Hello, Clark," Darrow said phlegmatically, then waited for whatever might come next.

Faced with Darrow's coolness, Durbin sounded shaky. "I wanted to congratulate you. I mean, you're my successor. It feels odd we haven't talked."

"Not so odd," Darrow answered in an even tone. "You're accused of stealing nearly a million dollars. That's why I'm here. Given that, I have a say in whether you're indicted. It's not as though you're passing me the baton so I can run a victory lap."

A brief silence ensued. "That's why I need to talk to you," Durbin said.

The simple statement held a pleading note. "Under the circumstances," Darrow said, "I can't meet with you alone. There can't be any misunderstanding of what either of us may say."

Durbin exhaled. "All right."

Darrow glanced at his calendar. "I've got an hour free at ten. Meet me at my office—I'll ask Lionel to join us. Bring a lawyer, if you like. In fact, I'd advise it."

"All right," Durbin repeated. He sounded like a beaten man.

Hanging up, Darrow called Farr. "Durbin wants to meet with me," he said.

"No surprise," Farr said with an edge of disdain. "He's been insisting, however incongruously, on his innocence. You're a new audience, potentially the difference between jail and mere penury. No doubt he wants to appeal to whatever quantum of mercy you haven't lavished on Steve Tillman. The only question is whether he'll try to make you feel like you're about to execute Bambi, or whether he'll float all the sympathetic reasons he chose to steal our money. Perhaps he was drunk."

The remarks were so caustic and so comprehensive that Darrow laughed aloud. "Ten o'clock," he said. "My office. After that you can tell me which president of Caldwell is the bigger fool."

To DARROW'S SURPRISE, Durbin came alone.

Darrow sat behind his desk; Durbin, in one of two wing chairs facing him. Farr settled in the other, studying Durbin while the former president focused on his successor. Always slight, Durbin looked diminished, his hair dyed an unconvincing black, heightening the contrast with his thin but sagging face. With a tepid smile, Durbin said, "I can't help but think about the first time the three of us met together. Strange, isn't it?"

Darrow thought so, too. Then, he had been hardly more than a boy, sickened and confused, grateful for Durbin's kindness; now, at least in theory, he was the most powerful man in the room, Durbin his supplicant. "Well," Darrow said, "at least this time no one's dead. But the school's been shafted. If you were me, what would *you* do about you?"

Darrow caught the flicker of Farr's arid smile, perhaps at the toughness of his protégé, perhaps because the reversal of fortune was so complete. But the chill look in Farr's blue eyes suggested that he was not amused by the subject of the meeting—or, Darrow surmised, by the fact that it was he who had once saved Durbin's presidency. Still watching Darrow, Durbin leaned slightly forward, fingers steepled in a precatory gesture. "No matter what you have been led to think," he said slowly, "I did not do this."

"Clark," Darrow answered softly, "there's a paper trail that followed you here. The orders are from your e-mail. Money went to your bank accounts—"

"I didn't send those e-mails," Durbin interrupted. "I didn't open those accounts—"

"Don't bullshit me," Darrow cut in. "For that to be true, some mastermind would have had to know where Caldwell had parked nine hundred thousand dollars in CDs, used your personal computer to ask Joe Betts to transfer them, and forged your signature for two different banks, all in an elaborate effort to frame you. Got anyone in mind?"

Durbin ignored his sarcasm. Stubbornly, he said, "It would have had to be someone on the investment committee."

"That certainly narrows down our list of suspects, doesn't it? Aside from you, that leaves Ed Rardin, Paul Johns, John Stewart— and Joe, of course. None of whom live in Wayne. Which one had access to your computer?"

Durbin seemed to rock in his chair. "None that I know of. But they were often here."

"Let's skip over that, then—as well as the slander inherent in suggesting that one of four honorable and wealthy men is a crook. Who among them has the skill to forge your signature?"

Durbin grimaced. Tightly, he said, "Someone could have traced it."

Farr, Darrow saw, was staring at the rug, as though he could no longer stand to look at Durbin. "Clark," Darrow said with renewed gentleness, "your investments went bad. Your son was in rehab for heroin addiction. Your wife was terribly sick. You needed money."

Durbin shook his head. "I'm not a thief, Mark. If I were, I wouldn't be that stupid."

Darrow gave him the glacial stare he had perfected in the court-room. "Desperate men do stupid things. You had no other source of money. In my experience, embezzlers imagine they can cover themselves before they're caught, often by moving around more cash. This embezzler was smart enough to game the system—which, as you pointed out, suggests an insider, someone with access to the information held within the investment committee. Which gets me back to the question you can't answer: which one had a key to your office?"

"I don't know."

"Then I can't help you. So help yourself, Clark. Tell us where the last eight hundred and fifty thousand went."

Durbin stared at him, his expression slack. "I don't know *where* the money is."

"Too bad," Darrow said in a pitiless tone. "Should you remember, please come back. Bring a lawyer with you next time, and do be quick about it. After this morning's performance, I'm an hour closer to calling up Dave Farragher."

Mechanically, Durbin rose, not trying to shake hands. "By the way," Darrow inquired casually, "who was supplying your kid with smack?"

Durbin's eyes were moist. "I don't know that, either. But maybe it was Carl Hall. Ironic, isn't it."

Still sitting, Darrow shrugged.

Farr stood, opening the door for Durbin. As Durbin paused there, looking back at Darrow, Farr placed a hand on his shoulder, a gesture that, to Darrow, combined a fleeting compassion with a reminder to leave. Somehow this moment reminded Darrow that, just yesterday, he had heard another plea of innocence. Perhaps there was nothing else Steve Tillman or Clark Durbin could have said.

Farr closed the door behind Durbin. "Human wreckage," he remarked, then looked at Darrow intently. "I haven't seen that side of you."

"A professional necessity. If Durbin's smart, he'll drop the fantasy that he's somehow getting away with this." Darrow waved Farr to his chair. "Can you stick around a minute? There's something else we need to talk about."

Farr sat back down. "Concerning?"

Darrow paused a moment. "Taylor," he answered. "We've been spending time together."

Farr's expression was neutral. "So I understand. I'm pleased you've become friends."

"We're certainly friends. But this may have a little more texture."

Farr raised his eyebrows. "How so?"

Darrow considered how to answer. "When I'm with Taylor, I don't think about Lee. For the first time in a long while, a greater part of me is living in the present."

Farr seemed to look inward, as though monitoring his own reactions. "Can I ask how far this has gone? Emotionally, I mean."

"It's still very new. But we're going to Boston together." Darrow waited until Farr met his eyes. "This isn't the Dark Ages. In any other situation, I wouldn't owe Taylor's father an explanation. But it's you, and you're the provost—college presidents generally don't pursue their provost's daughter. I'm not sure if the fact that this involves you and me makes it better, or more awkward."

Farr smiled slightly. "Some sort of incest taboo, you mean?"

"Jesus, Lionel. That *is* weird."

"Excuse my wan attempt to make light of this." Farr paused, seeming to gather his thoughts. "Given our relationship, the idea that you, as president, are involved with my twenty-eight-year-old daughter doesn't qualify as a scandal. The main complication for me is that I care for you both—I want both of you happy, and neither of you hurt. The chances are good that one of you will be; that's the inevitable outcome of almost every romantic relationship between a man and a woman. And either outcome would be hurtful to me. So forgive me for having mixed feelings."

Darrow felt deflated. "You mentioned happiness. The only way to get there is by assuming the risk."

Farr studied him. "Then how do you assess the risk with Taylor?"

"To her? Or to me?"

"Both."

Darrow leaned back. "For myself, all I can say is that I feel more open. Even before I had to deal with Lee's death, I never found it that easy. I very much want to see where this goes."

"And Taylor?"

"I'm not sure yet. There are remarkable elements to her personality."

Farr nodded. "I agree. Like her mother, Taylor has many gifts. But I also worry that she has a tendency toward melancholy that perhaps you've yet to see." Pausing, Farr added quietly, "Also like her mother."

Darrow managed a smile he did not feel. "Are you warning me off?"

Farr frowned in thought. "Merely cautioning you. For your own sake, but also for Taylor's. I believe that life has made both of you more vulnerable to hurt than others might be."

Darrow watched him. As remarkable as the conversation was, he sensed that there was a second conversation hidden beneath the first, the words to which remained unspoken. "Is that all there is?"

Farr looked down, studying a patch of sunlight on Darrow's Persian rug. "Perhaps not," he said at last. "Perhaps, in a non-Oedipal way, I'm a little stung—or at least saddened—that your new relationship with Taylor may be stronger than my own. I hope that's not affecting me. But self-knowledge is, at best, imperfect. Never more so than when the entire truth about oneself may be less attractive than one hopes."

Darrow felt a wave of sympathy. Though armored in his confidence and reputation, Farr might well be lonelier than he allowed. "That's only human, Lionel. Thanks for being honest."

Smiling, Farr stood. "Then I've fulfilled my obligations—as provost, father, and friend. Should you and Taylor defy the odds, nothing would please me more."

Darrow nodded. "I know that."

Farr looked relieved. "Then go with God, my son. And do go over those budget figures I prepared."

When Farr left, Darrow gazed at the door, lost in thought. Then he picked up the phone and called Mike Riley in Boston.

"I'm coming to town," he told the accountant. "Can you make time to see me?"

"Always. You still grappling with this embezzlement?"

"Yes. Durbin came to see me today, to assert his innocence. It was fairly pathetic. He tried to blame some unnamed person on the investment committee, as I'd guessed he might. So I challenged his suggestion with several questions, none of which he could answer."

"Did you expect him to?"

"Of course not. But I thought you might be able to do better."

Riley chuckled. "Still not quite convinced he did it, are you?"

"Not quite yet. I'll put all my questions in an e-mail. If I give you a couple of days, can you look over all the documents and tell me what you think?"

"Sure. What brings you back to Boston, by the way?"

"The hope of better meals."

"You might try San Francisco," Riley said, and got off.

Pensive, Darrow placed another call. "This is nice," Taylor said cheerfully. "I woke up this morning, and there was nothing to look forward to but my thesis. What made you think to call?"

"I've been bonding with your dad," Darrow informed her. "I told him. He seems to be feeling a little tender, even threatened. Like he's become the odd man out."

Taylor was quiet. "Do you find that a little curious?" she inquired coolly.

Against his will, Darrow heard Farr say, *She has a tendency toward melancholy.* And then heard Taylor telling him, *I worry about losing myself, or giving any man too much power over me.* In a casual tone, he answered, "I think he means well. But Lionel's a complicated person. As are we all, I suppose."

"Him most of all," Taylor responded in the same voice. "Don't worry, I'll tread lightly with him. In the end, we're all he has."

21

O N WEDNESDAY EVENING, DARROW SPOKE TO A HUNDRED alumni at a hotel ballroom in Columbus. "Almost everyone," he told them, "had a professor who influenced the course of your life, like Lionel Farr did mine. That's why you're here; it's why I'm here. So my first mission as president of Caldwell is to earn your trust. My second mission—which I hope becomes yours—will be to ensure that Caldwell has the resources to build state-of-the-art facilities, endow chairs for the most gifted teachers, and fund scholarships for any deserving student who entrusts us with her future.

"Next year I'll be back with a blueprint for this endeavor. If you'll give me your help, together we'll build a Caldwell College that offers the next generation of alumni even more than it gave us."

The crowd's applause was warm, its questions respectful. But, as at several recent events, the good feeling was punctured by an aggressive businessman who asserted that *his* trust was contingent on the prosecution of Clark Durbin. Deflecting the question, Darrow guessed that these challenges—similar in wording—reflected a pressure campaign orchestrated from within the board of trustees. Whoever it was, they meant for Darrow to yield Durbin on their timetable.

Afterward, Darrow mingled with the group, connecting stories with names and faces and, he hoped, lodging each detail in his memory bank. Then a bleached blonde about his age approached him with a smile at once bright and tentative, as though worried she would evoke no response. "Mark, I'm Laurie," she said. "Laurie Shilts. Would you have recognized me?"

Fifteen years and twenty pounds added up to "maybe not"—at least if Darrow had not asked alumni relations to ensure that Laurie was coming. But the blue-green eyes were still those of the sad and angry girl with a dull bruise on her face, telling him at the fateful party about breaking up with Joe Betts. Kissing her on the cheek, he said, "With those eyes? Always."

She drew back, examining him with the proprietary expression of a fond old friend. "Imagine this—you as the president of Caldwell."

Darrow grinned. "'The Decline of the West,'" he said lightly. "Can I buy you a drink? Meet me at the bar in fifteen minutes, and we'll review the last fifteen years."

Laurie's smile contained a dollop of flirtation. "Better late than never," she said.

IT WAS A half hour before Darrow entered the bar, delayed by several pledges of increased support for Caldwell. By the time he sat with Laurie at a small but unsteady wooden table, she had a glass of white wine in front of her, and a flush to her cheeks that suggested this was not her first. Signaling the waitress, Darrow ordered a glass of cabernet.

Laurie summoned a smile of knowing sadness. "So how *are* you, Mark?"

He could not miss the allusion to Lee. "I'm okay. As I guess you know, I lost my wife."

She touched his hand. "I do know. And I'm sorry."

Darrow shrugged. "A lot's happened to all of us since we left Caldwell."

Laurie sipped her wine, pensive now. "A lot happened before we left."

"I remember," Darrow said quietly. "What I don't have a clue about is the rest of your life."

With a faintly rueful laugh, Laurie said, "Oh, that."

"That. So start anywhere you like—job, married or single, kids, where you live, hobbies, criminal record, bizarre quirks you're concealing from your neighbors."

In truth, Laurie's alumni file had already told him much of this. Leaning forward, she said, "Let's skip the fetishes and the conditions of my parole. My ex-husband was—and is—a drunk. So I'm a single mom with a twelve-year-old daughter."

"Twelve?"

"I started making mistakes early." Quickly, Laurie amended this: "Or *continued* making them. Not Chloe—her dad, the deadbeat. It's not easy raising an adolescent girl alone, especially on a teacher's salary."

"I can imagine. Which grade?"

"Ninth-grade English in a nice suburban high school filled with largely uncurious white kids. They're probably not so different than me at that age, though I find that more depressing than comforting." Her smile resembled a grimace. "The prospering classes move there to escape. I guess it's some comfort that their kids are smoking pot with their socioeconomic peer group. But why should I complain? The school's safe, and so's my job."

"And Chloe?"

"She's bright and pretty—actually, she's beginning to look like my old yearbook pictures, back in more innocent times." Laurie frowned. "But she's getting a case of the sullens—if my teenage self is any guide, she'll spend the next six years despising me, all the more so because I'm the only parental game in town." Her voice softened. "It's sad for both of us, I guess. For a long time she was my only company—I leaned on her more than I should have. No boundaries, as they say.

"But now she makes me feel lonely. I guess that's what girls and their moms endure on the way to becoming human again." Laurie summoned a falsely bright smile. "Tales of a Mundane Life. I shouldn't squander the chance to see you on feeling sorry for myself."

Darrow shook his head in demurral. "Sometimes being alone is hard."

She gave him a solicitous look. "For everyone. On the surface, you still seem like the golden boy, so good-looking that I was always surprised by how nice you were. But maybe that helps you cover pain. Even back in college."

"Maybe so. Things happen all your life that no one else can fix." Then Darrow thought of Farr and Taylor, and wondered if this was true.

Laurie's gaze became open, curious. "But you're okay now?"

"Better. Part of that is the Caldwell job. It's a daily challenge, and it keeps me busy and engaged—there's nowhere for a college president to hide."

"It seems like you really care about Caldwell, Mark."

"I do. I just hibernated for sixteen years."

Laurie sipped her wine. "I don't blame you."

To Darrow, this sounded more like a shared emotion than sympathy. "It was tough on all of us, Laurie. We weren't prepared for what happened."

She put a curled finger to her lips. "I still think about that party, talking with you. It was only a few hours later . . ." Her voice trailed off, and then she gave him a sideways look. "Do you ever see Joe?"

"Quite a bit, lately."

"How is he?"

"Pretty good, I think. As far as I can tell, he's got a stable marriage and two nice kids." Darrow paused, looking at her. "It probably helps that he sticks to sparkling water."

Laurie bit her lip, nodding toward her empty glass. "I don't, clearly."

Darrow felt caught between the desire to keep her talking and misgivings just as deep. "So let's have one more for the road," he said, and hated the sound of that.

Laurie nodded. As Darrow caught the waitress's eye, she said, "I'm a friendly drunk, you'll be glad to know. Not like Joe."

"Yeah. I remember how he was."

"Maybe so," Laurie responded with a somber tone. "But not as well as I do."

When the wine arrived, Darrow took a sip. "I also remember," he ventured, "Joe talking about his father getting drunk and beating on his mother."

Laurie's mouth twisted in a smile that made her appear both hard and tired. "He never said that to me. But everyone needs a role model, I guess."

Darrow met her eyes, feeling torn between acceptance and dread. "Joe hit you?"

"Not in the beginning." She shook her head, as though to clear it. "This is pretty hard to talk about. I never really have—for a whole set of reasons, I guess. Is this anything you really want to know?"

"Yes. At least if you'd like to tell me."

The fleeting look she gave him was both grateful and reluctant. "When I first left Steve for Joe," she said at length, "he was gentle. But part of the attraction was that Joe was wounded—I believed that beneath the spoiled rich kid was a boy who'd been hurt. I was the girl who could help him heal." As she paused, Darrow noted the slight slur in her voice merging with a delay in choosing words. "One night he got really drunk at a party, and he said he wanted to 'fuck' me right away. So he bent me over a chair in someone else's room, all the time saying disgusting things. It felt more like rape than sex." Briefly her eyes closed. "He kept asking if he was better than Steve. And bigger."

Darrow felt uneasy. "Yeah," he said with gentle irony. "It's the fear that haunts us all."

"You're not like that," Laurie said emphatically. "Steve wasn't either." Abruptly she paused, the flush of her cheeks deepening. "At least not with me. When I dumped him, he was angry, but I never thought he'd hit me—not once. Instead he just felt terrible."

Darrow paused. Quietly, he said, "So Steve tells me."

She looked up again. "You saw him, too?"

"Yeah. He's changed a lot—bitter, but also thoughtful. There's more to Steve than most people got."

"Not me. I always knew that Steve saw and felt more than he said—like you, I guess. When I was with Joe, sometimes, I wondered why I'd left Steve. My ex-husband is the answer. Meet a prick, and I still imagine seeing a wounded boy."

Weighing how much to press her, Darrow looked around them. The crowd in the bar, commercial travelers in the final stages of enforced conviviality, was dwindling. "That night," he said, "I thought Joe might have hit you."

As though remembering, Laurie touched her face. "He had. But it happened the night before."

"*What* happened, exactly?"

"It wasn't the first time. He'd get drunk. Then suddenly he'd be jealous of Steve, like alcohol flipped a switch in his brain—I think he even scared himself a little. My father used to say, Never be with a man who scares you. That night was when I got scared for good."

The quiet fervor with which she pronounced this intimated something left unsaid. Softly, Darrow asked, "What was different?"

As Laurie drained her wine, Darrow signaled for another. A long silence ensued, Darrow waiting her out. In a monotone, Laurie said, "I've never told this to anyone."

"Then maybe it's time."

Laurie averted her eyes. When the chardonnay arrived, she took a quick swallow. "I was alone in his room, studying. I didn't expect him for an hour. So I did what a lot of other girls would do—started going through my boyfriend's drawers. The first two drawers only told me what I already knew—college boys are slobs."

She stopped abruptly, fingers twisting a strand of frosted hair. "And then?" Darrow asked.

"I opened the last drawer." Her voice became pinched. "It was filled with magazines. Pornography."

She looked so disturbed that Darrow hesitated. "And that was what scared you?"

Laurie's expression became self-questioning. "Was I scared then? Or just disgusted? I can't put myself back there when so much has happened. I just stared at the magazines, one after the other, until all I could hear was the way he talked when he was inside me." Her voice softened. "Except I couldn't have been in the pictures."

Puzzled, Darrow watched her. "Because?"

"Because I wasn't black." Laurie's throat twitched. "It was like something from a slave-ship fantasy, white men degrading black women in chains, sodomizing or whipping them. When I felt myself wanting to vomit, I closed the drawer.

"Joe came back an hour later, drunk. He wanted me. I told him no—because of how he was, and because of the pictures. His eyes got wild, and he asked if I still wanted to do it with Steve. I was so disgusted I said, 'Only when I want to feel like a woman.' Then he hit me across the face."

"What did you do?"

"I said I never wanted to see him again." She paused again, looking up at Darrow. "He started to cry, almost sob. Then he said in this kind of whisper, 'Tell anyone about this, and I'll kill you.'"

Darrow felt a chill. "So you didn't."

"No." Laurie took a sip of wine, unable to look at Darrow. "I was like Joe. Too ashamed for people to know what he was like, or the things I let him do."

Darrow tried to find something to say. Finally, he said, "I think I understand."

Laurie shook her head, rejecting easy comfort. "After you found

Angela Hall, I thought about telling someone. But then it turned out she was with Steve."

Darrow was silent until she met his gaze again. "So you didn't have to say anything about Joe hitting you."

"Yes," she answered dully. "Or those pictures."

So the police had missed it, Darrow thought, as had Steve Tillman's lawyer. Both, it seemed clear, should have scoured Joe Betts's life much harder. How many people, he wondered now, had been served by Steve's guilt—if only to salve their conscience or put unspoken misgivings about Angela's murder safely behind them. He understood Laurie Shilts well enough: she had never wished to speak of these things, just as part of Darrow wished that he had never heard them. But now he bore the weight of knowing. Gently, he said, "In the end, it only mattered to you."

She gave him the bleakest of smiles. "You're such a good guy, Mark. You always were."

A useful attribute, Darrow thought uncomfortably, if you wanted to manipulate someone. "So tell me," she continued in a throatier voice, "does a nice guy like you have anyone now? I hope that's not a tasteless question."

Darrow smiled, shaking his head. "After two years, a fair one. The answer is maybe. But I don't know whether it's real yet, or how long it can last. She and I are in very different places."

Saying this, he realized that he had spoken of Taylor to no one save her father. Hearing himself say the last phrase aloud, he realized how true it was.

Perhaps it showed on his face. "Only time will tell," Laurie said. "Sorry if I unloaded on you."

Darrow heard the regret in her voice, perhaps the fear of making herself less attractive. "It's been really nice to see you," he assured her. "If you ever need to talk, just call me."

Hope and doubt mingled in her eyes. "Better go now, huh? It's a school day for us both."

Standing, she teetered for an instant. "Let me get you a cab," Darrow said.

Laurie steadied herself. "Am I really that bad off?"

The bar was empty now, Darrow noticed. "No," he answered. "But I had a bad experience with this once, and you've got Chloe to look after. Call me overresponsible."

She took his arm, grateful to depend on him but still working out the logistics. "Tomorrow I have to drive her to school."

"Don't worry," Darrow said firmly. "I'll send a car for you and Chloe in the morning, and another one after school's out. You can tell anyone who cares that you've got car trouble, and a paranoid new boyfriend."

Laurie smiled. "That would keep them guessing, wouldn't it?"

Darrow walked her outside and hailed a cab. As she got in, Laurie kissed him on the cheek.

Darrow stood there for a time. It was just as well, he supposed, that Taylor was not sleeping over. He had far too much to think about.

22

Darrow barely slept. Late the next morning, after several more hours of thought, he decided to telephone Carl Hall.

To Darrow's surprise, given that Hall conducted his business by cell phone, the number was listed. To his greater surprise, Hall answered. "This is Mark Darrow," Darrow said without preface. "We need to talk."

Warily, Hall asked, "About what?"

"I'll save that for later. Alone, and in person."

The attenuated quiet that followed, Darrow knew, could be professional caution or something more. "Give me a clue," Hall demanded. "I don't want to be wasting my time."

Darrow thought quickly. "Among other things, your sister."

Hall's voice became quieter, less derisive. "What about her?"

Darrow decided to take a chance. "You can talk to me, Carl. Or I can go to Garrison."

"I guess you know where I live," Hall said at length.

"I can find it."

"Tonight then. Say ten o'clock."

Hall hung up.

Darrow sat at his desk, motionless, wondering what mistake he might have made, what secret Angela's brother might harbor. All he knew was that Carl Hall had one.

DARROW SPENT THE day on autopilot. He met with the chairs of the English and history departments about their needs; wrested more time from Ray Carrick, albeit with increasing difficulty, to dispose of Clark Durbin; importuned a wealthy but irate alumna not to strike Caldwell from her will; began recruiting a committee of alumni, faculty, and board members to address Caldwell's goals and more sharply define the school's identity; spoke to a specialist in minority recruitment; coordinated with Taylor to find dates for their trip to Boston; then asked the alumni relations director to schedule meetings during those days with prominent alumni. After normal working hours he reviewed potential budget cuts over dinner with Josh Daily, Caldwell's chief financial officer, and Joe Betts, who also suggested ways of further protecting Caldwell's endowment from adverse market conditions. Pushing his disquiet to the edges of his consciousness, Darrow did not mention Laurie Shilts. By the time he reached home, it was well past eight o'clock, and the house felt more lonely than normal. Contrary to his usual custom, he did not watch the news.

Something was badly wrong, he believed, and had been for sixteen years. Whatever that was, Darrow had the sense—more intuitive than reasoned—that it shadowed Caldwell still. But until he learned more, he could trust no one with his thoughts, not even Farr or Garrison. Neither man, he was sure, would feel this unease as keenly as he; both might reasonably question his preoccupation with Angela Hall's murder and—given Caldwell's very real problems—Darrow's judgment in stepping outside his role. He could not yet put a name to his suspicions, or risk his own or another person's reputation by accusing someone other than Steve Tillman.

He sat in the living room, glancing at his watch, turning facts and surmises over in his mind, arranging and rearranging them in a kaleidoscope of possibilities. The ones that troubled him most were those he could least afford to speak aloud.

At nine forty-five, Darrow left the house.

CARL HALL LIVED in a ranch-style home surrounded by several acres of fallow land, sequestered at the end of a cul-de-sac on the outer reaches of Wayne. Everything about it served the interests of a man running an illegal business: the gravel drive was long, and the house itself, shrouded by trees, could not be seen from the road. At night, Hall's normal business hours, a visitor could come and go without being identified. But as Darrow parked near the house, his footsteps crunching gravel, it struck him that for a man in a dangerous business this solitude could be a problem, depriving Hall of the protections offered by living on an urban block. No doubt Hall had weapons.

There were no lights on inside the house. Perhaps this was defensive; perhaps not. But Darrow felt pinpricks on the back of his neck. More clearly now, he saw the risk inherent in having told no one of this visit to an isolated place. If the threat he posed to Hall was greater than he knew, Hall might well make him disappear. Darrow did not like the stillness all around him, the darkness of the house itself.

He stepped up to the porch and stopped. Eyes adjusting to the thin moonlight, he found the doorbell. The ring inside chimed through what must have been an open window.

Nothing. Darrow tried again. Aside from the bell, the only sound he heard was the chirping of crickets.

He pressed the door latch with his thumb. To his surprise, the door was unlocked. Carefully, Darrow slipped into the dark inside, the door still open behind him.

"Carl?" he said quietly. His own voice sounded forlorn to him, hollow in the darkened space.

Still he heard no sound. Instinct told him to leave; nothing—at least nothing good—would come of staying. But he could not seem to move. Still facing a room too dark for sight, he felt for a wall switch by the door.

Finding one, he hesitated, stopped by fears he could not define. Then he chose to flick the switch.

He stood in the entry to a half-furnished living room. Carl Hall sat slumped in an overstuffed chair, as if asleep. For an instant, he reminded Darrow of his own father, save for the absence of an alcoholic's ragged snores.

Darrow felt his skin crawl. "Carl?" he said again, then recognized how foolish this was.

He stepped forward, softly, as though concerned with startling his host. But Darrow was acquainted with the dead: first Angela Hall; then murder victims at crime scenes; last, the body of his pregnant wife, lying in an Iowa morgue. In every case there was a terrible difference between slumber and death. Hall's lips were parted and his eyes wide, as though surprised by his own fate. On the arm of his chair was a hypodermic needle.

Darrow felt the shock wearing off. Unlike other deaths, Carl Hall's evoked no sadness or pity. What seeped through Darrow was a deepening fear of the unknown.

He took out his cell phone and, with a calm that surprised him, called George Garrison at home. "George," he began, "I'm at Carl Hall's house. I think you'd better come."

THE POLICE ARRIVED, then the team of specialists familiar to Darrow since he had found the body of Angela Hall. "First Angela," Garrison murmured. "Now Carl. Only their mother left."

For a time Garrison left Darrow with a detective. Standing outside the house, Darrow heard Garrison directing the others. Then the chief joined Darrow and the detective, his eyes keen in an emotionless face. "Let's hear it," he demanded of Darrow. "Starting with why you're here at all."

Darrow gave them the minimum: facts stripped of surmise; nothing about anyone but Hall. "You know I've been looking at Angela's murder," he told Garrison. "Carl's role seems pivotal. His own sister—who he lives with—is murdered, but Hall won't talk to the police until Fred Bender leans on him, and even then he tells Fred nothing. His mother says a white guy called for Angela; Hall doesn't know who. His mother says Angela kept a diary; the diary's missing, and Hall claims not to know it ever existed. Angela starts disappearing at night; Hall says he doesn't know why or where. I think he was lying about it all."

In an even tone, Garrison inquired, "Why would he do that?"

"Because he had something to lose by talking or to gain by keeping quiet."

"But you don't know what the 'something' is."

"Look," Darrow said, "every problem Caldwell has seems to involve Hall. Angela was murdered after a party; Carl was at the party. Griff Nordlinger tanked Steve's defense because of a cocaine problem; you think Hall was Nordlinger's supplier. Ditto Clark Durbin's son, only the drug was heroin. Part of Durbin's motive for embezzlement, the story goes, was to pay for his son's rehab."

"Carl sells drugs," Garrison said with muted impatience. "Carl likes money."

"So why is he dead?"

His eyes slits, Garrison examined the ground, as though debating whether to answer. "Looks like he died from a heroin overdose. We found the makings for an injection in the kitchen."

"Why would Carl use his own product? He'd know too well what it does." When Garrison said nothing, Darrow added, "I couldn't see track marks on his arm."

Garrison shoved his hands into his pockets. "You can also smoke the stuff. Or snort it."

"Then why change delivery systems? Because he'd started worrying about lung cancer?" Darrow softened his voice. "I'll make you a bet, George. Once toxicology runs their tests, they'll tell you that there's no other sign Carl was using, and that he died from an overdose massive enough to kill a basketball team. If so, there's a good chance someone murdered him."

Garrison glanced at the detective, scribbling notes at Darrow's side. "With Carl's cooperation?" Garrison said curtly. "Why not suicide?"

"Because Carl lacked the requisite self-awareness."

To Darrow's surprise, Garrison laughed softly. "That's another problem—people liked Carl a whole lot less than he liked himself. Anyone might have decided to kill him—a rival dealer or a customer wanting drugs."

"Maybe so. But they'd have put a bullet through his brain."

The front door opened as two paramedics carried Hall, shrouded on a stretcher, to an ambulance waiting in the driveway. Darrow and the police chief watched until the doors of the ambulance slammed shut, echoing in the night.

"I walked right through an unlocked door," Darrow said. "Any sign of a robbery or break-in?"

Garrison exhaled. "No. Guess that means that Hall let somebody shoot him up, after he was nice enough to let him—or them—in through the front door."

"He *knew* him, George," Darrow said urgently. "Bear with me. I called Hall this morning, threatening to go to you. He sounded worried; he couldn't know how little I knew. Suppose he told somebody I was coming—someone who knew everything I don't, and couldn't let anyone else find out. If so, you won't find his fingerprints."

The detective glanced at Garrison. "Of course not," the chief said flatly. "Or any evidence that he exists. Be nice if you'd give this nameless ghost a motive."

Darrow tried to remain unfazed. "I can't. But do me a favor and I'll give you my best guess."

In the moonlight, Darrow saw Garrison's hard stare of distrust. "What's the favor?"

"Keep my name out of this, for now. For Caldwell's sake, and also mine. There's no good explanation for me meeting a drug dealer."

"That's why you shouldn't have," Garrison snapped. "Bad judgment; tough luck. You should have called me."

"Maybe so. But you get nothing from making me look bad."

Garrison shrugged in indifference, moving his heavy shoulders. Tiredly, he said, "What's your guess?"

"It's possible Hall killed his sister, though I can never work out why. But if Carl didn't kill her—and Steve Tillman didn't—then Carl knew who did." Darrow's voice gained force. "I think Carl was blackmailing someone. Look for the diary, and for secret bank accounts or anywhere else where Carl might hide money."

Garrison stared at Darrow. "You should have called me," he repeated softly.

"Would you have listened?"

Garrison fell silent. "I'll cover you for now," he finally said. "As a favor to an old teammate. Unlike Tillman, you were never a prick."

Darrow left without mentioning Joe Betts.

The Spire

1

For days Darrow went about his life, busy on the surface, preoccupied beneath it. No one but the police—and, perhaps, a murderer—knew his secret.

He made speeches, chaired meetings, pushed his new committee into life. He saw Taylor often, enjoying each new intimacy of thought and feeling, yet fighting back the knowledge—most intense when he was with her—of concealing that which consumed him. His interactions with Joe Betts were shadowed by things he did not wish to know, suspicions he did not wish to have. He visited Steve Tillman, saying nothing new about the case. The principal salve to his conscience was that he had placed the matter in Garrison's hands. But even there he had hidden much. For now he would wait to see what Garrison did, then decide what else to do.

The character of Joe Betts preoccupied him. Abusing Laurie Shilts and obsessing about black women did not in themselves implicate him in Angela's murder. But Joe could have been the caller mentioned by Angela's mother. Nor had he any corroboration for his assertion that, in the last hours of Angela's life, he was alone in his dorm room. It was disturbingly convenient that, by Joe's account, he had awakened just in time to become the witness who put Steve Tillman in prison.

That was Darrow's dilemma. For now, he was caught between his belief that Steve might be innocent and the reluctance to accuse a prominent member of Caldwell's board, a man with a seemingly sound marriage and blameless life, of an ugly murder. Especially when one basis for the accusation, Laurie's account, might change that life for good.

At several points Darrow was tempted to confide in Lionel Farr. The closest he came was when Farr, remarking on newspaper accounts of Carl Hall's death, expressed puzzlement that "a man who lived off other people's misery would inflict it on himself." Given his own misgivings, the remark deepened Darrow's unease. Joe Betts had been in Wayne on the night of Hall's death. But though Darrow tried to envision Joe with a needle in his hand, he could not easily imagine the mechanisms of a murder by heroin injection. More than anything, this was what kept him from confiding in Farr a theory so lurid yet so speculative that it could transform Farr's concept either of Joe or of Darrow himself.

Eleven days into Darrow's paralysis, Garrison called him. "I want to see you," the chief said brusquely. It was not a request.

THEY MET IN Garrison's office, alone. Garrison closed the door behind him.

At once, Darrow feared that his role in Hall's death was about to become public. The chief sat behind his desk, his gaze penetrating and cool. "Well?" Darrow said.

"We've got things to talk about. Some of which you can't tell a living soul." Sitting back, Garrison regarded Darrow in momentary silence. "You were right about Hall's death. There's no evidence that he used heroin before that night—no tracks, no sign in his blood or tissues. The dose he took would kill anyone. An experienced user would know better, and so would Hall."

Though unsurprising, the revelation heightened Darrow's unease. "We pretty much knew that."

Eyes hooded, Garrison continued: "There were also abrasions on Carl's wrists, bruises on his ankles. It's possible that his arms and legs were bound or handcuffed at the time he was injected."

Absorbing this, Darrow asked, "How would that have happened?"

"If it did? Someone could have held a gun to his head and made him shackle himself. But that's only a guess—not many folks carry handcuffs around with them." Garrison paused, then continued in a lower register: "The point is that we can't rule out your idea that someone killed him. And that Hall knew the man who did."

Quiet, Darrow gazed out Garrison's window. The day was sunny; traffic moved at its normal pace, people going about their lives. But Darrow felt his world changing. Facing Garrison, he said, "You've got no reason to tell me this. There's something else."

After a moment, Garrison nodded. "We found a safe deposit box. Inside was a bag of diamonds worth over half a million dollars."

"So that's how Carl converted drug money."

"Maybe. But Carl knew how to launder money through the Alibi Club. Plus, from the record of entry for the box, he'd apparently begun depositing diamonds thirteen years ago and stopped five years later. Pretty rich for a guy whose drug business was small-time way back then."

Absently, Darrow touched the knot in his tie. "Same question, George. Why are you telling me all this?"

Still watching Darrow, Garrison opened his desk drawer. He took out a single piece of paper and slid it across the desk. Glancing down, Darrow saw a typed schedule, showing numerous transfers of money into seven different bank accounts for businesses Darrow did not recognize. "What is this?" Darrow asked.

"Keep reading."

As Darrow did, a pattern emerged. The transfers had occurred within the last year. By Darrow's swift calculation, that total exceeded six hundred thousand dollars, all in amounts less than ten thousand.

"What this suggests to me," he said at length, "is an effort to avoid transfers above the threshold that triggers an automatic inquiry by federal bank authorities." Looking up at Garrison, he asked, "Who's the signatory on these accounts?"

"Carl Hall."

Edgy, Darrow scoured the schedule again. "All these transfers," he said slowly, "happened after Caldwell's money disappeared."

A glint appeared in Garrison's eyes. "You'd be the one to know. No one from the college has taken the embezzlement to Farragher. At least not formally."

Darrow did not respond to this. "Who transferred the money to Hall?" he asked.

"The Security Bank of Geneva. Familiar?"

It was a different bank, Darrow recognized at once, than the one that had transferred money to an account in Clark Durbin's name— the last piece of evidence in the case against him. "Only by name," he said. "It's also a dead end. A Swiss bank will never disclose whoever controls this account. Only Carl could have told you what this means."

Garrison sat back. "Any idea what Carl might have to do with Durbin?"

"Other than that Hall supplied Durbin's son with heroin? That's the only connection I can make between Hall and Caldwell College— except for Angela's murder, which happened sixteen years ago. I can't get to why Durbin would be siphoning Caldwell's money to Carl Hall."

Garrison propped his chin on folded hands. "What about Durbin's son?"

Darrow shook his head. "He would've had to use his dad's computer to e-mail Joe Betts, then forge Durbin's name to open bank accounts. Pretty sophisticated for a twenty-something drug addict. Beyond that, you'd also need an inside knowledge of Caldwell's financial system.

"Obviously, the members of Caldwell's investment committee had that, including Durbin. So maybe Durbin's kid went through his father's files. But he would have had to figure out that Joe Betts's firm had $900,000 in CDs, and that his father had authority to move it by sending Joe an e-mail. Which gets us back to the question of why Durbin—or Durbin's kid or anyone else at Caldwell—would embezzle money to pay off Carl Hall."

Garrison fixed him with a gelid stare. "Remember what you told Hall you wanted to talk about?"

"Angela."

"Angela," Garrison repeated softly. "I think you know things you're still not saying. Just like you seem to know everyone involved, back from college days." He reached into the drawer again. "I want you to read something. You can't tell anyone you've seen it, and I don't think you'll want to. But after you're through maybe you'll want to tell me more."

Standing, Garrison placed a sheaf of Xeroxed pages, bound by a rubber band, in Darrow's lap. "Take your time," he said.

Without saying more, Garrison closed the office door behind him.

Removing the rubber band, Darrow felt a jolt. In his hands was what appeared to be a journal, written in a clearly feminine hand.

Alone, Darrow began reading. The nightmare began on the second page: an account of bondage and sexual sadism, supposedly inflicted on the writer by a male figure known only as "HE." Briefly, Darrow paused, touching his half-closed eyes.

The woman's tormentor, if he existed in life, was a man of considerable inventiveness. His techniques were varied, all calculated to produce humiliation without leaving a mark; all, in the diary's account, excited him in proportion to their debasement of the victim. But HE remained nameless, more a force of domination than a man with human characteristics and emotions, so defined by his obsessions that Darrow wondered if he was reading an elaborate exercise in sadomasochistic fantasy. The voice of the narrator was detached; it resembled the accounts of rape victims Darrow had heard as a prosecutor, wherein the woman, helpless during the act, has willed her conscious mind to go elsewhere. Yet the details were quite specific, meticulously recorded in the toneless voice of a concentration camp survivor, too resigned to inhumanity to respond with outrage.

On the last page, the only words she had written were: "There is such darkness in the chamber of stone."

Shaken, for some moments Darrow sat alone in the silent office. His thoughts kept returning to Laurie Shilts, the magazines she'd found in Joe Betts's drawer—which, for Laurie, had exposed Joe's deepest self, transmuting sympathy to fear.

The door opened, startling Darrow.

Garrison stood there, reading Darrow's face. "We found that in Carl's safe," he said. "We don't know what happened to the original."

Slowly, Darrow nodded. "Is this her handwriting?"

"Yeah. When we showed it to her mother, she just shriveled up."

Darrow waited for a question that never came. "It could all be fabricated," he said. "There's plenty of literary precedent for that."

Garrison laughed without humor. "So that's what this is. Something Angela wrote for fun."

"There's only one alternative: that HE was a real person."

Garrison crossed his arms. "Then maybe Carl was blackmailing him, just like you said. So HE bought him off with Caldwell's money, to hide that he was a murderer. If that's right, the question is why HE killed her."

It was odd, Darrow realized, to feel more horror in Garrison's office than standing over Carl Hall's body. "The diary tells us almost nothing," he replied, "except about this man's pathology. There's no person in those pages. Maybe HE was angry. Maybe HE went too far. Or maybe, as Fred Bender believed about Steve Tillman, HE killed Angela to prevent exposure."

Garrison gazed down at Darrow. "So tell me this: If the man used Caldwell's money, who could he be?"

After a moment, Darrow stood. "I'll think about that very hard, George. For Angela's sake, and Steve's."

2

O<small>N THE FLIGHT TO</small> B<small>OSTON,</small> D<small>ARROW AND</small> T<small>AYLOR WERE</small> companionable but quiet. No doubt, Darrow thought, Taylor was contemplating her interview. Unable to shake the images conjured by Angela's diary, Darrow pondered the psychic landscape—real or imagined—that had produced the faceless HE. For the next four days, he promised himself, he would focus on Taylor as much as he could.

The days would be full. They had dinner reservations, tickets to a Red Sox–Yankees game, plans for walks through Darrow's favorite parts of the city. But he, like Taylor, had work. Aside from meetings with his partners and selected Caldwell alumni, Darrow had two appointments he had mentioned to no one. His forensic accountant, Mike Riley, had analyzed the transfer of money to Hall's bank accounts and, more critically, would try to answer Darrow's questions. Of more speculative value was a meeting with the psychiatrist whose skill and rigor had helped Darrow after Lee's death.

When Darrow turned to her again, Taylor was asleep.

He studied her, pensive. After some misgivings, he had proposed staying at his town house. A shadow had crossed her face. "Will that be all right?" she had asked.

"I think it's time," Darrow had answered simply.

That night, Taylor had awakened from a nightmare she chose not to describe. The next morning, after she left, Darrow called his housekeeper in Boston.

DARROW AND LEE had lived in a handsome three-story brownstone on the first block of Commonwealth Avenue, near the Public Garden. Standing on the sidewalk, Taylor gazed at the town house. "You must be glad to see it," she said. "The location is lovely."

"I just hope you approve of the decor."

She gave him a sideways look, smiling a little. "Compared to where you're camping out?"

They entered the house. Stopping in the living room, Taylor took it all in—fourteen-foot ceilings, crown moldings, a large stone fireplace, and hardwood floors, brightened by Chinese carpets and bold modern art on the walls, accented by the black grand piano only Lee had played. Taylor admired the piano for a moment, then followed Darrow upstairs.

The rooms—a library, a master suite and two guest rooms, offices for Lee and Darrow, the exercise room where both had worked out— had been, as much as practical, scrubbed clean of any trace of her. Putting their suitcases in a guest room, Darrow wondered if Taylor sensed this.

"I like what you've done," she told him. "Instead of filling a hundred-and-fifty-year-old house with antiques, like you were communing with somebody's ancestors, you made it your own. You'll be pleased to know," she added wryly, "that I even like the art."

"That *is* a relief."

They descended the spiral staircase to the living room. Pausing by the piano, she rested a fingernail on the black enamel, tracing a line that bisected a light sprinkling of dust. Without turning, Taylor said quietly, "You needn't have done that."

"Done what?"

Facing him, Taylor answered, "Remove her pictures."

Darrow tried to smile. "Are you some kind of witch?"

"I hope not. Maybe I'm more sensitive to my surroundings than most, to spaces where something's missing." Her tone was even. "I can still feel her, Mark. I don't need to be part of an exorcism."

Darrow felt at sea. "Maybe we should go to a hotel."

"That's not what I'm saying," Taylor replied. "She's part of your life, and you love this house. So why pretend?"

Briefly, Darrow spread his hands, a gesture ending in a helpless shrug. "You're the first woman I've brought here, Taylor."

"Somehow I'd guessed that." Moving closer, she touched his wrist. "Living in my father's house, and remembering my mother, is much harder. This is something I'll get used to."

"Will you?"

"Yes." Briefly, Taylor smiled. "Of course, I'm looking forward to dinner out. The wine will help, too."

"Then you can choose it," Darrow promised.

TAYLOR CHOSE MEURSAULT. It was clear she liked the Federalist; they relaxed into dinner, talking easily again. It struck Darrow that he had dined here with her father, two days after Lee's memorial service. Farr had gently implied that, in time, there would be another woman for Darrow. Now Lionel's daughter sat across the table.

After dinner, Taylor and Darrow walked through the Common and the Public Garden. Dusk had fallen; the swan boats on the duck pond became shadows in the fading light, and an evening breeze stirred the branches of the willows. Away from Wayne and Caldwell, Darrow felt lighter. "Truth to tell," he said, "I sometimes think about selling it."

"The house? Setting aside that I feel like a trespasser, it really is very nice."

Abruptly, Darrow realized that he did not yet wish to go back. They sat beneath a willow, gazing at the first faint moonlight on the pond. Sensing his mood, Taylor let him be.

"About the photographs of Lee," he said at length. "That was also for me."

She turned to him, head tilted. "Yes?"

Darrow drew a breath. "When I look at them, I don't just feel sad. I feel angry, and guilty."

"Because she died?"

"Because of how she died, and why." Darrow felt repressed emotions coming to the surface. "Lee was the most engaging person I never completely knew. She grew up with an alcoholic father and a mother who took her own misery out on Lee. The result was a childhood almost as bleak as mine.

"Lee's reaction was to become completely driven—always in motion, never looking back. She was as perceptive about the politicians she covered as she was scared of looking at herself, especially when the truth was hard." Darrow turned, gazing at the pond. "In the context of our marriage, one of the hard truths about Lee is that she never wanted kids."

Taylor was quiet for a moment. "But she was pregnant when she died."

"She was also drunk," Darrow said flatly. "Not just a little, but a lot, driving faster than she should have. And it was dark. So she hit that patch of ice and lost control."

Taylor touched his hand. "I'm sorry, Mark."

"So am I," he said with quiet bitterness. "Also about the seat belt she wasn't wearing when the car flipped. One act of carelessness after another, resulting in two deaths—hers, and the son I very much wanted.

"I knew Lee didn't, without her ever saying so. She'd learned too well from her mother that kids were a form of enslavement." Darrow's voice softened. "Of course, I overlooked that. And Lee, being who she was, enabled me. Perhaps she loved me enough to violate her own instincts. But once she was pregnant, I could feel how much she hated it."

He felt Taylor watching him. "Had drinking always been a problem?"

"No. Living with an alcoholic father terrified her. Even before the pregnancy, Lee didn't drink much. Except on the night she died."

Softly, Taylor asked. "What happened that night?"

Darrow hesitated. "The facts are pretty banal," he began. "She was drinking with the press pack at a hangout near where the candidate she was covering had camped out for the night. Lee was more vivacious than normal—almost manic, I'm told. And she was with old friends, the ones who must have sensed how much she feared what motherhood would do to her career." Darrow's tone flattened. "Maybe she wanted to escape being pregnant; maybe she was running from our marriage. Whatever, she broke her rule about abstaining during pregnancy. She had a drink and just kept on going."

"And no one tried to stop her?"

"Not that anyone's willing to say. But Lee's biggest mistake was driving. Or maybe it was becoming pregnant." Darrow's voice lowered again. "We'd never really talked about that. If we had, I'd have promised to do more than my fair share of parenting.

"That would have been okay. Instead, Lee died, and I hated her for it, and still loved her. As screwed up as this may sound, I've even wondered if I helped kill her." Darrow exhaled. "So there it is. And here *I* am, awash in self-pity."

After a moment, Taylor said gently, "And you never talked to anyone about all this?"

"No one. Somehow I couldn't. Except the psychiatrist I found to keep myself sane."

"Did that help?"

"Some. Our friends tried to help, too—it wasn't their fault they didn't know. The same with the women I eventually started seeing." Darrow studied the swan boats, silver in the moonlight. "Maybe I'm like Lee. It's hard for me to lean on anyone. Except, at times, your father."

"But not about this. Or anything like this."

"No."

"Yet it's okay for people to lean on you," Taylor responded softly. "Like the night I talked about my mother—too much, I thought—and you were so sensitive to how I felt. Just as you were when I was twelve."

A catch in his throat took Darrow by surprise. "Maybe I knew something."

"Maybe I did, too."

Tears surfaced in his eyes. As he fought them back, Taylor leaned her forehead against his. After a time, she said, "Let's go home, Mark."

THEY TRIED TO sleep. Neither did. Late at night, they found each other. It was sweet and intense.

In the morning, as Taylor slept, Darrow went downstairs to make them coffee. The house seemed different, he realized. He liked knowing she was here.

3

THE NEXT MORNING DARROW MET WITH HIS EX-PARTNERS, while Taylor window-shopped on Newbury Street, "practicing for when I have a job." After lunch together, Taylor went to her interview, Darrow to the psychiatrist who had once helped him.

Jerry Seitz was a lean, bright-eyed man in his mid-forties whose attentive stillness seemed imposed on a naturally energetic nature. Darrow and Lee had known him socially. Before turning to Seitz in the aftermath of her death, Darrow had seen in him an ingenuous sweetness, almost a naïveté, which did not square with his profession. But within the confines of his office, Seitz was incisive and bracingly direct. Darrow liked him a great deal.

For the first time in a year, they faced each other in Seitz's sparely appointed office. "So," Seitz inquired bluntly, "are you still blaming yourself for Lee's death? Or have you managed to accept that Lee also fell short in your marriage?"

Darrow shifted in his chair. "I understand that Lee had her own difficulties. But the accident kept us from facing up to things." He stopped, shaking his head. "You knew her, Jerry. If she'd missed that patch of ice, would we have made it?"

Leaning forward, Seitz clasped his hands, weighing his answer as he looked into Darrow's face. "Maybe. I know you would have tried, Mark—awfully hard."

"And Lee?"

Seitz gave the slightest of shrugs. "Would have done the best she could. But I always felt that more of the burden would have fallen on you."

Darrow absorbed this. "I'll never really know, will I? I was talking about that just last night."

Seitz's eyebrows shot up. "That's new for you, isn't it?"

"One could say that."

"Who is she?"

Despite himself, Darrow laughed. "My provost's daughter. She came here with me."

Seitz's eyes lit with interest. "Is this serious?"

"It could be. But she's twenty-eight—looking for her first full-time job, completing her PhD dissertation, and intent on living in a major city when I've just moved to the place she never felt at home. Those are pretty serious impediments."

"So what is it about her?"

Darrow smiled a little. "As near as I can tell in a month's time? Everything else."

Still watching Darrow, Seitz smiled too, signaling encouragement. "If she's the right one, Mark, see if you can make things work. It says something that you've opened up to her." His smile vanishing, Seitz picked up a piece of paper from the table beside his chair. "On to a grimmer subject. I took detailed notes on what you told me about this diary. You're right that the whole thing could be fiction—the abstract quality of the narrative might suggest that. Still, you've asked me to assume it's real. So let's reprise the rules."

"All right."

"First, you want me to speculate on the character of the narrator and the man she chose to call HE. Second, you asked me to assume that HE killed her." Seitz briefly checked his notes. "Finally, you're trying to compare HE with a man you *know* to be real: a former classmate who was frequently inebriated, physically abusive to women, and obsessed with bondage involving African-American females. But who also, by your account, gave up drinking shortly after the strangulation of our narrator, and since then has led an ostensibly productive life that includes a highly successful career and a wife and kids he appears to cherish. Does that about cover it?"

"Pretty much."

Seitz puffed his cheeks. "This isn't psychology, Mark—it's more like divination. We should be doing this in a bar. But I'll try."

"All I can ask, Jerry."

"Though we know nothing else about him, the acts Angela ascribes to HE are clearly aberrant. Equally apparent, this man feels a deep contempt for women, however well masked in his so-called normal life. A common background begins with a hard-handed father who exploited a codependent mother. These guys often hate their fathers but also despise their mothers, for being weak."

"That's my old classmate, Jerry. Or so he told me in college."

"Interesting. The next step is that the son adopts the contempt of his father toward his mother, while Mom, replicating the pattern, placates him." Seitz grimaced. "In an adolescent boy there tends to be an erotic element in his subjugation of Mom—her submission begins feeling sexual to him. And because he hates his father, he begins to compete with Dad for power.

"This can get pretty tangled. When he was sixteen, a patient of mine came home from a date and found his mother in a negligee, drunk. So he pulled up her negligee and fucked her. She responded, and he liked cuckolding Dad. But he and Mom never spoke of it again. Perverse enough for you?"

"It'll do."

Seitz cocked his head. "By the way, what do you know about your classmate's wife?"

"Never met her. As near as I can tell, her role is to be wife and mother."

"Well, maybe they're the Cleaver family. Of course, you just can't know what happens once the kids are in bed. So I'll move on to the difference between a sociopath and a psychopath."

"Think HE is one or the other?"

"Only one of them," Seitz said succinctly. "As a lawyer, no doubt you've met your share of sociopaths—superficially charming but wholly lacking in empathy. For a sociopath, the only function of other people is to fulfill their own needs. If you're perceptive, they're pretty easy to spot. Most critical here is that they tend to be nonviolent—their sense of caution is too great."

"That would be Carl Hall, actually."

"Which brings me to the psychopath." Seitz's voice softened. "Psychopaths are very special people."

Beneath Seitz's words Darrow heard a warning. "In what way?"

"To begin, they're pretty rare. Like sociopaths, they tend to grow up in an abusive and hostile environment." Seitz paused, then added quietly, "So did you, I know. But psychopaths experience other people solely as objects. And they have absolute mastery over emotions that most of us can't control."

"Such as?"

"Fear. Put an ordinary person in a frightening situation—say, someone draws a knife—and their heart rate jumps. But a psychopath's anxiety level actually *decreases*. They thrive on danger, and tend to be absolutely fearless."

Imagining HE as a real person, Darrow felt uneasy. "How do they relate to women?"

"For a psychopath, sex is power. He needs and despises women at the same time. So he seeks out submissive women—perhaps prostitutes." Again, Seitz paused. "As the diary also suggests, he can get off on the thrill of it, until the need for sexual dominance becomes an addiction."

"What about their willingness to kill?"

"It's often very high. That, too, typically originates with a harsh father. But because a psychopath feels neither anxiety nor guilt, he can kill without remorse. And once he does, he can go to bed and never lose a minute's sleep." Seitz looked hard at Darrow. "By nature, psychopaths aren't anxious people. They don't tend to act on impulse. Instead, they're typically brilliant planners, meticulous in what they do. The man who murdered Angela Hall and her brother—assuming it's the same man, and that Hall was, in fact, murdered—may well be a psychopath. All he'd require is a reason that compels him."

"Would blackmail do?"

Seitz nodded. "Blackmail," he said gravely, "would do very well."

Reflective, Darrow sat back, steepling his fingers to his lips. "It was after Angela's murder that Joe Betts became sober. Maybe he was reacting to being dumped by his college girlfriend. In either case, that doesn't feel consistent with what you're saying."

Seitz tilted his head, as though examining Darrow's question with a jeweler's eye. "If your classmate was moved by shame or conscience, I'd agree. But simple self-preservation is sufficient for a psychopath. Pretending to honor the rules can enable them to conceal who they are. Given the proper motivation, psychopaths are capable of incredible self-control, even over their own deepest desires. Often for years at a time."

Darrow felt a nascent sense of dread. "You're saying HE could have lived a seemingly normal life after murdering Angela Hall. Including succeeding in a demanding career, as Joe Betts has."

"Sure," Seitz responded with an ironic smile. "In the annals of psychopaths, success as a financial adviser is pretty small potatoes. Consider Hitler and Stalin, both paragons of the breed. We remember them as mass murderers. But both also managed to outmaneuver their rivals—and, indeed, entire countries—until they dominated a fair share of the world."

"They were also obviously nuts."

"A lot of people didn't think so. And their form of insanity helped them." Seitz got up, cracking his window to admit a measure of fresh air from another sunlit day. "For one thing, they loved power and had a talent for exploitation—show weakness, and they'd only become more cruel. The only people they respected were those who shared their ruthlessness and lack of fear.

"For them, a couple of murders and a little embezzlement would have been light work. Yet they were often brilliant at reading other people. Neither felt any sentiment that would interfere with their insight and discernment. Faced with Hitler, Neville Chamberlain never had a prayer."

"Ruthlessness is one thing," Darrow retorted. "Charm is another. Sociopaths have that."

"So can psychopaths. And their confidence—concealed arrogance, really—inspires trust in them." Seitz slowed his speech for emphasis. "Stalin and Hitler survived in a much harsher environment than Wayne or the financial services industry."

Darrow fell quiet. After a time, he said, "I'm trying to square this with Joe Betts. For that matter, with his present family life as he presents it."

Seitz pondered this. "The man you describe is engaging, and capable enough to be a great financial success at a very young age. So much so that Caldwell made him a trustee in his mid-thirties, then asked him to oversee the school's investments.

"What you can't know is what he's like to be around in his most unguarded hours. As you concede, you don't know Betts's wife at all. But if she's perceptive, a spouse may realize there's something off. Best to have a wife who's somewhat otherworldly and trusting. Family members see more than the rest of us."

Darrow was still for a time, staring at a watercolor he did not truly see. "Outside the family circle, would HE have any weakness?"

"Arrogance. Psychopaths tend to have superior intelligence. They also know it. So every success they have in getting away with something increases their feeling of omnipotence." Seitz's tone became clipped. "As I noted, they excel at reading other people. But, because they can, they tend to underrate those around them and overrate themselves. They get caught, if at all, when they finally encounter someone as smart as they are."

Darrow took this in. "Tell me about Angela Hall."

"Sure," Seitz said promptly. "Unlike HE, we know Angela was real. What we don't know is whether the narrator in the diary is Angela or a surrogate for fantasies she never actually experienced. But a fair chunk of the populace gets a rush from a modest amount of pain, as long as it's not too dangerous. So in 'normal' S&M, there are rules.

"The problem for our narrator is that HE seems to have no rules. His pleasure comes not just from scaring, but from hurting. Thus his entwinement with her becomes more dangerous, his techniques ever more sadistic."

Darrow nodded. "At the beginning of her diary," he said, "the game seems somewhat manageable. What I was feeling was a process of seduction—Angela could take it, perhaps even be intrigued by it. But by the end, beneath her tone of eerie dispassion, she sounded frightened to me.

"My problem is that I knew her—or thought I did. I know we flatter ourselves by thinking that we understand people based on seeing a tiny fraction of their lives, that which they allow us to see. But the Angela I perceived wouldn't have signed on for this. At least not voluntarily."

"What do you know about *her* family?"

"Nothing."

"So for all you know," Seitz said pointedly, "Dad beat Mom. Like spousal abusers, their victims tend to replicate what they grew up with."

"Suppose that doesn't apply here?"

Seitz shrugged. "You know the alternatives. One, she liked it. Two, HE had some kind of leverage. Three, HE paid her."

Darrow sat back. "Joe had no leverage I can think of. If Joe was HE, they either met each other's needs or he was paying her. God knows Joe was rich enough. But the cops found no sign that Angela was getting money from anything but work."

"What about those diamonds?"

"Those were her brother's—" Darrow stopped himself. "Let me think about that."

"Let's return to Betts. How well does what I've told you fit?"

Darrow organized his thoughts. "Some pieces do. The abusive dad, contempt for women, hitting his girlfriend, an interest in S&M involving black females. And Joe was always smart enough and—at least when he was sober—personable.

"But could he have done all this? Beneath the arrogance you describe, Joe seems vulnerable and insecure. That's what I still struggle with."

Seitz nodded. "Anything else?"

"Your point about dormancy is important—the idea that a psychopath, if faced with danger, might have sufficient self-control to swear off S&M for years. Or, equally, important, alcohol . . ."

"That would especially be true," Seitz asked, "if he'd killed someone while drunk—either in a rage, or because he didn't know how to stop. He might well not kill again until Carl Hall threatened to strip the cover off his Norman Rockwell existence." Seitz paused, then admonished Darrow: "As you know better than anyone, *facts* are what you need here. The best you can do is take what I've given you and use it as a guide. Never forgetting that all our theorizing could be a pile of garbage."

Despite the darkness of his mood, Darrow smiled a little. "I'll still pay your bill, Jerry. But there is one thing I'm certain of. The personality you describe is *not* Steve Tillman."

4

DARROW AND TAYLOR DINED AT EXCELSIOR, ENJOYING A table by the window overlooking the Public Garden. Over cocktails, Taylor described her interview.

"They're very serious," she said, her tone sober and a bit surprised. "The museum wants to expand its collection of contemporary art, and they have the resources to do it."

"And they also seem serious about you?"

"Definitely. I don't have a lot of experience with interviews like this, but they were very thorough and interested in probing my ideas." She smiled, acknowledging a pride she could not contain. "In fact, they asked me to come back tomorrow, to meet with the head curator."

That she would be leaving Wayne, Darrow told himself, was inevitable; whatever his real feelings, his role was to be pleased for her. "If they offer you a job, would you take it?"

Taylor bit her lip, her look of pleasure succeeded by perplexity. "I wasn't expecting to make a decision this soon—either about a job or a city I barely know. But jobs like this are hard to find."

"Can you hold them off for a while?"

Taylor shook her head. "Not if they want me. They'd like someone to start tomorrow, if they could, and they're interviewing other candidates."

Darrow gazed out at the greenery of the Public Garden, his eyes following a young couple holding hands as they walked a meandering pathway. "Sometimes," he observed, "it's easier when decisions get made for you. It's far more difficult when *you* have to make them, not knowing what else may be out there."

Taylor gave him a curious look. "What was it like to live in Boston?"

The question made Darrow feel oddly glum. "As a single person? Fine, I guess—there's enough to do. Compared to a lot of cities, Boston's a magnet for young people. It's where I met Lee." Darrow gave her a somewhat rueful smile. "It seems like we're headed in different directions. Thanks to your dad, I'm a citizen of Wayne, Ohio."

Catching his mood, Taylor covered his hand. "If you hadn't come to Caldwell, Mark, we wouldn't know each other at all. At least not in this way."

Darrow tried to make his smile less equivocal. "I'd have missed that," he said.

THE THOUGHT OF separation, Darrow realized, brought new sensuality to their lovemaking, the sweet but sad awareness that, next month or the month after, they would be unable to reach for each other in the middle of the night. Though he told himself it was childish, he could not help but feel cheated. They had really just begun.

Lying beside her, he pondered this deep into the night. "What are you thinking?" she whispered.

He turned his face to her. "How did you know I was awake?"

"Because you breathe more deeply when you're sleeping."

She slept less well than he did, Darrow was learning, often restless until early morning. "I was thinking about you," he said. "Hoping this job prospect turns out however it's supposed to."

That seemed to make her thoughtful. Softly, she said, "I'll miss you, too."

They remained quiet until Darrow drifted off. As he did, he remembered Lee saying that most men were like Norsemen—they could eat well, make love with gusto, then fall into a dreamless sleep, untroubled by their own stirrings.

Suddenly, Darrow started awake.

It took a moment to orient himself. Then he realized that Taylor was sitting on the edge of the bed, still naked, her face in her hands. Placing his hands on her shoulders, he felt her flinch, heard a stifled sob.

"Taylor," he said with quiet urgency. "What is it?"

For a long time, she did not answer. "The same dream," she murmured. "Ever since I was twelve."

"What happens?"

She did not turn. "I find my mother dead. I try to get her to talk to me, and she can't."

He rested his chin on her shoulder, his face against hers. "Is that how it happened?"

"I don't think so—not the talking part. But I've had the dream so long I don't even know what's real." She paused, then said with muted despair, "I thought I'd finally outrun it."

"How do you mean?"

She turned sideways, staring out into the darkness. "The last year, at NYU, it seemed to have gone away. Returning to Wayne revived it." Her voice held a note of self-contempt. "It's just so arrested. It's like I'm twelve again, stuck in the worst part of my life."

"Did you ever go to a therapist?"

"At twelve? I wouldn't have known how to ask, and then I went to prep school." She turned, speaking softly. "What's there to explain, really? I lost my mother in adolescence, when I had no equipment for dealing with it, no one I could bring myself to talk with. Instead I ran away to Trumble, trying to shut off all my feelings. But they just migrated to my dream life. Living in the house where I found her body is bringing it all back."

She sounded close to devastated. "Be kind to yourself," Darrow said. "You lost the parent you loved most at the time you were least prepared. If you need help, Taylor, why not get some?"

She said nothing. But afterward, neither slept.

The next morning, over breakfast in his kitchen, Taylor remained silent. She did not finish her cereal, or even seem to know he was there. It was as if she were walled off.

She has a tendency toward melancholy, Farr had told him. Darrow did not know quite what to do.

Gazing at the table, Taylor said tonelessly, "I still have an interview, don't I."

MIKE RILEY'S OFFICE was jammed with manila folders in stacks, tomes on finance, and manuals on forensic accounting. Small, dark, fidgety, and often amused, Riley defied Darrow's image of a certified public accountant. He was also brilliant.

Sitting in front of Riley's cluttered desk, Darrow inquired, "Where's your pocket protector?"

"Lame," Riley replied. "Especially from a recovering lawyer who needs my help."

"So you believe what everyone else does?" Darrow said. "That Durbin is a crook?"

"He may be," Riley answered. "Just not indubitably."

"Explain."

"First, the facts inculpating Durbin look pretty persuasive. He was on the investment committee, his e-mail address is on the directive to Joe Betts, and what appears to be his signature is on the bank account where the proceeds went. As well as on the second account that received fifty thousand dollars wired from a Swiss bank."

Darrow took a swallow of black coffee. "What else?"

"There are still some holes." Riley spoke more slowly now. "The missing piece in the chain of evidence is that we don't know who controls the Swiss account. Obviously, the Swiss will never tell us. A new piece, also unexplained, is why over six hundred thousand came back to Carl Hall from another bank in Switzerland, and what, if anything, that has to do with Caldwell College. Given that the transfers to Hall happened *after* the embezzlement may suggest that the same person transferred money from one Swiss bank to the other. But that leaves us to wonder why Durbin would siphon money to Hall." He gave Darrow an arid smile. "That Carl died from a shitload of heroin is also inconvenient."

"Which brings us to my alternate theory," Darrow rejoined. "Blackmail, with the embezzler using Caldwell's money to pay off Hall."

Riley took out the schedule of transfers that Garrison had given Darrow. "What's interesting about these transfers is that they suggest a certain level of sophistication. Whoever moved the money understood that individual transfers of over ten thousand to or from a Swiss bank would trigger a federal inquiry."

Darrow looked at him keenly. "Anyone in the financial services industry would know that. Certainly anyone on Caldwell's investment committee. Except, perhaps, Clark Durbin."

Picking up a pen, Riley held it to his lips. "And so, you ask, could someone like Betts have framed Durbin?"

Darrow nodded. "You know the problem, Mike. Who else but Durbin would have access to his computer and e-mail account, plus the ability to 'forge' Durbin's name? No one believes Clark when he says it wasn't him."

"I don't believe him," Riley said flatly. "Or disbelieve him. Ever hear of 'spoofing'?"

"No."

"Not many people have. In brief, it's a very clever technique through which, by changing the settings on your PC, you can send an e-mail using someone else's address." Riley looked at Darrow keenly. "Someone *could* have done that to Durbin."

"What about Betts's reply? I've seen the e-mail trail; Joe e-mailed Durbin in response."

"Sure. But the sender of the original e-mail, by rigging his computer, can ensure that the reply goes to his PC. In my scenario, Durbin would never receive it." His eyes were bright with interest. "That would work particularly well, I suppose, if Betts were replying to himself."

Darrow reflected. "But anyone with inside knowledge could have done it?"

Riley grinned. "Anyone in central Ohio," he corrected. "I had my IT guy take a look at this. He tells me that's where Durbin's e-mail to Betts originated. Aside from Durbin, who on the investment committee lives in central Ohio?"

Darrow felt his instincts quicken. "Betts," he answered promptly. "And Ed Rardin. But our investigators obtained access to the PCs of everyone on the committee."

Riley waved a dismissive hand. "Of course they did. But that proves nothing if a member of the committee used a separate computer with a false account. Which is exactly what he would have done."

"What about Durbin's signatures?"

"I showed the copies you sent me to a handwriting expert." Riley gave a fatalistic shrug. "Inconclusive, he says. If someone forged Durbin's name, he varied the script enough that he must have been working from multiple examples of Durbin's real signature—no one signs his name the same way twice. But my expert also thought the pen tracks appeared heavier than Durbin's normal script, creating the possibility that someone was imitating Durbin's signature with painstaking deliberation. Bottom line, he isn't sure."

Pensive, Darrow eyed the Harvard coffee mug where Riley kept his pens and pencils. "So where are we?"

"Limbo. I can't tell you that any of this happened. I'm just saying it *could* have." He flashed a brief but jaunty smile. "Bring your laptop with you?"

"Sure."

"When you get home, open up your e-mail. Check out what pops up."

"I'll do that," Darrow said, and left.

WHEN HE ARRIVED home, the house was quiet, and Taylor had not returned.

Restless, he went upstairs to his office and opened his e-mail. Amid the cluster from Caldwell was one from Mike Riley. Opening it, he found a separate e-mail to Riley from Darrow's own address. "Mike," it began, "this will explain how I stole Caldwell's money. Being a lawyer, theft comes easy. I first learned by sending bills to clients."

Caught between amusement and unease, Darrow replied, "Lawyers also sue people. Please look up 'libel' in the dictionary."

Which, if Joe Betts knew what Darrow was doing, Joe might also suggest.

WHEN TAYLOR CAME through the door, Darrow was dressed for the Red Sox game. Though she looked tired, she seemed to have recovered her aplomb. "So?" he asked.

"So I'm sorry for the morning's séance."

"I liked the quiet," he said lightly. "How was your second interview?"

"Depends on your point of view." Taylor's smile was tentative. "They offered me the position, Mark. For better or worse, no one's making this decision for me."

Despite himself, Darrow was surprised. "This is major," he said. "Shall we skip the game and talk this over?"

Taylor shook her head. "I'd really like to go—we can always talk between innings. After all, I've got a whole week to decide."

They drove to Fenway Park, Taylor describing the offer and her impression of the curator. "It all sounds good," Darrow said as they arrived.

"If I let this go," Taylor responded, "I may regret it. But I also regret that it comes too soon. As they say, I'm torn."

The night was balmy, perfect for baseball. They sat between home and first base, three rows back, gazing in a direct line at the pitcher's mound and, beyond that, the left-field wall known as the Green Monster. "I love baseball," Taylor said. "The people, the smell of beer and hot dogs . . ."

"What about the game?"

"Especially the game," Taylor said. "It's performance art—there's a beautiful geometry to how it's played, the lines and angles. Every game is a creation, different than whatever came before. But there's a wonderful history, passed through generations." She smiled a little. "I never saw Ted Williams play. But my father could describe his swing so perfectly, I felt as if I had."

Once again, Darrow had the sad sense of potential lost—a father and daughter who, their lives altered by the same event, were unable to transcend it. "I have no memories like that," he said. "My father and I never played a game, or went to one. He just disappeared one day, leaving nothing behind. I don't even know if he's alive." And when his mother died, Darrow thought but did not say, all he had felt was emptiness.

Taylor glanced at him. Judging from his expression, she realized that he had said this less from personal sadness than to make a modest point about Farr. She chose to focus on the game.

It was unusually well played, a pitcher's battle between Josh Beckett and C. C. Sabathia in which, with the game tied 1–1 in the eighth inning, both pitchers finally yielded to the bullpen. "Why don't we do this," Darrow proposed. "If the Red Sox win, you take the job and never look back."

Taylor smiled. "That would be a relief, actually. Let the gods of baseball decide."

In the ninth, Alex Rodriguez put the Yankees ahead with a shot over the Green Monster. Taylor bit her lip. "Guess they want me in New York."

"Give Boston a chance," Darrow said.

The Red Sox got through the rest of the top of the ninth with no further damage. With one out in the bottom of the ninth, Dustin Pedroia singled. Then, with two outs, David Ortiz hit a towering home run off Mariano Rivera that won the game for Boston. Amid the tumult, Darrow gave Taylor a hug. "Seems like they're excited for you."

Taylor leaned back, her smile uncertain. "Want the decision back?" Darrow asked.

"No." Taylor kissed him. "It's a perfect job for me. I'm just thinking how much I'll miss you."

5

THERE WERE CERTAIN MORNINGS, DARROW THOUGHT, WHEN the world at first light seemed as fresh and new and awesome as creation.

This Monday morning was one. Walking from the President's House to his appointment with Lionel Farr, he crossed the gentle hillock between two older red-brick dormitories, taking in the scent of flowers, the deep greenness of oak trees, the seeming closeness of an unsullied blue sky, the glistening wet remnants on the grass from an overnight thunderstorm that, with the stiff breezes that followed, seemed to have purified nature. Light and landscape had always affected Darrow's moods: dank, dark enclosures depressed him; a mountain vista or a pristine beach or even a bright morning like this could exhilarate him. He had learned to savor such moments. And so, instead of meeting in his office, he had suggested to Farr that they walk there together.

Farr was waiting outside his house. Casually dressed for summer in slacks and a polo shirt, at first sighting the provost looked much younger than he was, his gray-blond hair still thick, his stomach flat, his profile clean. Even at a closer range that revealed the deep lines on his skin, the angles of his face seemed hewn from granite, the light blue eyes penetrating and clear. Lionel Farr would not slide gently into his dotage; he would fight against old age until he exhausted his last resources. But today the sight of him, usually welcome, jolted Darrow from his reveries. The conversation he intended would be difficult, its outcome unclear. Darrow had no script for this.

They headed toward College Hall, two men of roughly the same height and build, walking with the same easy rhythm. "How was Boston?" Farr inquired.

"Fine. What does Taylor say?"

Farr gave him a brief, sideways look. "Taylor," he said carefully, "can be a woman of shifting moods, somewhat difficult to read. At least for me. But she seemed a bit preoccupied, I thought." He paused, then added with an undertone of regret, "I'm in the odd position of asking Caldwell's president how my daughter's doing."

Taylor, Darrow realized at once, had said nothing about her job offer. "If you're asking how we are," Darrow said, "the answer's that we're still quite new. And running out of time."

The words seemed stiffer than Darrow had intended. "I don't mean to pry," Farr responded with parental dignity. "But I care for you both. I think you know that. Perhaps, at some point, Taylor will, too."

Darrow turned to him, trying to refine his sense that Farr was obscurely wounded. "I think she does, Lionel. But her mother's death seems to have been a fault line in both your lives. She's lived with her own thoughts for a very long time."

He could not find his balance this morning, Darrow reflected; he had said more than he had meant to. Quiet, Farr seemed to withdraw a little. "Anne was fragile," he said at length. "Not just physically, but emotionally. In some ways, so is Taylor—it's as if she believes that I could somehow have protected the mother she loved from the ravages of heart disease. It's a child's way of looking at the world."

The comment nettled Darrow. "That's a little harsh, Lionel."

"Perhaps so. But I think Taylor sees her mother as the princess in the tower, a helpless woman allowed to die. In the mythology, I'm less a human being than a marble statue, with the emotions to match." Farr's voice softened. "Anne's death devastated us both. The added price I paid with Taylor was my recompense for surviving. I, not Anne, was supposed to die."

The statement stunned Darrow. "For God's sake, Lionel."

They had reached the edge of fraternity row, the head of the walkway leading to the main campus. Abruptly, Farr stopped, looking not at Darrow but at the steeple of the Spire. "No doubt you think I'm being melodramatic."

"No," Darrow said bluntly. "Hurt, and a little resentful."

Farr's eyes narrowed, and then he nodded slowly. "Fifteen years of distance can do that. I have no doubt that had Anne lived, Taylor would not have left so soon, or remained alienated for so long. I still believe that as she got older, I might have done better as a father. Things could have been quite different."

"She did come back, after all."

"I know that," Farr said at length. "Perhaps some good will come of it—whether for Taylor and me or for the two of you." He faced Darrow, his expression somber. "You know she won't stay here, Mark. Not just because of work, or even the place itself. In her heart she believes that Anne depended on me too much. I hope you understand that Taylor is determined to control her own psychic space, to have a piece of her life that is hers alone."

"I don't expect anything else," Darrow said. "And don't want it. When the summer's done, Taylor has to move on."

"Which may not be bad for either of you," Farr responded. "In your case it will give you the time to better comprehend Taylor—both her strengths and her vulnerabilities." Farr's smile, faint and fleeting, seemed directed at himself. "I know I sound like the pompous father in *Love Story*. But if you and Taylor are meant to be more than you are now, it will stand the test of time and distance."

Darrow tried to untangle his own reaction, a shifting compound of irritation, sadness, and amusement. "Worse than *Love Story*," he said dryly. "Nonetheless, I'll hold the thought."

Farr laughed softly, and they began walking again. "There was something else," Farr prodded. "You wanted to speak in confidence."

"I do." Though Darrow had gone over what he meant to say— editing and rearranging the sequence of his explanation—he found that starting did not come easy. "Mind if we sit somewhere?"

They found a stone bench in a manicured garden, incongruously Asian in character, between the library and the student union. At this hour, a little before eight, few summer students were ambitious enough to surface; effectively deserted, the site afforded Darrow the privacy he needed and yet kept him from feeling claustrophobic. The subject was bad enough.

"There's no good place to begin this," Darrow said. "So I'll start with the most recent events. There's a fair chance that most of Caldwell's stolen money was siphoned to Carl Hall."

Farr raised his head slightly, as though looking at Darrow from a new angle. Something about his pupils reminded Darrow of drill bits. "Go on."

Succinctly, Darrow outlined Garrison's schedule of Hall's transactions: the timing and disbursements of money; their connection to a Swiss bank; their apparent structuring to avoid federal oversight. The skepticism in Farr's gaze seemed to border on antagonism. "The man was a drug dealer," he said curtly. "I assume you've given this information to Joe Betts and Greg Fox."

"Not yet."

"And why not, for the love of God?"

Darrow tried to remain calm. "I'll get to that," he said. "In the meanwhile, please withhold judgment. You can have a coronary once I'm done."

Farr inhaled slowly. "All right," he said in a neutral voice. "Tell me why the police entrusted you with this delicate information."

"Several reasons. One is that I found Hall's body."

Farr's smile, a rare show of teeth, held more anger than his hardened tone. "Of course. What better job for the president of Caldwell College."

"Part of my job," Darrow snapped, "is being smarter than the people you and Carrick chose to investigate this mess. I wish *that* part were harder."

The fury and frustration in Darrow's tone seemed to give Farr pause. In a frosty voice, he said, "Please justify that statement."

"Joe and Fox are masters of the obvious. 'Obviously,' Durbin embezzled money—after all, he sent an e-mail to Joe Betts, then signed his own name to bank accounts. 'Obviously,' Durbin's not only a criminal but criminally stupid. But the fact is—and I have an expert to confirm it—that a reasonably savvy person could have replicated Durbin's e-mail and forged his signature, leaving Durbin none the wiser. If you don't know you stole the money, it's hard to cover your tracks."

Farr crossed his arms. His voice soft and ironic, he asked, "So who did steal it, Mark?"

"Someone on the investment committee."

Briefly, Farr closed his eyes. With the same quiet, he said, "We're talking about business leaders of considerable wealth and unquestioned probity. I may be cynical about human nature, but your thesis borders on hallucinatory. Pass over whether any of them have the inventiveness you posit. What could possibly motivate one of those men to steal nine hundred thousand dollars, then try to ruin Clark Durbin's life, at considerable risk to their own?"

"Blackmail."

Farr propped his elbows on his knees, staring at the garden. "Let me grasp this. A black drug dealer from the southeast side of Wayne was blackmailing a prominent white alumnus. Makes perfect sense. Just tell me what connects two such disparate men."

Darrow steeled himself. "That's one reason I went to see Hall. After I found his body, the police located a safe deposit box in Carl's name. Inside was a small bag of diamonds, and a Xerox copy of a diary written by Angela Hall."

"Angela kept a diary?"

"Yes. It's not very pleasant to read. Or to describe."

In unsparing detail, Darrow did. The blood drained from Farr's face, making him look older. Tonelessly, he said, "Pray God this was an experiment in creative writing and that those things never happened to her."

"And if they did?"

"It defies every notion I had of this young woman." As he considered Darrow's words, the grooves in Farr's face seemed to deepen. "From what you say, the man she calls HE seems barely real."

"His perversions sound real enough." Darrow paused. "A couple of months before she died, Angela began disappearing at night. No one knows where she went. But her mother believes *that* was when she began this particular diary. After she was murdered, it disappeared."

"From which you posit . . ."

"That Angela went out to meet the man called HE. After she died, Carl stole her diary. That was his tool of blackmail."

Farr gazed straight ahead. "By your own account, the diary gives no clue to the man's identity. Even were he real, how would Carl know?"

"I don't have any idea. But I believe that Carl *did* know, and therefore knew that the same man might well have killed her. That's why HE murdered Carl."

Farr's mind moved quickly now, following the rules of Darrow's logic. "Making HE a member of our investment committee."

"Yes." Darrow paused and took a breath. "Joe Betts."

To Darrow's surprise, Farr was expressionless. "For which accusation, I assume, your reasons go back sixteen years. Joe was at the party. Joe and Tillman fought over Angela. No one saw Joe during the hours when Angela died. But Joe claimed to see Tillman returning from the Spire, sealing Steve's conviction." He turned to Darrow.

"We've always known these things. But what on earth makes you think Joe was capable of the practices depicted in Angela's diary?"

"Joe hit his college girlfriend," Darrow answered softly. "He also collected pornography involving black women and sadomasochism."

Farr pinched the bridge of his nose, rubbing it as though trying to erase a headache. "And you know this because—"

"Joe's ex-girlfriend told me."

"When?"

"About two weeks ago."

Turning again, Farr examined Darrow steadily. "You have been busy, haven't you?"

"Yes. Sorry it's so inconvenient."

"This is no time for petulance. Tell me why Angela wished to satisfy Joe's desires."

Darrow shook his head. "I don't know."

"He wasn't paying her?"

"Not that I know about."

Farr grimaced. "Outside the fateful party, do we know if Betts and Angela Hall had any relationship at all?"

Darrow hesitated. "Her mother remembers a youthful-sounding white guy calling Angela at home . . ."

"But not Joe."

"She just doesn't know." Once again, Darrow marshaled his arguments. "We know Steve had sex with her. But everything else, factually and psychologically, makes Joe as plausible a murderer as Steve Tillman. We know Steve didn't shoot up Carl Hall. Throw in the diary and the embezzlement, and a web starts tightening around Joe Betts."

Farr looked around, as though fearful that they might be overhead. "So what you're asking me to believe is that, by whatever means, a financial adviser from Columbus subdued Carl Hall inside his home on the outskirts of Wayne, prepared a heroin injection that—for reasons not apparent to me—he knew was lethal, and then put Carl to sleep like a terminally ill house pet."

"Essentially, yes."

"Your theory is a house of cards," Farr said tightly. "Change a single fact or eliminate one assumption, and the whole thing collapses. You become, if not the biggest fool in Caldwell's history, one of the most arrogant and presumptuous. The man who smeared an innocent man with wild accusations in order to save a guilty friend." Farr paused, then continued in a tone of deliberate calm: "We'll pass over all the leaps in logic. I won't ask you to decipher the baroque description of 'darkness in the chamber of stone.' We'll even forget the incongruity of converting a member of Caldwell's investment committee into a forger, a specialist in computer fakery, a sadomasochist, and an expert in preparing and administering heroin, all packaged in a man as nerveless as a brain surgeon. Just tell me why the 'blackmail' commenced only in the last year."

Farr's self-control, Darrow found, was more daunting than his anger. "It didn't start this year," he answered. "Hall opened the safe deposit box over a decade ago, and converting cash to diamonds is a classic technique for laundering money. I'm assuming that's how the payments began—"

"When Joe was barely out of school? Where did he get the money?"

"Inheritance, I'm guessing. His father died in our junior year."

Farr scowled. "At least you have him using his own money. So why would he risk embezzling Caldwell's investment funds?"

"I don't know. Maybe Joe no longer has the money we think he does. Or, after he got married, perhaps his wife started keeping an eye on their finances."

The day was becoming warmer, Darrow realized. He could see the dampness on Farr's forehead, feel it on his own. "Then take your central assumption," Farr countered, "that Betts killed Hall. Were that disproven, would you agree that your entire theory evanesces?"

"It wouldn't help," Darrow acknowledged. "But Joe was here in Wayne that night. We had a meeting to discuss our finances."

"Which ended when?"

Darrow tried to remember. "A little before eight, I think."

"What time did you find Hall?"

"Around ten."

"So sometime between eight and ten, you posit, Joe drove across town to Hall's, then subdued and killed him. All while escaping detection." Farr put his hand on Darrow's shoulder. "Let me propose an alternative theory. It would have taken less than an hour for Joe to drive back to Columbus. By nine o'clock, rather than killing Carl, Joe was watching the Disney Channel with his kids. Why don't you ask his wife?" Farr's tone became softer yet. "Of course, she might wonder why you care."

Darrow was silent. "Depending on her answer," Farr said, "your theory could be in deep trouble. I hope you've not been so careless as to share it with anyone else."

Darrow shook his head. "No. Not even the police."

Farr looked into Darrow's eyes. "Well, at least you retained the judgment to tell me. So, for all our sakes, hear me well.

"I understand why Tillman's conviction troubles you. But there's no way for you to know what really happened that night. Just as there's little reason to believe—and no way to prove—that Carl Hall's possibly accidental death relates to the college's sad history. My ultimate question is this: Why do you insist that Durbin's apparent theft must connect to Angela's murder?" Farr's grip on Darrow's shoulder tightened. "Take this fantasy to Chief Garrison, if you must. *He* can blow it up. But once you do that, you may destroy your presidency and, given all that's happened, jeopardize Caldwell College itself.

"That's not what you came here for, Mark. Angela Hall's dead; the money's gone. Your sole responsibility is to secure our future. Just as, after Angela's death, I did everything in my power to keep this school alive."

Darrow met his eyes. "I care about Caldwell, too. Perhaps as much as you."

Farr released his shoulder. "This isn't just about Caldwell," he said quietly. "You and Taylor are the most important people I have left. For either of you to suffer for this is more than I can bear. Please, tread lightly."

Slowly, Darrow nodded. "I will."

6

SHORTLY AFTER LUNCH, DARROW RECEIVED A CALL FROM RAY Carrick. Without preface, Carrick demanded, "When are we turning Durbin over to Dave Farragher?"

"When I know everything I need to know," Darrow answered simply.

"What else is there to know?" Carrick said with weary disgust. His voice became flinty. "At this point, Mark, you can either prosecute Durbin or explain why not. The governance committee of the board is meeting next Monday. We look forward to hearing from you."

Still raw from his confrontation with Lionel Farr, Darrow briefly wondered if his provost had telephoned Carrick, agreeing on a strategy to force his hand. Perhaps this was paranoid. But whatever the case, Darrow was trapped—he could not explain himself fully without accusing Joe Betts, and Carrick had given him one week. "Then I'll look forward to seeing you," Darrow said.

This reply, temperate but uncowed, induced in Carrick a momentary silence. "While we're on the phone," Darrow continued, "is there anything else you want to talk about?"

The question seemed to catch Carrick off guard. "Yes," he said defensively. "This whole business with the Tillman case—poking around in Farragher's files. We didn't hire you to do Dave's job."

Darrow held his temper. "They're not Dave's files," he replied. "They're public. Steve Tillman was my friend. One reason he's in jail is that everybody did their job except the lawyer who was defending him. If that bothers me enough to take a second look, that's my privilege as a citizen. I'm sure you agree that the man serving life for murdering a Caldwell student should actually have killed her."

"Dave Farragher has no doubt," Carrick said testily.

"He mentioned that—as I think you know." Darrow softened his tone. "I hope this isn't an issue for the board, Ray. But if it is, we can make it a subject of Monday's meeting as well."

Carrick's silence made it clear that he had heard Darrow's message: Darrow was willing to risk a public confrontation that, perhaps, could spin out of Carrick's control. "I'll reflect on that," Carrick said slowly.

Darrow wondered again whether, by private agreement, Farr was using Carrick to protect Darrow from his own excesses. But he felt Ray Carrick becoming his adversary. "I'd be happy to discuss this further, Ray," Darrow said in his most amiable tone. "On the phone or over lunch. I'd hate for us to misunderstand each other."

"So would I, Mark. If you have anything else to tell me, please do."

Very soon, Darrow knew, he would have to stand on something more concrete than his authority as Caldwell's president. "I will, Ray."

Hanging up, Darrow wondered what else he could learn in seven days.

Late that afternoon, Darrow called Joe Betts's office.

As he expected, Joe's assistant answered the phone. "Hi, Mr. Darrow. Looking for Joe?"

"You, actually." He sat back in his chair. "I'm trying to put together my expense reports, and I think I've scrambled some dates. Including a dinner with Joe."

"I'm sure I can help," Julie said with maternal good cheer. "I'm used to looking after boys."

"No doubt. Specifically, I'm showing a meeting with Joe at eight o'clock on the twenty-fifth. But that somehow doesn't seem right to me. Mind checking Joe's calendar?"

"Just a minute."

Waiting, Darrow calculated how to maneuver the conversation. At length Julie came back on the line. "The twenty-fifth's right. But Joe's calendar shows six o'clock, not eight."

"Bizarre," Darrow said, his voice puzzled. "It couldn't have been eight o'clock?"

"I don't think so. I'm showing that he drove to Cleveland that night, for a client meeting early the next morning." She gave the knowing but affectionate chuckle of an assistant attuned to her employer's eccentricities. "Joe doesn't schedule things late—he's a stickler for his full eight hours of sleep, especially on the road. I keep telling him to pack his fluffy pillow."

It was possible, Darrow saw at once, for Joe to have murdered Carl Hall before driving to Cleveland. As Farr had suggested, all that would require was some very surprising skills and the nerve of an assassin. "Thanks for the help," Darrow told Julie.

"You're welcome." Swiftly, she added, "Hold on, Mr. Darrow." There was a brief pause, then Julie explained, "Joe was passing by. When he heard it was you, he wanted to say hello."

Darrow hesitated. "Great. Please put him on."

"Hey, Mark," Joe said cheerfully, "Guess you need Julie to tell you where you've been."

"Yup. And all I need now is for her to tell me where I'm going."

"All of us could use that." Betts's voice changed pitch. "Anything new that I should know about?"

"Nothing in particular."

Joe hesitated. "Ray Carrick called me today, checking on the whole Durbin fiasco. He was wondering if we'd learned anything new that would keep us from seeking prosecution."

"Why am I not surprised?"

"So do we? You were going to see your forensics guy, I know. Ray seems to want this buttoned up."

"We're all on the same page, Joe." Darrow's tone became placating. "It's been three weeks since I told Durbin that he should come to Jesus. His time is running out."

The brief silence that followed suggested that Betts had caught Darrow's evasion. "And your guy in Boston," he prodded.

"Can't say that Durbin didn't do it."

The small equivocation seemed to unsettle Joe still more. "So I guess you've got nothing more to tell governance next Monday."

Darrow gave a short laugh. "News travels fast. Ray's not bashful, is he?"

"Not when something sticks in his craw. And Durbin does." Joe's tone became sympathetic. "This may be a time to give Ray what he wants. Still, if you think prosecuting Clark would hurt Caldwell more than help us, I'm more open to that argument. For whatever my opinion might be worth to Ray."

Darrow noted this change of attitude. Suspicion followed at once: if Joe had murdered Carl Hall, perhaps he no longer wanted the police or prosecutor to dig more deeply into the embezzlement. If so, Joe and Darrow were both ensnared in the crosscurrents of what might be an agreement between Farr and Carrick to prosecute Clark Durbin. But Darrow's confrontation with Farr had jarred him—he had a shade less confidence in the logic of his intuitions, and his interpretations of behaviors with multiple explanations.

"I'll let you know," Darrow said easily. "There's a decent argument that indicting Durbin would shake loose where the money went."

"It could," Joe agreed. "Or we could shut this down and let Clark just go quietly. You have to weigh recovering the money against ongoing negative publicity if Durbin goes to trial. For Caldwell's sake, I'm now willing to swallow my pride."

"Thanks, Joe. And I'm sorry to have bothered Julie."

"No problem," Joe said amiably. "Except on weekends, that was my only dinner out the entire month."

"Even with clients? You're leading a quiet life, Joe."

"By design. Dinner with Katie and the kids is pretty close to sacred." Joe's voice became serious. "In college, I told you about the old man. He'd come home on the train from Wall Street, spending a good hour in the bar car. I don't know who was more scared when Dad came through the door—Mother or my sisters and me.

"It stays with you, Mark. Once the kids were born, Katie and I agreed that dinner would be a time for us and the kids to enjoy each other, talk about the day, or just hear what's on everyone's mind. I can't change my childhood, but I can make theirs different."

However gratuitous in context, Joe's tribute to family life sounded heartfelt. Joe might be sincere or an extremely practiced actor—in either case, he very much wanted Darrow to know how completely he had changed, and how much his family relied on him. "As I said before," Darrow said, "I envy you."

"It'll come," Joe said almost gently. "Someday."

Deeply reflective, Darrow said good-bye.

Turning, he gazed out the window at the tree-shaded lawn in front of College Hall, recalling, as he did, walking with Joe across this lawn on the day of Joe's confession. HE was a psychopath, Jerry Seitz had surmised—amoral, adaptive, attuned to danger, gifted at outwitting others, able to restrain his deepest desires in order to survive. If Joe was guilty, these were among his attributes. In that case, Joe's claim of familial closeness was a complete and utter fraud.

Darrow tried to untangle his thoughts, let them lead wherever they would. But they kept gravitating to Laurie Shilts, the bondage magazine, the pathology detailed in Angela's diary. *There is such darkness in the chamber of stone.*

It was early evening, Darrow realized. He picked up the telephone and called Fred Bender's office.

The chief of security was in. "Mind if I walk over?" Darrow asked.

"Sure," Bender said laconically. "Been wanting to discuss our budget."

WHEN DARROW ARRIVED, Bender was leaning against the building near the doorway, smoking a Camel. Darrow joined him, looking across campus toward the sandstone base of the Spire.

"I've been thinking about our conversation," Darrow said.

"About Steve Tillman?" Bender moved his shoulders. "So have I, to no great purpose. What's bothering you now?"

"It's more a question. Back at the time of Angela's murder, who had access to the Spire?"

Bender gave him a curious glance. "Far as I know, things were pretty much the same as they are now. And had been ever since some drunken fool took a swan dive from the bell tower." Bender took a drag on his cigarette. "Security is supposed to have the only keys. But the president, administrators, trustees, and faculty members can borrow one to show alumni or special guests—anyone dumb enough to risk a heart attack by climbing a couple hundred steps."

"I recall each step," Darrow said with a smile.

"I bet you do. The day you climbed there, Durbin got a key from security to open the door himself. By tradition, that's the president's job whenever we beat Ohio Lutheran."

Darrow nodded. Facing him, Bender said, "I guess you're wondering if someone got inside there the night Angela Hall was murdered."

Darrow kept his face blank. "I've been grasping for a reason why I found her near the Spire."

Bender gave him a skeptical smile. "It's like a prison in there.

Who'd want to be inside the Spire at night? Anyhow, once you came back down, Durbin locked it and gave the key back to security."

"You asked him?"

"Yeah. You weren't in any shape to notice, but it was locked when we showed up in response to Lionel's call."

A fragment of memory surfaced in Darrow's mind: Taylor's amusing account of how a prep school friend lost her virginity in the chapel, supposedly sacrosanct, when her boyfriend managed to obtain a key. "Were students ever allowed to borrow a key?" he asked.

"Not without an authorized person." Puffing his cigarette, Bender added with a note of humor, "I don't claim it never happened. If there's one thing I've learned, it's to respect the enterprise of college students in the face of adult obstacles."

Darrow nodded. "I remember well."

Bender's eyes grew serious. Softly, he said, "Can't say we asked Tillman if he had a duplicate key. Or, for that matter, Joe Betts. If that's what you mean."

"I don't know what I mean, Fred."

Bender finished his cigarette. Glancing at his watch, he said, "Quitting time."

"For both of us," Darrow said. "Thanks."

He started back to his office. Over his shoulder, Bender said, "About the budget. You going to give me the extra man I need?"

Turning, Darrow smiled, giving a careless wave of the hand. "Anything you want, Fred. Fuck the English Department."

Bender emitted a skeptical laugh, and ground out the Camel with the heel of his shoe.

7

Ｉ N PLACE OF AN ELABORATE DINNER, TAYLOR AND DARROW prepared a picnic of red wine, Gruyère cheese, bruschetta, and cold shrimp. They ate at a wrought iron table behind the President's House, the twilight gathering around them.

"You look tired," Taylor said.

And also preoccupied, Darrow reflected, with both the burden of his secrets and the strain of withholding them from Taylor. "I've got a lot on my mind, I guess."

"Care to talk about it?"

"Maybe later. I'm curious about your final answer to the museum."

Taylor's brow knit, her expression becoming abstracted. "I'm accepting the position tomorrow," she said. "Or the next day. The salary's decent and the acquisition budget is more than that. Having sniffed around in the last couple of days, I can't see anything else where I'd have this kind of autonomy."

"Then congratulations," Darrow said, raising his glass. "When do you plan to start?"

Taylor touched her glass to his, looking more serious than pleased. "I'll try to get another six weeks here, to finish my dissertation." She sipped her wine, adding, "And to spend more time with you while I can."

Despite his worries, Darrow felt relieved. "I thought you couldn't wait to blow this particular pop stand."

"In most ways, I can't. Wayne isn't a good place for me." She hesitated, the doubt on her face replaced by candor. "We haven't had much time together, and I'm not sure what either of us is ready for. But I like you very much, Mark—more, at this stage, than I've ever cared for anyone." As though to cover her embarrassment, Taylor finished lightly: "Of course, you had a head start on anyone else. You're the only guy I had a crush on even before I knew what sex was."

Darrow laughed. "We met when you were seven, Taylor. I had to wait for you to catch up."

Taylor's smile did not quite reach her eyes. "So how do you feel about long-distance relationships?"

Darrow pondered the question. "Lee and I had one, every election cycle. Maybe she needed that. I didn't, really." Reading the disappointment on Taylor's face, Darrow took her hand. "I wasn't looking for someone who lived in another city. But the way I feel about you may end up mattering far more."

Taylor tilted her head. "It might be hard—me in Boston, you here, both of us with demanding jobs."

Still holding her hand, Darrow shrugged. "We're two smart people who seem to be able to talk pretty openly. I've already had one career, and I'm into my second. Launching yours is pretty important. We'll figure out what's right to do."

"Then I guess we're taking this as it comes."

"Starting now," Darrow said. "Have your dad's permission for an overnight?"

Taylor rolled her eyes. "That's still a little strange," she answered, then continued in a musing tone: "When I came back to Wayne, I thought Dad and I might become closer. Instead there's this weird constraint between us, partly because of what's happening with me and you. Sometimes I feel guilty, as though the energy I should be putting into healing my relationship with my father is going to you instead." She managed a smile. "I guess the truth is that you're just easier."

Darrow felt regret that this three-sided relationship had become more complex than he wished. "At one point," he replied, "I had this illusion that I might help things. In the end, I hope I can."

"I hope so, too."

Dusk had come, Darrow noticed, and with it a surprising coolness in the air. "So things are no better between Lionel and you?"

"A little, I suppose—I think he appreciates that I came home. But there's something Olympian about my father, a distance."

"That's not just with you, Taylor. Lionel is a man of his time—even with the people who most admire him, and that's pretty much everyone around the place."

A corner of Taylor's mouth turned down, lending her expression a trace of sadness and frustration. "But shouldn't it be different with a daughter who's also an adult?" Taylor's voice sharpened with annoyance. "He still treats me like a child, Mark, sometimes even in the smallest ways. The other day, I found him struggling with something on his computer. It's painfully obvious that the Internet is like a foreign country to him. But he absolutely refused to let me touch his dinosaur of a laptop."

Darrow smiled, recalling the many times when some contemporary had complained that a personal computer had reduced a parent to their babbling infant. "Once a child," he said, "always a child. And never more so than when a parent resents you for knowing more than they do."

Taylor did not smile. "Maybe so. But he was that way with my mother, I've begun to remember. Like he couldn't trust anyone but himself to do things right."

"Maybe that's one reason you've been so slow to trust."

"With men? I admitted that, didn't I." Taylor thought for a moment. "Maybe it's my father. But probably that's too simple. I loved my mother completely. But I realize now I never wanted to be as passive as I thought she was." Taylor shook her head, as if to clear away confusion. "Maybe she was just worn out, from a heart that had never worked right. A child's perspective is skewed by the limits of a child's perceptions."

"Speaking for my own childhood," Darrow agreed, "that's true enough. To me, my parents weren't human. Even now, it's hard to sort them out." He paused, then added simply, "At least Lionel's still alive. The two of you have time yet."

Taylor gazed at him, and then her expression softened. "Whatever else, I like the way *we* are. You and me."

"Does that mean you're staying over?"

Leaning across the table, Taylor kissed him. "Of course."

THEY LAY TOGETHER in the dark. The shared warmth of lovemaking and the comfortable talk that often followed had begun to feel familiar to him.

"You never told me about your day," she said.

Darrow composed his thoughts. "It's not so much about today. Or any particular day. It's much bigger than that, and much more draining."

"Can you talk about it?"

"I'm not sure." Darrow paused, then repeated softly, "I'm just not sure."

Something in his tone caused Taylor to sit up, leaning on her elbow as she looked at him. "You've been holding something back, haven't you? I could feel it in Boston."

"I had no choice, Taylor. For many reasons."

"Is this about Steve Tillman?"

Darrow weighed his answer. "And Angela Hall. And several other things, all of them pretty volatile. I don't want you to become part of this."

"You're sounding like my father." She caught herself, then said more evenly, "Maybe that's not fair, either. Even lovers are entitled to zones of privacy. I know I have mine. But, spoken or not, they still affect the other person."

"Like your nightmares, you mean."

"Exactly like them. You may not always know what they're about, Mark. But they're still with us, as you're well aware."

Darrow fell silent. Though he could not see her expression, he could read it in Taylor's voice—serious, intent, unwilling to let this go yet. "So I've begun to tell you things," she continued. "That's not easy for me. But I felt that you wouldn't exploit my candor, and that what goes on with me really matters to you. So, okay, this isn't a transaction. But what goes on with you really matters to me, too."

Darrow tried to unravel the mix of fact, intuition, and suspicion that ate at him. "Some things I'm not free to reveal, Taylor. Others could badly damage at least one man's reputation. But here's the essence: I don't think Steve killed Angela, in part because I believe the same man killed her brother."

He felt Taylor sitting up straighter. "Carl died from an overdose, I thought."

"True. But I don't think Carl did that to himself."

"Then you believe Angela's murderer is still out there."

"He may be, yes."

Taylor absorbed this. "How much have you told my father?"

"Most of it." Darrow hesitated. "A lot of this bears on Caldwell, in the present as well as the past."

"What *can* you tell me, Mark?"

Darrow hesitated. "Angela kept a diary," he said. "After she died, no one could find it. Now it turns out that Carl made a copy. The contents were pretty disturbing."

"How?"

"It suggests that she may have been involved in a fairly pathological relationship with an unnamed man. If he's real, he may know more about her murder than anyone still alive. The last page ends abruptly, and quite strangely. A single sentence: 'There is such darkness in the chamber of stone.'" Darrow paused. "I can't make sense of it. But I've started relating it to the Spire, maybe because I found her body there. Of course, I've never forgotten climbing to the top on the day she died."

"I remember, too. I was standing between my father and mother, looking up at you."

"I'd rather have been where you were. I'm pretty claustrophobic and don't much like heights. The stairway was so dark and gloomy I half-expected to encounter druid priests." He touched her arm. "But enough about the Spire. About my worries, I've told you all I can. At least for now."

Taylor did not answer. She lay on her back, staring into the darkness, toward the ceiling. "What is it?" Darrow asked.

Taylor's voice was muted. "I was recalling childhood fears. At some point I became terrified of the Spire."

Darrow rolled onto his side. "Because of Angela?"

"Before then," Taylor said softly. "Don't ask me to explain it. Maybe it's a child's imagination. For better or worse, I had quite a vivid one, and frightening fairy tales often feature stone towers."

She asked him no more questions. Nor, Darrow sensed, did she wish to talk. He held her until he fell asleep.

Suddenly he awakened. Crying out, Taylor struggled in his arms, trying to break free. "Taylor," he said urgently. "It's me—Mark."

She twitched and then was still. He felt new dampness on her skin. "You all right?" he whispered.

She seemed to shiver. "Just hold me."

For the moment, Darrow realized, that was all he could do.

8

FOR THE NEXT FEW HOURS, DARROW KEPT HIS THOUGHTS TO himself. When Taylor left, still preoccupied, Darrow called his assistant, asking her to clear his schedule and then track down every file concerning Angela Hall's time at Caldwell and to deliver it to his home. "Do it yourself," he told her. "It's absolutely critical that nobody else know about this. No one at all."

After hanging up, he telephoned George Garrison. "Got anything for me?" Garrison asked bluntly.

Once again, Darrow thought of all he was concealing. "I was hoping you did."

Garrison grunted, refusing to answer. "Why do I feel like you're still playing games with me?"

Darrow considered the risks of antagonizing a policeman who could, whenever he chose, place him at the scene of Carl Hall's death. "What I'm sitting on," Darrow said slowly, "is theory, not facts. If my theory's wrong, it could be very damaging to Caldwell, and at least one innocent person. I'd like to feel more certain about this before I come to you."

"If you even think you know something new about Angela or Carl," Garrison said, "*we* should sort it out. How you 'feel' about that isn't my priority."

His time was running out, Darrow knew. "Watching out for Caldwell is one of mine," he answered. "Just give me until Monday. Six more days isn't a lot to ask."

Steve Tillman studied Darrow through the Plexiglas window. "I wasn't expecting you," he said. "They don't make it easy to visit on short notice."

"This wouldn't keep."

Something in Darrow's voice caused Steve's gaze to harden. "I guess this isn't a cheer-up-the-prisoner visit."

Darrow watched his face. "There's something I've never told you—or the police. The reason I avoided your trial."

Surprise stole through Steve's eyes. With unconvincing sarcasm, he said, "At last I get to know."

"Yes. Then I want the truth from you."

"About what?"

"The night Angela was murdered," Darrow said flatly. "I called you from the fraternity house at about three A.M. That's roughly when the waitress saw someone laying Angela's body by the Spire. The same time, basically, that Joe claims to have seen you outside the dorm. You didn't answer the phone."

The smile Steve deployed at last was a movement of lips. "And *you* didn't tell anyone."

"Only Lionel Farr."

To Darrow's surprise, Steve laughed aloud. "So you and *Lionel* covered for me?"

"Lionel thought you were guilty," Darrow said succinctly. "He stayed quiet for my sake, and helped keep me away from the trial."

"What did *you* think?"

"I didn't know. But I couldn't be part of putting you away for life. Tell me where you were that night."

Steve's bitter smile returned. "Maybe you should have asked me then."

"I'm asking now."

Steve shrugged. "If I don't remember screwing Angela, why would I remember that? I was pretty fucked up that night. Maybe I was just passed out."

Darrow leaned closer. His face and Steve's, now inches apart, were separated by Plexiglas. Under his breath, Darrow said, "Bullshit."

Steve's smile vanished. "The phone was right by your bed," Darrow went on. "I called twice—fourteen rings, then fifteen. Anyone but a dead man would have answered."

Given Steve's blood alcohol level, Darrow was not sure of this. But Steve's gaze broke. "Like I said, maybe I went outside to breathe."

"But that's not *really* what you said, is it. What you keep on telling me was what a fucking liar Joe Betts was." Darrow's tone became cutting. "You're the liar, Steve. You were outside the room."

A vein in his friend's temple throbbed. "Maybe I was," he allowed. "Even then I couldn't tell real from unreal."

"So why accuse Joe?" Darrow snapped.

"Because I didn't kill her." Briefly Steve's eyes shut. "At least I know why you didn't visit all those years."

"That's not the reason."

"Well now you've got a good one. Please don't feel obligated."

Darrow stood. Softly, he said, "But I am, pal. We're not done yet."

DARROW DROVE HOME, doubt and depression seeping through him.

On the way, the only call he took was from Lisa, his assistant. Retrieving Angela Hall's records, she wanted him to know, had required a trip to a storage facility on the outskirts of Columbus. But the files would be inside his door when he got home.

They were. Opening the package, Darrow found Angela's application to Caldwell, memos of scholarship committee meetings, transcripts of grades, and the beginnings of graduate school applications prematurely interrupted—a draft letter of recommendation, a list of prospective law schools. Feeling spent, Darrow spread the files on his dining room table.

He had no idea what he was looking for. From his first conversation with Fred Bender, Darrow knew that he would not find obvious signs of emotional problems—behavioral issues or plummeting grades. Sorting the files, he tried to clear his mind.

Angela's first year, he discovered, was like that of many freshmen. A stellar student at Wayne High, she had struggled to maintain the 3.0 GPA necessary to retain her scholarship. Like Darrow, she had difficulty with the required science and math courses; unlike Darrow, her expository writing, though adequate for high school, had necessitated extra work at Caldwell. Nor had her choice of a prospective major, political science, seemed to suit her. None of this surprised him. Nor had it alienated the scholarship committee headed by Lionel Farr. Instead, the committee had allowed her to achieve the minimum grade point average by taking, without charge, a summer school classics course known as an easy mark.

For a moment, Darrow paused, imagining the challenges she'd faced.

Money was a constant problem. Unlike the full scholarship Lionel Farr had obtained for him, Angela's package covered tuition but not room and board. Darrow was not forced to work during the school year; Angela was compelled to, and the thinness of her resources required her to live at home. The necessity of a scholarship, and her trouble in maintaining a 3.0 average while working, had her dangling over a precipice as she entered her sophomore year.

Scanning her transcript for the fall semester, Darrow felt an odd relief. Three B's and an A in Farr's entry-level philosophy course had left Angela with some margin for error. The second semester enhanced this—along with two B's in basic courses she had received a B plus and an A minus in two philosophy classes, the latter taught by Lionel Farr. Darrow wondered if Farr, a stickler for high standards but a man with his own sense of justice, had, as with Darrow himself, responded to Angela's effort and ambition by reading her exam papers with a merciful eye. By the end of sophomore year, Angela had made Farr her academic adviser and had switched her major to philosophy.

This, too, evoked a memory in Darrow. Finding a kindred spirit in the head of the history department, he had switched his major from economics and made Dr. Silberstein his adviser, taking every possible course from him. Only an honest self-evaluation—and Charlie Silberstein's amusing but caustic description of academic life—had helped dissuade Darrow from considering a career in academia to parallel that of Farr, still his principal mentor. Farr's own judgment had proven definitive: "You're not cut out for our cloistered world, Mark. You have the mind and instincts of a lawyer."

Darrow closed the folder. He was tired, he realized, his concentration wandering. After brewing a strong cup of French roast, he turned to Angela's junior year.

From its beginning, she blossomed as a student. Her skills in composition improved exponentially: an A in an expository writing class was accompanied by a B plus in advanced Spanish and two A's in philosophy courses—one based on a take-home essay exam; the other, taught by Farr, on a rigorous final exam concerning Friedrich Nietzsche, a topic with which Darrow was all too familiar. Angela's second semester, almost as strong, was topped by another A, in Farr's Philosophy of the Enlightenment class. By the end of the spring semester her GPA was just shy of 3.5.

Her reward, as Darrow now recalled, was a summer job as Farr's research assistant. From the file, her contribution to his scholarship was unknown. Darrow smiled at this a little: that same summer Farr had helped secure Darrow a job at the admissions department—the compensation for which, combined with modest work hours, had allowed him to do some remedial carousing.

Reaching for the last folder, he reflected that, on paper, Angela was still alive.

The thought renewed his sadness and foreboding. When was it,

Darrow wondered now, that Angela Hall had first met Steve Tillman? Or, for that matter, Joe Betts? In the fall, he supposed, the period of her unexplained disappearances, when it seemed she had begun her final diary.

By this time Angela's path toward a scholarship at an elite law school was becoming clear. She had conquered her writing difficulties; dramatically raised her academic performance despite working at the Alibi Club; and secured an assistantship with a respected professor— who, as he had for Darrow, would no doubt write a forceful recommendation to the law school of her choice. There seemed to be little in Angela's way: no medical issues, visits to the school psychologist, or other hints of stress. All that remained was for her to nail the fall semester. Knowing that the transcript in the last file would be blank, Darrow hesitated to open it.

Nonetheless, he did. The courses she had chosen, including a senior seminar from Farr, would likely have raised her average still higher. Reading Farr's draft letter of recommendation—as laudatory as that he had written for Darrow, but distinctive in its endorsement of Angela's character and abilities—Darrow could feel still more the depth of his mentor's sadness at her murder.

Closing the file, Darrow's hand froze.

For a moment, losing all sense of time, he sat still. Against his will, the pattern of his thoughts began to rearrange itself.

Keep an open mind, Farr had once admonished him, long ago. *Don't impose your own narrative on the world all around you.*

Rearranging Angela's files, Darrow started from the beginning, again, this time inverting the prism he had brought to them before. In the interstices of fact, he realized, he had woven a story of Angela's progress that paralleled his own. But a different story, far more troubling, might be hidden by the first.

That story, were it true, had not ended with her death.

The telephone startled Darrow. He hesitated, then went to the kitchen and answered.

"So I accepted the job," Taylor informed him.

It took a moment for Darrow to focus. "How does it feel?"

"Great. They seemed absolutely ecstatic." Her voice softened. "This will be good, Mark. I'm sure of it."

In the future, perhaps, but in the present, Darrow reflected, he was parting from Taylor much too soon. "Then I'll take you out to celebrate," he proposed.

"Are you sure? I was so caught up in my own news I didn't even ask why you're out today."

"Just working at home." He paused, then added softly, "I feel like I need to see you."

Taylor was quiet. "Is everything okay?"

"I'll meet you at the Carriage House. Seven o'clock."

Saying good-bye, Darrow paused in the kitchen doorway, staring at the files on the table. For an odd moment he thought of the bones of some prehistoric animal through which, using facts and guesswork, archaeologists summoned a living thing from the dead past. Darrow loathed what he had conjured, and himself for his worst thoughts. But his new story of Angela Hall, imagined or real, was too deeply embedded in his own past, and in the present of Caldwell College.

Reaching into his coat pocket, Darrow retrieved his cell phone.

His law school roommate, David Rotner, had been the best man at his wedding. David's ambitions had taken him to Washington, as deputy to the general counsel of the Defense Department. Whenever they managed to get together, once or twice a year, Darrow asked Rotner where Bin Laden resided now.

After dialing the number, he waited, as always, to be transferred at least twice. To his surprise, he found Rotner within two minutes.

"Is this about Bin Laden?" his old roommate inquired. "If so, I can reassure you that Caldwell College is well down on his list."

Darrow managed to laugh. "But not on yours, I hope. I'm calling to ask a favor."

"Which is?"

For an instant, Darrow paused. "I need you to tell me how to access the files of a former army officer."

"How former?"

"He would have left the military in the early seventies."

Rotner thought. "There's a depository of records at Fort Benjamin Harrison, in Indiana. Likely that's where they are. Who is this guy?"

"A Special Forces officer who served in Vietnam. I'd like to know what he did there. Including whether, for some reason or another, he got involved in moving money around."

"Vietnam," Rotner answered, "got pretty funky. But what's all that to you?"

"He's affiliated with Caldwell. Among other problems we've had a major embezzlement. My predecessor looks good for that. But there are two other people, at least in theory, who could have done it if they had the skills. This man's one."

"Then why not leave this to the authorities, whoever they might be?"

"Too sensitive."

"That's a problem. Any prosecutor would have an easier time getting this file than you would. When do you need it?"

Darrow hesitated. "By the end of this week."

Rotner laughed. "This is the federal government, Mark. Not to mention that there's a separate bureaucracy for requests like this. Try the end of this *year*."

"No time for that." Darrow began pacing. "Suppose you wanted to see this thing tomorrow. Could you?"

"If I was really curious and really lucky? Maybe. But I'm not the secretary of defense." In a tone of caution, Rotner inquired, "What are you asking me to do?"

"To look at his records, then tell me whether there's anything of interest. This is very serious, David, and not just to me. Or else I'd never ask."

"I can look at them," Rotner finally replied. "But I can't describe the contents. All I can do is tell you whether they're worth a written request."

Darrow rubbed his temples. "Then that's all I can ask." He paused, then said quietly, "The man's name is Lionel Farr."

9

DESPITE TAYLOR'S NEWS, BOTH DARROW AND SHE WERE listless at dinner. On the drive home, she asked, "What's making you so quiet?"

Darrow pulled into the driveway. "A lot of things," he answered. "You, for one. You don't seem all that happy."

"I've been thinking about Angela's diary," she said simply. "You called it 'pathological.' But you've told me almost nothing. Mark, please—I need to know what's bothering you so much."

They sat in the car in front of the darkened house, silent for a time. "By itself," Darrow answered, "the diary doesn't prove a thing. Not even whether the man she describes is real."

"And if he is?"

Darrow did not answer. In a low voice, she repeated her request: "Please tell me about the diary."

Gazing into the darkness, he tried to untangle the reasons he wished to tell her yet feared to do so. At length he turned and faced her directly. "If you want me to," he said.

For the next few minutes, Darrow described the diary in detail—its specificity, its flatness of tone, its depiction of ritual subjugation slipping out of control. Taylor leaned her head back against the car seat, her eyes half-closed, until his narrative was done.

"I think it's real," she said simply. "Angela didn't just make it up."

"How do you know that?"

"If this were some writing exercise, she'd describe her own feelings. Instead she's removed herself." Taylor faced him again. "She was traumatized, Mark."

Darrow thought of Angela on the night of the party—her drinking, her edge of desperation, her refusal of a ride home, the tears in her eyes when she gave him an impulsive hug. *Gonna be a long night for me, I think.*

"Is there something else?" Taylor asked.

As best he could, Darrow reprised this memory. Finishing, he asked, "What do you make of all that?"

Taylor's voice remained quiet, her manner contained. "The same thing you do, I imagine. Angela may not have expected to die. But that night she was afraid of something, or someone. I'm not even sure that what happened to her was wholly a surprise."

By silent consent, they went inside. But, as on the morning in Boston after her nightmare, part of her seemed absent. Alone, she went to his bedroom.

He found her there, naked, sitting on the edge of his bed with her arms crossed. Lying beside her, Darrow touched Taylor's shoulder. "It's not you," she said. "Maybe I'm just tired."

Darrow turned out the light. After a time she slid into bed with him, their bodies apart. All that he knew was that Angela's diary had taken her somewhere he could not reach.

To his surprise, she slept. Darrow did not. Lying awake, he felt her restless stirrings, heard small cries that were not words escape her lips.

IN THE MIDDLE of the night, Taylor shuddered. Only when Darrow heard her stifling sobs did he know she was awake.

Darrow put his arms around her. She lay there, silent.

He reached for the bedside lamp.

The light made her flinch. Then she turned on her back, eyes open, as though reorienting herself. A strand of hair stuck to her dampened skin. "The dream?" Darrow asked.

Her lips parting slightly, she gazed up at the ceiling. "A part I've never told you."

"Maybe it would be better if you did."

"Better?" she asked softly.

"What could be worse?"

He felt her shiver. In a monotone, Taylor described the dream.

HER PARENTS WERE in their bedroom. She did not know how old she was; dreams have their own logic. But, in life, it would have been before her mother slept in a separate room.

Her parents' voices, though raised, were too muffled for Taylor to understand. She pressed her face against the door. Then her mother spoke in voice so intense, and so unlike her, that Taylor could hear. "We're done. Look for your ideal woman somewhere else."

Taylor turned and walked away so softly that her footsteps made no sound, certain only that her parents were not as she hoped, but as she feared.

"I DON'T KNOW what it means," she told Darrow now. "If anything."

"How do you know it's a dream and not a memory?"

She turned, looking wordlessly into his eyes.

"You said they started sleeping apart." Darrow took her hand. "You were a child, Taylor. There are whole pieces of childhood I simply don't remember. When you've got no other means of escaping, dissociation provides one."

"Do you ever dream?"

"Not if I can help it." His tone softened. "My parents are both gone. There's no one living to remind me."

Taylor said nothing. Reaching across his body, she turned out the light.

*   *   *

WHEN SHE SLIPPED out of bed into the darkness, Darrow did not follow for a time.

He found her on his couch, a blanket draped around her. Darrow sat beside her.

"I don't think it's a dream," she said.

"The argument?"

"No." Her eyes narrowed with the effort to remember. "Something else. In memory, it's the last time the three of us went to the riverbank."

HER MOTHER WAS painting, her father reading pages from his manuscript on Friedrich Nietzsche. Though that spring was unseasonably warm, the water was still too chilly for swimming. Alone on a blanket, Taylor read a Nancy Drew book, restive because the mystery seemed transparent. She looked up, intending to complain to her mother.

Her father stood behind her mother, staring at the painting. His expression was dark. Seeming to ignore him, her mother added brushstrokes. Her eyes were grave, the half smile on her face oddly bitter. Taylor had never seen this look before.

"WHAT WAS THE painting?" Darrow asked.

"A tower. The only one I'd ever seen."

In Darrow's silence, Taylor pulled the blanket tight around her shoulders. "I could swear the painting was real, Mark. But I never saw it again."

"When was this, do you think?"

Taylor shook her head. "I can't tell. But in my mind, it's days before she died. Maybe that's part of my aversion to the Spire."

Darrow asked nothing more. At last they both slept.

In the morning, leaving, Taylor smiled sadly. "This must be like living with the insane," she said.

"No," he answered. "My mother was insane. I can tell the difference."

TRYING TO WORK, Darrow could not concentrate. He made the scheduled telephone calls to alumni. Though his mind drifted, he was grateful for the distraction from his own thoughts. Pleading the press of work, he canceled a meeting with Lionel Farr.

Instead, he called Carly Simmons, the medical examiner in the Angela Hall case. Simmons was not in; all he could do was leave his number. By midafternoon, Simmons still had not responded.

When his telephone rang, Darrow snatched at it.

The caller was not Simmons but David Rotner. "I've got the file," Rotner said at once.

He sounded somber. Surprised, Darrow asked, "And?"

"There's nothing to suggest that Farr was laundering money," Rotner said. "Though the last outfit he served in was run by the CIA. As you probably know, the agency moved money around in all sorts of ways. But your man's specialty was on the operational side."

"Meaning?"

"I told you what my constraints are." Rotner's voice lowered. "All I can say is that you'd find the files interesting. But there's nothing here that makes him an embezzler."

Sitting in his chair, Darrow gazed out at the rolling grounds. "What about a double murderer?"

For a moment Rotner was silent. "Why do you ask that?"

"It's nothing I can be sure of. But a second murder—if it is one— happened about three weeks ago."

"Then you've got me in a bind, Mark."

"How so?"

"Because you're one of my closest friends, and I'm not supposed to tell you a fucking thing." His tone became emphatic. "But I will say this: based on these records and what you just told me, you may be dealing with a very singular personality. I strongly suggest that some appropriate person request them."

Darrow made himself stay calm. "I don't have time for that, David."

For a moment Rotner said nothing. At length, he asked, "Have you ever heard of the Phoenix program?"

"No."

"It was a very special, very secret operation during Vietnam. Under the auspices of the CIA, Special Forces personnel carried out targeted assassinations of Viet Cong, alleged VC agents or sympathizers who gave them information. Your man was in the program."

Darrow felt his nerves come alive. "How were these killings done?"

"As I understand it, the techniques varied. A bullet in the head, or maybe a slit throat if silence was important."

"What about pumping someone full of heroin?"

"No idea. But it could have happened. It might make for a quiet death, and Vietnam was awash in smack." Rotner sounded defensive. "The work was dirty, dangerous, and stressful. Our guys got through it by believing that they were protecting their fellow soldiers, the mission, and our country, maybe even Vietnam itself. That's how they stayed sane."

"Did Farr remain sane?"

"The question you need to ask, Mark, is who he was going in."

"What do you mean?"

"Dammit, Mark." Rotner paused, then said with resignation, "Your guy exceeded orders. He seemed to like his work too much."

Darrow felt caged. "Meaning?"

"They'd go into a village at night to kill a VC agent. The orders would be specific to that person—you'd have to put in an application for a particular target and have it approved up the line. It was *not* a hunting license—neither the army nor CIA nor the guys doing it saw this as a form of recreation or a license for mass murder. The idea was to create fear, not hatred.

"Farr was different. Tell him to kill a VC and somehow the tar-get's entire family would end up dead. The army concluded that Farr was a liability."

An image of Farr in Vietnam, those years he would never speak of, made Darrow feel queasy. "You mean they thought he was insane."

"They believed," Rotner answered flatly, "that Farr was danger-ous. Let someone damaged step outside normal societal boundaries and it might be hard to bring him back. For many in the Phoenix program, Vietnam was a nightmare. But a man like Farr might be-lieve it was the rest of us who were living in a fairy tale."

"Did anyone use the word 'psychopath'?"

"The Special Forces never wanted guys like that, and they screened their candidates with care." Rotner paused, then added, "Still, it's al-ways possible for a psychopath to slip through, especially someone with a very high IQ. Witness Jeffrey MacDonald, the Special Forces doctor convicted of killing his wife and kids, then planting evidence that they were murdered by intruders. My understanding of psy-chopaths is that the moral dimensions of murder don't occur to them at all. What was scary about Macdonald was that he was so smart and so persuasive, he damn near got away with it."

Darrow stared at the papers on his desk: budget figures, the draft of a speech—the stuff of normal life. "Was that why Farr left the military?"

"Not exactly." Rotner hesitated. "There was also the murder of a prostitute in Saigon."

Head bent, Darrow rubbed the bridge of his nose. "What were the circumstances?"

"The killer tied this woman to her bed. The evidence suggested she was strangled during sex." Rotner tried to keep his voice neutral. "The woman who ran the brothel identified a photograph of Farr. So did a friend of the dead girl's."

For what seemed to him a long time, Darrow was quiet. "Mark?" Rotner asked.

"I was wondering why Farr wasn't prosecuted."

"The army was set to bring charges. Then both women retracted their stories. It seemed clear they'd been intimidated, but neither would say so. Without them a court-martial was pointless." Rotner's tone contained a quiet awe. "The army threatened Farr with prosecution anyhow, hoping to compel his resignation. Farr called their bluff. What's plain is that the man had the nerve of a cat burglar, completely without fear.

"In the end, all the army could do was arrange an administrative separation, effectively burying the reasons. The only trace of what must have happened is the file on my desk. To the rest of the world, Lionel Farr was just a war-weary soldier, like so many others in those times."

"He's not like the others," Darrow said quietly. "He's much more remarkable."

"And much more dangerous," Rotner said. "According to these files, he must be in his sixties. But he's not someone who's passive when cornered. Be cautious, Mark."

Darrow promised he would.

FOR THE NEXT few minutes, Darrow thought of many things: the moment when Farr offered to change his life, Farr kneeling beside Angela's body, Farr helping Durbin take charge of Caldwell's response, Farr promising his help on the day the police arrested Steve Tillman. But Darrow's mind kept returning to Taylor, both the child and the woman.

Picking up the telephone, he called Carly Simmons again. "Got your message," she said brusquely. "But the dead have their ways of demanding my attention. You'd think they'd be more patient than the living."

On another day, Darrow might have laughed. "I'll make it quick," he said in an apologetic tone. "Fifteen years ago, would an unattended death in Wayne County have automatically triggered an autopsy?"

"Automatically?" Simmons sounded mildly amused. "We certainly autopsied Angela Hall."

"This isn't about Angela. My question pertains to a woman in her mid-forties with a history of heart disease."

"You've sure got a wide-ranging curiosity," Simmons said dryly. "In the case you describe, it depends. Back then the old doctor who'd come out and sign the death certificate, Rodney Harrison, might not have called for an autopsy. Especially if he knew the woman and her history and nothing seemed amiss."

Darrow's mouth felt dry. "One last question. If you wanted to kill someone in her sleep and leave no trace, how would you do it?"

"Last time *I* did that," Simmons replied in a quietly caustic tone, "I used a pillow. Of course, an autopsy would give you the cause of death. But there's a good chance nothing would be apparent to the naked eye." More sharply, she said, "Mind telling me what *this* is all about?"

"I will," Darrow promised. "Just not yet."

"Then let me get back to my corpses, Mr. Darrow. They're generally more informative."

Darrow thanked her. Without putting down the telephone, he called Taylor on her cell. "Where are you?" he asked.

Taylor sounded puzzled. "My dad's house. Working on my dissertation."

"Stay there," he said. "I'm coming over."

10

TAYLOR MET HIM AT THE DOOR, HER FACE DRAWN FROM LACK of sleep. Her voice anxious, she asked, "What's wrong, Mark?"

He brushed past her, tense as she, glancing around the living room. "Where's Lionel?"

"At work." She paused. "It's not even four o'clock."

He turned to her. "I want you out of here. Pack up what you need."

She folded her arms, visibly striving for a deliberate calm, her eyes flecked with doubt and worry. "Tell me what's going on."

"Later."

"Now," she said tightly. "Is this about my father?"

Darrow made himself pause, searching for words. "And your mother," he said. "Do you remember if she had an autopsy?"

Taylor stared at him. She could not seem to move. "Why are you asking?"

Silent, Darrow placed his hands on her shoulders. For a moment, she looked into his face. Then, haltingly at first, Taylor began speaking.

THE WHITE-HAIRED DOCTOR stood with her father by her mother's bed, touching Anne Farr's wrist. Taylor watched from the doorway, gazing at her mother's lifeless face, a ghastly yellow in the light through her bedroom window. In a dispassionate tone, the old man said, "I'm sorry, Lionel. But Anne appears to have died quite peacefully. I guess her heart just gave out."

"So it seems. Taylor found her like this."

Neither man, Taylor realized, had noticed her. "Dear God," Dr. Harrison said in a sorrowful wheeze. "That must have been hard for her."

"It's what we always feared," her father responded. "But this came too soon. We're not ready, Taylor and I."

"At least she has you." The doctor placed a consoling hand on her father's shoulder. "Are you curious about the precise cause of death? If so, we can perform an autopsy."

It took a moment for her father to answer. "If you feel compelled to do it, Rodney."

"And otherwise?"

Turning, her father spoke in a voice thick with grief. "She's dead, for God's sake. Will carving up Anne's body bring her back to life? We both know her heart betrayed her." His speech slowed. "Forgive me. But remembering her like this is hard enough. I don't want to think about an autopsy."

Awkwardly, Dr. Harrison patted his shoulder. "I understand."

"Good," her father answered. "As you say, there's Taylor to think of now."

TAYLOR LOOKED AT Darrow, the cloud of anguish darkening her eyes. Darrow felt the entire foundation of his life being upended by the same man, her father. "Your dreams are about something," he told her. "I'm not sure they're dreams at all."

Taylor shook her head, less in denial, Darrow perceived, than dismay at what she had never acknowledged. He spoke with gentle urgency. "You were a child, Taylor, unable to face your doubts, and without anyone to hear them. All you could do was repress your deepest fears, then run away as far as you could go. At least until now." He paused, then added quietly, "I think your mother knew what he'd done—or believed she did. That's what you've been sensing."

To his surprise, Taylor backed away, saying in a cool, clear voice, "Dreams aren't proof, Mark. Tell me what else you know."

"There's no time for this—"

Her eyes filled with pain and rage. "Tell me, dammit."

"All right," he said. "The money embezzled from Caldwell went to bank accounts controlled by Carl Hall. Somehow Carl knew that your father was the man in Angela's diary. Lionel used the weakness in Caldwell's financial system to pay off Carl and frame Clark Durbin by fabricating his e-mail—"

"How?" Taylor interrupted. "When it comes to computers, my father struggles just to cope."

"Or so he's made us think. It seems he's very good at that."

Taylor took this in, her gaze intense with thought. Briefly, she shut her eyes. Then she seemed to stand straighter, controlling her emotions with an act of will. With icy calm, she said, "We have to check his office, Mark."

Darrow stared at her. Moments before, she had confronted her own suspicion that one parent had murdered the other, which must have been lodged in her subconscious since adolescence. Now, eerily, she had begun to function as her father did in moments of crisis or danger—detached from her own emotions, thinking swiftly, so devoid of doubt or fear that it sharpened Darrow's edginess. "We need to get out of here," he said. "Go to the police."

"And tell them what?" Taylor stared into Darrow's eyes, speaking with the same dispassion. "I finally know why he keeps his study locked. I also know where he keeps his keys. If we don't look, he'll destroy whatever's there. Just like he cremated my mother's body."

Turning, she went to her father's bedroom. Darrow followed and found her reaching into a small drawer in a rolltop desk. She held up a set of keys. "When I was a child," Taylor said, "this was where he hid things. He never knew I saw him."

This enmity, Darrow realized, was years deep, practiced by two quiet adversaries. "How do you know what these open?" he asked her.

"One day my laptop shut down. He wasn't home, and I needed to check my e-mail on his computer. He never knew I'd violated his sanctuary." Swiftly, Taylor walked to his study. "How many men, I wonder, lock their study at home to keep their family out."

Darrow stared at the dead bolt. "I don't remember seeing this."

"You didn't," Taylor answered tersely. "He installed it the day after we scattered her ashes. It was one of the things we never spoke of."

Though made gloomier by the absence of light, the office was familiar: the map of Vietnam, the oil painting of Mad Anthony Wayne, the leather chair where Farr had sat when he offered the teenage Darrow a new vision of his future. The sense of trespass caused Darrow to pause. He watched Taylor pull out her father's desk chair and log in to Farr's laptop. "You won't find anything," Darrow said. "To imitate Durbin's e-mail, he'd have needed a different computer."

Glancing up, Taylor handed him the keys. "Then look in his drawers."

These, too, had locks. Finding the key, Darrow unlocked three drawers. Two were empty save for writing utensils and printing paper; the third was stuffed with bank records and extra checks. Wedged into the fourth was a small laptop. Darrow remembered a report prepared by Greg Fox and Joe Betts; Farr's spare computer, he realized, was identical to the one Clark Durbin had used as president of Caldwell. Glancing up, he discovered that Taylor was watching him.

"We should take that," she said. "Someone can look it over later."

"Then let's go. I don't want you anywhere near here, Taylor. Let Garrison do the rest."

"What will you tell him? If I understand what you've told me, my father set all this up perfectly, including Swiss bank accounts. Then he murdered the only witness."

"That's my point."

"And mine. If dreams and instincts and pages from a diary added up to anything, you'd have already gone to the police." With the same frightening calm, Taylor refocused on her father's laptop. "There's a reason he didn't want me touching this."

Darrow glanced at his watch. It was nearly five o'clock. "What time does he come home?"

"Usually around six." Taylor tapped the keyboard, summoning her father's files—research papers, records of bills, student essays. "When I began my dissertation," she told Darrow, "I was absolutely paranoid that someone might steal from it. So I encrypted it with a password: 'Anne,' after my mother. No one could have guessed it unless they knew me very well."

She could have been discussing the last novel she had read or her favorite restaurant in the West Village. Only the way she held her head, still and focused on the screen, betrayed her feelings. Quietly, she said, "He must have hidden a file using a separate password."

Watching her, Darrow flashed on his first financial fraud case. The chief financial officer of a major company had mapped out the falsification of profits on his home computer, in a file entitled "Liberal Accounting Adjustments." The man was more arrogant than inventive; too accustomed to believing himself smarter than his adversaries, he thought himself impervious. In this he had been wrong. The password he had chosen, the name of his graduate school, had embarrassed Wharton deeply when Darrow revealed it in court. Taylor looked up. "I just tried to open a file called 'Family Pictures,'" she told him. "But the computer is asking me for a password. Any ideas?"

"No."

"We both know things about him," Taylor insisted. "What password would he use?"

"Try 'Nietzsche.'"

Swiftly, Taylor did this. "No," she told him.

She tried several others. Edgy, Darrow went to the entrance of the study, half-expecting Farr. Darrow had betrayed his thoughts, though not quite all, to a man with a feral sense of danger. He thought of all the ways Farr had covered himself, even within his own family, in part to keep his daughter's doubts at bay. An ambiguous but disturbing image came to Darrow: Anne Farr painting beside the river; Lionel Farr staring at a depiction of the Spire that Taylor had never seen again.

Over his shoulder, Darrow said, "Try 'Spire.' "

He walked into the living room. Opening the front door, he stood on the porch and looked up and down the street. Though blocks away, neither of the two men he saw on foot had Farr's erect posture or martial stride. How many times, Darrow wondered, had the sight of those things made him smile? With a leaden feeling, he closed the door, carrying the burden of his fears and memories to Farr's office.

Taylor had turned from the screen.

In profile, her skin was unnaturally pale. She did not move. All that distinguished her from a mannequin was the single tear running down her face.

"What is it?" Darrow asked, and then looked at the screen.

Her back to a dark stone wall, Angela Hall stared back at him, naked but for the leather straps that bound her wrists and ankles. Stunned, Darrow placed his hand on Taylor's shoulder and felt the tremor running through her. With unearthly quiet, she said, "Imagine calling this file 'Family Pictures.' "

His hand resting on her shoulder, Darrow clicked to another photograph, then several more. Her face frozen when it was not turned away, Angela was captured in different poses. The photographs suggested varied possibilities. But their common theme was exposure and helplessness—the man behind the camera could tell her to perform the act suggested and Angela could not resist. The photographs could have illustrated her diary.

Darrow clicked again.

The next set of photographs was of a young white woman he did not know. From the length and style of her hair, Darrow guessed, she had entered Caldwell before him. He supposed that she, like Angela, might have majored in philosophy.

Darrow stopped clicking.

"Keep going," Taylor said in an ashen voice.

She had turned to the screen, the streaks of wetness on her face glistening in its gray-blue glow. "No," he answered.

Reaching past him, Taylor clicked the mouse. Rather than looking at the screen, Darrow watched his lover's face.

Her expression, he thought now, was like Angela's: oddly stoic, eyes frozen in shock. Suddenly she flinched, crying out, then bent forward with her eyes shut.

Darrow faced the screen. Naked, Anne Farr hung by the wrists from the chain of the Spire's bell. The bell was behind her head; had Farr pushed her, Darrow thought, it might have rung.

Darrow shut off the computer.

Resting his face against the crown of Taylor's head, he murmured, "Take both laptops, Taylor. That's all that's left for you to do."

There was nothing else to say, Darrow knew, or the time to say it. Taylor seemed to grasp this. After a moment, she raised her head to look at him.

"Go to the police station," Darrow directed. "Tell Garrison what we found."

Moving slowly, Taylor unplugged the laptop. Her voice muted, she said, "Where will you be?"

Darrow did not respond. Instead, he picked up Farr's desk phone and dialed a number he knew from memory.

On the third ring, Farr answered his private line. "It's Mark," Darrow said. "I need to see you."

For an instant, Farr did not respond. "Concerning what?"

"Family pictures. The ones on your computer."

As Darrow absorbed Farr's profound silence, Taylor's eyes widened in fear. "So this is what we've come to," Farr said at length.

"Yes."

"Then I'll meet you at the Spire, Mark."

Abruptly, Farr hung up.

Taylor grabbed the lapels of Darrow's suit coat. "We know what he is," she said in desperation. "Please, don't do this."

"I have to," Darrow answered. "Because of all he is to me."

11

WHEN DARROW REACHED THE SPIRE, THE OAKEN DOOR AT its base was ajar.

He stopped, afraid of what might follow if he entered, dreading the claustrophobia that had enveloped him in the tower sixteen years before. Farr would know this; he knew Mark Darrow well. Breathing deeply, Darrow filled his lungs and then crossed the threshold.

The dank smell of moist sandstone flooded his nostrils. The winding stairs above him, lit dimly by lamps placed too wide apart, disappeared in shadows. Darrow began climbing, his loathing of close spaces tightening around him like a vise. This time, he could not distract himself by counting the steps. This time, Farr awaited him.

As he climbed the Spire, Darrow thought of finding Angela Hall's body. From the moment a stunned Mark Darrow had run to him for help, Farr had taken control, improvising with what Darrow now understood was a psychopath's nerveless brilliance. Perceiving that Darrow's account of the party led directly to Steve Tillman, Farr had prevented Darrow from warning Steve by taking him to Durbin's home. There Farr had taken charge of Caldwell's response, making himself as indispensable to Durbin as he was above suspicion. When Steve was arrested and Mark had asked for his help, Farr had sent Steve to a lawyer he knew to be incompetent. The last piece of Farr's lightning adaptations was the sacrifice of Mark's closest friend to a life in prison.

Briefly Darrow paused in the darkness, recalling the night Farr had first approached him. Moments before that, he had thrown the winning touchdown pass to Steve; barking signals, Mark had shut down his emotions, banishing all thought except to execute this play. The crowd noise had vanished; the task before him became no more daunting than a video game. Mark had first done this as a boy, shutting out his mother's frightening shifts of mood, the sudden violence of his alcoholic father. Perhaps that was why his coach had called him the "mentally toughest guy around." Except, perhaps, for the man at the top of the Spire.

He was not quite ready, Darrow realized. In his reasoning mind he understood who Farr had been in secret. Murder was nothing to him. And yet this same man had saved Darrow from a life so dreary that it frightened him to recall. He could not make two decades of affection vanish in an hour.

Darrow kept climbing. The only sound he heard was the echo of his footsteps. He must not think of Taylor, or anything outside the Spire.

Why had Farr chosen this place, Darrow wondered. He kept expecting the provost to appear on the darkened steps above him. Surely he was near the top; the sound of Darrow's breathing, more labored now, whispered against the stone. But there was no way of knowing where Farr was—the staircase kept winding upward, vanishing from sight. Darrow bent in a semicrouch, preparing to dodge or leap.

He suddenly stopped, the pit of his stomach hollow. At the top of the staircase he saw the door to the bell tower, slightly open. Farr had entered Angela Hall's "chamber of stone."

Darrow climbed the final steps. As before, his footfalls caused a thudding echo; the element of surprise belonged to Farr alone, a man who seemed to have retained his assassin's skills.

Abruptly, Darrow pushed open the door.

He saw nothing but the brass bell and the chain from which Anne Farr had been suspended. Edging forward, Darrow looked to each side. The door shut softly behind him.

Flinching, he heard Farr's mirthless laugh.

Darrow turned to face him.

Farr stood beside the door, his blue eyes glinting with keen appraisal. But for this, he looked disconcertingly the same. Something in Darrow's expression caused him to smile slightly.

"You were expecting me to start speaking in tongues?" Farr inquired sarcastically. "Or perhaps a disjointed rant?"

He was utterly calm, Darrow realized. Mildly, Farr asked, "Are you afraid, Mark?"

Darrow found his voice. "You murdered at least four people."

"Four?"

"I'm counting the prostitute in Vietnam."

The trace of amusement vanished from Farr's eyes, replaced by heightened attention. "I've underrated you, it seems."

Once more, Darrow willed himself to feel nothing. "Maybe so. I'm the one you left whole."

"Unlike Taylor, you mean."

Darrow nodded. "At least she's still alive. You must have always watched her, wondering if you'd be forced to choose between her life and yours."

Farr stepped closer to Darrow, grasping the chain of the bell. Then he leaned against its metallic mass in a pose of relaxation that, to Darrow, seemed explosive in its stillness. "When did you divine all this, Mark?"

Darrow did not move. "I'm not here to impress you. I came to tell you that it's over, and that killing me is pointless. I want you to come down with me."

Farr's eyes became a chill blue. "Then persuade me. Enthrall me with all you know."

"What's to say, Lionel? You're a sexual psychopath. The rest followed."

Farr's expression became blank, almost bored. "Spare me the lecture on pathology. If we're both to leave here alive, I want facts, not stereotypes."

The explicit threat was so casually delivered that it made Darrow's skin clammy. Against his will, he absorbed the gloomy shadows, the heavy bell, the dingy stones against which Angela had died. The sole light came from the four openings in the stone—through one of which, decades ago, a young man had fallen to his death. Finding his voice again, Darrow said, "Angela, then."

"Yes," Farr concurred. "Angela."

"A bit at a time, you brought her close—saving her scholarship, taking a professorial interest, giving her grades she feared she hadn't earned, reviewing her papers, then making revisions until she was no longer sure whose work it was. Pretending to help her, you eroded her sense of self. Whether or not she needed you to succeed, she came to believe she did. Helping her financially was part of the endgame. That, and the draft letter of recommendation you dangled."

Watching Farr's expression, keen with interest, Darrow stopped there. "Go on," Farr demanded.

This, too, was a game, Darrow realized, its stakes obscure but perhaps lethal. He shrugged his assent, continuing with a casualness he did not feel: "Your psychic stalking had worked before. Whatever her reasons, Angela let you bring her here, becoming little more than robotic as she submitted to what you needed." Darrow's voice became cutting. "She wrote the diary to record what you were doing to her. By its end, she loathed you as deeply as you deserved."

Behind Farr's opaque mask, Darrow sensed an anger he was fighting to control. "Is that what you think?"

"*You* read the diary," Darrow retorted. "You killed Carl for it. Angela was so young, Lionel. Before you found her, she was filled with hope. Maybe that came back to her. Maybe sleeping with Steve

Tillman, even drunk, made her skin crawl at the thought of you. When she left his room to come here, she was done with you." Darrow softened his voice. "Fred Bender thought Steve killed her because she threatened to charge him with rape. Right theory, wrong man. Angela threatened to expose you to Clark Durbin. So you beat her, then strangled her to death where we're standing now.

"After you carried her body down, the waitress saw you laying it on the ground. Even then, you'd had the presence of mind to lock the door behind you. No one but Carl Hall and Taylor's mother ever imagined what had happened in this place."

Farr's glacial eyes remained on Darrow's face. "Are you expecting me to comment? Or are you simply trying to dazzle me?"

The questions jarred loose Darrow's anger. "We're talking about murder and sadomasochism. If you still imagine I'm who you need me to be, you're a fool."

A flush appeared on Farr's cheekbones. "It's not that easy to insult me, Mark. Your story's incomplete."

"So's your comprehension," Darrow responded. "DNA lasts the longest in dark places. I'm sure there's a genetic trace of both of you still here."

Farr's eyes narrowed. "And Carl?"

"Gazed into his sister's coffin and saw dollars. I imagine he'd followed her here, no doubt on an earlier night, and seen you leaving. After her murder he came to you, asking to be paid." Darrow paused. "You couldn't risk a double murder that soon. Worse, you were married to a woman who was afraid you'd strangled Angela Hall. When Anne painted the Spire, you knew."

Eyes cool, Farr shook his head, miming disapproval. "Your tale's becoming gothic."

"Gothic novels don't turn on life insurance policies. Anne had one, I suspect, to help cover Taylor's education. You killed her for the proceeds, eliminating the threat that she'd expose you and giving you money to buy off Carl Hall. But transfers of cash create a paper trail. Diamonds don't."

A moment's surprise surfaced in Farr's eyes. "Tell me the rest, Mark."

"The other problem was Taylor. She loved her mother, and she was as sensitive and intuitive as she was bright. I wonder which of you frightened the other more—the remote father or the haunted child who knew in her subconscious that something wasn't right. I suppose Taylor's fortunate she didn't 'drown.'"

Farr crossed his arms, his face now pale in the fading light. "At least it's fortunate for you. Or was."

Darrow did not respond to this. "If you were to let Taylor live," he went on, "you needed to separate her from her memories. But you had no money to send her away. So Anne's parents paid for her education, and gave her a second home until they died. Only Carl was still in Wayne."

The remark evoked in Farr a smile of contempt. "Yes, Carl. As Heraclitus once said, 'Character is fate.'"

"Carl's *and* yours. He kept wanting more money, and was too street-smart for you to kill easily—especially because he kept to a neighborhood where a white college professor would be conspicuous." Pausing, Darrow watched Farr closely, both men tense and alert. "Over time, you must have become quite desperate. Then you saw an opportunity to embezzle money and frame a man with severe financial problems, including a son whose heroin addiction was conveniently fed by Carl Hall. Everything Joe Betts could have done to implicate Durbin, you did. And everyone believed it. Which brings the story back to me."

Farr's expression changed again, betraying the faintest regret. "That was unfortunate for us both, wasn't it."

"Certainly for you," Darrow retorted. "Your chief concern was that Caldwell's next president be as malleable as Durbin. You couldn't count on controlling a stranger, or even remaining as provost. I was young, presentable, well-known to the board and alumni, and, most ironic of all, sophisticated in criminal and financial fraud cases." Darrow spoke quietly, reining in his anger. "But I had another qualification no other candidate could match: the admiration and affection you'd imbued me with since I was seventeen. You saw me as the person least likely to suspect you, the one you could deflect from any area of danger.

"That was a miscalculation, Lionel—quite a bad one. Not just because I was also the most likely to sense that something was wrong. You still can't believe that anyone else is as smart as you, can you?"

Farr gave the brass bell a shove, propelling it toward Darrow. "You did alter the balance of things, Mark. You got a man killed."

"Carl got Carl killed," Darrow said flatly. "He became too greedy and told himself you were too old to be a threat to him. He didn't know you'd murdered people as a vocation. Once you grasped my doubts about where Caldwell's money went, you couldn't risk letting him live.

"That left only Taylor. You never expected that she'd return. And the last thing you wanted was for me to spend much time with her." Darrow's voice softened again. "Maybe she suspected you, Lionel. But maybe she just hoped to know you better. Thanks to me, she does."

"Meaning?"

"She took your 'family pictures' to Garrison. You couldn't be more finished."

Farr shoved the bell again, swinging it closer to Darrow's face. "When I snatched you off the football field," Farr told him, "I chose well. It was almost like choosing my own son." His voice became oddly gentle. "You claim there's little point in killing you. Instead, you've persuaded me you shouldn't live. If you're the one who's ruined me, why give you the pleasure of watching me come to an inglorious end? One victory celebration in the Spire is enough for a man's lifetime." Pausing, Farr shook his head. "The sad part is that I loved you. More than anything, that's why I brought you back. Now both of us are finished."

Shaken, Darrow backed away from the swinging bell. "What about Taylor, Lionel?"

Farr smiled in disbelief. "Even if you lived, do you imagine your relationship could possibly survive this?"

"If how I feel counts for anything, it will. Taylor's the one woman you didn't destroy."

"Do you really think so?" Suddenly Farr gave the bell a violent shove toward Darrow. Reeling backward, Darrow reached for the wall, trying to brace himself. To his horror, he found himself framed against an opening in the tower.

Farr came swiftly toward him. Frozen, Darrow crouched as Farr grasped his shoulders with both hands. Swinging behind them, the bell tolled sonorously.

Farr looked deeply into his eyes, as though trying to hold a memory. In a tone tinged with regret, he said, "Good-bye, Mark."

Darrow wrenched from his grasp and staggered sideways.

Farr let him go, staring at him with the thinnest of smiles. Softly, Farr said, "You still don't understand."

The bell kept tolling. As it echoed through the tower, Darrow watched Farr move to the opening, turn, and sit on the ledge. For a last moment he gazed back at Darrow. Then Farr closed his eyes and toppled backward into space.

Shocked, Darrow stared at the opening, seconds before filled by his friend and mentor. Then, despite his fear of heights, he willed himself to peer down at the grass below.

Farr lay on the grass, his body crumpled. Much as Darrow had knelt over Angela, Taylor knelt beside him now, her raven hair almost touching her father's face. Only then did she look up toward Darrow.

12

Taylor had her father cremated. She let the cremato-
rium dispose of his ashes as they chose.

The museum gave her an extra month. She would visit friends in
the East, she told Darrow—she could not stay in Wayne. Darrow understood this. She had suffered the greater loss; he would have to deal
with his own confusion and grief alone. For now, it was enough that
Taylor had survived.

There was much for Darrow to do. At his direction, Joe Betts and
the investment committee filed a claim against Carl Hall's estate. As-
sisted by George Garrison, Dave Farragher petitioned for Steve Tillman's release; days later, Farragher postponed his run for Congress.
When his friend was released, Darrow drove him away from the
prison.

Though Steve thanked him, he said little about Farr. The whiplash
of his emotions, combined with sudden freedom, had left him troubled and confused. "What will I do now?" he asked Darrow.

"There's a room at my place," Darrow said. "Seems only fair."

Steve managed to smile. "Football season's starting," Darrow told
him. "Caldwell needs a receivers coach. If you want the job, it'll give
you some time to sort this out."

Steve considered this. "I haven't seen a game in sixteen years."

"Nothing's changed. Our team is still white; the receivers are still slow. You'll catch up."

At length, Steve nodded. His reactions seemed delayed, Darrow realized, as though he could not trust his own perceptions of reality. "Then I guess I'll take it," Steve finally said.

The next day, over lunch, Darrow described Steve's state of mind to Garrison. "If I'd come to you before," Darrow added, "I'd have accused the wrong man. There's been enough of that."

Garrison sat back, hands folded across his stomach, his expression curious and not unkind. "Lionel Farr," he said. "How are *you* dealing with that?"

Darrow shrugged. "It's taking a while. But Farr made me responsible for Caldwell's future. That tends to get me through the day."

But not the nights. A few evenings a week, less often than he wished, Darrow called Taylor. Their conversations were halting; it was as though Taylor, like Steve, had been paralyzed by Lionel Farr's death. "I can help you through this," Darrow told her once.

"Can you?"

There was neither challenge nor hope in her voice, only a dispassionate curiosity that Darrow found disheartening. He said good-bye that night without knowing what else to say.

That weekend he flew to Boston and sat down with Jerry Seitz.

For several hours Darrow told him about Taylor and his own relationship to Farr. "This man didn't make you," Seitz responded. "Maybe Caldwell did. But you made yourself a very different man. That's why you were finally able to see him as he truly was."

Darrow was quiet for a time. "Farr killed himself, Jerry, instead of trying to throw me off the Spire. Explain *that* to me."

Seitz shook his head. "I'm not a mind reader. But he didn't kill Taylor, either. One could argue that he kept you alive for her."

"Do you believe that?"

Seitz gave a short laugh. "Not really. Nor do I think for a moment that what he felt for her—or you—was 'love' as most of us define it.

No doubt he saw himself in you, his quasi son; no doubt the admiration you gave him was a source of considerable pleasure. Still, even psychopaths have a subconscious. Maybe he wanted to be a better father than the one he had."

"I don't know anything about that."

"He'd never tell you." The light of new thought appeared in Seitz's eyes. "Know what I think, Mark? Farr admired you. In your own way, you can be very cold-blooded. Maybe Farr saw in you someone almost as smart and ruthless as he."

Darrow's own smile was bleak. "Are you saying that to make me feel better?"

"Don't worry, Mark. You can turn that side of you on and off like a switch. You've learned to use it only when you need to. At your worst, you can never be as subarctic as Lionel Farr." He paused. "The ultimate reason for Farr's suicide, I think, is that he refused to let you win."

The thought chilled Darrow; he still could not shake the image of Farr's ruined body, Taylor kneeling over him. "What did the Spire mean to him, I wonder."

"God knows. Theories abound—maybe he wanted to appropriate Caldwell's most important symbol. I don't need to dwell on the sexual imagery. But the Spire became his private realm; no one could stop him there. In terms of the subconscious, it's also a place where a man can fall from the greatest heights. In the end, that's literally what Farr chose for himself."

Darrow became quiet. "Farr's dead," he said at length. "I can deal with that at leisure. But Taylor is still alive."

"Give her time, Mark."

"I know that. But how much time?"

"Whatever she needs." Seitz's tone was quiet and compassionate. "You have to face that it may not work out with Taylor. Before this happened, she admitted to her own issues with trust. Knowing that your father killed your mother has to be deeply traumatic, and you're at the core of it.

"Maybe she'll get through this once she sorts it out some more. Maybe you can help her. But she'll always be more than a little cautious."

Darrow nodded. Since Farr's death, Taylor and he had barely touched each other.

This conversation, with its unanswered questions and sorrowful doubts, followed him back to Wayne, and into a meeting with Ray Carrick and the governance committee of the board of trustees.

In the wake of Farr's death, Darrow and Carrick had agreed that, because of Darrow's own involvement, Carrick would speak on behalf of Caldwell. The statement, largely drafted by Darrow, had traced Farr's role in Angela's death and the embezzlement, absolving Clark Durbin of wrongdoing. Carrick had added his own coda: "The shadow on our school is lifted. It was the work of a single man, and that man is gone from our community. Caldwell's healing can now begin." Darrow thought this utter horseshit.

It was in this mood that he faced the committee, knowing that he, like Farr before him, had become indispensable. Looking at Ray Carrick, Darrow informed them that—were he to remain here—he intended to demolish the Spire. "There's been too much idolatry," he said. "This school was never about a stone tower, any more than it was about its provost. The heart of Caldwell's campus should look to the future, not the past."

Darrow glanced at each trustee, five men and a woman. No one—including Carrick—challenged him. "Good," Darrow said. "I think we can also agree that we need more women on the board. But that's for the fall meeting. The immediate problem is to find a new provost. I have one."

Surprised, Carrick asked, "Who?"

"Clark Durbin."

"*Durbin?*" Carrick repeated with astonishment.

"Yes. Once we get used to the idea that he's not a crook, Clark makes perfect sense. He knows the school, the faculty always liked him, and he's a good fund-raiser. From my perspective, another advantage is that he lacks Lionel's belief that a provost should run the school." Darrow looked at Carrick, adding, in a sardonic tone, "Besides, it'll keep Clark from suing us for firing him without just cause. If *I* were Clark, I would."

"Would he even take it?"

Darrow smiled. "He says he would. I could certainly use his help. Are we agreed?"

Carrick hesitated. At the other end of the conference table, Joe Betts leaned forward to speak. "We all owe you a lot, Mark. A mistake is a mistake, and we made a big one. I, for one, don't want to lose you. You're the guy who saved our ass."

Without destroying your reputation, Darrow thought, or your marriage. "Thank you," Darrow said simply. "But there's still a lot ahead of us. At least for the next three years, I'll do my best."

Carrick looked from Darrow to Betts, once a reliable ally. The balance of power was shifting; if Carrick did not like it, Darrow thought, he damn well could pretend.

"Three years?" Carrie Goode inquired.

Darrow nodded. "That's the most I can promise. Three years is enough time to launch a capital campaign, get the school in order, and find the long-term leader Caldwell needs. After that, I hope to have a different life."

A day later, Taylor called him.

THEY MET IN Boston.

Over dinner and long into the night, they merely talked, describing as best they could what each had gone through, without speaking of the future. To Darrow, Taylor's intentions were opaque. Though they slept beside each other, sometimes touching, they did not make love.

In the morning, they sat on the brick patio of Darrow's town house. Once Darrow and Lee had enjoyed this, heedless of what awaited them. Now Darrow was acutely aware of not knowing if what he wanted could still exist.

"I haven't wanted to ask about Caldwell," Taylor said. "How is that now?"

"All right." Darrow hesitated. "Next week they're tearing down the Spire."

For a moment, her eyes were haunted and deeply sad. "That's the easy part," she answered.

She said nothing more. In their silence, Darrow felt Taylor studying him. There was a new clarity in her eyes, as though she had awakened to find him sitting there. "What are you thinking, Mark?"

He smiled a little. "I was thinking about you. That happens fairly often."

"I know. And I'm sorry."

Darrow felt a stab of dismay. "Sorry?"

"I know how I've been," she said quietly. "At least you know my excuse."

"I do know." Darrow hesitated. "This hasn't been easy for me, either. But the fact that Lionel wasn't my father lends me a certain clarity."

"About what?"

"You." Darrow felt his caution overcome by emotions he could no longer defer. "I don't want to lose you, Taylor."

Silent, she watched him, her expression wary yet not closed. Darrow's words came swiftly: "I'm not a mystic, so I don't know how to explain this. But I think we were meant to be together from the beginning. Even when I was in college and what's happened between us now was unimaginable.

"I think you feel it, too. To let Lionel destroy us gives him too much power. Maybe looking at me forces you to remember him. If so, at least that's better than nightmares and repression." He forced himself to speak more gently. "Together, you and I can face whatever happened. Who else could understand each other as well as you and I do?"

Doubt surfaced in Taylor's eyes. "I really mean that much to you?"

"More than I can express." Darrow drew a breath, deciding to take his time. "I'm in love with you, Taylor. When we're in the same space, no matter what you're doing, I feel at peace. I've never had that before. Without you, I don't think I ever will. And I don't think losing me would be any good for you, either.

"You want kids. I want *our* kids. Together we can give them what we never had. We can do that because of all we've learned. And because we can tell each other and our children the truth as best we know it." Darrow took her hand. "I've got three years at Caldwell, and then I'm done. We don't have to wait. America still makes airplanes, and I still have a home in Boston. Our life can be what we choose; you'll have the career you want. All I know is that the life we can have together will be much richer than the lives we'd lead apart."

Taylor tilted her head, the slightest smile at the corner of her lips. "That's more than I've heard you say at one time since I was seven. Are you quite sure you're done?"

Darrow watched her, caught between a feeling of release and a deep fear of losing her. "Only for the moment."

Head bowed, Taylor touched her eyes. "I'm not sure how to answer."

"You can start by looking at me."

"Another willful man," she murmured, and then raised her gaze to his. "This is hard, Mark. It *will* be hard, at least for a while."

"I know that," Darrow answered. "All we can do is try."

To his surprise, Taylor kissed him. "Then let's go inside," she said.

AFTERWORD AND ACKNOWLEDGMENTS

One of the deepest pleasures of writing *The Spire* was returning, after over a decade away, to writing a psychological suspense novel intensely focused on characters, story, and setting. So I'm grateful to all those who helped me along the way.

Among them were old and new friends affiliated with my undergraduate school, Ohio Wesleyan University, and the small town in which it is located, Delaware—both of which supplied considerable atmosphere without the dire history. Interim President David Robbins helped me grasp Darrow's challenges and Lionel Farr's duties, while Dr. Carl Pinkele lent a faculty perspective. Dr. Erin Flynn gave me advice on Farr's philosophy class, while Dr. Carol Neuman de Vegvar lent Taylor Farr a background in art history. Two college friends who became prominent lawyers in Delaware, Dan Bennington and Tony Heald, conspired with me to bring the Tillman case to life, and Delaware County Prosecutor Dave Yost cordially shared a prosecutor's perspective. I'm also very grateful to Chief of Police Russ Martin and Officer Sean Sneed, who helped me imagine the investigation, as well as the challenges facing Chief George Garrison. Finally, thanks to all the members of the wonderful Ohio Wesleyan community—students, alumni, faculty, administrators, and board members—with whom I so enjoyed working during my tenure as a trustee.

Others helped me create the world of *The Spire*. My friend Derek Bok, former president of Harvard, was generous with his advice, as was Bob Edgar, president of Common Cause. Invaluable insight into the Tillman case came from prosecutor Al Giannini, defense lawyer Jim Collins, homicide inspector Joe Toomey, and forensic pathologist Terri Haddix. My son, Brooke, and daughter, Katie, shared some anecdotes from college and prep school that I was happy to learn after the fact. Retired General Hugh Shelton was kind enough to impart some needed military background. Dale Walker explained to a computer illiterate how Darrow and Taylor might get into Farr's PC. Researcher Cristin Williams helped reconstruct the cultural background of Darrow's college years. And, as always, my friend Bob Tyrer helped me investigate varied areas of ignorance.

Psychiatry and forensic accounting are worlds unto themselves. Dr. Rodney Shapiro gave me a fascinating insight into the psychological possibilities presented by Lionel Farr. Several members of the splendid firm of Deloitte & Touche helped me create the accounting scenario: Pat Brady, Karen Kennard, Richard Miller, and Rick Potocek. Similarly generous were Jeff Raymon and Elliot Rosenfield of the firm that bears their names, as well as Ted Bunn and Bryan St. Germain, who otherwise spend some of their time protecting me from the vagaries of the stock market.

As always, I owe a great debt to my figurative board of directors: my assistant, Alison Porter Thomas; my agent, Fred Hill; my editor, John Sterling; my splendid copy editor, Bonnie Thompson; and my wife and discerning reader, Dr. Nancy Clair.

Finally, there are my cherished friends—and one of our favorite couples—Justin Feldman and Linda Fairstein. For several years now, the four of us have enjoyed long and wonderful evenings together. Justin has been a constant source of friendship, warmth, humor, and advice—as well as some of the best legal and political anecdotes ever told. As for Linda, it is not enough that she, as a lawyer, helped establish the Manhattan DA's Sex Crimes Unit, or that she has since written numerous engrossing and best-selling novels. Linda also wrote the vows for our wedding this summer, which—thanks to her and Justin's generosity—took place on the grounds of their beautiful home on Martha's Vineyard. For all of that, and more, Nancy and I dedicate this book to them.

ABOUT THE AUTHOR

RICHARD NORTH PATTERSON is the author of *Eclipse, Exile,* and fourteen other bestselling and critically acclaimed novels. Formerly a trial lawyer, he was the SEC's liaison to the Watergate special prosecutor and has served on the boards of several Washington advocacy groups. He lives in San Francisco and on Martha's Vineyard with his wife, Dr. Nancy Clair.